TAKEOVER

THE LEGACY BOOK ONE

BY: LANA GRAYSON

To My Husband...

Yes, this is a book about a step-brother romance,

and no, it didn't turn out as weird as you thought. ;)

CHAPTER ONE
SARAH

It wasn't just a hostile takeover.

It was war.

The email jolted my phone. A flurry of text messages and calls rumbled it off the library's desk.

I let it fall. My laptop dinged and threatened to blue-screen as it lagged over the invasion of alerts. A blizzard of emails flashed over the desktop, all attaching stock reports, portfolios, bond liabilities, and profit and losses. My life was a tangled disaster of graphs and spreadsheets that, until this quarter, predicted a booming year for my family's farm.

"You've got to be kidding me!"

My voice bounced off the library walls, followed by a particularly angry hush from the students studying below. My apology carried too far, and I cringed as the next shush hissed into an unfriendly word.

God, did I envy the students just fretting over their midterms.

My thesis minimized under the mess of emails, reports, and numbers. The lab would have to wait. Again. I rubbed the exhaustion from my face. I'd have to redo the titrations before I finished the damn thing. That'd set me back another day.

It was okay. I could handle it.

I flipped through my planner and scribbled a quick note for Wednesday. The little block was filled with names, notes, and numbers. I scrawled in the margin instead. *Titration.* I could fit it in between my Soil Fertility exam and the presentation for the irrigation proposal designed for our south cornfield.

My phone didn't stop vibrating. Maybe the battery would drain before I was forced to take a call from a nervous investor? A girl could hope. I snapped the buckle around my planner and shoved it into my laptop bag.

Dad warned about this. He knew it was coming, but he thought Darius Bennett and the Bennett Corporation would make the move when he announced the cancer. They didn't, and the suspense poisoned us as much as his chemo. We prepared anyway. In the hospital, Dad told my brothers every last secret about our company, the farm, and the Bennetts. They were ready when he died.

But no one prepared for Josiah and Mike dying in a private plane crash just four months later.

And Dad never thought to share his secrets with me.

I shouldered the bag and burst from the library, nearly tumbling down the steps leading from the Agricultural and Biosystems Engineering loft. Studying in the loneliest section in the library didn't bother me. No one was around to watch the CEO and prime shareholder of a multi-billion dollar company crash on her behind. Even better, no one spied me taking a hit from my inhaler.

The albuterol sucked, but it was effective. I blamed my trembling on the meds.

The Bennetts targeted my family for the past thirty years, but never once stole a single stock from my father's control.

But Dad was dead now.

I hid the inhaler in my purse. In a way, the tightness crushing my chest composed me. I couldn't rush, and I took greater care saving my breath on the most important words—all sound business practices according to my father. Fleeing from Broughton University's library in a burst of paperwork and bumbling backpacks was not proper Atwood behavior, and I would not grant the Bennetts the satisfaction of seeing me rattled.

That bastard family deserved only the same grief they caused me.

My phone rang three times before I made it to my car. Our attorney, Anthony Delvannis, did his job well, but he had a bad habit of calling me during lectures and labs. He charged enough that he could have purchased some patience while I failed my classes for his conference calls. And it wouldn't have hurt to buy a little bit of good news every so often. Apparently, that wasn't part of the attorney/client privilege.

"We have a problem." Anthony didn't greet me. He never did—a relic from Dad's time. Josiah had inherited the same abruptness, but Michael used to tolerate the pleasantries. "Bennett held a press conference."

My fingers tightened over the steering wheel. "And?"

"You better get over here."

"How bad is it?"

"I'd advise an immediate response. And I'd convince your mother to make a public appearance."

"She hardly gets out of bed—"

"Force her, Sarah. The marriage spooked the board and dropped your stock prices. And now Bennett's making these statements. Best not to hemorrhage any more money."

Like we had any money left to lose.

"I'll be there in five."

Uttering an uncouth word might have relieved some stress, but my chest still ached. Darius Bennett didn't deserve a single breath wasted over his name.

"Damage control," he said. "Start thinking."

The call ended. I hated this. I wasn't Sarah Meredith Atwood anymore. I became Sarah *Damage Control* Atwood, though Sarah *Criminally-Underprepared-But-Faking-It* Atwood was probably more apt.

The University faded in my rearview mirror. What had been my life's ambition now shifted. I was Mark Atwood's only living heir, the last member of my family competent enough to act as owner of the farm—even if I was never intended to touch the books, make the decisions, or involve myself with the corporation. My role was to help Mom, study, and distract the guests at our parties with my pretty dress and sensible conversation.

I had a lot to represent. Our farm grew from a little homestead out west into a major, multi-thousand acre empire of diversified crops and ranches stretching throughout Southern California and encroaching deeper into the Southwest. The Atwoods didn't trade seeds for a pail of milk anymore. And, once I finished my degree and conducted my own research, our seeds would be the foundation for an entirely new division of the company.

Genetically modified, drought-resistant, high-yield seed. My research would be something that could really make a difference, a true legacy that would secure the Atwoods for generations and help the farms in Southern California survive. Maybe even in other arid places throughout the world.

Dad sent me to the best schools, put me in the best agricultural engineering university, and ensured I had every opportunity to place the family first. But, instead of working in the lab, I was on *damage control*. Investor problems. Worker grievances. Irrigation administration. We had vice-presidents to handle the day-to-day, but only an Atwood could ease the trigger-fingers of our stock holders.

I much preferred the lab.

Anthony's paralegal waited for me outside. I tossed him the keys to Josiah's Mercedes and hurried inside as he parked. The receptionist handed me a bottle of water, and I cracked it open before bursting into Anthony's office without knocking. He hated that.

Anthony wasn't a man who tolerated interruptions, impropriety, or disrespect. He was far too handsome for such strict business practices. If Anthony was anywhere near as intimidating in the court room as he was frowning at his desk, I pitied his targets. Luckily, he represented us.

His office hid under a stack of papers and thick files. Dad hired his family's firm based on their superb organization. Now? Rolled plans, endless contracts, blueprints, and banking statements cluttered Anthony's tables. Dad's death didn't just leave our house a mess. The remnants of his legacy mixed in the papers and clutter left behind by my brothers.

Nothing was where it should have been, and everything that made sense was lost in redundant duplications.

Except the paper trail telling me where most of our money went.

That documentation, conveniently, was missing.

The television paused on an image of Darius Bennett. The clean-cut, aging business man decked himself out in imported suits, diamond cufflinks, and a sleek smile that bared more teeth than genuine excitement. His only honest quality was the grey in his hair, and that hadn't spread fast enough.

I sunk into a spare chair. "A press conference?"

"Classic Bennett," Anthony said.

He pressed play. The staged conference was meant to be a resource for the company—one of Dad's initiatives. Face-to-face contact wasted time, but Skype meetings calmed irritated stock holders and quieted jittery investors. Darius adopted it—like he tried to adopt everything else.

"*Family.*" Darius Bennett's serpent tongue rolled over the word as if it meant anything to him. "*It's the most important connection in this world. The past few months have been a difficult time for my family—all our families. Tragedy shadowed our hearts, but, slowly, we've begun to heal with new projects, new friends, and, of course, new love.*"

"What's the point of this?" I couldn't look into his slimy, toad-brown eyes even when he was only a digital representation. I wrinkled the one paper that hadn't been lost amid the clutter on Anthony's desk. The marriage certificate weighed as heavily on both our minds as any of the contracts or negotiations Darius could ruin with his publicity stunt. "What's he trying to do?"

Anthony tapped the desk and ordered me to be quiet. I huffed.

Deep breath in.

Deep breath out.

It didn't calm me, but it kept me from choking. Even over a video, Darius wielded a malicious power. The coiled rage pitted my stomach. He didn't deserve *any* reaction from me—not disgust, not rage, and certainly not a response from *my* stock holders.

"Since the unforeseen and tragic deaths of Josiah and Michael Atwood, the Bennett family has supported, comforted, and loved the Atwoods. Nothing replaces the loss of two children, but the compassion of a new family has lifted the veil of mourning and encouraged a new era of prosperity."

I sipped my water. The chill did nothing to extinguish the flaring of my temper.

Compassion?

Mourning?

Michael and Josiah weren't even buried before the vulture circled their gravesites and scavenged what remained. But what remained was me, and I hadn't given him a single taste of our company.

The water bottle crumpled in my grip. I didn't answer Anthony's glance. Nothing Darius Bennett said shocked me anymore. Anyone not drugged into oblivion on Vicodin and a cocktail of other soul-sucking pills should have realized what he wanted.

The grief and drugs had to be the only reason Mom was blinded to his charm.

"The Bennett Corporation is committed to the same excellence and success which created Atwood Industries so many generations ago. Family built this farm, and the blood, sweat, and tears of its children forged an empire of new technology blended with good, old-fashioned hard work."

Darius Bennett spoke the truth. He was a snake, but even the ultimate tempter graced the world with honesty every once in a while.

"Just a few months ago, I joined my family with the Atwood's in a quiet ceremony, and this flicker of happiness has blossomed into a unique partnership between two souls lost in a life of darkness and...dare I say, solitude?"

I bit my lip and tasted blood. The copper twang of Atwood pride prevented me from pitching my water at the screen.

"I wish to extend that partnership." Darius softened his voice for the camera. It sounded false and sour. *"The Bennett Corporation and Atwood Industries have lived in competition for far too long. As our families have merged, so have our hearts, ambitions, and visions for the future. Beginning today, I am announcing a new conversation—one between business partners. Friends. Family."* He lingered over the implication. *"A business proposal between a father and his new daughter."*

My profanity wasn't dignified.

I didn't remember standing. The room swirled a bit too quick, and my cough silenced the string of un-pleasantries bitter on my tongue.

Anthony stopped the video. The coughing intensified, but he respectfully waited until I recovered.

"Never," I said.

He nodded. "I assumed as much. This is not a formal offer, but the message broadcast to your Board of Directors. Has your mother said anything about Bennett's end game?"

"Mom's not..." Not the mother I remembered. "I can't talk to her. She trusts Darius. Always did, even before..."

Before she drugged herself beyond the pain of losing most of her family. I was still there, still trying to keep her in one piece. But she was the first battle I lost to Darius. It'd be the last.

"He has no claim over the company," I said. "Doesn't matter how many times Mom flashes the ring. Atwood Industries is independent of the family. He gets nothing but money. At least I can thank Josiah and Mike for being thoroughly irresponsible and losing it all."

Anthony exhaled. "You aren't destitute, Sarah. What money remains buys influence."

"The Bennetts are wealthier than us. Always have been."

"Certain members of your board might be interested in this partnership." He anticipated my frown with a raised hand. "It would make for one very powerful, very wealthy company."

"All under Darius Bennett's control."

"It doesn't have to be—"

"It's what he wants. Atwood Industries destroyed, ripped apart piece by piece. He doesn't care about the money or the company. He can't wait to cast us out into the street after he's robbed us of our land."

"He doesn't have that power."

"Nothing will stop him until he has it," I said. "I'm not indulging this. He has no right to call me...to talk about me like I'm his...his..."

I wheezed. Anthony had the discretion to pretend he didn't hear it.

My foot bumped my book-bag as I collapsed into the chair.

I was only twenty years old. Even Dad was closer to thirty when he took the company from Papa, and he had worked with him from his teens to learn the business.

I picked through my memories of dinners where Dad sat still long enough to offer wisdom. Never to me though. He looked to my brothers to protect the company like the warriors our success demanded. Atwood Industries wasn't supposed to be mine, but it sure as hell wouldn't fall prey to Darius Bennett.

"We have to make the clause public."

Anthony rolled away from his desk. He shook his head, but he didn't argue as he pulled my father's will from his shelf. Until two years ago, I had never seen the damned thing. Now, it felt like all I did was pour over the intricacies of Mark Atwood's Final Will and Testament and the poorly defined agreements my brothers had only started to organize for themselves.

"This clause makes it harder on you, Sarah," Anthony said. "Legal issues, trusts, every difficulty. We could argue against it—the company can be yours."

"I would rather lose everything than let Darius Bennett touch a single share."

"This is your farm too, Sarah."

"That's why I'm doing this." I took the copy of the will. "It's what my father wanted."

Anthony never showed frustration, but he tightened the dashing pony tail that swept most of his dark hair from his face. Neither of us was used to doing business with the other. Anthony was once just the charming attorney who visited us at home and brought Mom and me a box of chocolates before dealing with Dad and my brothers. Now? We were sick of each other—spending too many hours trying to fix too many problems. I hadn't had a piece of chocolate since the plane crash.

"I'm well aware of what Mark wanted for your brothers and what he expected of you," Anthony said. "But he's gone. You can take control of your own life now. So the question is...what do *you* want?"

I stuffed the will in my bag next to the homework I had forgotten to complete and the paper I'd never turn in.

"I want my father back." My voice hardened. "And I want Darius Bennett rotting in jail for his murder."

CHAPTER TWO
SARAH

"Did you win?" Dad asked.

I hid the red ribbon behind my back.

"Almost." I couldn't meet his eyes. "Second place. But most of the kids were older than me. Like, fifteen. They were in high school."

He waited. I offered him my prize. He didn't take it.

"I can't display that in my office. Throw it away."

"But, Dad, it...it's still good. They said so."

"I don't want you to make me look good." He packed his briefcase and left me at his desk. "You're an Atwood. You're meant to make me look great. You'll have to try harder."

"I will. I promise."

He didn't answer, but I earned his proud nod.

It was better than any stupid ribbon.

I grabbed my keys from Anthony's secretary and hit my inhaler the instant I reached my car.

Early summer was a bad season with all the pollen on the farm. Staying at school was easier on my lungs, but Mom made the worst decision of a lifetime without me being there. I moved home and thought I could balance both school and my family's mess.

I learned that lesson fast.

The add/drop forms were signed by sympathetic professors, but I hadn't returned it to the administrative offices. Dad said Atwoods never quit. As long as we had sun, water, and dirt, we'd survive.

But Dad never took thermodynamics and organic chemistry while managing the entire corporation. Dad hadn't dealt with Mom slicing her wrists the day of her sons' funerals. Dad never had to bathe her, dress her, and force her to eat. He didn't watch as a loathsome man more snake than human took advantage of her depression with superficial words.

Ten miles outside of Cherrywood Valley, and our fields traded the buildings, industrial districts, and diners for swaths of green. We owned acres upon acres, but the corn, alfalfa, and almonds still felt like Dad's, not mine. At least when Josiah and Mike squandered most of our money, they hadn't lost the most important things: the property, the soil, the crops.

Our future.

My phone rang. I couldn't avoid her forever.

Mom's sweet voice dulled—about three hours into her latest dose and already itching for another.

"Sweetheart," Mom said. "Are you coming home?"

Her newest obsession was always knowing my exact location. I couldn't blame her. We hadn't realized Josiah and Mike went to Vegas until the cable news channels broke with a story about their private plane crash. The police called an hour later.

"Just turned into the driveway."

"Good. I have a surprise for you."

If she meant to smile, it didn't translate over the phone. Mom's grin used to schmooze Dad's business partners. Dad said I had her features, but I saw more of him in me—especially our hair, as pale as corn peeking up in the fields. Mom's went grey before Dad's diagnosis. She pulled most of it out when he died.

Fortunately, it grew back for the wedding.

She didn't let me hang up and prattled on about Grandma's fancy china she found in storage. She'd be using the plates for dinner, but I didn't question why.

Then I saw the limo.

I didn't bother pulling into the garage. I wouldn't be staying long.

The curtains were pulled back. Mom gave me a wave from the foyer. I didn't return it.

"Is he here?" I demanded.

"Who?"

"*Him.*"

"Your father?"

I couldn't tell if it was the drugs or her warped mind that made the mistake.

"*Step*-father."

Mom cleared her voice. "I hoped it'd be a surprise—"

I disconnected the call. She waited by the window. My once beautiful mother, reduced to a dumb shell of a woman, orange pill bottle clutched in her hand.

I parked the car and counted my blessings.

Darius was here, and it would be easier than I thought to shut him down. Whatever game he played, whatever trigger he threatened to pull, it wouldn't matter. The Atwood fortune and company was as secure as kicking his ass out of my house and locking the door behind him.

Mom ushered me through the foyer, boasting about her roasted pork loin.

"Your father's favorite," she said.

It wasn't. Dad liked veal.

"Where is he?" I asked. She pointed to the kitchen—the little dinette area she begged Dad to remodel for her.

Dad favored the finer things. Large houses. Nice cars. Expensive trips overseas. Mom liked the simple, country living that supported the Atwoods for generations. They compromised. Mom got her farm house—Dad had his luxury. I grew up in a southern plantation antebellum home—columns and wraparound porches, winding staircases and sitting parlors.

The kitchen bathed in a down-to-earth, folksy atmosphere. The wooden table sat eight, far more than the blended atrocity that was my new family. Mom begged me to drop my bag and change before attending dinner.

No dice.

I pushed the doors open, but my steps crashed to a halt.

Darius wasn't alone.

"My dear!" His fake, plastic expression was better suited for ribbon cuttings and photo-ops. He didn't hide his distaste well. "I'm glad you've decided to join us."

Mom curled behind me, squeezing my hand. "Isn't this great? Your brothers are all here, for the first time since the wedding!"

They weren't my *brothers*.

My brothers were dead and buried.

These men were Bennetts.

Mom had toasted me at the wedding—sloshed on wine and dulled to incoherence with pills—claiming I was lucky to have *five* older brothers now. At the time, Josiah and Mike refused to answer. My new *brothers*—Nicholas, Maxwell, and Reed—weren't thrilled about the addition either.

Darius and his sons trespassed in my kitchen. The house was big, but in his oppressive presence, the walls shrunk and the ceilings collapsed. Every bit of air I managed to sneak into my lungs squeezed out, useless and stale.

Four Bennetts or four million. It didn't matter. I had Dad's will and final wishes.

I had won.

"You remember Nicholas, Max, and Reed?" Mom acted as if the men in her kitchen were life-long friends or her own flesh and blood. "Well, say hello, Sarah!"

"Hi."

Darius grinned. I hadn't seen them since the wedding four months ago. I considered it a good thing, especially as my mother pushed me into each of their arms for a dance while Josiah drank himself into a stupor and Mike stormed out after the ceremony.

Nicholas was the oldest at twenty-nine, and he was everything I expected from Darius Bennett's heir. Handsome. Cultivated. Reserved. He danced with me first at the reception, and I hated how polite he acted. He mentioned nothing of the marriage or how I wore the same mourning blacks I had for my father's funeral.

Without the aid of the champagne, I had nothing to brace me against his stare. Nicholas didn't share his father's eyes. His strong jaw and dark hair framed a majestically golden gaze—almost a toasted almond and far warmer than I expected.

He nodded but didn't offer more. That was fine. Nicholas had every reputation of his father. Word on the street was he was as ambitious as he was cruel. Our business partners warned when Nicholas assumed leadership of his family, I'd have one hell of a rival.

He didn't scare me.

In fact, had I encountered him on campus? I might have blushed instead of glared.

"Max, darling," Mom said. "Your drink is empty. Sarah, get your brother more iced tea?"

Max chuckled. Not a gentle, hospitable laugh.

He extended the glass, forcing me to cross the kitchen to pour him tea from the pitcher right beside him on the counter.

But that was Max. At the wedding, he had been an absolute force of masculinity and testosterone. His dance was an experiment to see how rough he could lead before I pushed from his arms and stalked away. He didn't even dance correctly. His steps jolted stiff, and he practically dragged his leg when he moved. Probably deliberate, just to annoy me. I might have slapped him, but I hadn't trusted the dark bands of tattoos swirling up his arms. Even now, the stylish dress shirt beneath his vest couldn't hide the hint of his ink. He seemed much older than twenty-seven.

He didn't scare me either, but I wondered if he should have.

"Tea it is." I gave him a refill of the chilled lemon tea. Max's dark eyes studied me. I ignored him. "Anyone else?"

Darius rattled his glass. The ice clinked. "Another whiskey, my dear."

I froze. Mom nodded toward the dining room.

She wasn't serious.

Dad's whiskey? The last of the special cask? The whiskey wasn't just rare—it wasn't made anymore. Dad savored each and every drop and reserved it only for special occasions like births or funerals or major, multi-million dollar deals.

And Darius had the nerve to slosh it around his glass like two bit moonshine.

I seized his tumbler, but the final straw rested at the feet of Reed.

Hamlet—my fuzzy goldendoodle—betrayed me. He rolled over and begged for tummy rubs from the youngest of my step-brothers.

Reed shared his father's callous poise, but when he grinned he seemed playful, a brightness that belonged at a beach barbeque, not boardroom. He had a dimple, but only one, on his left cheek. His right side tugged his smile differently, and a scar tore from his neck through his ear. But it didn't disfigure him.

I remembered he had actually enjoyed the wedding. Unlike Nicholas and Max, he danced most of the night with whatever girl was available. He grabbed me twice. Grandma loved him and lamented that a twenty-four year old man was a bit too young for her.

He was charming for a Bennett. Then again, Reed and Hamlet probably shared the same litter. Reed scratched his tummy, Hamlet fluttered his leg, and that was all the bullshit I was about to tolerate.

"Hamlet." I had to snap his name twice before he peeled himself from Reed. I pointed to the corner. "Go lay down."

"He wasn't bothering me," Reed winked. "Nice pup."

I slammed the tumbler against the table. Darius folded his hands.

"Why are you here?" I asked.

"Sprout, Darius has a rule," Mom whispered. My step-brothers smirked at the nickname. *Great.* "No business at dinner."

And my real father had his own rules. Don't put off what needs to be done. The corn would rot without harvest, and the animals would suffer without water. Atwood Industries wasn't a *business*. It was a living, breathing ecosystem that would wither and die in the hands of Darius Bennett.

"It's okay, Bethany," Darius said. "I expected this from Sarah."

Max crossed his arms, but Reed ignored the conversation. Nicholas gestured for me to sit.

I declined.

"I watched your press conference today, Darius." I tried to speak civilly and failed. A soft cough forced its way out. I hid it behind my hand.

"Are you well, my dear?"

"You had no authority to speak for Atwood Industries."

"With all due respect..." Nicholas said. His voice rumbled deep with the smoothness of melting wax. God, it was disarming. "My father was speaking for the Bennett Corporation."

"About *us*."

Mom started to fret. She stumbled over Hamlet and trembled to the stove. She reached in, forgetting the oven mitts. Reed stopped her

19

before she grabbed the roasting pan. He stole a towel from the counter and removed the dish. Mom thanked him, and he grinned again.

"Aren't you sweet," she said.

"Just hungry." He took the carving knife from Mom before she picked it up by the blade. "Let me?"

"Sarah, come sit so we can eat," she said.

"I don't have much an appetite, thanks." I reached into my bag, but Darius interrupted me before I pulled the will.

"My dear, I intend to buy your company."

The words sliced through me, as if he ripped my heart out and stuffed it in our fields' tilled dirt.

He thought my father's legacy was for sale, that he could scrape out the memories and hard work and blood from our own kitchen with a handshake and serpentine leer.

"Get out of my house."

Mom covered her mouth. "Sarah, listen to your father."

"He is *not* my father."

"And she will never see me as such, Bethany. I told you she would be hostile to this idea."

"*Hostile?*" Now I did sit if only so the few breaths of air cramming into my lungs did their work. "You come in my *home* after making statements about my family's company as if you are a spokesperson instead of a goddamned demon. How dare you!"

Nicholas raised a hand, as if he could silence me with the graceful motion.

He could, but that didn't mean I'd ever surrender to their proposal.

"Ms. Atwood. We've prepared a very generous offer for your company. Above and beyond its value, and more than what your father would have considered an accurate reflection of your assets. We aren't trying to undermine you."

I knew better than to trust a Bennett, even when Nicholas's steady demeanor shared none of the false bravado Darius wielded as both sword and shield.

"I'm not interested."

Mom touched my shoulder. "Sarah, we were never meant to manage this company."

"Mom, you aren't running the company. I am. And I'm not selling."

Darius chuckled. "Child, what you do know of directing a multi-*billion* dollar business?"

"I'm not a child."

"Your mother is right. You aren't meant to control Atwood Industries."

"Neither are you."

Nicholas braced me with a glance before reaching into the laptop bag.

"We aren't insulting you." He let the vindictive bite in my words pass. How much patience did he possess? "This is an opportunity to secure your future."

He pushed the contract toward me. I didn't read it, but I hadn't pulled my gaze from his quick enough. His confidence might have been attractive if he hadn't thought himself infallible. Nicholas actually believed his presented offense was an offer of freedom, wealth, and *charity*.

I didn't need Bennett charity.

And I wasn't comfortable trapped within the shadow of his stare or the buttery smoothness of his voice.

"When my father died..." I let the word linger. Darius, the bastard snake he was, didn't flinch. "His will was very specific."

"And we'll do our best to honor his conditions," Nicholas said.

No golden eyes or caramel cadence could save his deal. I set the will on the table. Darius inhaled.

Josiah managed to get power of attorney before Mom married. That passed to me, and I locked the will up tight from Darius with a perverse pleasure. My step-brothers watched as I flipped the pages to the clause that would either protect or damn my father's company.

I pushed the document to Darius. His expression slimed into a forced civility.

"In the event of Mark Gabriel Atwood's death, Atwood Industries and all assets as defined in Section 3 (a), shall be passed to his blood male heir."

"A *male* heir?" Darius's voice scraped over the word.

Nicholas cast a glance to his brothers. Max frowned. Reed tossed Hamlet a piece of the pork loin. I waited for the hammer to fall or a mic to drop.

"A technicality, my dear," Darius said. He cleared his throat. "He didn't specifically name any of his children. And rightly so. He believed the company would pass to one of his sons, but no one anticipated their untimely deaths."

"The clause stands." I hoped I was doing the right thing. "And I'll honor my father's wishes. As of today, I will hold Atwood Industries in a trust until I have a son."

Mom shook another pill from the bottle. Darius said nothing, but the rage, condemnation, and frustration in his clenching jaw read easier than the rest of my father's will.

The only thing more glorious than Darius's failure would have been to witnessed such *hatred* with him behind bars, where the murdering son of a bitch belonged.

Nicholas wasn't deterred. He flipped through the rest of the pages with a cursory glance.

"You could fight this," he said. "Ms. Atwood, I understand your aggravation, but we are offering you...everything."

"Everything can't bring my father back." I stared at Darius. He took my mother's hand, bringing her fingers to his lips with a sneer. "But this is his land. His legacy. Selling it would be no better than selling his memory. I won't do it."

I stood. Nicholas followed, but Darius burned where he sat.

"I have work at the office," I said. It was true, I just wasn't sure how to do any of it. Damage control, investors to call, reports to write, labs to turn in at school. I nodded toward my *brothers* and relished a deep breath that rejuvenated me more than any hit from my inhaler. "Excuse me, I won't be able to stay for dinner."

I lashed the bag over my shoulder. Darius didn't dare watch me leave, but my step-brothers stared as I stalked from the room. Suddenly, I wasn't the only one tense in Darius's presence.

Nicholas, Max, and Reed silenced, minding their father like the good little sons of the devil they were. Victory tasted sweet, but I didn't envy their ride home.

I made it to the car before the bittersweet laugh bubbled inside me. Dad would have been proud. My brothers ecstatic.

But me?

I collapsed in the driver's seat, staring at a home where I couldn't stay and land I relinquished to an imaginary son that bluffed my way to momentary freedom.

But at least the Atwood name, fortune, and future were safe. I almost hoped the Bennetts would try to fight for what didn't belong to them.

If only to watch them fail.

CHAPTER THREE
NICHOLAS

Life was a struggle to secure two necessities.

Family.

Power.

With one came the other. It was a simple formula my father preached since I was born, and one I repeated each day as I grew into the man he decided I would become.

My father declined Bethany Atwood's offer to stay for dinner after my new step-sister made one very impetuous mistake.

She challenged him in a way not even Mark Atwood had ever dared.

She'd stake her life on a company that wasn't hers and a name that bullied, intimidated, and stole every ounce of begrudged respect it earned. My father wasn't a forgiving man, and hers was an insult he wouldn't soon forget.

The limo ride to the airport commanded silence. I studied Mark Atwood's will, marveling in how brilliantly he wove his final wishes to honor his *sons*. Sarah's name wasn't mentioned. If she knew or cared, it didn't show. The girl waved the will like a flag, as though a strip of paper would protect her.

It wouldn't. And she'd soon learn what a terrible, regrettable mistake she had made.

I handed the paperwork to Max. He didn't care to read it, but, under our father's scrutiny, he took the papers and shuffled the pages. He wasn't a man who studied contracts and parsed the law. That was my role. I doubted he'd find any other conclusion.

Sarah Atwood played her hand all in—no bluffs, no cheats, and every scrap of luck the Atwoods had saved since they clawed their way into an elite world which didn't belong to them.

Mark Atwood rotted in hell and danced in glee at this turn of events. It wouldn't be long until my father lost his patience and sent Sarah there as well.

The private jet waited to depart. My father boarded in silence and slipped into his cabin. My brothers left him to brood. My attention drifted to the window and the fading airport below. The cornfields extended even this far from their farm. Acres upon acres of land—all under the control of one little girl who had no idea how much trouble she caused.

"She's cuter than I remembered." Reed kicked his seat back.

Max smacked the ass of our private flight attendant and earned her giggle. "Careful. That's your sister."

"Family first, huh? What'd you think, Nick?"

I poured over the will. How the hell had we lost this? "I wouldn't want to be Sarah Atwood at the moment."

Reed shrugged at Max. "Didn't look like she wanted to be Sarah Atwood either."

"How bad is it if we don't get this deal?" Max asked.

I wouldn't discuss the possibility, not with our father so close. The cabin wasn't soundproof, and I couldn't insult his judgment within earshot. Family and power were the most important aspects of life to him—and it was his reason for marrying the Atwood widow and debasing our name to offer the girl more money than their company was worth.

"We'll devise a new plan," I said. "A new course of negotiations. This isn't over."

Max lowered his voice. "He has me talking to investors."

"I am as well."

His fist clenched. "You and me got different ways of talking, Nick."

"And neither method is effective at the moment."

Reed stole the will and flipped around the document. "So we expand. Do something besides agricultural support and engineering."

"For how long?" I asked. "We don't have the luxury of time. The best we can do is free a couple million and form a project outside the corporation."

Max raised his eyebrows. "The Atwoods had the assets we needed."

"That money is gone now."

"And her bastard brothers knew just how to fuck us with it."

Reed leaned forward. "What the hell is Dad gonna do to that girl?"

"Not our concern," I said.

"Bullshit."

I tightened my jaw. I loved my brother, but sometimes he didn't think like a Bennett, and that was more troublesome than Sarah Atwood.

"What wouldn't our father do to acquire that company?" I said.

Reed and Max fell silent.

The plane delivered us to San Jose in an hour and a half. We landed, and our driver wove through the redwood forest and private land that separated the Bennett Estate from the rest of the world. The gated monstrosity ruled from one of the tallest points in the forest, surrounded with wilderness and streams—the clean, fertile grounds the Bennett family promised to sustain with our research and products designed to assist agricultural enterprises across the country.

Our father hadn't spoken since leaving the farm. He burned with insult. I understood. Mark Atwood had been the specter of grief that haunted our family for the past seventeen years. We celebrated his death, but none of us anticipated the littlest Atwood carrying on her father's legacy.

Reed was right.

Sarah defined pretty—a feisty little blonde with more fight in her than freckles on her nose. She was better suited for college textbooks, not contracts and reports—as if she understood anything about the power they contained. She never raised a hand against my father, but her simple smile was the cat-scratch of her nails against his face.

No one ever claimed her family fought fair. In another world, my step-sister might have made an excellent Bennett.

We crossed the foyer, our steps echoing over the imported marble. The split, grand staircase presided over the entry hall, an impressive and immense structure carved for the simple purpose of displaying our wealth and the extravagances built for our pleasure.

My brothers lived outside the estate as the grounds would pass solely to me. In the rare instances we were brought together, we each possessed our own private wing. But twenty-five thousand square feet wasn't enough space. Not when Max refused to live off his inheritance, and Reed fought to travel overseas—to find a place beyond our father's influence. It didn't exist.

My brothers knew their places within the Bennett's realm of influence. Max, two years younger than me, entered the service, but he never saw combat. Even now, he attempted to hide his limp, but our name failed to secure him a position on the front, regardless of how beneficial it would have been for our image. Instead, Max oversaw security for the Bennett Corporation.

Reed garnered enough sympathy from the fading scars over the right side of his face, neck, and ear that his charity work came easily. His charm helped as well.

We had our roles to fill in the family.

It was the first time in twenty-nine years I had failed at mine.

I staked everything on the assumption she'd sell—not initially, not even amicably—but eventually. We'd wear her down, offer her more money than they deserved for their empire, and treat the Atwood name with a delicacy they hadn't earned.

But I didn't anticipate my father gloating at a press conference and announcing our intentions, and I hadn't realized how much she hated our family. The feeling was mutual, but our rivalry existed between Mark and his sons. Undoubtedly, her father had twisted her, confused her, and used her.

Sarah didn't even realize the legal complications she created. The stock would tank. Investors would run. Customers would pursue safer companies.

Of course, my offer would stand.

At a substantially reduced price.

"Follow me." Our father's voice didn't echo, but it boomed over the foyer.

Reed clapped me on the shoulder as he crossed into the study, but Max shared my glance, recognizing our father's strained cadence.

While Mark Atwood built his home with every decadent and gaudy architectural mistake, the Bennett estate hadn't changed for generations. The French manor, framed with Corinthian stone and imported marbles, was beautiful. Spanning foyers and elaborate halls separated vast wings of meticulously sculpted woodwork and refined parlors. Dark woods and darker colors warmed the mansion, and the masonry forged a certain stonework elegancy.

The study surrounded a roaring hearth with floor to ceiling book cases and mementos of my family's world travels. The most recent addition was a photograph upon the mantle, dressed in a solid silver frame and held in a strict reverence of coiled garland.

My father's wedding picture—an image of him and Bethany Atwood embraced in their first kiss.

We hadn't questioned the photograph.

My father motioned for me to sit in the wingback mirroring his leather chair. He made no such arrangements for Max or Reed.

He rarely smoked, but a cigar clipped and passed to me first. He left the box for my brothers and reclined. I let the smoke settle over me. Max puffed and relaxed. Reed waved the smoke away from his neck.

"Our family is being tested." My father's rage blazed like the red-hot end of his cigar. "This company is facing a series of challenges we haven't encountered in many years. It is up to you, my sons, to save us."

Max nodded. Reed stood, motionless. My father awaited my reply.

"Of course," I said. "We'll do whatever is necessary."

"The company bears our name. It is the source of our pride, and our face upon this world. And now? We find ourselves in a precarious position." He drew on the cigar. "We need Atwood Industries. I *want* Atwood Industries."

Max spoke first, a mistake he consistently made. "Christ. Atwood Industries will *bankrupt* the family. We can't keep throwing money at the rat's nest and hope it burns through the trash."

My father's fist clenched. I didn't have time to intercede.

"Mark Atwood was a blight upon this world. You should be grateful the demons snarled through the dirt to drag his worthless, miserable hide to Hell."

Max didn't hesitate. "I am."

"It is a benefit to this family that his sons have died and the scourge of the Atwood name has been scoured from the earth."

"What about Sarah?" Reed said.

My father silently seethed, his wrath centering upon whatever memory he harbored of the girl.

"In this lifetime, we'll face two sets of people. Those who oppose us, and those we may use for our own advantage. The Atwoods opposed us." The chill in his words would extinguish the cigar. "I will spend every cent, pursue every outlet, and spill blood to redeem our family and ensure the Atwoods are cast into the gutter of their own shame."

Reed frowned. "And so that means giving them more money than the accounts are worth? How does that vindicate us?"

I waved a hand. "Money is nothing. It's made and spent, wasted and created every day. But there is only one Bennett family. And now, only one Atwood remains."

My father exhaled. "And had the cunt taken the offer, their land, crops, animals, and livelihood would have been ours to burn. Instead, we're faced with greater challenges."

Max nodded. "Then we make her sell. I'll do whatever it takes."

And he did, often and ruthlessly. But no violence would aid us, not when she twisted the circumstances and bound herself in awkward legality. Inheritance law was difficult enough, especially following her brothers' deaths.

"Selling makes no difference now," I said.

"The company is held in her trust until..." My father twitched. "She presents a male heir."

Reed pulled his phone and made a note. "So we scour their family tree. Find a cousin or something."

"No."

My father offered nothing more. I lowered the cigar.

"No?" I hesitated. "We let her retain the rights to the company?"

"No, we are not searching for a male heir."

"Then how—"

"We have no *time* to waste. We have less than a year before our influence and shareholders are compromised." My father shook his head. "We could divert resources to find a distant relative willing to sell, but Atwood's little bitch would thrive during months and months of litigation."

I straightened. "It is the cleanest solution. A clear-cut buyout. No unpleasant bartering for investors' votes. No crises. No stock crashes. We'll present to whomever we can find."

"And it will fail again!" His voice cracked over the room. "She refused our offer. Worse, she humiliated us. Buying the company is no longer an option. And now, we are forced to regain our honor from the Atwoods." He pitched a goblet of wine into the hearth. The glass shattered. "From the Goddamned *Atwoods*!"

Reed shifted away from the sputtering fire. "Then what do you—"

"I want Sarah Atwood's male heir."

The fire popped. My father's rasping breath echoed against the crackle of the fire.

The blaze fueled the rage churning within him. He stared, but the Darius Bennett I recognized—the man I emulated and respected—no longer existed. A demonic shell darkened over him as fury crept into madness.

I hated myself for the question I was forced to ask.

"You want her *heir*?"

My father spoke into the fire. "She forced the clause. Atwood Industries belongs to her yet-to-be-conceived *son*. All rights and wealth, institutions and assets will be granted to an unborn child."

A chill slowed my thoughts.

It should have silenced me.

It should have prevented me from understanding *exactly* what my father wished.

Unfortunately, my conscience flaked to ash years ago. I was Nicholas Bennett. The heir to the Bennett empire. My sins, my crimes, and my regrets existed only to protect the family.

Reed didn't understand. "She doesn't have a son yet."

Max exhaled a curtain of smoke to hide his realization. I shared his shiver. My father's grin would desecrate everything pure within his power.

Like Sarah Atwood.

"She will have a son," my father said. "Her heir will belong to the Bennetts."

I stilled my movements and wished my heart had ceased with it.

"And one of you will create it."

The clock on the mantle chimed ten o'clock. Not nearly late enough for talk of this nature.

Max hesitated. He posed the question to me to avoid the wide-eyed insanity of our father.

"You want us to seduce Sarah Atwood?"

No.

Seduction never crossed his mind.

Until Bethany, my father never expressed any sympathy for the family. Their deaths enthralled him, and their misery entertained him. Any misfortune was a cause for celebration.

No one would *seduce* the girl.

"I will have an heir to Atwood Industries." My father didn't lower his voice, despite the evil he summoned. "I'll control everything and everyone within that family."

"But—"

"Everything she loves, and everything she has worked so hard to build and maintain, will be lost the instant that girl bears a Bennett for a son."

My father stared at each of us, unshakable and unblinking.

"I want that Atwood bitch to regret challenging me. We offered her everything. She refused." His words haunted the room with vulgar threat. "She will regret crossing me every second of every minute of every day it takes her to grow a Bennett in her womb." He laughed.

"And then I'll watch as her world is destroyed the instant my grandson is born into this world."

"You want us...to fuck her," Reed whispered.

"No. I want you to breed Sarah Atwood."

The fire crackled. The charring pop didn't disturb me. I would hear it for all eternity as my father damned our family to the deepest, blackest depths of hell.

Max stood too quickly, wincing as he forced his weight over his bad leg. "Holy Christ, Dad."

I poured a glass of wine, offering the Pinot Noir to my father. He accepted.

"Dad, you've married Bethany," I said. "Sarah is technically our sister."

"*Step*-sister,"

"*Step*-sister. But don't you think the relation is—"

"Do you plan for this family to fail, Nicholas?"

Did he? What did he think he'd accomplish besides serving us with life-sentences and corrupting a young woman's innocence?

"Of course not," I said.

"Do you intend to let the Atwood whore spit on the generous agreement *you* created?" He tilted his head. "She did not insult me, son. Her refusal voided your contract. She disrespected *you*."

"And so I should impregnate my step-sister?" I braved a chuckle. "You said it yourself. The clause is a technicality. She holds the trust. If we present that a sale of the company positively benefits Atwood Industries, she would be within her right to accept—"

"Enough." My father never raised his voice. I gave him his respect, taught through years of agony endured under his crop, molding me into

35

his perfect son. "She'll never sell. She'll control the company until she bears a child and raises it with the same delusions that indoctrinated her into the Atwood philosophy." My father exhaled. He gestured to my brothers. "Leave us. I will discuss this further with Nicholas."

Max and Reed stiffened, unceremoniously dismissed from the conversation.

I envied them.

My father appraised me with the grace of an executioner sharpening his blades.

"You would disobey me in this," he said.

I lowered my wine. "No. But I question your motivations."

"Why?"

"It is not...honorable."

My father laughed. "And what Mark Atwood did to your mother. That was honorable?"

I didn't answer.

"Life is a war, Nicholas, and death is too often the only solution," he said. "Imagine when a birth is the ultimate conquest."

"She'll never do this willingly."

"And?"

I expected it. "You're asking us to rape Sarah Atwood."

"I'm asking you to protect this family."

"She'll go to the police. We'll be ruined."

"Then don't let her talk to the police!" My father waved a hand over the parlor. "This will be *your* estate, Nicholas. Your home! If you can't find one place to hide a scrawny little girl—"

"Dad, listen to what you're saying!" I stood. His gaze followed—invisible shackles binding me to our name, our home, our pride. "You're asking us to abduct, rape, and impregnate our *step-sister.*"

"For the family."

"Absolutely not."

He asked the impossible, and yet his eyebrows rose, as if he realized the obscenity of the plan. Still he chose to ignore every modern convention of rationality and decency.

And for what?

The family?

No.

This wasn't for the Bennetts. And it wasn't for the company.

This was vengeance. Pure sadism. He planned an end to a bitter feud that began before I was born and was bound to continue after I died.

"We won't do this."

My father said nothing. He stared, and I struggled to endure the uncompromising commands. I braced for the worst, but I hadn't anticipated his brutality. I was twenty-nine years old, and he yet surprised me.

Horrified me.

"Nicholas, you are my eldest son. You are my heir, my legacy to this world." He spoke softly, intentionally forcing me to hold my breath just to listen. "But understand, I have two other sons."

"Perhaps they'd prefer to do this crime," I said.

"Doubtful."

"Then you realize this is a mistake."

"Nicholas, you will control the company and this family *alone*, as it has been set for generations."

"I understand."

"I have no real need for two additional sons."

The implication struck like a blade to the throat. I didn't doubt his threat. A Bennett lost his naivety at a young age. My father had no cause to lie.

"You would harm your own flesh and blood?" I asked.

"You would deny your family the ultimate wealth, security, and vengeance?"

My father stood, a lurking devil.

"I love this family," I said.

"Then protect it."

"From you?"

"From any danger. The decision rests with you, Nicholas. Convince your brothers to capture and breed Sarah Atwood, or..." His pat to my shoulder suddenly gripped, pinching hard against a nerve he favored to bring me to my knees as a child. I didn't wince. "You will be responsible for what happens to this family."

He sipped the rest of his wine and left me to the silence of the study.

What choice did I have?

I would always put my family first.

CHAPTER FOUR
SARAH

I fell asleep at the lab.

My first time at the facility in weeks, and I wasted it collapsed on the black laminate table, trapped between a microscope, a couple test tubes, and Lady Gaga blaring on my laptop.

I checked for drool and groped for my phone.

Midnight.

What a productive four hours.

I stretched. The perpetual ache in my shoulders wouldn't ease if I didn't get some sleep in a bed. Last night I curled up in the university library, but I hadn't studied a word for my midterms. Instead, I blinked through as much of the new agreement Anthony's office worked up to announce the trust. It granted me executive power to operate the company in lieu of whatever imaginary baby I concocted, but it wouldn't help me pass Ecology.

At least Atwood Industries was safe from Darius Bennett. That made the exhaustion, misery, and complications worth it. Nothing was going to tarnish my father's legacy—certainly not any empire the Bennetts shaded with their vulgarity.

I blinked at the laptop. The measurements were supposed to upload directly into the program.

"Damn."

I alt-tabbed through the open applications. Facebook. iTunes. An Amazon product confirmation for a case of K-Cups I didn't remember ordering but made sense. My head throbbed with a horrible caffeine withdrawal. I spaced out, but I swore I opened the correct spreadsheet.

My Biosystems Design coursework stared at me.

Great.

I was such a mess I wasn't even doing the right work in the right lab.

Frustrating.

I closed out the program. My back ached, my laptop overheated, and I was pretty sure I forgot to eat lunch and dinner.

Something had to give.

And I had a bad feeling about what it'd be.

The state-of-the-art lab belonged to Atwood Industries—and Dad promised my own office once I earned my PhD.

It wouldn't happen now.

No matter how much work I had done in the lab, no matter how much I researched and developed, I had a bigger responsibility. When it came time to publish, patent, and sell, the credentials were more important than the private, basement lab.

Dad forbade me from working on anything for Atwood Industries at school, and I understood. Less risk for the campus to claim experiments at the university belonged to them. But peer reviews and testing and all the hassle that came from developing a commercial product—*especially* anything genetically modified—turned into a nightmare and a half.

What started as something fun and exciting became an exercise in litigation, patent wars, and corporate level secrecy. Dad insisted nothing about my research leaked beyond the family. Josiah was supportive. Mike called me a nerd. It didn't matter as long as Dad was proud of me.

"If Mike and Jos get the company when they grow up…" It was the first time ten year old me had thought about it, and my nose scrunched up in confusion. "What do I get?"

Dad parsed through his papers. "Your brothers were made for the company, Sprout. I needed sons."

"Then what was I made for?"

"I wasn't expecting a little girl. It's only proper for the company to go to my boys." Dad winked and pushed my textbook toward me. "But you like science, and that helps me."

"It does?"

"Sure, Sprout. Daddy has all kinds of people helping to make the corn better before we plant it. You'll work in the labs and do research."

"But I want to be a baker."

"Nonsense. It'll make Daddy happy to have you working hard for the company. Don't let me down, Sarah. You're the future of the Atwoods."

Some future.

I rubbed my face. I hadn't drooled on my research journal. Good. The scrawling gibberish? Not so much.

Half of my notes didn't pertain to the research I *knew* would revolutionize Atwood seed and product. Most of the notebook now filled with scribbled leads on what my brothers worked on and where they had tucked or spent so many millions of dollars. Anthony warned we'd be hit with an audit from the Board if we didn't get it sorted out soon.

Just the thought of an audit gave me a headache—especially after losing most of my credits last semester because of the funerals.

My email blipped. Anthony, torturing me after hours again.

S—Bennett hired a private investigator to research into Josmik Holdings. I'll find out more, but be careful with information on open networks. —Anthony

"Good luck." I closed the laptop. "He'll need it."

Like I had any information about Josiah and Michael's joint venture. Whatever money they took, spent, or invested was gone. Anthony and I had no success figuring it out.

But Darius shouldn't have even known about Josmik Holdings.

The shiver tingled over me.

Why would he investigate my brothers' lost investments?

He wanted something they had. Something he failed to obtain before Dad died.

And that something was worth murdering for.

A crash echoed from upstairs. I checked the time.

Midnight?

A door slammed from the ground floor offices. Who in their right mind was working so late?

I zipped my bag, listening over the clicking pumps working hard to maintain a vacuum for the projects stashed in the corner. The lab existed in a state of pure noise. Chemistry wasn't all mixing compounds and dissolving solutions. I spent more time waiting for the machines to finish their tests than doing fun experiments. Erlenmeyer flasks were a lot more exciting when I wasn't washing them.

I listened.

Nothing else echoed.

I hadn't studied in the lab in a few weeks, but usually no one darted into the offices upstairs in the middle of the night.

All the more reason to head home. It was way past the time I was comfortable being out alone, especially when the last warnings Dad gave was about my security as I had grown into such a *beautiful woman.*

I wasn't about to think of those implications. Another bump shattered the stillness.

This time it didn't come from upstairs.

This time, the slice of a boot crashed on the stairs just outside my lab.

The few techs and chemists who used the lab didn't wear steel tipped boots. They also didn't lurk in the hallways. And they certainly didn't take the steps agonizingly slow, clopping a heavy-footed echo in the bare basement halls as though hiding.

My chest tightened—the worst moment for that to happen. I edged away from the door with a wheeze. The light switch waited under my hand, but drenching the lab in darkness would be just as suspicious as me bursting out of the room in a dead sprint.

Instead, I searched my purse for the phone. Mike and Josiah always carried guns. I regretted never taking up their offer to learn to shoot. A small canister of mace jingled on my key ring. I had no idea if it even worked anymore, but I tossed the cap away. If it was empty, maybe my aching lungs wouldn't swallow enough mace to hurt me?

Or maybe it'd cause a full-on attack.

Only one way to find out.

Glassware stacked around me, but my only real weapon was a lab stool. The acids and strong bases locked up tight in the storage room. The windows didn't open completely, and we converted our second cubby into a larger eye-wash station and emergency shower. No hiding in there.

The footsteps snapped against the cement hall.

My pulse fluttered.

I was trapped.

Thud.

Quiet.

Thud.

I counted my breaths. Far too few to be effective. I heaved the nearest stool over my head.

The door kicked open. I screamed and slammed the stool against a man dressed completely in black leather. He grabbed the chair before it crashed against his ski-mask. He jerked me off-balance.

I spun from his grasp, but my laptop clattered to the ground. The book bag followed.

He lunged. My soil ecology books swung into his jaw.

I thought I was quick, but my attacker was bigger, stronger, and far more aggressive. His hands laced over my waist and lifted me from the ground. I screamed, throwing fists and kicks against anything soft and squishy.

Except nothing about the mugger was soft.

"*Let me go!*"

Something connected. Hard. My toes felt like they broke, but the attacker slumped. I kicked again, missing the fleshy bits I had already pummeled. I nailed his knee with a swift, deliberate aim.

He dropped me, but I picked myself up faster than the asshole clawing who needed the wall to stand on his injured leg.

The mace didn't mist so much as it jetted, but the shot of liquid capsicum dosed him with aggravation.

Run.

The pepper spray showered the lab, and the spiced air tore razor-bladed pain in my throat and lungs. I coughed and abandoned my bags.

He didn't follow. I sprinted up the basement steps, collapsing at the top in a wheeze that scared me more than the attack.

I groped for my inhaler in my pocket.

"Fu—"

I didn't have the strength to swear. The inhaler tucked in my freaking purse which was probably long gone with the mugger. Damn. I didn't carry that much money on me. The idiot attacker would make off with forty dollars, a student ID, and my emergency medication. Hell, the biology textbooks that clattered against his face were the most expensive thing in the lab.

I burst outside and bolted to my car. The clicking locks echoed. A symphony in my fear. My fingers trembled as I pushed the ignition, but the rumble reassured me. Like my father's casual whistle as he kicked my butt in tennis or my brothers' fist-fights at the base of the stairs.

Comforting. Normal.

I managed to breathe. Kinda. I'd just drive home. Find my medication. Calm down, call the police.

Recover my damn lab journal and laptop before the thief made off with something more important, more valuable, and absolutely crucial to the survival of my family.

Christ, before the mugger ruined something that had the opportunity to revolutionize agriculture and significantly raise yields in dry, arid climates. Not the most riveting way to save the world, but it'd be enough to put food in a lot of people's bellies and conserve a hell of a lot more water.

My chest ached. I had to get home.

Breathe in.

Breathe out.

I peeled out of the parking lot and sped down the deserted main street.

Twin headlights blinded me from my rearview mirror.

A car?

No. I swore again, wasting more air on useless fear.

Motorcycles.

Goddamn it.

I lived in Cherrywood Valley long enough to realize the Atwoods weren't the only powerful force dominating the markets. I avoided the bikers as Dad instructed.

But these guys weren't the local Anathema thugs.

The bikes roared beside me, and I reflexively jammed the breaks as one cut in front of the car. The rider dressed in solid black, and a shaded helmet covered his face. He swung toward me, and I drifted away, slowing enough to drop a gear. I made it too easy for them to chase me.

My vision darkened as the cough squeezed my chest and head.

Not good.

I accelerated, but the bikes kept up—speeding, edging close, and risking their own lives to drift ever closer to my car.

What did they want? To kill me? To steal the car?

Hurting me would do nothing. They couldn't even kidnap me, not when I was the only one able to release the ransom money.

Oh, God.

Ransom.

It made sense. All the instability, all of Darius's damn speeches. It was a chance for a criminal to make a move against me—especially if they thought Darius would seize control of the money and company.

I was the easier target.

God, that pissed me off.

Dad didn't raise me to be a victim. I hid weakness beneath the Atwood name, and I utilized my gifts to forge a stronger image. A better image. Sarah Atwood—gifted student, charming philanthropist...

Lost and struggling daughter trying her damnedest to do what she could to keep her mother from slicing her wrists and the company from dissolving to our family's greatest enemy.

I jerked the wheel toward the asshole biker treading too close to my side. I scared him off, but not before the clatter echoed inside the car.

The bang terrified me.

They punctured my tires!

I lurched the wheel again. Wasn't a great idea. The busted tire shredded over the rim.

The car fought and thudded. I waited until the last possible moment before shoving my foot flat against the break and riding through the dangerous shudder that skidded the remaining good tires.

I twisted the wheel and accelerated. My turn from the main drag surprised them. The bikers screeched to a halt and spun to chase, but I had a quarter of a mile on them.

Even with my lungs cramping and shoulders tightening, I found my way through the city in the darkness. The bikers hung back. They weren't Anathema, and that gave me some hope. I sped past the opera house and industrial district, heading south instead of taking the bridge across the river. The town limits blurred by. A couple aching breaths delivered me a mile outside the city.

The pain in my lungs didn't ease until the first of our thigh-high corn sprouted in the distance. The night hid most of our property, but I didn't care. I was close to home.

In my breathless fog, I realized my mistake.

Damn it. I led the bikers right to my house.

The crushing sob didn't emerge from my chest. I swallowed another harsh breath. I couldn't turn around. Stopping so suddenly in the rattling car would allow my stalkers to dive from the bikes and get too close.

The car rumbled. Something charred and filled the interior with acrid fumes.

I couldn't make it to the next town over on three wheels. Home seemed to be the best option, and I prayed I'd get there with enough of a head start to find Dad's old hunting rifle. Maybe Mom knew how to shoot.

Maybe Darius would be there?

Fuck.

I slammed my hand on the wheel.

Jesus Christ. Crawling to *Darius Bennett* for help? How much oxygen had I lost?

A flash preceded the second blowout. The back tire popped in a horrible burst of sparks and an explosive thud that stole complete control of the car. I spun out, fish-tailed, and bumbled over the road. The speedometer read a number somewhere between idiotic and absolute disaster.

The car skidded off the shoulder. The wooden fence didn't stop me. In the darkness—in my blinding, aching, oxygen-deprived fear—I slammed on the accelerator instead. My wheels tore into the acres of corn, and the stalks thudded and cracked and beat against my windshield.

Screaming did nothing. The car careened into the dirt, sinking deep into our fields and rutting through the crops. My headlight shattered on the fence and what remained dulled with mud and shredded leaves.

The frayed tires bounced against the mud before imbedding in the irrigation equipment. The car juked, tossing hard to the right. I shielded my face as it flipped, crashing and shattering every window.

The engine still hummed.

But the car stopped.

I fell against broken glass. The airbag hadn't deployed, my only salvation. The dust would have killed me…unless the men chasing me did it first.

My vision blurred. The coughing did nothing to clear my lungs. Twice I attempted to turn the car off, missing the ignition and pressing furiously against the radio. Lady Gaga roared against the nightmare. I didn't have the energy or clarity to shut it off.

I was close to home.

I thought.

Maybe?

Get out of the car.

Deep breath. Didn't help.

I twisted against the steering wheel. The movement strained an already spasming chest. I had to get out. I had...the door...

I pulled myself up, measuring each breath with a slight motion. Couldn't overexert myself. Not with the pollen.

Dust.

Debris.

I crashed Josiah's car.

My brother would have made sure I was okay.

Dad would have been so pissed. At least he was dead. Didn't have to worry about getting in trouble. I was in enough for a lifetime.

My shocked laugh pulled me from the stupor. I shivered, but my legs untangled from the seat. I climbed up and forced my weight against the passenger door.

The bikes rumbled from the road.

They *still* chased?

What did they expect to find? A wreck like that should have turned me to corn-meal mush. I grunted and shoved the door open, heaving myself up and using my ribs to prevent the door from closing. My lungs hardly worked anyway. Why should they get protected?

I clattered to the ground and sputtered in the dirt. My fingers grasped the soil of my family's land. It gave me strength. Something my brothers never understood and Darius Bennett would sooner salt than experience.

I took a step.

One step.

Then another.

And a third.

I stumbled into the corn, away from the car blaring techno pop in the shadows of the field.

Another step.

Where was I?

West field. No. North field? I left town traveling south.

Something cold slithered against my ankle. My cry didn't squeak out. Not when a web crossed over my lips.

Corn silk.

Pretend its corn silk.

Breathe.

Run.

Too much to do.

Someone called my name. Maybe Mom saw the crash? She'd come running if she had managed to pull herself out of bed.

But the voice was deep—a melting wax of shadow and heat.

Not her.

I dodged the thrashing slap of corn as I ran. Destructive footsteps slammed behind me.

Did I cry? I hoped the wetness on my cheeks wasn't blood. I didn't stop sprinting through the endless, darkened fields of cold, dew-kissed corn.

My name again. Closer. I tripped over the stalks and crashed to the ground.

Get up.

My fists dug into the dirt again as the shadow burst after me. I tossed the handful, but the man in the helmet sidestepped the throw. I kicked. He grabbed my leg.

The panic attack won out. My puffing chest hyperventilated me before the asthma stole my vision. The biker dove to my side, picking me up. I swung another fist, but I struck only black riding leathers, protecting him from the road and my weak hits. He held me close. The dark helmet muffled his call.

"She's over here!"

That delicious voice again. Familiar. I struggled to turn over, to crawl away. He called my name and shook me once as my head lolled in his arms. He ripped the helmet off.

Golden eyes swirled in my mind.

I swore my kidnapper looked like Nicholas Bennett.

CHAPTER FIVE
SARAH

A needle pinched my skin. I jerked awake.

Where was I?

The blood drew too slowly, delicately stolen from my vein. They tried to be gentle and failed.

Hands poked at me. I shifted, but I couldn't move. Thick bindings strapped me down, the material stretched taut over my chest and wrists.

A hospital?

No. The shattering fear shredded me inside and out.

This wasn't a hospital.

The hands rolled over my stomach. They tested the few bruises on my skin. My vision blurred and the dark splotches blended into the hazy darkness surrounding me.

The fingers moved to my belly.

Then lower.

Far, far too low.

What was happening?

And why...

It was too hard to think. Hard to see. I didn't want those fingers. I squirmed from another needle.

I groaned. They didn't care. I stayed at enough hospitals to expect a greeting or kind word or even a brisk order from the doctor to stay still while they finished their examination.

Something was wrong. My pulse leapt, though the sheer exhaustion of waking up layered my body in a strange weight. My mind screamed. Nothing escaped my trembling lips.

A doctor moved over me. The white coat fluttered as he reached for a pair of purple latex gloves.

I closed my eyes.

A chilled invasion sliced through me. I whimpered, but I didn't have the strength to scream or to shift away.

I still cried.

The doctor's fingers prodded *inside* me.

Oh, God.

I struggled. It didn't bother him. He pressed hard on my navel and withdrew after a moment, passing beyond the cold, artificial light aimed between my legs.

Exposed.

So exposed.

A metal tool jingled on a tray next to the bed. The doctor rubbed where the needle prickled. He checked his watch and nodded.

And pushed my legs open.

"N—no."

"Hush."

My vision darkened again. My head fell against the pillow. I couldn't yell. Worse, my body refused to fall asleep again.

The tool forced inside me. I tensed, but he worked fast.

"Virgin," he said. "She's healthy."

"St—*stop*."

They ignored me. A shiver of sickness bound in my stomach. He scraped the tool inside. I lost myself in terrified shivers, but the exam was done.

The shock faded after my first gasp. I could *breathe*.

One. Two. Three amazing breaths.

Each breath chased the tears of shame with a rush of relief.

The doctor spoke in a hushed tone, but I listened only to my inhalations. No wheezing shadowed my lungs. He hadn't treated the attack. Did I survive on my own?

Where was I?

The fatigue blinded me, and it decimated my patience. I couldn't speak. I kicked instead. The doctor frowned.

"—You have two weeks." He answered questions I hadn't heard asked. "Give her folic acid."

Another needle punctured my arm. I yelped, but the liquid slurped through my veins like syrup, deadening everywhere it touched. I fought, but the doctor patted my arm.

He shifted my pants over my hips.

The button remained unfastened. It disgraced me more than anything.

A voice spoke from the shadows. "That's a good girl, my dear."

No.

I tried to rise. The drugs hardened my muscles into stone.

Not *him*. Darius Bennett's words barbed my mind with a living nightmare that followed me into the darkness.

"Rest now. We need you healthy, Sarah. You have a very important job to do."

***

It wasn't my room.

The tall ceiling with delicate moldings wasn't my own. The bay window overlooked a vast wilderness, not my familiar cornfields. The poster bed stuffed with down comforters. I hated down. I kicked it away before it triggered the asthma.

The motion dizzied me. Moving was bad. Whatever drugs sloshed through my system hadn't fully cleared. I flexed my arm. Someone replaced my blood with molasses, but I was alive.

And whoever dared to imprison me would regret leaving me whole.

I shivered. I had been kidnapped. Of all the idiotic crimes.

Did they expect me to write a check in exchange for my safety? Did they expect me to beg for mercy? Cower and promise never to tell a soul what happened?

Fuck that.

I was Sarah Atwood.

Atwoods didn't surrender.

We rose at dawn to start working and didn't sleep until the job finished. My ancestors made our millions tilling, hoeing, planting, and harvesting from sunup till sundown, breaking our backs and sweating our lives away in the summer heat. Once we tamed the land, we tended to the economy. Millions became billions, acres became miles, and corn spun into gold.

And still, my father spent his every waking moment inspecting the littlest details of our farms, our books, our crops, our workers, our animals—*everything*.

If my father poisoned himself through chemotherapy while securing a partnership with Sugarweed Corn Syrup, I wasn't about to *beg* to save myself from an asshole who imprisoned me but didn't have the common sense to tie me up.

I forced myself to stand. The drugs pumped heavier than my blood, and my balance pooled in my feet. The wooziness jeopardized my bravery, but at least I regained my dignity.

The button on my jeans remained unfastened.

My stomach heaved.

I didn't remember what happened.

I fled from the lab, but the asthma attack turned to fog. My car crashed. That hurt, but I peeled myself from the wreckage and hid within the cornfields. I collapsed, and then...

Nothing.

Flashes though.

A strong chest cradled me—smelling of leather and rich shadow. I liked the scent, but I fought until that first prick of the needle.

It should have frightened me, but waking terrified me more.

Hands poking. Cold instruments. Blood drawn.

I hated doctors' appointments—if only because I was *always* there. Breathing and X-rays and allergists and every specialist obsessed with the bits of me that never worked right.

I surveyed my arms, chest, and tummy. I hadn't checked everywhere, but I felt generally unmolested. Still, the tension returned in my lungs. This time I earned the fear.

I didn't know where I was or who had taken me, but I swore no one would touch me again.

Ever.

I studied my prison. The digs were far nicer than I expected from a kidnapping. In my mind, I imagined dusty cement and rusted chains, darkness and rats.

Instead, I woke in a poster bed puffed with soft mattresses and softer pillows. Muted golds blended with the aristocratic scarlet wallpaper, an older style. Whoever designed the room painstakingly refurbished the elegance without losing the gothic edge.

Dark woods and hauntingly beautiful paintings of fairy tales and villains added to the room's antique sophistication, and my window overlooked acres of shadowed forests and mountainous peeks.

We weren't in Cherrywood Valley.

No corn fluttered in expansive fields. No flatness stretched beyond our sight. The farm was rural, but not isolated.

Empty wilderness surrounded us.

Fear was messy. It stole what tenuous control I held over my breath. I didn't have my medications which meant I couldn't get upset.

I scoured the room. No phones or weapons, indications of names or locations or clues about what psychopath kept me prisoner.

The private bathroom might have dazzled me, but why did they give me such luxury? What use would I have for a separate, brass footed tub outside the stylishly tiled shower? I hesitated before the cherry vanity. The drawers layered with brand new brushes and hairdryers, make-ups and creams, lotions and perfumes.

It felt...permanent.

The carved dressers contained clothes. My size. My favorite books tucked within a case next to a cold fireplace. A towel rested on the nightstand, folded with a bottle of shampoo, conditioner, and a shower gel containing flecks of pure gold.

The door wasn't locked.

My captors hadn't kidnapped me.

They *housed* me.

What the hell was happening? This was no petty crime, no mad desperation for ransom.

I had no idea why I had been captured, but a simple, damning, terrifying truth festered in the darkness.

They didn't want my family's money.

They hunted *me*.

I'd make sure they regretted every moment of it.

My insides chilled. The pleasant room and comforts were more warning than hospitality. They dressed me in elegance and stole samples of my blood after violating me from the inside. I shivered.

I peeked into the hall. The sophistication of my room bled into the rest of the home. High-ceilinged hallways arched tall, beyond what seemed practical. My home was big, but this gothic-inspired, decadent prison wasn't a house. It was an estate.

They maintained the mansion with a pride that had long shifted into arrogance. The dark rugs would have been stitched with gold if it was fashionable, and painstaking care crafted the lanterns on the walls, wiring electricity through the original sconces. The manor existed in a timeless, dreamlike perfection of antiquity and modern reflection.

A winding staircase yielded to a grand foyer. Chiseled tile and marble columns stretched well beyond the first floor, extending to a ceiling dominated by not one, but three extravagant chandeliers. Their prisms of light filled the impressive hall with a gentle radiance.

This was more than anything the Atwoods ever built. Who had this much money?

And why would someone so rich kidnap me?

The truth prickled at me. I ignored it.

My torn, bloodied clothes and muddied shoes didn't belong in a hall this beautiful. Each step echoed in the isolation. I searched the hall expanding to my left. Every room sealed shut, formal and uninviting. The hostility radiated down the hall to the right as well, but a single door opened, and a cold, flickering firelight cast gold into the hall.

It wasn't polite to force a guest to wander a home. It also wasn't proper to kidnap her.

But it made sense.

I knew *exactly* who had me.

I burst through the doorway. The masculine study housed the obligatory bookcases and hearths, worldly mementos and every other indicator of *old money* they stuffed inside the bloated parlor. The elegance existed only to flaunt their wealth, and whatever beauty I thought existed within the estate rotted in the gluttony of Bennett greed.

"Of course it's you," I whispered.

Darius Bennett greeted me, a medieval king surveying the bounty of his hunt.

He claimed an executive leather chair and shadowed himself in the glow of the fireplace. His gaze revolted me. He looked at me like a piece of meat.

He wore a suit, but I expected the shining scales of a serpent to burst from the seams. He slithered down to his den like I was a mouse clamped in his jaws.

His sons waited for me as well.

Reed crumpled under my glare. Max wasn't as easy, but I puffed with pride as he tucked an ice pack over his knee.

So he was the one who tried to pluck me from my lab?

I hoped he learned a valuable lesson.

But I ignored both Max and Reed. They weren't the ones who deserved my ire.

Nicholas Bennett watched me in silence.

His inspection beat in my chest with a profound, unforgivable fury. I couldn't easily breathe in his presence, and I hated that we shared the same air.

He traded the riding leathers of his motorcycle for a pristine, meticulously crafted suit. He looked just as good in the tight leather that cradled his every muscle as he did drafted in decadence.

But clean-cut and regal or muddy and violent, it didn't matter. The Bennetts were criminals. I didn't need a ranch's worth of polished leather to prove their deviancy.

"How are you feeling, my dear?" Darius spoke only to watch me squirm.

He expected me to be frightened. I was, but damned if I'd let him see it.

"How dare you." I hissed at the snake. He didn't flinch. "Take me home, *right now.*"

Darius preferred his silence. My first breath stuttered. I coughed, but it was the last time he'd ever see that weakness. I borrowed Dad's pride and stared down the men in the room.

They were supposed to be my step-family.

But step-families didn't abduct their little sisters in the middle of the night.

They didn't slash her tires and nearly kill her in a car crash. They didn't drug her, transport her across the state, and sic doctors on very private, very *off-limit* areas.

Whatever game they played, whatever intimidation they planned, was absolutely inappropriate, illegal, and stupid. They'd learn quick I wasn't just a twenty year old pushover.

I hoped.

"Kidnapping?" I snorted. "That's low. Even for you."

Darius offered me nothing. He waited while I twisted myself in fear and rage.

I didn't like the way he looked at me.

Before, he saw me as little more than an annoyance, an obstacle he'd destroy just as he ruined everything else in the Atwood family. The blood on his hands terrified me, but I'd fight him. Not just to protect myself and Mom, but because Darius Bennett was the reason Dad died.

But now? The hairs prickled on my neck. He let his attention...linger.

He looked at me as a woman for the first time. His slimy scrutiny left filth over my curves. He imagined what hid beneath my clothes.

His voice echoed in my mind. The memory assaulted me like the doctor's fingers. I squirmed. They revealed me. *Virgin.*

Darius's *Good girl* sickened me with his pride.

"What the hell is going on here?" I demanded.

Nicholas gestured to an empty chair. He was lucky I didn't kick the leather monstrosity into the fireplace.

"Ms. Atwood."

He hadn't dropped the spine-tingling warmth from his voice. The deep baritone wrapped over me like the shackles they neglected to snap over my wrists.

I didn't look into his eyes. The last time I did, he held me in the cornfield, protecting me from the cold, the injuries, and my fading breath. He dared to comfort me in the darkness, and his honeyed gaze actually *calmed* me before I slipped into unconsciousness.

He didn't share Darius's stare, but I didn't trust his brand of oppression. Nicholas was, undoubtedly, the most dangerous Bennett.

He lured instead of conquered. Nicholas wasn't a man who favored fists and aggression, not when the confidence warming his voice struck through me like a heated blade. He anticipated my fight, but his endless patience shielded him from my defiance.

I could torture him with silence, beat him with my every strength, or sit and rationally negotiate my freedom. He'd outlast me.

I had no idea how to best him, and he had only whispered my name.

He gestured to the chair once more.

I wouldn't sit. We were beyond cordiality and honest expectations. My backpack and laptop rested at Max's feet. The brute was more muscle than brains. He kicked off his suit jacket in favor of a t-shirt. Raging bands of tattoos coiled against his skin, thick and angry. I didn't dare rush for my belongings.

They left my bag unzipped. The Bennetts greasy hands had rifled through all my notebooks.

My research journal rested on the table next to Darius's whiskey.

"Ms. Atwood," Nicholas tried again. He had no right to speak my name, but his voice rumbled over the syllables with a refined grace. "You had a bad accident. You should sit."

"You bastards." I stared at the journal before glaring at Darius Bennett. "I know what this is about."

Nicholas offered a dry chuckle. "I don't think you do."

"Sons of bitches!"

Reed seized me before I launched myself at his father. Somewhere between my kitchen and the attack on his motorcycle, he lost the playful smirk and dimple that separated him from the other lunatics in his family.

"You kidnapped me for my *research*!"

Reed dropped me when I pushed from his arms, but it wasn't like I posed a threat to Darius. Without a weapon, I'd never escape four men, each stronger, larger, and more imposing than the last.

I was a drop of blonde in a den of shadows. I made no excuses for my medical conditions, but I also knew my limits. Getting angry—letting the injustice and pain and inconceivable violation upset me—would land me on the floor, wheezing and humiliated.

I would never, ever let a Bennett see me in such a state.

But my *research*? The bastard terrorized me, threatened me, and stole my work.

"Are you really that evil?"

Darius's lips curled into a monstrous leer. He reached for the journal, flipping through pages and pages of notes I had scribbled for the past three years. Every initial calculation that led me to a working, testable, and experimental hypothesis rested in his hands.

So much work.

The entire future of Atwood Industries.

And Darius Bennett pawed through my notes as if he didn't even *care* that he held the potential for millions—maybe billions—of dollars under his fingertips.

"Most of my family is dead, and you think you can steal the company with an insulting offer. I refuse you, so this is your solution?" I studied each of the Bennetts. "You kidnap me and steal my research. Is it a ransom? You'll hold my work hostage until I agree to cooperate?"

Darius thumped the journal against his hand. "We'll find a use for it."

The rage tinted my vision. I traded air for the edge in my voice. It was worth it.

"You won't get away with this. I have patents."

I bluffed. Not everything had been protected like Dad insisted. After his funeral, I used the lab to mourn. What happened there was private—my own homage to him. I stopped patenting, and, once Josiah and Mike died in the accident, I hardly had the energy or time to protect my work. Half my journal pages weren't signed. Most of the experiments hadn't been replicated.

If they took it, I'd lose everything.

Darius waded through my indignation. His sneer silenced me.

"It isn't about the research, child," he said. "You know why you're here."

My stomach turned.

Something had changed.

The fire roared. It burned cold.

The silence crackled. It hurt my ears.

Nicholas stood. He loomed tall, strong, and utterly inescapable.

"Ms. Atwood, we didn't bring you to our home to steal your research."

Max shrugged. "That's a windfall."

Protecting my journal wasn't nearly as important as protecting me, and I suddenly realized I had no defense against my step-brothers.

"You want my company," I said.

Nicholas nodded. "Yes."

"You'll scare me into negotiations?"

His eyes hardened, cracking the gold into bitter amber.

"No, Ms. Atwood. Unfortunately, your actions have prevented a sale of the company."

"Then why am I here?"

Nicholas stepped close, and I stared up at him. Trembling, though I didn't understand why.

He presented himself as a solid, masculine, impenetrable force. Bennett ruthlessness was legendary. He encapsulated everything dangerous and merciless that existed within the family, twisted into his own uses and balanced with a grace undeserving of such a monster.

Because he was handsome, he seemed kind.

And because he was my step-brother, I trusted he wouldn't hurt me.

But because he was a Bennett, he was neither kind nor trustworthy. And he would hurt me.

"You've forced us to make a difficult decision, Ms. Atwood."

Nicholas's voice constricted like every binding I expected and every threat I'd have to fight to survive. But he had me pinned already, restrained and helpless without raising a hand.

The kidnapping. The doctor. The blood tests.

Only Darius would be so cruel.

Nicholas wasn't his father, but he was a Bennett. And that meant he was the nightmare of his father, brought to life and wrapped in a false comfort, a subdued dominance, and a promised brutality.

"Atwood Industries belongs to a *male* heir." Nicholas spoke as though we were the only two within the room. As if that would gentle his intentions. "The Bennett family will acquire your company, your lands, and your wealth. Ms. Atwood, your heir will also be ours."

I stepped away.

"Y—you think I'm going to...*marry* you?"

Nicholas's expression crested, almost to remorse, almost softening, as if a monster could emphasize with the fear crippling me to incomprehension.

"No. I won't marry you," he said.

"I'm not...I won't sleep with you," I said. "You're technically my *brother*."

"You have no choice, Ms. Atwood."

"No *choice*?" I stared at him. Was he dangerously proud or an unrepentant criminal? "I don't have a choice in conceiving my own child? What are you going to do?"

He didn't answer.

I wasn't fast enough to escape them all.

"You wouldn't rape me."

The damning silence sheathed me in untasted violence. The Bennetts cast their noose, but I stumbled into the rope. I stood only because the shock tensed my legs and the remaining sedative pumping in my blood numbed me to the absolute insanity.

"You can't do this," I whispered.

Darius laughed. "Sarah, my dear, what choice did you leave us? The clause bound our hands as much as it did yours. Your company requires a male heir. We will give you that son."

"Absolutely not."

The words sounded stronger in my head. My whimper intimidated no one.

"This isn't a negotiation," Darius said. "You did your best, but even your father understood you weren't capable of managing his company. He raised you only because he knew you'd eventually pump out more Atwood swine, and, I'm sure you're going to do very well at it."

My heart pulsed hard, but it delivered nothing where it needed to go. Tears seared my vision, and I was grateful. At least then I wouldn't stare at the devil who threatened me with every horrible and despicable evil in the world.

"You're my step-father, Darius. Why would you do this to my mother? You don't have to love her, but for God's sake, you still married her, you fucking—"

He raised a hand. "Please, Sarah. No need for such language. I respect your mother, and I will honor my vow to her."

"Even you aren't sick enough to rape your own step-daughter."

"Of course not." He gestured to his sons. "Your brothers will undertake this task."

"No."

"Three Bennett men. It doesn't matter to me *who* has the heir, only that it is created. Behave yourself, honor our wishes, and you won't be harmed."

"You're delusional."

"Fight this, and I guarantee you'll come to regret it."

"I'll call the police." The threat didn't frighten him. "I'll call my mother."

He shook his head.

"Jesus Christ, Darius!" I gripped the chair. I wasn't even strong enough to puncture the leather with my nails. I hoped they didn't notice. "I *am* Atwood Industries. You think you can touch me and I won't immediately bury this family in every legal, civil, and public relations nightmare money can buy?"

"Of course not," Darius said. "But you'll behave."

"Why?"

"Because you love your mother."

My stomach dropped. "So you'd threaten your *honored* wife?"

Darius nodded.

"You're pathetic." I pointed to them all, wishing I had chosen a more profane gesture. "I'm leaving, and I'm going right to the police."

Nicholas blocked my escape. His expression reserved no kindness, only dark intent. If the devil hid within beauty, I stared into a golden halo of absolute evil.

"Ms. Atwood, you are our guest for the foreseeable future." Nicholas's voice promised a false and sinful gentleness. "I'm afraid you aren't permitted to leave the grounds."

"Not for some time, of course," Darius said. "Unfortunately, we have a few weeks before you are...of use to us."

I swore. That invasion was worse than the doctor's prodding fingers.

"So you'll hold me here until you rape me," I whispered.

If Nicholas felt any remorse, any human emotion behind his handsome cast of regal stillness, he let none escape. I mimicked his stoicism if only so I could shatter his confidence and dance over the shards of his broken pride.

"What happens when you fail?" I asked. "You'll never control me."

Darius folded his hands. "My dear, it's nothing personal. Fight us or spread your legs willingly. The torment is yours to create."

"And my revenge is yours to suffer."

He sighed. "It doesn't matter if you fight. It doesn't matter if you deny my sons. As of this moment, you belong to them. Your body exists only for their pleasure and your womb for the child that will carry the Bennett name."

I swallowed a surge of bile. Darius laughed. My step-brothers didn't share his amusement.

"My dear," he said. "You'll remain here as our prisoner, bound within our walls and trapped in your brothers' beds, until the day you bear a son."

CHAPTER SIX
NICHOLAS

If I was a monster, I found success in my evils.

I no longer recognized the man in the mirror, but at least the sins I committed and the lives I destroyed would protect the ones I loved.

I never pretended to be a good man; I simply cared for my family.

But I wasn't born as Nicholas Bennett. I was always recognized as the heir—the firstborn son and the future of our family. My father sculpted, perfected, and beat me into the right temperament to serve as his replacement. He influenced politicians, bought out his competitors, and imprisoned his enemies, but he couldn't outrun time. One day he would fade.

Then I would become his legacy.

Except when I'd seize control, no innocent girl would be held captive in her bedroom, waiting for the theft of her innocence and the destruction of her body.

I fastened my cufflinks and buttoned the suit jacket. The vest and trousers fit better than riding leathers and concealed weapons. We called for the helicopter, but Max rapped at my door before the pilot prepared to take off.

"Reed's about to split," Max said. "You grabbing him this time or me?"

Max tugged at his suit. He fit in the leather with more ease, but my father hadn't asked for his usual assistance. He attended me today— crammed between investors and crystal glasses for a lunch meeting. I preferred him at my side. Anything was better for him than crouching in the shadows, drenched in another's blood.

I didn't have time for my youngest brother's antics. "Where does Reed think he's going?"

"Anywhere Dad isn't."

If such a place existed, I hadn't found it yet. And if Reed ever did, I'd let him go. I'd also order Max to leave with him. Unfortunately, my father's rule anchored us within the shadow of our estate and under his unblinking stare.

Reed knew better. The situation hadn't set well with him, but he endangered everyone with his behavior.

He endangered the girl.

I had no reason to hurry. Reed wouldn't escape without telling me. The south garage housed our bikes, all three meticulously scoured and cleaned of debris from the cornfield.

He leaned against his motorcycle. He hadn't opened the garage yet, but his bag rested at his feet. It was a step farther than he made before. Usually, he came to his senses before leaving his bedroom. I once caught him on the stairs.

Reed seldom lost his smile. The scar on his cheek and ear aged him, but not enough. He wasn't much older than the girl we captured and locked away. He wasn't that different either.

"I'm gone."

Reed didn't look at me. He hadn't, not since Mark Atwood's death and our father's sudden compulsion to marry his widow.

He said I was too much like him.

I believed it.

"This is bullshit, Nick."

"Get off the bike," I said. "Max and I have an appointment at noon. We don't have time for this."

"You know this isn't right." His gloved hands twisted. The leather wouldn't protect him. No matter what he hid or how far he rode, the Bennett name bled into him deeper than any tattoo or scar. "You can't tell me you're okay with this."

"It's done, Reed."

"You're going to hurt that girl?"

"Get off the bike. We'll go in the house and talk."

"You are actually going to *rape* that girl?"

I checked my watch. I didn't have time to justify my actions or pretend to defend anything my father had planned.

Max crossed his arms. "You leave, and you make it harder on everyone."

"Maybe." The keys flipped into Reed's hand. "But me and my conscience will just have to deal."

"Why do you care so much about an Atwood?" Max pointed to Reed's scars. "After everything Mark Atwood did to this family—"

"That *girl* isn't Mark Atwood." Reed drew himself up to his full height. He could look me in the eye, but I owned the extra inch and the extra years. "That girl is...a girl. Jesus Christ, she didn't understand. She thought we planned to steal her fucking research material."

Max smirked. "She took that harder than the news about the heir."

"Fuck this." Reed shouldered his bag. "If you imprison and rape an innocent girl..." He swore leaned over his bike. "If you want to *impregnate* your goddamned step-sister? Fine. Do it for Dad. Be his little minion and pound your humanity away. I'm won't be a part of it."

Max moved too quickly, and Reed's punch swung quicker than he anticipated. Reed's fist connected with his chin, and Max spat blood on the cement. I raised a hand before the retaliation began and held Reed's shoulder. He didn't dare strike me.

"This is repulsive to me as well." For more reasons than one. "But this is how he's planned for it to be done."

"What about you?" Reed shared Mom's green eyes. It made this harder. "How the hell did he talk you into this? I fucking hoped..." He pushed away. "Nothing's gonna change when you get the company."

That's where he was wrong. It would change. Given the opportunity. Given the time.

But it wouldn't do any good if my brothers were dead.

The company wouldn't matter. Money, power, politics—a waste. My father existed in a world where cruelty created opportunities for those brave enough to shed their decency and devour those less ambitious. He groomed me for that life, exercising one rule.

Family first—at the expense of all else. Pride. Compassion. Sarah Atwood.

Until his sons interfered.

Some blood had more worth than others.

"This is about more than the girl," I said. "I'll find a solution, but you aren't leaving. Not now."

"If you have to *ask* me to stay, you're more fucked in the head than he is."

Max rubbed his face. His knuckles scarred from the last vendor lunch we attended—when my presentation hadn't swayed our guest, Max's fist secured what we needed. It was important, my father said, that we experience business first hand. I would present the numbers, and, when solid facts and figures failed, Max delivered the final options with as little mercy as he had patience.

Reed understood. He was a smart man—probably smarter than me if he had applied himself in the way our father chose. Instead, he focused on colleges and research, the same experiments the girl had concocted and different avenues for the company. It was appreciated, but it wasn't his place. We had our roles. Heir. Muscle. Charity. Deviating wasn't an option.

And freeing Sarah Atwood wasn't a solution.

"If you leave, you'll damn her," I said. Reed didn't believe me. I envied his naivety. "He's demanded *all* of us do it. Three men. Three times the chances."

"Guess he'll only have two."

"No." I tilted my head. "He'll ensure she's taken by *three* men."

Reed exhaled once he realized what I meant.

"You would never hurt that girl," I said. "But our father would."

"You can't be asking me to do this."

"If he takes her, she probably won't survive it."

"Goddamn it, Nick."

"Get inside. You have a conference call at three."

Max tapped his cell. "Helicopter's here."

Reed pitched his bag across the room. Something shattered in the pocket. He gave it a solid kick, but he returned to the house with a profanity reserved more for himself than me.

I wouldn't savor this victory. I laid the bag at the doorway and struck the switch to lower the garage's gate.

Sarah Atwood wasn't the only one imprisoned within the estate, but once my father sated his perversions, after we stole her innocence and invaded her body, she'd be released.

If she behaved.

If we all behaved.

Ten years ago, I might have had the same crisis of conscience as Reed. Cruelty existed in many forms. This was just the basest, the most animalistic and vulgar form of power.

The personal touch sickened me. I held no respect or love for the Atwoods, but Reed was right. Sarah was a reckless twenty year old girl, but she reserved every bit of her father's strength, her brothers' ambition, and her own imaginative solutions to her family's problems.

She was also the most beautiful woman to ever hate me.

Even panting and muddy, lost in a cornfield with a cut to her brow and hyperventilating as my brothers and I terrorized her, Sarah was lovely—pale and delicate with hair the same color as silken gold. I lamented that it was her name that would destroy her.

She was a fluttering fairy trapped within a garden of stone. Even the tiniest suffered.

The helicopter flight would be quick, but my father's text message vibrated my phone the instant the pilot lifted us from the roof. Instructions. Reminders. Orders.

Life was little more than a schedule, and a rigorous one by intent. The Bennett Corporation thrived on out-pacing, out-innovating, and out-maneuvering our rivals. My grandfather built the empire, my father expanded it, and I was born to defend it.

To me, that meant security and diversification.

To my father, it meant imprisoning the daughter of our greatest business rival and then asserting our control by beating, raping, and breeding the poor girl. Neither of my brothers approved of this plan, but they had as little a choice as the girl.

If I was to keep them all alive, including Sarah Atwood, we needed to obey my father. Do as he said. Act like the monsters he raised.

I ignored the text message.

…Or maybe I'd find another way.

The helicopter delivered us to San Jose, landing on the rooftop of a partnered hotel chain. The top floor restaurant might have entertained those who hadn't just seen the skyline from the air, but it amused the investors. Pleasing those willing to drop millions on our corporation was as important as winning them over through presentations and slide shows.

A handsome smile, charming conversation, and direct, no-nonsense negotiation style usually secured our investments. We choreographed the lunch. One cocktail before ordering, a sensible wine with a light meal, and mineral water with a refreshing sorbet for dessert. I permitted the discussion to tread from business to family, but no further than memories of *alma maters* and, if the occasion permitted, gentle enthusiasm for children—especially if adult, female, and unattached. Professional matters were kept discreet, approximated numbers offered, and official figures promised at a later date within the corporate offices.

And it usually worked.

Usually.

Our target was an important board member—one of my father's initial contacts. Samuel Peters approached retirement age with a shuffling gait dancing between arthritis and gout. Max lost his patience the second time Samuel called him Matt, but he remembered me. He liked me.

That's what made his decision all the more puzzling.

"Nicholas, I'll be straight with you." Samuel scooped a spoonful of the sorbet to his mouth, but missed the cream that lingered in the corners of his lips. "The Bennett Corporation has been good to me and my family, but I had an offer to sell my shares, and, I'll tell you, it was a *good* offer."

We expected it. It didn't stop the disappointment from pitting my stomach.

"Our company has seen a seven percent growth each year for the past five," I said. "It's a solid investment. Selling now will secure you, but retaining your percentage could see your profits double within the next ten years."

"Doubt I'll be around in ten years, my boy." Samuel cracked a laugh as dry as the wallet he pulled from his pocket. He fiddled with the leather and held a photograph toward Max. "I'm trying to take care of my bunny."

He didn't refer to an animal. The blonde in the picture somehow scrunched her legs onto his lap and pressed more silicon than actual skin against his wrinkles. Max perked an eyebrow, hiding his grimace with a well-timed throat clear.

"With all due respect..." I earned Max's amusement. "Bunny would benefit from the stock as well."

"True. Don't I know it!" Samuel cackled. "But she doesn't have a mind for numbers, you see."

Obviously.

"They offered me a good price." He hocked a cough and sipped his water. "You can understand that, Nicholas. I'm an old man. I want to take care of my family and treat them well."

"I understand." More than anything, I understood. "But you are a voting member of our stock holders, and the company that wished to purchase your shares..."

"Josmik Holdings."

I steadied my expression. "Yes. They represent a private corporation which was formed by the recently passed Atwood Brothers, Josiah and Michael."

Samuel nodded. "Messy business."

"Indeed."

"Nicholas, I'm sorry. I signed the contract before the boys died. My attorney is preparing the agreements now with their executor. Everything should be settled within the year." He rapped a finger against the table. "Have you met their sister? Young thing. Pretty. Smart too."

"She's actually..." I hadn't admitted it since locking her inside her room. "My new step-sister. You attended my father's wedding a few months ago."

"Ah! That's right, that's right. Well, good, it's settled then. Speak with Ms. Atwood. She may be willing to halt the sale."

Yes. Sarah probably would, given my father's persistence. Then again, if his original threat hadn't crippled her, I doubted we could do much to rattle Sarah Atwood.

Max's hands usually stained with blood, but mine seldom dripped with crimson. My soul, of course, withered and died years ago. I might not have swung the punch, but my orders busted car windows, broke jaws, and threatened more than one family with financial ruin. All in the name of business. All to protect the Bennett Corporation.

Samuel shrugged and tossed his napkin on the table. "It's not the news you wanted to hear. Nothing personal."

He stood, but I raised a hand. "Is there any chance you might be able to cancel the deal. Any chance at all?"

"You put me in a tight spot."

"Are you selling for the money?"

Samuel returned to his seat. His hand shook over his cane, but he glanced from Max to me.

"I'll be honest. I respect you, Nicholas. I do. But your father..."

Max leaned away from the table. We both tensed like we were kids again, sneaking into the pool after curfew. The sting of the crop burned through the years, the precise strikes that hid too well beneath a child's suit.

I urged him to continue the thought before he lost it in a fog of dementia. "My father?"

"Darius is not a classical businessman, not like you. We know how the company made those seven percent gains. The research division was slashed in half. Distribution's contract negotiations were messy and costly. And the union problems?"

I steadied my voice. "Price of doing business in this day and age."

"Maybe." Samuel sighed. "Darius took a proud company, retained the polish on the outside, and rotted the interior. And that's hard for you to hear, but his leadership is reactive and quick to burn. His temper gets him in trouble, and, in this economy, his methods won't stand the test of time."

Max hid his agreement in a quick swig of his water. I didn't have the luxury of denial while face-to-face with one of our largest investors.

"Drought hit the West bad, Nicholas. Farms already had their fertilizers and products purchased, but this year coming up?" He shook his head. "The farmers are gonna need more than rain to stay afloat, you hear?"

He was right. I knew it. Reed knew it. That was why he fought to shift our developmental focuses to new aspects of the industry. It was also why he attempted to study law, engineering, something beyond business and numbers.

He saw it coming. The rest of the family and the stock holders anticipated it.

Even the Atwoods waited for the inevitable.

And my father focused only on the short-term profits and quarterly analyses. It wouldn't always distract the stock holders. Samuel was right.

Which meant an opportunity existed that hadn't before.

"What if..." I leaned into the table. "What if Darius no longer led the Bennett Corporation?"

Samuel chortled. "Darius Bennett? Retire? Son, he'll be older than me and still guarding his office with a bottle of whiskey and a loaded gun."

"Not necessarily."

For the first time in the seven years I had known Samuel, he sharpened. He wagged a finger at me, rasping a dry cough.

"Now you sound like your father."

"The Bennett Corporation impacts many people's lives. My family, but also our stock holders and investors and their families. Their...bunnies."

"Very true, son."

My voice lowered. I had no reason to protect hypotheticals. My back ached, an imaginary pain I would ignore. The strain tightened along the largest scar tracing my shoulders, itching as though it had ruptured.

"If the stock holders aren't pleased with the direction of the company, changing leadership is the easier and more rectifiable choice. I can't have all our voting members selling stock because of a presented offer that seemed more tasteful than dealing with the issues at hand."

Max hadn't moved. I ignored the text message buzzing in my pocket. The adrenaline flooded my blood. Our blood. Bennett blood.

Either excitement or betrayal would poison me.

At least it wouldn't target my brothers.

"What are you proposing?" Sam asked.

"Stop the sale."

"Why?"

"Because I can offer you better than the Atwoods."

"How?"

"A different vision for the company. Safer investments. More sustainable profits regardless of environmental conditions which may impact our largest customers."

"You'll need help." Sam scratched his chin. "And a majority of the shareholders are loyal to your father."

"The company is mine by right."

"Not yet, my boy, not yet."

I sipped my water. The thrill that shocked through my body wasn't fear. It was pleasure. Pure strength.

A newfound *freedom*.

"I'll put the company's interests before my own. Blood forgives, profits do not. If you give me your support, grant me a little time to speak with our other voting stock holders, I believe I can present you with a profitable solution. I'll guarantee your continued growth within our company."

"And Darius?"

"He's a businessman."

"He's also your father."

A fact he never let me forget. What was a more damning sin—the loss of profits or the destruction of a family? The Bennett family thrived on the power granted by our name, the influence of the men in our bloodline, and the shared secrets taught father to son. Generations of Bennetts wielded family like a sword and armor, and success was our ultimate victory.

But times changed. Economies changed. Politics changed.

And some Bennetts abused the honor in our name.

So why not herald the change and assume what belonged to me before the generations of success and wealth, power and glory turned to the same dust choking our customers' farms?

Sam nodded. "The stock stays."

Max stiffened. Even my brother—a man strengthened by every martial art money could train—folded under the implication. He frowned, but he said nothing. Like all Bennetts, he knew his place.

But mine wasn't right for me anymore. I wanted more. Something conquerable and profitable that would grant me more power than my father ever dreamed.

I liked it.

Too much.

"You won't regret this," I said. "And neither will the Bennett Corporation. A change like this benefits us all, Samuel."

He chuckled, shaking my hand—the age old business standard which sealed more than just a gentleman's agreement.

It offered me the opportunity to have everything.

To control everything.

To own *everything*.

Samuel clapped my brother on the shoulder. "Matt. Nice to see you again."

Max didn't correct him. His gaze burned through me, but the wine was cool, a rich vintage that the Bennetts preferred. I swirled the crimson and waited as Samuel shuffled from the table. Once, my brother's silence might have concerned me. But now?

I relished it.

He wouldn't be brave enough to offer me congratulations, nor would he break a rigid code of conduct and interrogate me in the restaurant.

A waitress fluttered past. I snapped a finger, and she nodded, hurrying past her other tables and darting into the kitchen to fetch another bottle of wine.

"I'll attend your investor meeting tomorrow, Max." I thanked the server with a hundred from my jacket pocket and nodded for her to leave. She studied Max, her lips parted ever so slightly, but he ignored the brunette as she shimmied away. "You don't have to come."

Max downed his wine. "No. I think I should be there. What the hell are you doing?"

"What's best for this company."

"What about the family?"

"One and the same, Max."

He didn't believe me, but it was the first moment in twenty-nine years I thought clearly.

I wasn't protecting the family anymore. The only way we'd survive was if someone *saved* it—from within and from the external threats that would only further destroy what control we held over the market, the investors, and our customers.

A change in ownership would preserve the standards we upheld.

And holding the girl captive? It eliminated the Atwood threat, but my father's long-term solution was cruel. Still, ruining Sarah to seize her company would win the war. Other options must have existed, but we didn't have time for the battles it'd require.

Sarah was almost twenty-one, and that made her dangerous. Her heir would secure us for generations, fortifying a legacy built of darkness, lies, and undeniable wealth. But a single mistake and she'd have the legal and moral power to rip us apart.

But I'd fix it. And I'd do it before only the ashes of success remained.

But a real plan required time. Management. Escaping the impenetrable will of my father.

Max stole the bottle and poured another glass. He preferred hard liquors, but it was unsightly for a man to drink more than a single whiskey at a business lunch. He chugged the wine instead.

"If Dad finds out what you just did, he'll kill you," Max warned. "What the hell possessed you to be that fucking reckless?"

"When have you ever known me to be reckless?"

"First Sarah Atwood, now this? You aren't acting sane."

"If I can secure enough investors to vote for a change in leadership, maybe the girl will go home. Eventually. Once this is done."

"Eventually?" Max ground his teeth. "What the hell do you mean *eventually*? Just tell Dad *no*."

And enrage him? He'd take his vengeance out on our prisoner, then he'd have my actions and correspondence, meetings and parties monitored and scrutinized by his own private investigators and personal associates.

No. We had one option, and I pitied the girl I couldn't rescue.

Sarah Atwood would save the Bennett Corporation in two ways.

She would either bear a child we created to secure a future which joined our assets—or her presence and inevitable resistance would distract my father while I forged a partnership to depose him.

Neither future offered the girl much hope, but I'd never ask forgiveness from an Atwood, even if she was beautiful, young, and completely innocent to the sin trapping her within our beds.

My phone vibrated once more. The message was just another complication. Max read my expression and stood as I did.

"Problem?" He asked.

Slight. Nothing I couldn't handle.

"Sarah Atwood has escaped."

CHAPTER SEVEN
SARAH

The mansion was easy to escape.

The estate? Not so much.

The Bennetts prided themselves on extravagance, independence, and privacy. Their home wasn't just a decadent manor comprised of dozens of rooms, wings, and glamour. They owned nearly as much land as us. But instead of planting crops or tending animals, they wasted good, fertile soil on meticulously crafted gardens with sculptures of dark creatures, aggressively coiling roses, and an endless path which stretched beyond the courtyard and into an overgrown forest of shadows and menace.

The Bennetts lived in the wilderness by choice, and they were rich enough to buy time. A car took too long to deliver them to San Jose. They installed a helipad on the roof of the estate.

A *helicopter*.

The Atwoods were wealthy, but my father wouldn't dare let his children gallivant across the world in a *helicopter*. My brothers had to wait for his death before they even felt comfortable traveling in a private jet.

The jet that ultimately claimed their lives.

Maybe Dad was onto something.

I stole a bottle of water before I bolted, but I drained it in a coughing fit as soon as I passed beyond sight of the house.

I couldn't run. A day without medication and the stress of the kidnapping scoured my lungs. The cool water helped, but nothing would combat the hardening of my chest. Even if I had my inhaler, I wasn't getting far.

My feet crunched against broken twigs and scattered pine needles. The cobblestone path wasn't used often, but I hoped the road beyond the private property would be populated. Tourists explored even the most scenic road routes, and the Bennetts lived just outside wine country.

Someone would find me. When they did, I would reward them for the opportunity to call the police, my stock holders, and my doctor.

My main priority was getting the hell off their property. Once I was home, I'd figure out how best to torch that prison to ash.

I coughed. The path blurred as the dry wheeze prickled me with a headache. I groped across the road and leaned against the base of a redwood.

The redwoods teetered over their estate, and the air chilled in the shade of the trees. Redwoods and firs, oaks and scrub, ferns and stones littered the forest. The view was more exotic than the acres of corn surrounding my home, but the mid-summer pollen stuck to my throat.

I'd have to go slower.

The Bennetts had no idea I suffered from asthma. For all I cared, they'd assume I died of starvation trying to crawl my way across their endless property. Some secrets were too important to reveal.

My hike wasn't the act of defiance I planned. My escape shifted into survival. I had to contact my doctor and fill my prescription. I fell behind on my pills, and I was already anxious without my rescue inhaler.

I wouldn't think about it. The pollen was bad, but as long as I was walking, I'd be okay. If I was free, I'd be okay.

Those bastards thought they could trap me in the house. Maybe they hoped I'd cower in the corner waiting for my step-brothers to rape me. Maybe they figured that I'd be too terrified to fight.

One thing was certain.

They didn't expect me pitching a chair through the dining room window to make my escape.

A Bennett could repair a window with the change in their pocket—but I'd give the Atwood fortune to watch Darius Bennett pop a vein in rage.

The rumble echoed in the distance. I pushed away from the tree as the bike thundered along the path. I cursed. My luck depended on whoever followed. Reed wouldn't hurt me. Max would, but he wouldn't kill me.

And Nicholas?

I missed a breath. I couldn't fear Nicholas. I refused to give any Bennett that pleasure.

But I wasn't comfortable around him. His golden stare shattered me and then examined every piece to determine how he could use it to his advantage. The cadence of his voice beat against my body harder than my frantic heart. His unbreakable poise rivaled my resolve.

Nicholas seared through my defenses with a reserved word and didn't flinch when I opposed him.

I'd rather face Darius than Nicholas.

Which was why I didn't answer the amber-eyed rider as he slowed to my side.

Whatever leathers and helmet my step-brother wore while abducting me were gone, cast aside for an imported, tailor fit suit, complete with navy blue pocket square and vest beneath the jacket. He might not have worn a cut displaying his city and club and every dastardly crime he ever committed, but the suit exposed more than he wished.

He was stylish. He was arrogant. He was ruthless enough to pursue me on a motorcycle.

I was the fox, he was the sportsman, and the twisted machine he rode the noble steed he whipped, tamed, and beat into submission. I hadn't made it far from the house. And yet he chased. He *hunted*.

He watched me with a wicked amusement.

"Ms. Atwood."

The words rolled off his lips—the crashing of thunder or the whisper of fire. Both left me chilled and hot and...flushing.

My steps slowed, but not out of respect for him. The quick pace and breathless anticipation of his chase clattered my lungs. I debated stopping to pretend to listen to his terms, or collapsing against the path, forcing him to drag me to my exquisite cell.

The bike surged forward, blocking my path. Nicholas must have anticipated I wouldn't climb on the beast willingly. He adjusted his tie and unbuttoned his jacket before dismounting.

No man had any right to be that handsome, especially a Bennett.

His mellow gold eyes, brush of dark hair, and regal smile would charm the last dollar out of a collections' box while crushing anyone that might have protested. Nicholas was built for sheer intimidation. I was small—and not just asthma tiny. My father teased that I was the runt of his litter, his little corn sprout in a bountiful harvest.

I had to look up to meet his gaze, and the effort didn't go unnoticed. His lip curled, but I couldn't tell if it was amusement or a challenge.

"It's dangerous to travel this path alone, Ms. Atwood," Nicholas warned. "You never know what's lurking in the woods."

"Probably the same evil inside your estate."

"Would you rather my company or the mountain lions' on this ridge?"

"Trick question."

He chuckled. "Where do you think you're going?"

"Home."

His eyebrow perked, but his voice never lost the tempered cadence. He liked this game.

"You're far from home, Ms. Atwood."

"Then perhaps you'd arrange for transportation to see me there safely."

"If you would climb onto my bike, I'll take you home."

I looked over my shoulder, glancing toward the estate. I realized my mistake too late. I'd rather turn my back on a mountain lion than Nicholas. I deliberately searched his expression, ignoring how just his glance bound me in his stillness.

"The Bennett Estate is *not* my home," I said.

"It is, for the foreseeable future."

"You and I have far different definitions of *future*."

I might have stepped away, fidgeted as I surveyed any chance to escape. Nicholas didn't move. Didn't shift. Didn't break my gaze. Every instinct I fought to squirm only strengthened him. Even Darius Bennett showed a weakness with the tensing of his lip or clench of his fist when I defied him.

Nicholas was unbreakable. He held me captive with honesty as intense as violence. He breathed a callous indifference.

I had no idea how to act around him.

Screaming would give him the victory. Silence was my implied surrender. His every steady breath cracked my confidence. Slowly. Steadily. Inch by fracturing inch.

I wasn't ready to combat whatever he planned.

"If you excuse me…" I swallowed as the words didn't carry the edge I wished. I hid the wheeze before he realized the pause wasn't a dare for his reaction. "Thank you for your gracious hospitality, but I must kindly decline your invitation."

I expected an arm around my waist and a threatening rasp in my ear, but he wouldn't defile himself with base violence.

"You're walking." His voice carried like shadow, but this darkness wasn't cool. It warmed whatever it touched. Wove over my body. Bound my wrists and legs with the shackles of his amusement. "You won't run? Not even from your captors?"

He admitted it without remorse. I didn't turn. If he wanted to listen, he'd have to follow.

And he did.

"I don't have to run," I said. "It's been over a day since the kidnapping. People will start searching for me."

"Are you sure?"

"You aren't untouchable, Nicholas. Even your family has limits on power. I own a billion dollar company. I'm expected to email and call and make decisions for various departments at any given time. Someone will notice I'm gone." I swallowed the pitting fear. "My *mother* will notice I'm gone."

"Your mother believes you are a guest of the estate while we conduct business."

"Of course she does." I didn't stop walking, but every step shoved a dagger of betrayal deeper into my side. "Enough Vicodin and anti-depressants will convince her of anything. But she hasn't been very useful for a few months. I haven't had the luxury of help since my father and brothers died."

"I admire your courage, Ms. Atwood, but the nearest public road is over five miles from here."

Five miles.

Five miles on no medications.

Five miles weakened, exhausted, and terrified.

"Then you should be a gentleman and call a taxi."

Nicholas laughed. "Or I have a pilot's license. I could fly you away in the helicopter."

He wasn't threatened by me. It was an insult, but what could I do against him? Nicholas's broad shoulders and muscular chest weren't hidden beneath the suit. The style accentuated every inch of his form. While Max bulked with the strength he earned punishing and training his body, Nicholas possessed a natural power. Something I never experienced—only bluffed.

The only charity he'd offer would be hauling me to the estate on his bike, and he'd grant me the privilege of clinging to his back.

He was hard. He was cruel.

And I envied every breath he stole from me.

"Take me home." My voice fell to a whisper. A *please* tempted my lips. "Why won't you take me home?"

"Come with me," Nicholas said. "I'll get you something to drink. We'll discuss this like civilized people in the comfort of a parlor instead of a stark wilderness."

"I like the wilderness." I spoke too quickly and showed a bit of myself I didn't mean for him to see. I licked my lips and tried again. "I prefer the forest to the barrenness of your estate."

"Hopefully it won't be barren for long."

Absolutely not. "Are you out of your mind?"

Nicholas gestured to the bike. "Ms. Atwood, it's time to return."

"I refuse."

"I understand," he said. "And so I am granting you two options. Either you come willingly, allow me to see you safely to our home, and we discuss these matters—"

"Forget it."

"—Or I subdue you, bind your hands, and you spend your days strapped to a bed, like my father prefers."

"I'm not afraid of your father."

My voice trembled. Nicholas heard. His amusement threaded me into silence.

"Are you afraid of me?" He asked.

I didn't answer. My chest hurt, and I allowed myself a pause to breathe anything but his question.

It didn't help.

I still imagined him tying me to the bed—helpless, naked, bound for his pleasure with only mercy to restrain him.

I had no compassion for the Bennetts.

God, what sympathy would they spare for me?

But maybe Nicholas was telling the truth. Maybe he wasn't like his father, didn't see me as a woman to rut for whatever animalistic desires overwhelmed him.

Maybe he hadn't imagined me more helpless than I felt now.

Maybe he didn't want me begging.

Whimpering.

The rush of heat didn't warm me. Whatever passed between us wasn't a mutual lust. His dangerous hunger coveted everything chaste and virtuous within me. I could try to hide, but Nicholas would always find me. That power was something no one should have possessed. Not a friend, not an enemy, and certainly not a Bennett.

I struggled against every sweaty, vulgar, and passionate image darkening my thoughts and tore my gaze from Nicholas. My breathing eased.

He had already invaded my mind. My lungs. How soon until he took my body?

"I'll make you a proposition," I whispered. "If you release me, *untouched*, and my research is returned, I'll forgive this insanity. We can talk about selling the company."

Nicholas prowled closer, his steps silent against the pine needles and cobblestones. I didn't run, but I prayed for even an ounce of his poise. I endured a calculated silence.

He planned it all.

Every soul-wracking moment, every tremble upon my skin, every hope and confidence that crashed before him. He *planned* it.

He captured me without touching me. He possessed me without violating me. He owned me without a word.

I should have run until my breath gasped into nothing and I collapsed in exhaustion.

Instead, I trapped myself within Nicholas Bennett's will.

And if I wanted to survive, I'd have to fight my every instinct to offer him complete and total obedience.

"You're in no position to make demands."

"Neither are you."

His chuckle rumbled, more threatening than his bike. "I'm not afraid of you, Ms. Atwood."

"You should be," I said. "You've invited me into your home. You've threatened to keep me prisoner. You haven't tied me to a bed, and I don't think you will. It's a mistake."

"Is it?"

"I plan to tear the Bennetts apart. I'll crush your estate to the ground brick-by-brick. I will have my revenge."

His voice lowered. "But we haven't done anything to you. Yet."

"You've done enough. You ruined my family."

"You think we killed your father."

"I don't think it." I coughed but regained my control. "I *know* it."

Nicholas frowned. I'd never understand his stillness. Where he waited, I tensed. While he quietly plotted, I braced to run. When he breathed, I struggled over everything betraying me—my body, my resolve, my courage.

He was stone, and I was the flooding stream pouring over any available avenue to escape.

Except I had nowhere to go.

The trees and forest, scrubs and ferns were just as dangerous as the Bennetts, despite how many years I spent studying ecology and agriculture. The trees wouldn't protect me, the weather wouldn't warm me, and the very plants I studied would poison me in pollen. I would wither and collapse in the dirt before I fled the shadow of the estate.

But I wasn't about to die.

"So what will you do about this murder?" He asked.

Plenty. "I'm an opportunist. My father taught me to take whatever luck the world offered and make up the difference ourselves. I'm waiting for my chance."

He stepped closer. I wouldn't let him see me retreat. "How can I help?"

"Screw your help. I'll earn my freedom, destroy your sick family, and I'll find the evidence to prove Darius killed my father. You won't be able to stop me."

"You're very confident for someone trapped in the clutches of apparent murderers."

"It's not confidence. I'm right. This is about justice and honor."

"You're defending Atwood honor?"

"Until the day I die."

"Then you're brave, foolish, and misguided." He paused. "But at least you aren't a monster like Mark Atwood."

The insult ripped through me. I welcomed the adrenaline as I confronted a man twice my size who teased me with the threat of captivity and violence.

"What do you want from me?" The forest seized the echo and veiled my words from the world. "Do you want to attack me? Hurt me? Do it. We're alone. No one would know. No one would see. You have me at your mercy so if you're going to rape me, just do it and get it over with—"

Nicholas rushed, seizing me within his grasp. The shock choked me, and I flailed instead of screamed. Trapped in his iron embrace, he hauled me from the path and slammed me against the base of a towering redwood. I dug my fingers into his suit. It did nothing. Nicholas shook me, forced me against the cool, uncaring tree trunk.

He dared to kiss me.

Not a gentle, story-book kiss meant to reassure my fears and redeem my trust in the man slinking into the overgrown forest to steal what I wasn't prepared to give.

Not a passionate, lust-crazed demand that would fuel our desire and trap us both in the carnal urges and natural cravings that existed only within the wilds.

Nicholas kissed me because I was his. He was my captor. Everything his family promised and everything he threatened would come true.

His lips crushed mine with a ragged, possessive heat. My body pinned against the tree as he slammed my wrists hard into the bark. He forced one arm to my side and drew the other over my head. I struggled, but his nibbling, expert pressure against my mouth forced a gasp.

From my parted lips, he attacked. His tongue stole a flick against mine. I twisted against his hold.

And I was punished.

Or rewarded?

Nicholas pushed, trapping me against his chest. I weakened in his power, amazed by the stirring unwelcomed sensations sizzling the tempted rapture over my skin.

Everywhere he touched burned—a fiery indignity and searing passion. He treated me with disrespect, and I seethed against the strength that so easily took my kiss.

The molten response bubbled inside me, folding and rising and taking me with more demands than his embrace.

My core tightened.

My legs trembled.

I tensed.

I hated him.

More than Reed or Max. More than Darius.

But my body surrendered everything sane and good and reasonable within my soul and blackened it with the corruption of the Bennetts. He held my hands. He pinned me. His strength moved against my petite frame as though he could break through me and the redwood with a single, vigorous thrust.

I imagined his ferocity.

And groaned.

But Nicholas pulled away. His breath tore through his body just as ragged as mine. I struggled to smack him, but he didn't release my hands.

I didn't think he'd ever release me.

I wasn't sure I wanted him to.

All the more reason to fight and escape before I decimated what remained of my pride.

His crisp scent enveloped me with a clean masculinity. My wrists bruised in his grip. I didn't care. The threatening promise of his form was too much, too fast, too overwhelming. His presence dulled my senses and forged forbidden and sensual fantasies that layered me with shame.

I tried to swear, but I had no strength left to speak. Instead I glowered, and he welcomed my resistance with a low whisper.

"I'm not going to hurt you, Ms. Atwood." He pulled my wrists to his chest, binding me to him. "When it comes time, I won't chase you. You'll come to me."

"I doubt that."

His predator grin layered me with goose bumps.

"I'll break you, Ms. Atwood, this is my promise. I will take you, mold you, and control you. You'll surrender to me. I won't hurt you, but that doesn't mean I won't devour you entirely."

"Why are you doing this?"

"Because I learned something about myself today." His lips pressed against my ear, his words a secret only for me. "I'm doing this because I *can*."

He pulled me from the tree and hauled me to the bike. My vision darkened, but the flush of heat and rage, passion and resistance provided me the strength to preserve my pride. Nicholas ordered me to hold him. I had nothing to clutch but his muscular chest as he returned me to the Bennett Estate.

He tried to intimidate me.

But I knew better. I saw through it, and the glimpse into his mind made every violation and suppressed pleasure worth it.

He wouldn't take me because he *could*.

He'd take me because he *wanted* me.

And because he dared to touch me, he'd be the first brick I destroyed in the Bennett Estate.

CHAPTER EIGHT
SARAH

Nicholas delivered me to the mansion. I stumbled off the motorcycle, but he pointed to the columned portico framing the front door.

"Wait there."

The brief ride was humiliating enough. I wasn't taking orders from Nicholas, especially if he thought I somehow *belonged* to him. He had tracked me down like a hunter stalking his prey and dared to kiss me without my consent.

At least, I didn't think I consented.

My lips tingled, along with other places I'd be damned to admit. Nicholas twisted my senses, but it wasn't just the indignity of his touch that chiseled my resolve into dust. He was the most sensual and attractive and *dangerous* man I had ever met.

My own *step-brother* trapped me in a perilous game I couldn't win, not if my body ached for something darker. I unsuccessfully exhaled the overheated air from my lungs.

I wasn't waiting for him. It was too risky to see him again before I learned how to endure the intensity of his stare without falling apart.

If I planned to survive this, I'd have to master Nicholas before he completely dominated me.

I studied the monstrous prison again. The spires clutched for the sky. The dark Corinthian stone blighted the natural beauty of the forest. The hundreds of windows stared at me in wicked accusation, as though they realized I wrecked an elegant dining room to escape from a dungeon of pure extravagance.

I edged through the front door. The foyer greeted me with silence. Nothing was bright in the house. No white marble, no delicate art or soft furniture. Dark tiles and splashes of crimson framed the centerpiece of the foyer—the grand staircase which would lead only to my ultimate violation.

Stairs. My chest hurt just looking at them.

I was certain Darius Bennett installed an elevator within his private sanctuary of opulence and secrets, but I'd be damned if they'd catch me using a crutch. God only knew what they'd do if I revealed the asthma.

One step.

Nice and slow.

A breath.

Second step.

This was pathetic. By the time I made it to my room, Nicholas might have found me, tortured me, and slammed me within my bed.

Third step—

"My dear…where do you think you're going?"

Of course Darius would find me. I missed my breath, but I didn't give him the pleasure of watching me pale. I continued my leisurely pace up the stairs.

"Get down here now, young lady."

His words lulled soft and the perverted whisper of *young lady* unsettled me. He didn't speak it to be kind. He meant it like a step-father.

And the implication sickened me.

I hid my disgust. "I'm going to my room to think about what I've done."

"I said *get down here*. I won't ask you twice, child."

"Fuck you."

He moved faster than I expected. I managed to rush only two steps before he was upon me. His hand tangled in my hair and yanked my head back.

I thought he meant to pin me.

I shrieked a breathless cry as he threw me down the stairs. I bounced once before landing hard against the tile of the foyer. I burned with tears.

No one had ever hit me.

Not my father. Not my mother. Not even Josiah and Mike when I would roughhouse with them. *No one* ever hurt me.

Or pushed me down stairs.

I had to get out of here.

I struggled to my feet, but Darius grasped me before I rose. He hauled me against him, twisting a hand in my hair and pinning me a thick arm over my waist.

His sneered whisper clutched my heart.

"You've misbehaved, my dear. I am very disappointed in you."

His fatherly, bitter tones rumbled felt dirty and wrong. I kicked, but even without asthma I couldn't match a Bennett's natural strength. Darius dragged me into the dining hall, aiming for where I tossed his chair through a plate window to escape. Glass littered the floor—a shimmering sea of danger.

I screamed as Darius pitched me to the ground. I tumbled onto the glass, and a thick shard instantly sliced my palm. He missed the worst of the pile, but the few crushed slivers tore at my skin. I bled everywhere, even from the smallest nicks on my exposed arms. His heel pressed against my neck. I struggled, but the movement only ground the glass into me. I stilled.

Darius Bennett looked too much like Nicholas—an older, greying, severe Nicholas who lost the amber tint to his eyes in favor of a lifeless brown. Darius didn't have the same strong jaw or Roman nose, but the similarities were enough. The brow, his drawn lips. But Nicholas hadn't played his emotions so vividly. Darius snarled, practically baring his teeth as he threatened to snap my neck with a steady kick.

My chest fluttered with useless breaths—hopefully fear and not the beginning of a serious attack.

A tear escaped as Darius knelt at my side, cradling a handful of glass in his palm. His voice lowered to a hideous threat.

"My dear, consider your circumstances. You are our guest because we need your cunt." A sharp shard of glass the size of a paring knife danced in his fingers. He pressed the serrated edge against my throat. "The rest of your body doesn't matter. Perhaps you wish to pick this glass up *piece by piece* with just your mouth?"

He wouldn't.

"No?" He pressed the glass against my cheek. "What if you cleaned this mess by hand?"

I shook my head.

"Then if you promise to be a good girl…" The glass drifted low. I tensed as it passed my throat but stiffened when he teased the edge over my chest. He swept over my breast and poked my nipple hiding beneath my shirt. "Maybe I won't have you sleep in this mess all night."

The shard traced down. Lower and lower, summoning a frenzied breath that forced a tremble over my body.

He dragged the tip over my stomach to the hem of my shirt. I swallowed bile as he focused on the crest between my legs. The glass prodded where nothing should touch.

Son of a bitch.

My hands curled within the glass shards. I swore and threw the dust at his face.

"Little bitch!"

The backhand struck harder than I expected. He laid me out before I had a chance to run, but his second strike never fell.

Nicholas loomed over us, his hand gripping his father's wrist. Reed rushed to my side, hauling me up from the glass. He pushed me behind him, just far enough to give me a momentary head start if his father dove at me once more.

Darius dabbed his eyes with a handkerchief, but he'd never admit that an Atwood harmed him. He snarled, pointing to the glass.

"Clean this up," he said. "Then come to us in the smoking lounge, do you understand, young lady?"

He didn't have the right to call me *young lady*.

"She'll clean," Nicholas said.

I blushed the instant he spoke. Darius growled and left me to my chore. Reed and Max followed, dutifully, as proper sons and lapdogs.

Nicholas waited, as though he expected a moment of gratitude for preventing the second blow. I hardly believed the first one had fallen, and the pain was only now blossoming over my cheek.

"I told you to wait for me," he said.

Was it an apology or another punishment? I brushed the glass from my clothing, amazed I wasn't more injured. Blood smeared, and the cut in my palm burned, but the sting distracted me from Nicholas's sharp glare, a prickle worse than any of the serrated shards scratching my skin.

"Next time, you *will* listen to me."

I didn't answer. He didn't offer to help. Was it all intimidation? He didn't threaten me, but what could hurt more than the damning kiss he forced upon me in the woods?

A kiss that took my breath then and now.

He followed his family and left me to my hell.

I fantasized about scratching the elaborate dining table with the glass, slashing through the original art decorating the walls, or simply leaving the shards for Darius to imbed in his feet.

But damaging a fine mahogany, ruining a precious painting, or forcing a maid to tend to my mess was just as distasteful as the vulgar words Darius whispered with wicked honesty. That revenge would be petty and would probably end with me locked in a room. I couldn't lose the freedom to explore the estate—to search for any reason, any evidence, for Darius Bennett murdering my father.

Running away nearly blew my chance.

I wouldn't be so selfish in the future.

I cleaned my injuries and swept up the glass. The activity exhausted me, and I hid within a powder room, wheezing. My body demanded a rest, but I didn't have the time.

Darius ordered me to his study once I was finished. God only knew what he wanted. I was more than content to make him wait, but my caution warned me to behave.

If I needed an inhaler—or a doctor—I couldn't give him reason to deny me.

And so I joined them.

Too many Bennetts waited for me in the dark shadows of the parlor.

The books on shelves darkened an already threatening salon, but the fire in the hearth roared. The bottles of bourbon and whiskey, brandy and cordials rested half-empty on a cart.

Darius obviously enjoyed this room—a private retreat for him and his sons. He ruled like a king, surrounded by decadence, scented by the charred wood from the fire and polished leather of the chairs. My step-family waited in silence, their seats arranged in a semi-circle framing the fireplace and ignoring the most precious piece of art Darius owned—the antique grand piano waiting in the corner.

A footstool was positioned in the center of their circle.

Darius didn't react when I entered. The hairs on my neck prickled. I hesitated.

I fucked up.

I fought him for a momentary victory. In my panic, I threw the glass and earned whatever punishment he plotted. The fight was as reckless as thinking I could escape from the estate to find any medication.

No.

It was never about the asthma. I lied to myself as ineffectively as I lied to Nicholas.

I tried to escape because the Bennetts terrified me. And now? The dread tore me apart before the men even touched me.

"My dear." Darius gestured to the ottoman. "Come join us."

"No, thank you."

"It's not an invitation."

I didn't let my gaze drift over Nicholas. Reed stared into the fire. His hair—a sun-bleached brown—matched the highlights and shadows within the hearth. He helped me from the glass. If I thought any Bennetts were capable of kindness, he might have been an ally.

But Reed was no friend. Neither was Max. For as prestigious and wealthy as the family was, rumors whispered of Max's personal touches to finalizing deals. Torched cars, shattered windows.

Broken bones.

Max walked with a severe limp, but he wasn't weak. A kick dropped me from his clutches once. He wouldn't let me get that lucky again.

This wasn't a parlor. It was a dragon's lair, carved for Darius and his sons, and it was the last place I should have entered.

I claimed the seat.

Darius nodded for Nicholas to continue reading from the tablet in his lap.

"Profits from production of the Weed and Wrangler division rose three percent from last month," Nicholas said. "It was our most significant growth overall, but down four percent from where we were this time last year."

"Reasons?"

"Distribution costs, supplier delays."

What in the world? I expected hellfire. Instead I got a board meeting. Lately, I started believing they were one and the same, but I didn't expect business from the Bennetts.

"Suggestions?" Darius snapped his fingers and pointed to the whiskey.

He gestured for me to serve them.

Son of a bitch. I curled my fist to hide the blood. The gash stung and my cheek throbbed where he struck me. Enough bruises would line my skin from the fall down the stairs, and I could only imagine how bad the rest of me looked from the car crash.

Whiskey was easy. I tipped the decanter and let the alcohol spill into his tumbler. I hoped it would poison him.

Nicholas swiped across the tablet. "I've created a three point plan to regain our ground. I've instructed our CFO to present—"

"One moment, son." Darius curled a finger for me to stand.

What now?

"My dear, as an honored guest in the Bennett home, you are welcomed to attend this meeting as a show of good faith."

Sure, I was. "What good faith?"

"You will soon carry a Bennett in your belly. You should be privy to the information discussed, don't you think?"

I shuddered. "No."

Darius's pleasure wrenched every last hope from my heart. "You will sit here. Listen to our meeting. Learn our business. And do you know why?"

I shook my head.

"Because you are insignificant. You are present because no matter what you do or where you go, we will find you, capture you, and restrain you within these halls."

My fingers dug into the leather beneath me. He savored his drink.

"You are nothing more than a pussy to fuck and a womb to seed, do you understand?"

I scowled. Darius didn't blink.

"Now be a good girl. Take off your clothes."

My heart stalled. My rough intake of air was neither asthma nor shock.

It was fear.

"Excuse me?" I whispered.

"Take off your clothes."

"No!"

Nicholas closed the cover on his tablet. Max stretched in his chair, but even Reed inspected me.

"I won't ask again."

"Good. I won't do it."

"The doctor said you are not ovulating yet, child." Darius perked an eyebrow. "At this moment, you are a centerpiece. However, if you insist on defying us, we will tie you down and rut you here like the animal you are. Is that what you would prefer?"

They wouldn't break me. I shook my head. "No."

"Good. We are not barbarians, my dear. This is not entertainment. It is business."

"Raping me is *business?*"

"It's purely for procreation." He laughed. "Of course, my sons may think procreating is quite enjoyable."

"You're sick."

"Take off your clothes, and you won't be harmed. Refuse, and the clothes come off, and you'll regret this delay. Your choice."

Damn it.

Hell wasn't the moment my hands tangled in the dirty material of my shirt, but the instant just before. The *decision*. The beaded thought of terror balanced between self-preservation and modesty. Four Bennett men meant to look upon my body, not as a form of lust or admiration, but because, like Nicholas said—they *could*.

I weighed my options. Weakened by the shade of my asthma, I couldn't fight them off. Stripping was mortifying, but I'd never handle their touch. Not now. Not until I had rested and prepared for the horrors of such violence.

Darius grinned as I tugged the shirt over my head. I ignored my burning cheeks and the bumbling nausea in my stomach.

My fingers trembled. I failed twice to unfasten the button on my jeans. Darius clinked the ice in his drink.

"My dear, the brassiere?"

Of course. They'd want a perverted show while I struggled to degrade myself. It wasn't like the bra hid much anyway. I was skinny and small and hardly *breeding* material. Why not reveal all my secrets at once? I bit my lip and unclasped the hooks.

And made the mistake of searching for Nicholas.

For the briefest of moments trapped in the woods, I almost made a foolish mistake. When Nicholas captured me against the tree—when he pinned my arms and stole my lips and whipped me with blended lust, confusion, and anger—I thought of this *exact* moment. I imagined revealing myself to him. Welcoming his attention.

It was another layer of hell, where all reason burned into cinders of lust and bestial instinct.

Now, the thought was wretched, a bottomless despair, a horrible realization.

I nearly surrendered to his kiss. My thoughts had blurred with a longing for his touch.

I was attracted to Nicholas, and nothing terrified me more.

The bra dropped to the ground, and my breasts were exposed to the wolves. The fire couldn't combat the sudden chill that only hardened my nipples and humiliated me in their responsiveness. My step-brothers were silent, but they saw everything.

Darius nodded. "And now the rest."

This wasn't my dishonor. It was theirs. *They* were the ones debasing themselves. *They* were the ones kidnapping women and destroying any morality that still existed within their family.

I yanked the jeans down, accidentally taking my panties with them. But what did it matter? They wanted to see all of me, as if it would frighten me.

So fine.

I didn't cry. I didn't scream. I didn't beg.

None of this pleased Darius Bennett.

It amused Reed. He gave me a wink. Max glanced over my form and dismissed me to read an email on his phone.

But Nicholas?

If his golden eyes had burned, I'd be cast in a molten shell of utter desire. He memorized every part of me with a nefarious eagerness. It wasn't as though he hadn't felt me through the kiss. Our bodies pressed together. My chest arched. My hips practically bucked.

First he claimed my kiss, and now he viewed my vulnerability with roguish excitement. The flush of pink embarrassment colored my skin, dancing over every bit of my exposure. Nicholas shared none of my shame for enjoying this. He actually believed, without a doubt or a moment of guilty humility, that I was *his*.

These men were going to rape me.

But Nicholas? He was honest to his word. He wouldn't hurt me, and I'd break the instant he touched me.

Their silence was a whip, and I wasn't about to get beat again.

"You were saying, Nicholas..." I didn't unclench my fists. "Your company's products are failing?"

Reed snorted. I swore he smiled at me. "I've always said farmers fear the runoff. We should make something *organic*. Capitalize on that market."

Like I hadn't heard that before. "And what will you do when that product also devastates the local ecosystem, pollutes the water table, and causes birth defects in cattle?" I shrugged. "There's a reason the Atwood's farms have never used your pesticides and herbicides. We *value* our crop."

Nicholas didn't flinch. "We've run numerous ecological studies, each of which have passed with no admonishment from any regulatory committees." He enjoyed this game. "Perhaps it was your farm polluting the water table? Your unhealthy breeding selection contributing to the problems with Atwood livestock?"

"She had best hope her breeding stock has no complications." Darius's voice hardened.

He was revolting.

Darius stood, circling me though I tried my best to ignore the sting of his stare upon me. The slap to my breast was quick and severe. I wished I hadn't shrieked. I had no time to defend myself before he cupped me between the legs.

Darius twisted his fingers in my delicate curls.

And yanked.

"This is disgusting." He tugged me off balance, gripping on the fine, blonde curls that obscured my slit. "Horrible."

Each word was a punch to my gut. I struggled away from him, but his next slap aimed directly between my legs. The shock of the strike drew tears. I dropped onto the ottoman.

"You think I would give you to my sons *unprepared?*" Darius leered at me as I struggled to cross my legs.

"Leave me alone," I whispered.

"You will take a bath and shave your pussy so your body will please your brothers. Is that understood?"

I couldn't speak. The demand was too mortifying.

The first time anyone saw my body—and they insulted it.

Horrible. Hideous. *Disgusting?*

This was beyond cruel. My stomach threatened to wretch, but I had nothing inside me but bitterness. I shook my head.

"No—that's...*no.*"

Darius kicked the ottoman from under me. I collapsed on the floor. I tried to cover my breasts. It only exposed more of me.

"You will not return until you're bare. Go."

Reed called for his father. His awkward shrug combined honesty with reluctance. "I don't want to verge on too much information here, but I'm...very okay with how she looks now."

114

Darius straightened his jacket. He nodded, gesturing toward Max. "And you?"

Max hadn't moved. He shrugged, glancing from his phone to search for the area I tried to hide. "A pussy's a pussy. I'm not picky."

I tensed as Nicholas and his father shared a glance.

Nicholas sat like a king. Regal and magnificent and absolutely unreadable in his strength. He became the epitome of stillness. His patience treaded so close to premonition I wondered if he saw how everything would unfold, bend, and break before it happened.

I searched for his mercy in a desperate, insane moment. He might have been my savior. A protector. A voice of *reason.*

Instead, his mellow baritone spoke only to fracture me.

"Go upstairs, Ms. Atwood, and tend to yourself."

Bastard.

Bully.

Enemy.

The indignity of the request was nothing compared to the insufferable arrogance of the man who demanded it. I pushed myself from the ground. Ungracefully, simply relieved my throat hadn't closed as I savored a particular choice phrase to utter. The frustration stung harder than Darius's hit, but I wouldn't test my luck while my flesh was so vulnerable to my step-father.

I ignored their admiration as I hurried from the room. I ran. A mistake. The fear chased like a shadow, and I had to sit on the landing between the floors as I wheezed.

This wasn't good.

Not the panic. Not the breathing.

But in a perverse way, they helped. I stumbled into my room and slammed the bathroom door. The scalding water poured from the bath. I savored the hot air.

My muscles relaxed in the familiar heat. A steamy bathroom used to slow my attacks. It wasn't medication, but it'd get me through this.

At least, I hoped it'd get me through.

Who was cruel enough to shame a girl about her own body? And who was stupid enough to believe the vulgar lies? Darius meant to get in my head. It wasn't his words that blinded me.

Nicholas's judgment was the razor to my vein.

What was a worse punishment—altering my body and surrendering? Fighting them and earning Darius's wrath?

I had too much to consider and not nearly enough air.

I gripped the razor, but I had no idea how to bend the right way to protect that softened skin. The warmth of the water comforted me from the first swipe to the last, but the end product wasn't as sexy as my friends insisted it'd be.

I looked young.

Vulnerable.

Weak.

I appeared like a woman the Bennetts preferred. It gave me confidence.

I'd use it to my advantage. I'd let the vulgarity be a disguise.

But I still shouldered a robe before leaving my room. It didn't prevent the chill as I clutched the railing and descended the stairs. One express trip to the foyer was enough. But Darius's shout echoed a dozen times in the expansive hall.

I wheezed as he ripped the robe from my shoulders and tore me from the pink terrycloth.

"You disobedient little *slut*." Darius kicked my knee, dropping me to the floor. I preferred it there, pressed against the cool tile while the world bashed helplessly against my lungs. "Do you think you're allowed clothes unless I specifically say it?"

He kicked me again. I shielded my head, but he didn't aim for my face. He bruised my thigh, but the strike successfully pried my legs apart.

"Jesus, Dad, she's down." Reed cautiously approached. "Don't hurt her."

I coughed, but only once. The rest was lost to a choked sob I'd never admit to rasping. My legs fell open, and everything revealed to them. The delicate curve of my hip trapped me in femininity. The softened skin, pale and silky from the bath, bared me as little more than a tightness for them to steal.

Every last fold and petal and virgin sight exposed to my greatest enemies.

"Excellent." Darius appraised me like I was a fine wine in his glass. "Unfortunately, I've just been called to San Francisco, but this lovely memory will keep me warm during my trip."

He clapped Nicholas on the shoulder. "Take her if you wish. Punish her if she requires it." He pointed to Max and Reed. "You as well, but ask permission from Nicholas. As eldest, he deserves the first night."

Sick.

Depraved.

Monsters.

I turned away and folded my legs, earning yet another kick from Darius. Nicholas intervened before he lunged for my hair.

"Don't bruise her." He studied me. "She's radiant now. I enjoy it."

The foot lowered. I edged closer to the damned stairs I'd never be able to climb again. My coughing worsened, but Nicholas said nothing. Darius pulled his cell to call his driver. He strode from the foyer and disappeared down the stairs to the garage.

My step-brothers waited as I shivered beneath them. Reed moved first. He dove for the robe while Max swore.

"Here." Reed laid it over my shoulders. "I saw enough."

The rage clouded my sanity. I shoved the robe into his arms.

"Screw you," I said. "You think you can dress me and everything will be okay?"

Nicholas offered his hand to get me up. Absolutely not. Crawling was preferable to his help.

"Ms. Atwood—"

"You're all demons," I whispered. "Especially you, Nicholas. Strap me to the bed now, I'll never submit to you."

Nicholas buttoned his jacket. I didn't have the strength to stand, but it didn't matter. The weight of the humiliation crushed me at their feet. I was no longer the admired centerpiece in their charade. I crumpled, weak and angry and flushed with embarrassment.

"Allow me to speak with her," Nicholas said.

Reed hesitated. Max had the right idea. He pulled his phone and nudged Reed to follow. Their steps faded, but the thudding of my heart would echo throughout the house.

Nicholas knelt only once his brothers passed from the room. He laid the robe over my shoulders.

"Consider this a lesson in strategic concessions, Ms. Atwood."

My expression blanked.

"Permit my father his small victories. Concentrate your strength on what matters. Granting him his perversions will protect you. Challenge him on every little thing? He will make you suffer."

I coughed again. Nicholas thought I cried. I didn't know which weakness was worse.

"Why don't you take a razor below the belt and then we'll talk?" I said.

"If we're being honest—"

"—I don't want your honesty—"

"I'd take you however I could get you."

His words wrapped me tighter than the robe, a heated promise. I tensed.

"I'd take you innocent with those beautiful pale curls, or I'd enjoy you completely bare, soft, and wanton. All that matters is that I'm the man who will ultimately taste you."

"Rape me."

"We'll see."

"Why did you side with Darius?"

He stood again. He might have thought I'd do the same, but my body locked. Pure adrenaline pumped my blood for me. I coughed again—unproductive and dry.

"My father expected me to side with him."

I spat the word. "Coward."

"In a few days' time, you will be bred by your three step-brothers. Is a bit of nudity the worst thing you can imagine?"

Well, when he put it that way—it sounded just as bad.

"You challenged my father when you fled. Had you stayed where I ordered and done as I said, I might have convinced him you were already sufficiently punished. Instead, you defied me, angered him, and suffered the consequences."

"Shaving my…" I gasped. "That's a *consequence?*"

"No. My father beating you senseless would have been the consequence. Hopefully you learned how best to behave."

"This is *not* my fault."

"But it is," he said. "You aren't thinking in terms of concessions, only pride. Why fight him on every term when you are negotiating for something far more important?"

"My freedom?"

"Your life."

"I'm not giving him any more victories over me. Once was enough."

"You're in his house, Ms. Atwood. You're at his mercy."

"He has no mercy." My words clipped without air.

"Not for you. But, if he thinks he's broken you, this might go easier."

"Why would I give in?"

Nicholas brushed my cheek with his fingers, so gently I jerked as if he had struck me. But Nicholas would never hurt me. I understood that now. He had no cause to beat me, no obsession to watch me bleed.

He offered me a single escape, but it wasn't freedom.

"Surrender, and when the time comes, I will be the only one to take you."

I coughed again. The gasp didn't return air. The thickness in my throat finally closed.

Then, the panic.

No matter how strong I believed I was, or how I once controlled it, or how much I understood about my body, my courage always disintegrated when I tripped over my first missed breath.

Nicholas knelt as my breath hitched—a quiet hiccup that made him chuckle. His smiled faded as I gripped his arm. I dug into his jacket. My nails tinted blue.

"Ms. Atwood, come with me. I'll get you some water."

I coughed. It caused only pain. Soundless agony bubbled in me.

"What's wrong?" Nicholas demanded. He shouted for his brothers when I didn't answer.

I clawed at my neck. The brief sip of air I managed did nothing. My head pounded. I fell forward, slapping my throat, my chest, trying to make him understand.

Reed rushed into the room first, diving to our side. "Sarah?"

Max limped after, watching from a distance. "What the hell's wrong with her? Is she choking?"

Nicholas shook his head. He helped me onto my back. It didn't help. My vision darkened, but the horrible coughing squeezed my chest. I pushed him away as much as I pulled him close, struggling against the pressure consuming me from the inside out.

Betraying me.

Destroying me.

Bennett wouldn't need to hurt me. My Atwood blood cursed me from the day I was born.

"*Sarah!*" Nicholas cradled me against him. Not the first time he did it. Maybe the last. "Sarah?"

I had no choice. It was stupid of me to hide the illness. I stared into his dark, caramel eyes—a color too beautiful for the man he was. The one I thought he was? I forced the words out.

"As—asthma." I beat my useless chest. "H—help me."

CHAPTER NINE
NICHOLAS

Sarah Atwood collapsed in my arms.

It was the second time I cradled her limp body to my chest.

"What the fuck did she just say?" Reed hovered over her. "*Asthma?*"

I batted him away and lifted her from the floor. Was that why she was so small? So fragile?

The girl weighed nothing. I rested her on the parlor chaise. Her cuts reopened. Blood leeched from her arms, hands, and neck onto the white couch. A thin line dribbled along her perfect breasts.

Almost perfect. Perfection wouldn't struggle and heave and choke to breathe.

Her lips turned blue, and her coughing rasped far too shallow to be effective. Her body lurched, but still she clung to me.

I had no idea what to do for her.

"Should we sit her up?" Reed knelt before her, trying to hold her still. He rushed to the kitchen and returned with a bottle of water. "Give her this."

We padded pillows behind her. Sarah slumped and turned her head. The water dripped from her lips, blending with the crimson cuts on her neck.

"Jesus." Max gritted his teeth. "You gotta call him, Nick."

My father was the last person who needed to know our prisoner slowly suffocated. I nodded, though the decision churned my stomach. He wouldn't care that she suffered.

Why didn't I realize she had asthma?

We studied the Atwood stock and bonds, hired private investigators to trace her brothers' activities, secured corporate allies and tucked them within her company. We knew everything about Atwood Industries and nothing about Sarah.

My father planned for us to bed and breed her. We purchased clothes for her, provided lotions and makeup, and prepared her room. But we neglected her most important amenity.

A rescue inhaler.

"Got a problem." Max lowered his voice as he spoke into the phone. "The girl's sick...Not sure....An asthma attack, I think." He paused. "No, definitely not faking it."

Max's frustration mirrored my own. He ended the call. "He said to call Doctor Rimes."

Absolutely not.

"Rimes is an hour away," I said. "She doesn't have that long."

Reed flipped through his phone. "Dude, this is serious. Every one of these websites says to get her to a hospital."

Max crossed his arms. "She's not getting out of the house. Dad will carve her lungs out himself. He's not risking her escaping."

"Look at her!" Reed stood. "She can't run away like this."

Sarah's grip weakened. I knelt before her, helpless as her delicate blue eyes widened, teary, and dulled to the color of a rich ash.

Last time I held her this closely, it wasn't terror that made her tremble.

It was rage.

Indignation.

Desire.

But I didn't see it then. The coughing. The walking. The weakness. The attack had lasted for a while, and she pushed herself beyond her strength.

She didn't tell us she was sick. She hadn't trusted us. And now, she was in trouble.

Unacceptable.

The girl was our captive, but she was the only woman—only person—I met who intimidated my father to violence. He loathed the Atwoods, but his hatred of Sarah bordered on personal obsession. She returned it, punch for punch, even when she could no longer defend herself.

She was the most remarkable woman I knew.

I tied her robe closed to calm her, though she was lovely, even in distress.

How beautiful would she be when we conquered her?

"Max, we're taking the helicopter," I said. "You fly. Reed, call the hospital. Tell them we're on our way and give them our flight information."

"Are you insane?" Max wove his fingers through his hair. "If she goes to a hospital, they won't just treat her asthma. Not when Dad punted her down the stairs and rolled her in glass. They'll ask questions. She'll tell people she's been kidnapped and fuck us over."

Reed offered the water again. She turned away. Gripped me harder.

"I'd rather explain a kidnapping than a murder." Reed exhaled. "We don't have a choice."

Max swore. "We take her to the hospital, and Dad will kill her himself."

"She won't talk." I cupped her chin. She choked and gasped, but she was still listening. "She knows if she tells anyone what's happened to her, our father will hurt her mother. She's not ready to lose the only family she has left."

"We're her family," Reed snorted. "Technically."

"And that's why we'll help her." I lifted Sarah into my arms and ordered my brother to the helicopter. "I'll make Dad understand."

Sarah didn't struggle. Either she understood I meant to help or she was in that much pain.

Or she was dying.

I wouldn't tolerate innocent blood on my hands.

The girl wasn't just a beautiful creature of fire and passion. She was an heir to a fortune and the key to the Bennetts acquiring a company that would preserve our name, wealth, and status for generations, despite the challenges facing us.

My motivations were selfish, vile, and cruel.

But that was business.

And losing our greatest asset to a secret illness wasn't an option.

I was the better pilot, but I wasn't releasing Sarah from my arms. Reed followed with bottles of water and warm compresses. She wheezed against my chest. I braced her for Max's flight.

Reed shouted what I didn't have the courage to ask.

"Is she conscious?" He fit a pair of sound-muffling headphones over her ears. They tumbled off until I held them against her. "Christ, Nick. She's gonna die."

Not if I prevented it.

Reed sunk into the seat, head in his hands. "This was fucked from the start."

"Stop panicking." Max shouted as he kicked the throttle and propelled the helicopter over the estate and to the east, toward the closest hospital in San Jose. Not necessarily the best, but we weren't in a position to research any pulmonary specialists of Northern California. "We'll be there in twenty. Keep her alive."

Twenty minutes.

Sarah's head lulled into my chest.

Did she even have twenty minutes?

I patted her cheek. She jerked away. Her frustration relieved me. At least she was still awake enough to realize a Bennett held her. Then again, she'd fight us until that last breath.

A shadow of blue faded over her lips. I felt her heart rate flutter, beating in terror and pain.

I was helpless while she was conscious, but I was terrified when she collapsed—when her chest ceased struggling and her body fell limp.

"Max!" I shouted. "Fucking land!"

The helicopter rumbled over the skyscrapers, and Reed stole the radio from Max. Swearing rarely earned landing clearance in private airfields, but the hospital made an exception. We touched down, and I leapt from the doors before we cut the engine. A handful of nurses and a concerned doctor waited for us at the roof access. I rushed Sarah inside.

"How old is she?" The stocky, balding doctor fitted a stethoscope over his ears.

"Twenty."

"Asthma attack?"

Apparently. "Yes."

"When did it begin?"

"Half an hour ago."

"Emergency medications?"

Jesus Christ, if I knew all this information when we stole her from the cornfield, I wouldn't have left her in the care of frantic nurses, shoving her onto a gurney while fitting an oxygen mask over her face.

"She had none to take." It wasn't a lie.

The doctor squeezed into the elevator with two nurses as a third prevented me from following. "What's your relation to the patient?"

My turn to cough. "I'm her…brother."

The nurse took my information and pointed to the stairwell. "To the waiting room, Mr. Bennett."

I wasn't leaving Sarah in the hands of strangers, not when I couldn't trust a word from her lips.

Not when I feared abandoning her, frightened and alone in the hospital.

I pushed past the nurse to the elevator. Reed grasped my shoulder, preventing me from making a mistake.

"Come on," he said. "Max is taking care of the helicopter. They warned we might get into trouble."

Trouble?

Someone dared to question me for saving a life?

And not just any life—a woman who belonged to us.

To me.

Whether Sarah Atwood believed it or not, whether she consented to it, understood it, or even realized the full extent of our ownership of her, she was mine.

It might have horrified me a week ago, but that was before I found her. Held her.

Before I kissed her.

A single taste of her pouty, peppermint pink lips, and she sealed her own fate. Her innocence teased me, and her strength challenged me. No other woman ever excited me into such carnal instinct. Pinning her against the tree? Holding her against her will as I kissed her? Nearly exploding when her body warmed and pressed into mine and bared her own simmering desperation?

She was pure temptation—a mistake, a crime, a sin.

I nearly let her die.

The memory of her kiss shredded me, filling me with the horrible, spine-chilling rasp of her broken breaths.

If she was still breathing.

The nurse led us to a sterile waiting room with pasty white walls and mottled blue carpets. Nothing changed in hospitals. No matter the cleanliness or order, each waiting room suffered through a depressing haze. It was too familiar, even after seventeen years of healing.

The last time I waited in a hospital, it was to say goodbye to our mother. Her heart failed before my father heard about the accident. Reed rested in the ICU. Max was taken to his second surgery.

Back then, the car crash rendered me helpless. I was twelve years old when my mother was murdered and my brothers injured. I had no means to help. But now I was a man, and I was responsible for Sarah's wellbeing. I had no excuse—not for my behavior and not for my inability to protect the one woman vital to my family's financial security.

The woman who enthralled me into sin.

An hour passed.

Then another.

And finally a third.

I didn't question where Reed found five pounds of chocolate. He offered me a soda, presenting a half dozen alternative flavors when I refused the first. He set his stash upon the table and sunk into a bag of corn chips.

"You okay?" The bag crumbled in his grip. "She looked bad."

"It was my fault." I knew why the phone buzzed in my pocket with the telltale persistence of a dozen hornets. I didn't answer. "I should have realized she was sick."

"She shouldn't have hidden it."

"She shouldn't have thought to hide it. The last thing I wanted was for her to get hurt."

Reed snorted, spilling half his chips. "Jesus Christ, Nick. Sarah was *always* going to get hurt. If it wasn't asthma, it was Dad's foot imbedded in her skull. Or a belt wrapped around her neck. Or, shit, I don't know. Internal injuries from when we fuck her half to death."

"Enough."

"This wasn't ending without her getting bloody." He tossed the snacks away. "This girl won't submit. She threw one of our dining room chairs through a goddamned window to escape."

And I caught her.

I had liked the chase.

"She's fighting for her life," Reed said. "And either she's going to lose hers, or we'll spend the rest of ours in prison. Those are the only possibilities."

No. Not the only possibilities.

Sarah's death would be nothing compared to the consequences for my brothers if she didn't comply, surrender, and ultimately conceive from our crimes. My father would murder his own flesh and blood if it meant securing something more valuable to him than our sacrifice.

His sons were pawns to achieve whatever success he envisioned.

The company was his real legacy.

Shouting echoed from the nurses' station. Reed swore, but he unwrapped a candy bar instead of moving. It wasn't as though my father would listen to him even if he'd decided to intervene. That task was left to me.

I buttoned my jacket as I approached the arguing nurses barricading themselves from my father with only the benefit of a half door between them.

"My daughter in is one of these rooms!" He pounded against the counter. "I demand to see her."

A redheaded nurse tried her best and failed. "Sir, I'm sorry, but the doctors are stabilizing her. She's resting now, but you'll be permitted to visit her shortly—"

"Unacceptable. The Bennetts own a wing in this hospital. I sat on the Board of Directors for three years. Bring out your supervisor, immediately."

I eased between my father and the irritated nurses and smiled.

He seethed. I pitied the poor nurses and doubted they'd have jobs once their shifts ended. I encouraged him to give me a moment with the women.

"Nicholas Bennett." I introduced myself and offered a business card with my credentials and a written cellphone number scrawled on the front. "Did I hear you correctly? Sarah is stabilized?"

The stocky head nurse took the card, but she fanned herself with it as she searched me over. She was twenty years too old for me and brandished pictures of her kids pinned to the corkboard behind her computer, but I wasn't above seizing an opportunity when it presented itself.

"She's stable, but she's weak and on oxygen. She'll need to rest."

"Oh, of course." The charm chipped away some of the nurse's ice. "She's a fighter."

"That she is."

"The thing is..." I lowered my voice. The nurse leaned closer. "My sister's asthma is very private. She doesn't like doctors or hospitals—they scare her, what with the history of her condition. She would rest better, and frankly, so would I, if I might be permitted to stay at her side. I'd hate for her to panic and trigger another attack."

The nurse perked an eyebrow.

"I'll keep out of the way. You won't notice I'm there. Sarah will thank you for it."

After a long pause, she sighed. "She'll be moved to a regular room in a few minutes. You can join her then." She fiddled under the desk and slid a "Care Partner" badge to me.

"Only you," she warned, nodding to my father.

Perfect.

"I understand, thank you." I tucked the badge in my pocket. "I'll let the rest of the family know she's doing well."

My father rushed me when I returned to the waiting room. He gripped my shoulder and hauled me into the wall. Reed didn't move.

"You listen to me, Nicholas." He edged close, sneering as his eyes flicked up to meet mine. I straightened, rising higher if only to irritate him. "I told you *not* to bring her to the hospital."

"She would have died."

"What do you think will happen if she breathes a word of this to the doctors?"

Reed should have known not to speak. "She can't breathe."

My father ground his teeth. "She can write. Text."

"She won't," I said.

My father over-annunciated when angry. He released me when a group of nurses crossed for the break room. "If she even *hints* to what's happened—"

"She knows better."

"You hope. Get in that room and remind her of what will happen if she displeases us. She doesn't speak. She isn't left alone." He pulled his cell. "I'll call Doctor Rimes and transfer her care into his custody. We'll take her to the estate to recover."

Reed tossed his food to the table. "She's sick, Dad. She shouldn't leave the hospital. What if she has another attack?"

"Then the little bitch will have learned her lesson."

I didn't like his tone. "Did you know she had asthma?"

My father snorted. "Of course. I had her emergency inhaler."

"*What?*"

"It was in her purse. Max picked it up after she eluded him and his crippled leg."

"You could have stopped this."

"And now she knows. We feed her, clothe her if we so choose, and we'll administer her medications. If she defies us, we'll take any combination of our generosity away."

"And if she still fights?"

My father waved a dismissive hand. "I disciplined my sons. Why should my daughter fare any differently?"

I said nothing. She wasn't his daughter, not truly, and she wasn't as resilient as us. Sarah wouldn't survive the belts, lashes, burns, and running mile after mile on treadmills. He'd have her sleeping without a mattress or going hungry while writing thousands of lines to apologize for a trivial mistake.

Sarah didn't deserve my father's brand of discipline.

"Let me speak with her," I said. "I'll control her behavior. It won't be a concern."

"And yours?"

"Excuse me?"

My father hissed his words through clenched teeth. "I will not be defied by my own son. You'll obey me when I give an order. That girl is not to leave our estate—not until she is fucked, bred, and your son is swaddled in her arms, do you understand?"

"I'll take care of it."

I turned, but my father caught my elbow. Squeezed. It didn't hurt, and I didn't react.

"That isn't what I asked." He growled. "Do you *understand*, Nicholas?"

I understood my father's madness. That wasn't a lie.

"I'll protect the family," I said. "You have my word."

My father released me. I left him with Reed and charmed a nurse to lead me to Sarah.

He would keep her prisoner, and he expected me to silence her cries before she had the breath to scream. And I would—only because I couldn't have her spoiling the Bennett name.

He'd secure our future through the suffering of the girl. I had a better plan. My phone chimed with two new voicemails from perspective stock holders sensitive to my vision for the company.

I didn't need an illegitimate heir to claim what would be mine.

The stock ticked into my favor. Ten percent, twenty percent, thirty-five percent of the holders. Allied to me. Respecting me. Offering me their allegiance in a fight to save the Bennett Corporation from the madness risking our future wealth.

My step-sister would be tamed, and she would return to the estate under my control.

A single word from her would bring down my family's empire.

No one would stop me from taking what was mine.

And Sarah Atwood was mine.

CHAPTER TEN
SARAH

I hated hospitals.

I hated hospital beds and their paper thin blankets. I hated the hospital's noise and beeping machinery. I hated hospital doctors with their cold hands and colder stethoscopes and the lies they spouted over and over.

I'd be fine.

Just breathe.

I was safe now.

They'd help me.

I wouldn't be *safe* or *helped*. I was hopelessly alone. Everything I had done was to preserve my company and maintain a sense of decorum and strength. Now? I fought for my life—both literally and for the freedom I couldn't earn even outside the estate.

Nicholas Bennett sat at my bedside, checking emails on his phone while I'd slept. My monitors chimed, and the air tickled my nose dry.

Oxygen. They only gave me oxygen when I was really sick.

Last thing I remembered was falling to my knees and begging Nicholas for help. That stung more than the ill-placed IV.

"How do you feel?" Nicholas didn't look up from his phone.

Awful. Horrible. Like someone kicked me in the ribs during an asthma attack.

"Fine."

"You're in the hospital," he said.

"You don't say."

"You didn't give us much choice. I thought you were going to die."

Yeah, I did that a lot. I eased onto the pillows. My body grumbled from a few hours in the lumpy bed.

"What time is it?"

"Time for you to rest."

It was the same response my father always gave.

"Ask a stupid question, Sprout." He checked his watch and rapped on the room's door. "Where the hell is your mother?"

"I'm okay, Dad." My words mumbled. It hurt to talk. I peeked under the hospital gown.

My chest covered in bruises!

"Oh no."

Dad frowned. "It's from the CPR. You have a few broken ribs. Sit still."

Good thing I was flat as a board or the doctors would have pounded me down. Was I supposed to feel so horrible? This wasn't like a normal attack.

"Nurse!" He called to a passing woman. "My daughter needs a sedative."

"But, Dad, I'm okay?"

"I can't wait for your mother anymore. There's ten million dollars riding on a deal at the ranch, I have to get back."

"But—"

"This nice lady is going to give you something to help you sleep." Dad patted the nurse. "Your mom will be here when you wake up."

My lip trembled. The tears fell. I wiped them away in case he thought I was being weak, but moving was pure agony. I cried harder, losing my breath to sobs and then crumpling in more pain when my chest tightened over the whimpers.

"Sarah, you're hysterical. This will help."

The nurse injected the medicine into my IV. I shook my head, but Dad rubbed my foot as my vision faded.

"I'll call later. Sleep tight, Sprout."

Dad hated hospitals as much as I did. He was always making excuses to leave.

The oxygen dried my mouth. I reached for the bedside pitcher of water but the finger monitor and wires bumped over the tray. Nicholas pocketed his phone and poured a glass. I pulled the tubes off my face before drinking.

"The doctors said you'd make a full recovery."

I nodded. "That's what they say every time."

"It looked bad."

It always did. I sipped again. The water didn't dilute the antiseptic bitterness on my tongue.

The doctors had me inhale more drugs and mists and steroids than I remembered from my past attacks. My chest hurt, but I could breathe. I suffered only from exhaustion now.

Josiah and Mike never understood that I was okay once I had the medicines and examinations. An attack scared them witless and usually filled my room with more provisions from home than the nurses felt sanitary.

This time, I had only one gift.

A dozen roses stashed in the window. Thick, crimson blossoms spilled from a crystal vase.

"Reed." Nicholas answered before I asked.

"They're beautiful."

"Like I said, you looked…worse for wear. Especially with the cuts and bruises."

I touched my cheek. It hurt as badly as my ribs. "Did you tell them my step-father molested and beat me?"

"We told them you fell down the stairs during the attack. Tripped over a glass statue." He folded his hands and studied me. His gaze grazed my skin and rejuvenated everything that was struck.

"A *statue?*" Even laughing caused pain. "Hopefully there aren't any more statues in my future."

"That depends on you."

"I doubt that."

I coughed. Just a residual strain, but Nicholas offered me more water. He acted kind, but he didn't sport the "care-partner" badge because he was my step-brother. He was no nurse. He was my warden. At least he didn't fret as much as my real family.

Then again, he'd have to care about me to fret. His only concern was that I stayed alive and gave him the child he demanded. Didn't matter if I was healthy, safe, or statue-free.

"It was a pleasurable kiss in the woods," Nicholas said. "But I didn't think you'd take it so hard."

I choked on my water. First asthma, now drowning. I wiped the dribble from my mouth and muffled my profanity.

Nicholas's smile was nothing like the harsh, violent menace of his father.

My heart thudded faster. The stupid monitors betrayed a quick blipping. Nicholas chuckled. I sipped the water again, tempted to spill it over his expensive suit, chiseled jaw, and perfect wave of dark hair.

Raising my arm took too much effort. I should've ordered him to dunk himself. Instead I leaned against the pillows and savored every freeing breath.

"Are you all right?" He asked. "I can call for the nurse."

"Stop hovering. It's unbecoming for a Bennett."

"If you insist."

I shifted. Nothing was more uncomfortable than staying in a hospital. I tugged on the blankets if only to distract myself from Nicholas's scrutiny.

"Does my mother know I'm here?"

Nicholas lowered his voice, but that didn't help. The smoothness of his words carried in the whisper—a warmed cocoa cadence that presumed it could solve any problem or subdue any opponent. And it probably could. I didn't have the strength to defend myself, let alone battle a man who matched me bite for bite and then swallowed me whole.

"We didn't tell her," he said. "She knows you're with us, but my father thought it best to wait until you were stable and at home before telling her—"

"No."

"You have no choice in the matter, Ms. Atwood."

I exhaled. It felt nice. "I don't want her to know."

"About the hospital?"

"The hospital or the attack. If she knew her only remaining child collapsed?" I hated to relive the memories as much as she did. "After Josiah and Mike…she's not capable of handling this sort of emergency anymore. Not her sanity and certainly not her liver."

"But she's your mother."

"She's not my mother anymore. My father's murder tore her to pieces. Obviously she's not in the right frame of mind. Look at who she married."

Nicholas nodded. "For what's it worth, my father does seem to…admire her."

"Every woman dreams of the moment a man finally admits that he *admires* her."

"When my mother died, my father's heart died with her."

"Your father never had a heart."

"He did for her," Nicholas said.

"What about for his sons?"

He arched an eyebrow. "We're off-topic."

"I like this topic better."

"If you'd rather not tell Bethany, I'll respect your wishes."

I smirked. "A first time for everything."

"I wouldn't get used to it."

His phone vibrated from his pocket. He ignored it. He gestured to the oxygen line cast over the bed.

"You should be wearing that."

"Florescent green doesn't match my hospital gown."

He picked it up, and I fell still. His hands brushed my ears, tucking the tube into place. His fingers grazed my cheek. I shivered. The monitor jumped again. My pulse fluttered ten beats higher.

"I'm not going to hurt you," he said.

Oh, yes, he would, in more ways than he intended. I shoo'ed his hands away and adjusted the oxygen myself—like an old pro.

"Why didn't you tell me about the asthma?"

I hesitated. "It didn't come up."

He didn't buy it. Neither did I. "It was important. The doctor said you're on three different medications."

Why would I have told the Bennetts I was sick? Should I have held a loaded gun against my head too?

I accidentally met his eyes. The warmth brushed over me like a sun-kissed field.

Not good.

"I didn't tell you because I didn't think I'd have the pleasure of being your extended houseguest."

Nicholas didn't fall for the sass. "You will be a guest for quite some time. Though, I assure you, the stay can be as difficult or...pleasurable...as you wish."

"You do know how to sweet talk an invalid."

He laughed. "Hardly. You're stronger here than half the men I do business with every day."

"I bet you say that to all the asthmatic girls."

"Only the ones who deserve the compliment."

The damn monitor beeped quicker. I changed the subject.

"How's Darius faring?"

His hesitation was worth the asthma attack. "He isn't pleased by the turn of events."

"Is he pissed I didn't die?"

"More frustrated that you almost did."

"I do love to disappoint him."

The coughing bubbled from deep—a rattle that alarmed Nicholas. He stood.

"I'll get a nurse."

I shrugged. "It's just inflammation. I'll cough for a while."

"You should sleep. I have work that will keep me occupied. You rest. I'll be right here."

Like I was that stupid. "How kind of you."

"I only want you to be safe."

"No. You want to guard me. To make sure I don't toss a chair through that window."

"We're ten stories up. I don't recommend rappelling in your condition."

"But nothing is stopping me from pushing this…" I grazed the *call* button on my bed's remote. "I could…find a nurse. Tell her everything."

Nicholas expected it. The hard angles of his face shadowed against the glow of the monitors.

He folded his hands. "You haven't yet."

"No. I haven't."

"Why not?" The cautious edge in his voice pricked over me, sharpening as I dared to challenge him. "The nurses would believe every word. The doctors insisted on admitting you for multiple days, but my father argued and had a nurse fired as he demanded your immediate release into our private family physician's care. I've pledged a new MRI machine to placate the staff for his behavior."

"How charitable."

"It was Reed's idea. He believed we had enough hospital wings in our name." Nicholas waited. I said nothing. "You're returning to the estate. You can't stop it, even if you push that button."

"Maybe that's what I want."

He took the bait. "Why?"

"I haven't finished what I started there."

"And what's that?"

"Proving Darius Bennett killed my father."

Nicholas didn't react. His contemplative, uncompromising stillness revealed nothing.

"Do you really think we killed your father?"

I shook my head. "It's the only thing that makes sense. He had cancer. Bad. But he fought it because he was strong and said he'd beat it. And he did. So he went into remission, and the doctors cleared him. But he goes to work one day?" My voice trembled. I swallowed, hard. "He goes to work and then dies in his chair. A *Pepsi* in front of him."

Nicholas waited.

"He never drank anything but *Coke* a day in his life."

"Hardly the cause for a murder allegation."

"The autopsy was inconclusive, but an hour before he died, he left my brothers a voicemail telling them he loved them. He believed something was going to happen to him, and he made sure they knew how he felt before..."

Nicholas nodded. "Did he speak with you?"

My chest hurt. Not the asthma. "No."

"What do you hope to find?

"Anything that would prove Darius had something to do with his death."

My finger rubbed the call button, brushing the pad in tight circles. Nicholas watched, waited. I considered my options.

Press the button. Scream at the nurse to bring the police. Have the Bennetts escorted from my room and locked behind bars.

Get lost in endless legal battles over kidnapping charges and their denials and defamation law suits.

Destroy what remained of my mother as I accused her husband of a conspiracy to rape.

Spend my life in whispers and lies as the business community, the Atwood social circle, the media, and the world gossiped about my ordeal.

I'd never get close to the Bennetts again. They'd serve time, but not for the crime I knew they committed. It wouldn't be enough. Not until Darius confessed or until a jury formally proclaimed him guilty.

But for that to happen, to see my father's death avenged, I couldn't lose the opportunity I had. If I stayed, I had the freedom to wander their house, get closer to Nicholas, Max, and Reed, and search for the evidence the police refused to believe existed.

"This is the second and last time I will ever ask a Bennett for help," I said.

"This Bennett has a name, Ms. Atwood."

I drew an unsteady breath. "Nicholas, I need your help."

"What do you want me to do, Sarah?"

I vaguely remembered him using my real name, calling to me, keeping me awake until they delivered me to safety. His caramel voice rumbled over the word, soft and silken and spoken with such familiarity it flushed my cheeks. I imagined how it would sound breathless, whispered in the masculine growl that he uttered while pinning me in the woods.

The monitor beeped again. If I had the strength, I would have tossed my pillow over my face and willed myself to suffocate again.

I was too tired to fight him. Too tired to rationalize my trembling so near to him.

I remembered my last gasp of air before collapsing. It laced with his scent—sharp and clean and rugged. I still tasted his lips, reveled in his spiciness, and warmed where his hands had captured me.

"I won't tell a soul what's happening," I said. "Promise."

"I doubt you'll keep that promise once I take you."

My stomach fluttered. I wished I hadn't already imagined my step-brother in such a way. It wasn't just wrong because he was an enemy. Nothing in our perverted arrangement made sense. Having those thoughts were as morally reprehensible as what they planned to do to me.

"You will help me find enough evidence to convict your father," I said.

"You're asking me to betray my family."

"Only Darius."

"He's still family."

I tilted my head. "So am I, and yet you threaten to harm me."

"Not threaten. Promise." He wasn't teasing. "But you aren't Darius Bennett."

"He's not a father. He's a monster. He wants you to rape me. To *impregnate* me. You watched him mistreat, hurt, and humiliate me. Help me find the evidence to put that lunatic behind bars, and I won't say a word about this insanity."

"That won't stop what we plan to do to you."

"Screw your plan. I don't care if you rape me. Avenging my father is more important than whatever happens to me."

For the first time, his professional, composed façade cracked. "Are you serious?"

My teeth chattered. I blamed exhaustion, but it was the memory's fault. I gripped the thin blanket and shivered.

"When I was twelve, I went with my father to tour one of our cattle facilities in Nevada. The dust caused an asthma attack. We were far from the hospital. I died twice in the ambulance and once when they finally had me in an emergency room. I was gone for three minutes. Completely flat-lined. The doctor almost called it."

He listened, intently. "That must have been terrifying."

"It wasn't my first attack, but it was my worst."

"You're very strong, Sarah."

I didn't feel much like it now. "Do you know what I saw while I was dead?"

Everyone wanted to know, but no one believed the answer. Somehow, I knew Nicholas would.

"What did you see?"

"Absolutely nothing."

His expression fell. So did mine. I tugged the blankets higher and looked away.

"Everything faded, like I fell asleep. And then instantly, I was back. There was nothing."

"Are you sure?"

"Without a doubt." I swallowed. "This life is my only life, Nicholas. And I'll do *everything* I can to survive it. I'm not ready to be…nothing yet."

"Sarah—"

"My father's life was stolen. I can't bring him back. I'll never see him again, and for that crime, I will not rest until I get justice. I'll fight you with every breath my body allows."

"I believe you."

I met his stare and strengthened into the same stone that sealed him in stillness. "If you plan on raping me, I'm prepared to battle. But if you succeed and get me pregnant?" I lowered my voice. "Imagine how hard I'll fight if I am defending my *child*."

Nicholas frowned before standing. He leaned over me only so he could whisper, only so he could listen as the betraying monitors revealed just how fierce my heart beat within his arm's reach.

"I admire your courage," he said. "But you don't have to fight me."

"Will you let me go?"

I pressed against the pillow as he encroached too close. I held my breath, but my aching lungs punished me more than his crisp scent. Nicholas's spice overwhelmed me. I stilled.

"Once I take you, Sarah, you won't want to leave."

"You overestimate yourself."

"You underestimate how much you'll enjoy it."

I pushed myself forward, though the effort ripped every last bit of strength from my body. I trembled, but I wasn't sure if it was the illness or how close I was to him.

"You can force me if you like," I whispered, "but I'll *never* enjoy anything you do to me."

"Trust me, Sarah." Nicholas dared to graze his lips against mine. I jerked away before my breath shuddered as badly as the sensations in my core. "One night in my bed and you will be begging me for your release."

He kissed me again, the lightest flutter against my lips. I froze. In the wilderness, he attacked. Forced me against trees and bound my wrists in his hands to keep me still.

This kiss wasn't a threat. He promised every word he said with the gentle, compassionate nibble.

He promised to rape me.

He promised I'd enjoy it.

I shivered a good shiver, but I was too exhausted to rub the goose bumps from my arms.

"I won't give in," I whispered.

"You already have."

I blushed as the door kicked open. I fell against the pillows. Nicholas stood.

Since when did the hospital pipe in hot air through the oxygen system?

Nicholas offered, but Max refused his help unloading the bags and packages tucked in his arms. I gripped the blanket. Reed, I could probably handle now. But after the kiss and the confusion and all the wicked and evil and sensual words Nicholas whispered, I couldn't fight two dangerous Bennetts at once.

I didn't understand Max at all. He hardly spoke to me. I thought he resented my kick to his leg, but he limped too heavily for that. A lifelong injury must have bothered him, even if he was built like some of Dad's old-school, indestructible tractors. He'd be handsome if he dared to smile like Reed.

He dumped a box of fast food onto the side table—a variety of brands and types, pizza and burgers, salads and tacos. While Nicholas tidied the spilled French fries, Max unfolded a blanket. He didn't ask before covering me with the softest, fuzziest, most unbelievably pink throw. He put the teddy bear on the bed last.

Not one purchased from the hospital gift shop.

An expensive, plush bear…dressed in overalls with a straw hat.

"A farmer bear?" I didn't know what to say. "What is…"

"Hospitals are cold."

So was he, even loaded with presents.

"I spent a lot of time in hospitals after my surgeries," he said. "Thought you could use this."

I was in love with the blanket. I nodded.

"And hospital food is trash," Max said.

Nicholas poked through the bags. "So you brought her junk?"

"Whatever the hell she wants. We're getting out of here tomorrow anyway." Max hesitated. He lost the suit jacket and tensed in just the vest and dress shirt. Every muscle flexed. "Good night."

He left before I could even thank him.

He left before I could ask him not to leave me alone with Nicholas. Not because I didn't trust him, but because I couldn't trust myself. I was too tired to suppress my attraction. Too tired to think rationally.

"Are you hungry?" Nicholas asked.

"Not in the least. What—"

"My brother isn't much for conversation." He moved the food from the tray, though I snagged a cup of French fries before they escaped. "But he's worried."

I snuggled in the blanket. He didn't look worried. He seemed inconvenienced. Impatient.

Thoughtful.

"You should rest." Nicholas pulled his phone and flicked through emails. "Especially if we're taking you home tomorrow. Our private doctor is good, but the estate isn't a hospital."

No, it wasn't.

The estate was a prison.

And an opportunity.

I wasted enough time and almost lost my life in a foolish attempt to break free from the greatest gift I'd been given. I'd brave the asthma, Darius Bennett's humiliations and beatings, and even Nicholas's threatened kiss if only to find the evidence to pin my father's death on the Bennetts.

Sacrificing my body to protect my family?

It was worth it.

Tomorrow, we were going back.

To war.

CHAPTER ELEVEN
NICHOLAS

My brothers slept in the hospital waiting room, iPads folded on their laps, unopened sodas and cold food scattered around their impromptu offices.

I woke them without a greeting.

"We need to alter our strategy."

Max blinked first. He cracked his neck and straightened his bad leg with a grunt. A soda can tumbled over, and Reed jerked awake.

"She okay?" Reed asked. "Fuck, she didn't talk, did she?"

"She's sleeping."

Max checked his watch and rubbed his face. "Want a break?"

"No."

"You left her alone?"

"Yes."

His expression twisted, a graveled grimace that might have warned me of dangerous ground had I not realized how deeply I already sunk into the mire.

"Dad's said not to leave her alone."

"Don't worry about Sarah Atwood," I said.

Reed checked the doors before speaking, as though our father would dare to rest within a hospital for an Atwood's benefit.

"She's got us by the balls, Nick," he said. "Don't give her the opportunity to ruin us."

"Oh, she's trying to ruin us." I claimed a seat across from my brothers, unable to hide my amusement. "She's plotting her ways to topple the Bennett Corporation."

"Fantastic." Reed rubbed his temples.

Max wasn't as threatened. "What's a little kitten like her going to do?"

"She's going to prove our father murdered Mark Atwood."

My brothers silenced for a long moment before their laughter chorused within the waiting room.

"And how's she gonna prove that?" Max asked. "I didn't know we were about to fuck Sherlock Holmes."

"She made me a deal."

"This outta be good."

I shrugged. "She returns to the estate willingly, and I help her gather evidence against Dad."

Max laughed again. "And the rape?"

"Presumably, she'll allow it to happen."

"What a little freak."

Reed shuddered. "Why would she let us do that? She knows we'll…" His voice lowered. "We're going to impregnate her. Why the hell would she surrender to something like that?"

"She has her reasons." I folded my hands. "I never said she wouldn't be a challenge."

"Doesn't make sense," Reed said. "What does she have on us?"

"Presumably nothing or she would have moved already."

Max didn't buy it. "She's smarter than that."

I nodded. "But she's also impetuous. Naive. She's a college undergrad, not a CEO. If we were battling Mark Atwood or his sons, the Bennett Corporation would face a significant threat. But Sarah Atwood is not her father or brothers. She's little more than a child, and she's too fraught with vengeance to understand how dangerous her circumstances are."

"So what are you planning?" Reed asked.

"Just what I agreed to. I'll help her find the evidence to prove her father was murdered."

"I don't know what's more frightening," Max said. "The fact that we might get away with raping an innocent girl, or that you've lost your damn mind."

"This will work. She only needs to trust me."

"No. She just gotta spread her legs for you."

"Can't have one without the other."

Max lived and dealt enough darkness. I recognized the growl in his voice, the unspoken intimidation he wielded. "Yes, we can. Dad won't rest until that girl is broken, bruised, and sobbing."

And there was the fundamental difference between my father's perspective on business and my vision for the future. He viewed Sarah Atwood with the same bloodthirsty aggression she reserved for our family—and it benefited no one. The Atwoods didn't rival our corporation directly, but their influence within the agricultural industry could secure or frighten customers. No love was lost between our families, and I was pleased when Mark Atwood was buried in the soil he loved so much.

But Sarah wasn't an enemy.

She was a tool.

A newfound asset.

And a liability, but all great opportunities came with substantial risk. The reward would be far more substantial than whatever problems the little field mouse created.

My father planned to destroy the Atwoods and claim everything for our family.

Sarah was worth more than a quick struggle and a nine month nightmare. A girl like her—with that determination and strength—wasn't an adversary.

She'd become an ally.

My ally.

Whether she realized it or not.

My phone buzzed. Seven AM and business already started. I answered the call with a warm greeting.

"Peter, how are you?"

Reed furrowed his brow. He mouthed Peter's name to Max with a shrug.

Peter Handalan didn't greet me with the same cordiality. He rarely offered pleasantries when discussing any business unless he pulled a minimum two over par on any course. Mid-June meant Peter toured the East Coast greens. I figured he had played a few hours before calling me.

"Nicholas Bennett, I don't know what stunt you're pulling, but I swear to God, if this dips our stock in any way, shape, or form, I'll pull every last share from your godforsaken company and invest in pharmaceuticals like I should have done ten years ago."

I braced for it. "I assure you, Peter. You'll be glad you stayed with the Bennett Corporation just as soon as certain technicalities and all these...unpleasant details are sorted and finalized."

Reed extended his arms. I ignored his questions.

"You want me to vote you in as the new CEO."

"I want the Board of Directors to initiate a vote of no confidence in my father, yes."

Reed bolted upright. Max grabbed a handful of his shirt and tossed him into the chair. I hoped Peter didn't hear his profanity.

"You're playing a risky game. Since when do the Bennetts supersede their elders? The company is yours when Darius retires."

"Some members of the Board are displeased in the latest financials. They have been for over two years. Eight quarters of struggling growth concealed with layoffs, alternations in management, and product distribution. They've noticed, and they feel their investments are mismanaged."

Peter cackled. "Your family is cutthroat, but it doesn't sniff for its own blood."

"My allegiance is to the company, Peter. Always has been, always will. I'll work hard to ensure proper growth and new opportunities for prosperity."

"You've got Darius's confidence."

"I have my own skills and abilities. This is the right move. I'm asking you for a pledge. A promise. Gentleman's agreement, no contracts."

"So your father doesn't sniff out a paper trail."

"Yes."

"This sort of change rattles a company, Nicholas. One false move and your stocks plummet and customer confidence takes a hit. Are you prepared for the fallout this will cause?"

I paused. "The public and investors will be told my father took an early retirement. He was recently wed, perhaps he wants to spend time with his new wife and family. Maybe he wants to sail around the world. Climb Everest. The Bennett Corporation will salute his years of dedicated service, honor him as he wills, and then organize the transition to me. I've spent my life preparing for this opportunity, and the investors will feel confident in my abilities."

Max crossed his arms. Reed held his head in his hands.

"I won't be alone in this," Peter warned. "You give me the names of the sons of bitches voting with me. Do you understand?"

"Of course. I need to speak with one last board member to secure their allegiance, and this messy business will be done quickly, quietly, and effectively, with no disruption to the company or its everyday operations."

"I'm too old for this bullshit, Nicholas. I should be lying on a beach somewhere, getting my cock sucked by some cute Filipino and my yacht refurbished for my wife."

"This deal will guarantee it."

"Yeah." Peter exhaled. I imagined him puffing a cigar as a golf cart puttered up the green. "I know you're right. Wouldn't want to be you though. Darius Bennett isn't a forgiving man."

"But he is my father."

"For how much longer?" Peter swore. "You get me those names, and we'll talk again."

The call ended as Peter cackled to his partner about a ball shanked hard to the left. I pocketed my phone. Reed started to laugh, bending over to catch his breath as Max raged at his side.

"What in the everloving fuck are you doing?" Reed said. "Holy shit, man, you didn't even tell us."

"I figured I had your support."

"For a *takeover*?"

Was my brother that naive? "Our profits are failing. Our investors are bolting. Dad is *kidnapping* and raping women. Is that the man you want controlling our future? Our wealth?"

"You don't have to tell me that Dad lost his goddamned mind," Reed said. "That happened *years* ago. But, Jesus Christ. He's going to find out what you're doing. Then I'll be chasing *you* down on a bike with the tire iron."

I wasn't worried. "He's a bit preoccupied with our house guest at the moment."

"It won't work. Sarah's nothing to him."

"She's *everything* to him," I said. "He's obsessed with her, her family, with what Mark Atwood's will unintentionally promised us. He isn't watching the Bennett Corporation. He's thinking about what we are going to lose a year from now. Right now he's planning how he'll finagle his way into being named regent of a stolen empire."

Reed shrugged. "How does this protect Sarah?"

Max answered for me. "It doesn't."

"If Nick seizes control of the company—"

"That will take *months*," Max said. "You're missing the point. This has nothing to do with Sarah. We can't protect the girl."

Reed wasn't often angry. His voice lowered. Even Mom's green eyes couldn't dull the intensity and indignation that scarred us all as our father's sons.

"I don't care what you say, I don't care about Dad. I am not hurting that girl. I've done a lot of sketchy shit for this family, but rape isn't one of them, and I'm not impregnating someone by force so *my* child can be manipulated for our gain. That's two lives I fuck over. It's not happening."

"You're right," I said. "Which is why we are changing strategy involving the girl."

Max rifled through his laptop bag and swallowed a handful of pain-killers. "Are we letting her go?"

"No."

"You want to keep her."

Like he hadn't had the same fantasy. "Very much."

Reed scowled. "So you can rape her?"

"No. I plan to seduce her."

He laughed. "You're fucked in the head. Why the hell would she fall for you?"

"Because I'm a Bennett. I have land. I have our business. I have our wealth…" I shrugged. "And I have my pick of the women."

"This isn't a woman. She's an Atwood."

"Perfect," I said. "Who better to seduce? Who better to have willingly spread her legs and offer me every part of her? I will seduce, bed, and take Mark Atwood's daughter as my own—a beautiful toy for my amusement."

Max perked an eyebrow. "Since when do you like that type of toy?"

I answered honestly. "Since the first time I saw her."

Reed tilted his head. "What makes you think you're the only one who'll have her?"

"I'll speak with Dad and convince him to let me have her to myself. Save her the indignity of serving three men in favor of submitting completely to me."

"What a hero," he snorted. "Steal the company, rape the girl."

"*Experience* the girl."

Reed and Max fell silent. I expected it. They didn't understand the gift that we nearly lost, the beauty nearly taken from the world.

I saw through her rage, the shattering shell of her confidence, the strength she bluffed and the simmering hate she wielded as an ineffective shield.

Beneath her admirable resilience hid a passionate woman, imprisoned more by her own hesitance than any chains and ropes I might have used to restrain her.

Sarah Atwood wanted me.

And I'd ensure that fatal mistake would ruin her with pleasure.

CHAPTER TWELVE
SARAH

It was a mistake returning to the Bennett estate.

The creeping stone mansion spilled into the otherwise pristine forest. The dark manor loomed within the shadows and spoiled the vibrant green of the mountain with its splashes of crimson and white blossoming flowers. It didn't belong here.

It was nothing more than a trap. Worse, I set the snare myself.

Nicholas carried me through the threshold. I ignored the implication and braced myself for whatever I would find inside.

The manor and everything it encompassed etched from unforgiving stone. The foyer. The columns. Even the men. They hardened themselves for endurance and intimidation, chiseling flecks of their humanity into dust. Nothing soft or kind existed in their world.

I needed to rest before I could defend myself from them.

Darius Bennett met us on the grand staircase, positioned exactly where I took my last full breath and begged his heir for help.

I wiggled from Nicholas's arms.

"Welcome home, my dear." He held a bag of my prescriptions and twisted it within his hand. "You look moments from death."

That I believed. Anger kept me on my feet. The pinpricks of hatred jammed into the base of my skull, but I said nothing, only stared at the bag that contained my rescue inhaler.

I anticipated this cruelty.

"If you want your medications, you'll ask for permission first." He waited for an ill-advised profanity. It wasn't worth the risk. "I trust we can come to an arrangement. I'd hate to see you in such pain again, my dear."

He hated that it wasn't a pain he caused. I didn't waste a word on him.

"I'll carry them," Nicholas said. "She's my charge at the moment."

Darius chuckled. "I know an excellent way for her to earn the medications, son."

Bastards. They could keep the meds.

Darius thought he could frighten me, that I wouldn't dare climb the steps he guarded. I stormed forward, but Nicholas grasped my hand.

His touch somehow relieved me. My strides weakened the instant we passed from Darius's view. I panted, slowing as Nicholas guided me into the depths of the house. The hall ended with steel doors, and he pushed a button to reveal an elevator.

"I can walk." It took two breaths to finish the sentence.

Nicholas tucked the prescriptions into his suit pocket. "Don't mistake pride for strength, Sarah. We should never have taken you from the hospital so quickly. You need to rest."

We rode to the third floor, and my stomach twisted. That area belonged to my step-brothers, each claiming their own wing for privacy. My fingers tightened over the railing.

They wouldn't dare try to violate me. Not when I was sick.

Then again, I had no strength to fight them.

"You're safe for now," Nicholas said.

Was I that easy to read? "Why should I believe you?"

His eyes burned a bit brighter, the gold hues crisp and demanding. I wished I hadn't noticed.

He led me through the east wing and rapped against the doorframe to a darkened room. The lights flared.

Of course the Bennetts had a private theater.

The room furnished with amphitheater styled seating, oversized leather chairs, and a screen the size of our barn doors. Max stood as we entered. Reed munched on popcorn made from the actual popcorn cart still spitting fresh kernels.

"Welcome to my sanctuary." Max waved over the wall-to-wall cherry cabinets which completely encased the room. The theater was dark, cozy, and housed a variety of liquors and snacks. He didn't share Reed's smile, but I swore he softened his voice when I edged closer to Nicholas. "You can use it while you recover."

"Oh, but—"

Max didn't let me answer. He flipped open a cabinet door.

If Heaven had existed, this was it.

"I lost count after a couple thousand movies." He pulled out a selection and showed me the titles. Action, comedy, foreign, classic. "Whatever you like, it's probably here."

Reed waved to a cabinet. "Playstation, Xbox, and Wii down there too."

Nicholas guided me to a recliner close to the screen, complete with fuzzy blanket, headphones, and a set of pink pajamas.

My stomach twisted. How did they get my favorite pajamas from my room at *home*?

"The doctor is coming at noon," Nicholas said. "You should be resting when he gets here."

I studied the offering with a guarded suspicion. What were they planning?

Popcorn?

Movies?

Games?

I hated myself for envying the setup.

I hated myself more for considering their gift.

How long was it since I let myself watch a movie? I always had too many classes and meetings and funerals and sharp objects to hide from my mother.

Once the farm and company unceremoniously fell into my lap, I'd been consumed by work and email, schedules and classes, reports and P&Ls. When my asthma flared and I was forced to bed on a bad day, I still had classwork to finish and paperwork to sign. My recovery days became opportunities to conference call with Anthony about legal matters.

And now the *Bennetts* were the ones to offer me a chance to rest?

Unbelievable.

And worse, I almost fell for it.

"Stop it." I pulled away from Nicholas. "You're creeping me out."

164

Reed stood, wiping the butter from his hands on his jogging pants. Max wasn't in a suit either. They wore workout clothes. Their shirts stretched over barrel chests, trim waists, and powerful forms. For a moment—a split second of weakness and oxygen deprivation—I wondered what Nicholas looked like beneath his regal suits.

"What's wrong?" Reed jerked a thumb toward the popcorn. He grinned. His dimple tugged so effortlessly. "We got junior mints too."

"This!" I said. "All of this."

"We're just trying to help. Give you a place to recover."

"Yeah, stop it. Christ." My lungs seized. "Tie me up in the basement. Chain me to a wall. Don't do *this*."

Nicholas hesitated. "Do what?"

I couldn't believe I was saying it.

"Don't act like you're my *brothers*."

Enough was enough. I reached for the door before I lost the strength to deny the salty beckoning of the popcorn. Max's words burned through me.

"Get in that chair, tuck in, and fucking rest," he said. "We're not playing."

Neither was I. "I'll be fine without your help."

"You walk out of this room, and our father will make your life a living hell."

"He already has."

Max's revelation laced with poison. "He'll make us fuck you even if you aren't fertile."

The hair on my neck rose. I turned, pretending the words hadn't twisted my stomach.

"*What did you say?*"

"Get in your pajamas and rest. If you think you're strong enough to fight, then fight and suffer the consequences. He *will* punish you for the hospital, and you won't like what he's planning, ovulating or not."

Reed no longer looked at me. He rubbed his face, massaging the lingering scars over his jaw and cheek. "The sicker you act, the safer you are."

I wasn't about to display any weakness before a Bennett, but the cough answered for me.

"He wants us to rape you." Max spoke the word so casually, as if it were already written in stone and predestined. I trembled when I realized it probably was. "But no one is going to murder you. If you look like you can't handle it…" He held his arms out. His muscles tensed, dangerously strong and completely inescapable. "We won't touch you. Use some common sense."

Nicholas said nothing, but his promise burrowed deep in my mind.

He wouldn't hurt me.

Nicholas was many things—ruthless, ambitious. But was he a man of his word?

Reed waved the Xbox controller again. Max brandished a number of blue-ray videos.

Though my insides turned on me, slithering in the cold fear of what I knew would happen but hadn't been brave enough to imagine.

They would take me.

They would try to breed a Bennett son into me.

I nearly died in Nicholas's arms, and, if I was going to recover, I couldn't risk the added stress of whatever depravity they planned for my virginity. I grabbed a title from Max's collection at random.

Reed called me forward. "What'd you pick?"

I held the movie up with a trembling hand. He grinned. He must have known he was charming.

"*Diehard*. Love it." He tossed me my pajamas and pointed to the powder room behind the screen. "Change in there. We'll take care of you."

Take care of me?

Nicholas nudged me when I didn't move. His mocha words breathed heat into me.

"Do you need help changing?" He whispered.

The goose bumps returned. I shook my head. "I think I remember how it works, thanks."

Nicholas didn't like my tone. He moved behind me, seizing my arms and pinning me against him. I didn't have the strength to fight, but I regained my pride far quicker than my energy.

"Now what do you want?" I hissed.

"Sarah, you're our guest." His voice rumbled in places that weren't fair for him to strike. Max perked an eyebrow. "More important than a guest, actually. Do you know what you are?"

"An enemy."

"Hardly. You're a gift."

"I don't give Bennetts charity."

"Not willingly." His grip tightened. "But we'll take it nevertheless."

"Of course you will."

"But now that you're in our custody, we'll do whatever it takes to keep you safe, protected, and healthy." He paused. "I won't guarantee happy. That's up to you."

"Don't count on it."

"You're in our possession, Sarah. You *are* a possession."

"For now."

His voice dizzied me. I hated the betraying tingles that revealed too much. My cheeks flushed as pink as my pajamas. He didn't release me, even as his brothers watched.

How was I supposed to fight a man like this?

Nicholas spoke of lust and ownership and captivity as though it were an offered romance. Everything he vowed to do was a crime, but yet every time he threatened me with a hint of his intentions, my defenses shattered.

Thoughts and feelings and *desires* rippled through what remained of my rationality.

His was a different breed of cruelty.

Nicholas deliberately teased me. He whispered with velvet promises laced in blood and wielded the menace of his passion like a blade to my neck. Part of me longed for the moment he finally decided to slice.

But I expected Bennett trickery. I braced for beatings and tried to forget the humiliations.

But movies? Popcorn? A pledge to ensure my safety?

Something didn't add up.

My eyebrow perked.

Not all the Bennetts were thrilled with Darius's plan.

Reed didn't touch me. Max hadn't approved.

Only Nicholas dared to act. He eagerly waited to take me, fuck me, breed me. He murmured those sordid words into my ear just to watch as his stare unraveled my barest threads.

I didn't realize it before.

My step-brothers were monsters, but what if I could twist my newfound family from my captors into my rescuers?

Nicholas already agreed to search for the evidence I needed to prove my father was murdered. What would I get out of Reed and Max?

I obeyed them without a protest, changing and returning to the theater just in time to offer them a pitiful little cough. Reed lunged over his seat to get me another blanket. Max fumbled with a bottle of water. Nicholas ripped open the prescription bag to find my inhaler.

I hid my excitement with another sad cough. They leapt to my aid.

These men, my step-brothers, weren't just my future rapists.

They would be my allies.

Even if they didn't know it yet.

***

They didn't hurt me. At all.

For five days, I recovered and just…hung out with my step-brothers. Between their trips to the city and appointments, jobs and company events, they'd catch a movie with me, play a game, or sneak me desserts.

It was like it a perfectly normal…family.

They didn't touch me. No one threatened me. I wasn't scared.

No one kissed me, despite the dreams that woke me in a frustrated heat.

I camped out on a leather recliner, hidden away in Max's theater sanctuary. One of my step-brothers managed to baby-sit me at all hours, either so I didn't escape or to keep an eye on my asthma.

Nicholas, of course, ran the company. He worked in and out of the estate, but Nicholas was the only one who lived with Darius in the mansion. Reed and Max, under orders from their father, had returned from their homes only to breed me.

Charming.

They all worked for the Bennett Corporation, though Max wasn't meant to join the company. Max was military, or had been, until whatever happened to his leg became too much of a detriment to serve. I didn't ask if it was a combat injury. He wasn't forthcoming with many details save for relentlessly mocking my skill at Call of Duty.

And Reed? God help me, Reed might have been my third brother. He worked the family's charity as the Director of Operations—a general saint in a family of demons. I liked him, even when he slaughtered me at Mario Kart and mocked me for going in reverse around the finish line.

"Just ask, and I'll give you a thirty second head start," he said.

Freaking Mario bopped me with a red shell. I threw the controller as the Princess avatar cried just inches from the finish as the race mercy ended.

Reed hopped over his recliner and made a sandwich from the platter stashed upstairs so I wouldn't hobble to the kitchen.

So I wouldn't cross Darius's path.

He held up the salami. I shook my head. Turkey. I scrunched my nose. He tossed a pepperoncini at me. I ducked. It slammed against one of the recliners and slid in a sticky mess down the back.

"Oh, Max is gonna be *pissed*," I said.

"I'll buy him a new chair. What do you want to eat?"

No more sandwiches. My step-brothers were carnivores. I hadn't seen a floret of broccoli in a week.

"Ever been to Cherrywood Valley?" I shrugged. "You know, when you aren't kidnapping me?"

"Sometimes."

"We have a farmer's market set up on Tuesdays and Thursdays. There's a restaurant that takes whatever produce is left over and grills it up. It's delicious."

He stared at the platter. "I can't take you home, Sarah."

I hadn't asked him that yet. "Are you sure?"

"Don't make this harder on yourself."

"I'd like to get out of the house."

"Turn your face blue again. That worked last time."

No thanks.

I stiffened as a silken voice chuckled from the doorway. Nicholas's amusement squeezed everything inside me, but enough of my strength returned that I could finally meet his stare.

"Are you bored already, Ms. Atwood?" He asked.

"So what if I am?"

"Then we can go to work."

"*We?*"

Nicholas motioned for me to follow. Reed tossed me a blanket. I wrapped it over me if only because my peppermint striped fuzzy pants and chemise didn't offer me an edge against Nicholas's suit.

My steps slowed as he led me to the study. I clutched the blanket. He did it on purpose—taking me to the same room where his father humiliated me. I had been completely exposed to him here. Bare. Vulnerable.

I wasn't ready to relive it. I recovered, but my breathing wasn't clear yet, and I slept fourteen hours a day. I'd still be admitted in the hospital if the Bennetts hadn't demanded my release.

My stay in their care had been relatively peaceful, but that didn't mean I was safe.

They counted the days. So did I. I hated that *time of the month*, but I never thought there'd be something worse than it—a time when everything I knew about life, men, and love would be forever destroyed.

My laptop waited in the study. He pointed to a spare chair and claimed the seat before my computer.

"You've got to be kidding," I said.

"We have emails to answer and a bit of work to do."

"Get off my computer."

"I like the desktop." He studied the photo I saved—a picture of Mike, Josiah, and I doing handstands next to a crumbling scarecrow. "You have a lovely smile."

"Get *off* my computer."

Nicholas ignored me. "First thing. Sign this."

He pushed my course add/drop forms toward me.

Was beating me to a pulp not a good enough torture for a Bennett?

"I don't like it either," he said. "But, even if you weren't in this situation, your family's tragedy and the company are too much to handle. You figured this might happen, or you wouldn't have carried these with you."

"I can do it."

He raised an eyebrow. "You're the acting CEO of a billion dollar company. Education is important, but it isn't necessary now."

"But I'm not majoring in business."

"You aren't passing either."

I would have hated it more if he weren't right. I wouldn't pass with so many incompletes and missed assignments.

"Sarah, we won't let you leave the estate until you have our son," Nicholas said. My stomach still lurched every time they said it. "You won't be going to college anytime soon."

My hand thudded heavy against the paper. I poked a hole through the flourish I added to *Atwood*.

Just another sacrifice. I blinked frustrated tears.

Nicholas placed the document in a folder labeled *Broughton University*. His attention focused on the screen. He scanned the emails with a harsh sigh.

"Did your father micromanage his company?"

"Why would I tell you that?"

He pushed away from the computer. "I should be at my office, working on my own projects. Instead, I'm behind so I might stabilize a rival company. I'd take more care with my tone."

"Oh bullshit," I said. "This isn't for *me*. This is a cover-up so no one realizes that I've been kidnapped."

"You're right."

"I'll return to the theater now, thank you."

He studied the emails. "You are involved in entirely too many corporate affairs. Where are your Vice-Presidents?" He scrolled through an email chain. "Your father and brothers wouldn't have dealt with this many minute details. No wonder you're behind on your coursework."

I seethed as he typed out email after email.

"What are you doing?" I demanded.

"Delegating."

"Well, stop it!"

Nicholas read one email more carefully. "Your attorney received a letter from an investor in Josmik Holdings. He says, *I might have something for us.*"

I didn't react. Nicholas arched an eyebrow.

"Any idea what that's about?" He asked.

He wished. Darius hired a private investigator to dig up dirt on my brothers' investment. The Bennetts wanted the same information I needed. Too bad I had nothing to give.

I shrugged. "Just one of the dozens of fires my brothers started that we've been putting out."

If he doubted me, he didn't show it. He closed the laptop.

"You won't like this next order of business."

"This takeover has been a blast so far."

He handed me another document. I didn't finish the first paragraph before I crumpled it and threw it at him.

"A leave of *absence*?"

"Undue strain from your asthma attack. Doctor recommended."

"I'll never sign it."

"My father knows that."

A chill sprinted over my spine, despite the pleasant fire crackling from the hearth.

"What's he holding over me?"

"Your medication."

Of course was.

"He'll try to scare you. More attacks, less recovery time. Multiple illnesses will weaken your Board's confidence." Nicholas didn't soften his voice. He didn't have to. His every word squeezed my chest like another attack. "Either you willingly take the leave and let your VPs do their job, or you'll lose their respect and money."

"I can live without the inhaler."

"Sarah, even your father took a leave of absence when he was diagnosed—"

"*Don't.*" I hissed through clenched teeth. "Don't you talk about him."

I stood, brushing my hands through my hair. I didn't have a lot of options. Making a run for it didn't end well last time, but at least I'd try to escape the worst decision before I lost all control of my life.

Was it worth it?

Leaving school? Abandoning the company?

Sacrificing my *body*?

Was it worth destroying *everything* so I could take down a man who deserved to experience every misfortune that befell my family?

Yes.

Because it's what Dad would have made me do.

"Sue him." My father spoke through a mouthful of mashed potatoes. He shoveled another bite before pointing his fork. "They insulted the Atwoods. Call Anthony. We'll set up a defamation suit."

Josiah reluctantly shrugged. "Just let it slide. We won't take a hit from a local paper."

"If they insulted our product, they insulted us. Nothing is more important than our name, son. Our farm, our company, our crops—it's all part of our blood. And we protect our blood, you hear?"

"Yeah. I got it."

Dad threw his fork down. "We'll do it now. Get up."

"We haven't even cut the cake." Josiah stood anyway.

"She's turned fifteen. She'll be fine."

Mike joined him, mussing my hair. "Catch you later, Sprout."

Dad shouted from his office. They wished me a happy birthday before following.

I was actually sixteen.

My father worked so hard, he accidentally forgot to care for anything but his job.

He would have made me cut out Darius's heart by now.

How was I supposed to avenge him if I had to leave everything behind?

My father deserved justice. I deserved a life. But the responsibility that fell to me was the very thing my father never planned for me to have.

He wanted a male heir to preserve the Atwood legacy.

So did the Bennetts.

"Sarah." Nicholas's baritone soothed me, a comfort I didn't want. "You've worked hard. No one will deny that."

"I didn't have a choice."

Nicholas stood before me. Too close, but I didn't give an inch. My breathing quickened. It only teased me with the crisp, sharp scent of him.

"I wish I had better news for you," he said.

"Let me guess. I don't have a choice now either?"

He shook his head. A shiver grazed me. I didn't know if it was good or bad.

"Your fate is decided, Sarah."

I bit my lip and stared at his. Mistake.

"And what fate is that?" I asked.

"You're mine."

For the first time in a week I took deep, healthy breaths, but my body refused them all. Nicholas towered over me. The button on his suit jacket slipped, revealing a trim waist and broad, muscular chest waiting beneath the dress shirt.

He was close enough to touch.

Close enough to be dangerous.

"I don't belong to anyone," I whispered. "Least of all a Bennett."

His attention lingered on the ottoman where his family displayed my nudity. I didn't react. He prowled closer, herding me toward the desk.

"I should bend you over right now."

"You wouldn't dare."

Why did I challenge him? I should have just run.

He seized me, and I twisted in his arms. Nicholas was far stronger than me. He forced me over the desk and I thudded on my stomach. He avoided an awkward kick and pinned me with an arm over my back.

My skin prickled in a sudden sweat as he moved behind me. His hips pressed against mine. I arched. Reflexively. Instinctually.

Completely inappropriately.

He curled his hand in my hair and chuckled. "You like this."

Yes.

"No, I don't."

"Why lie to me?"

"I'll scream."

"And who would save you, Ms. Atwood?"

No one.

"You're scaring me."

He didn't care. "Am I hurting you?"

Was *that* the distinction? *Hurting* me?

Physically, no. He simply held me against my will. Again. Wielded his strength over me and dragged my body where he liked. I couldn't scramble away without pressing harder against him. He chided me with a soft whisper of my name—an angel's voice with a devil's intent.

He liked that I still tried to struggle.

"This as an opportunity," he said. "We're offering you every luxury. No responsibilities. No commitments. Just a beautiful home for you to enjoy with every amenity at your fingertips." His hands slid over my hips. "This could be a life of pleasure."

I tried to focus on anything but how our bodies touched. "You think this would be *pleasurable*?"

"Exceedingly."

"Raping me?"

His voice lowered to a growl. "When I take you, it won't be by force. You will surrender."

My breath rattled in my chest. "Never."

"It'll happen. Soon. Why deny me?"

"Why would I ever give into you?"

His hands tightened. I resisted a groan. "I'm offering you a place in my bed. A partnership with a sweet reward."

"Nothing you ever do to me will be *sweet*."

"Another challenge?" Nicholas hauled me up only to sit me on the end of the desk. I groaned, too dizzy with fatigue to stop him from spreading my legs. He stepped in, pushing against the part of me he planned to capture. "Would you like a demonstration?"

Yes.

"No."

"You'll have to be more convincing than that."

"Don't touch me."

His fingers teased over my legs. I beat his hands away, but his warning prevented me from running.

"Just behave, Sarah."

"I will fight you every day until I die."

"Don't tempt fate."

"You plan to rape me," I whispered. "Impregnate me. Your family killed my father and stole my research. Believe me, Nicholas Bennett, you might take everything from me, but you'll never win. I'll bring you all down, man by man, brick by brick, dollar by dollar."

"I'm sure you'll try."

He gently caressed me, his hands tickling my thighs, hips, arms. Every swipe of his fingers cascaded goose bumps from his touch directly to my heating core. I clenched and didn't understand why. I debated kicking, but he was far too strong. He'd never let me escape, not when he had me where he wanted me.

"You're fighting the wrong battles." He drifted lower. I flinched as he followed the pajama's pink stripe along my inner thigh. It didn't lead to the trembling crest between my legs. It was either a relief or a travesty.

"Just relax, Sarah. I won't hurt you."

"Why should I trust you?"

"Because you're enjoying this."

The indignity of his words flushed my skin. His fingers teased, but not where they would do the most good. Or evil.

Christ, I didn't even know anymore.

"You're molesting me," I whispered.

"Another fight. Where do you find the strength?"

"Get used to it."

"I do enjoy a challenge." Nicholas's inspection traced up my body, the hardened devotion of his stare was a caress of my soft skin. He leaned in. "But I'd much prefer a taste."

"Don't kiss me."

His lips brushed along my throat. He respected my wishes, but the punishment was worse. He latched onto my neck. Hard. Expecting a squeak or protest.

He earned nothing but a cascade of shivers.

I arched, my chest bumping his suit. The warmth of his body charred every raw and exposed part of me. I filled with his scent, his strength, and the pleasure of his teeth capturing my neck.

I wasn't losing this battle.

I *couldn't.*

Surrendering to Nicholas Bennett wasn't an option.

I couldn't permit his touch, not when his hands brushed my inner thigh. He nipped at my tender neck. Heat overwhelmed me, but I'd never feel warm until I pressed against his chest without the barrier of his clothing.

What was wrong with me? I wanted, *lusted,* for the man who captured and threatened to claim me in every bestial way I could imagine.

I'd deny him.

He'd take it anyway.

"Consider this another strategic concession." Nicholas released my neck only to nibble on my ear. He wasn't gentle, but his sharp bite intoxicated me. "This is a system of incrementalism. Learn it, Ms. Atwood, it may one day protect your company."

"What are you talking about?"

"Little gains. Piece by piece. Grant me these simple pleasures." His lips trailed along my chin, tasting me as he spoke nonsense and business and threat. "Enjoy this and save your strength for when I take you to bed."

I bit my lip. If that night were anything like this moment—where his touch forced me to imagine every dark and traitorous delight lost beneath him—there would be no fight.

His hand brushed over my belly, tickling lower and lower. He waited for my protest.

I stayed silent.

He slipped under the waistband of my pajamas with a victorious hum. The barrier of my panties offered no protection as the tips of his fingers drifted to the softness between my legs.

Bare.

Completely smooth.

Just as he had requested days ago.

It humiliated me. It gave me a sultry innocence and sensuality.

It *worked*.

Nicholas exhaled a profanity. His every muscle tensed, strained against an urge to seize me with brute force.

I tempted him with a soft, silky trap. He'd never escape.

"Consider it a strategic concession," I whispered.

His finger flicked down. Beyond the shaven softness, I had no control over what happened with my body. I closed my eyes and welcomed the betraying pink over my skin.

Wet.

Too wet.

The damning, revealing desire sealed my fate.

As if it hadn't already been decided.

He kidnapped me. He stole my kiss. He saved my life.

And now?

Was it was a survival instinct that protected me from the ultimate violation, or simply my undeniable need for an unimaginable man?

A hardness pressed against my thigh. It was only a taste of what was to come, but the heat incinerated my logic and reason. His touch ground against me, and the cup of his hand claimed the secret it stroked.

I flinched as he slipped between the soft petals, exploring the offered wetness from my slit. I arched. It wasn't to escape.

My gasp revealed my every amazement.

Nicholas loomed over me, twisting his free hand in my hair. I parted my lips. He accepted the invitation. His touch gentled when I groaned, as though he understood I had never been pleasured beyond my quick, unsatisfying rubbing in the quiet dark of my room.

"If you knew how vulnerable you look..." Nicholas captured my mouth. He flicked a finger over my clit and tasted my whimper. His tongue mirrored his fingers, tracing an aching path within our kiss. "I may never let you go, Sarah Atwood. Not when you submit so perfectly to me."

I escaped his lips. "I haven't submitted to you."

"Why are you pretending to be so brave?"

"Why are you pretending you've won?"

"Because I have." His touch drew a hesitant plea from me. The shudder rolled through us both.

His finger drifted low, dipping into a wetness that should have been sinful and horrid, deceiving and humiliating. He offered me no warning before slipping into my desperate slit.

He swore as I clenched upon the intrusion. I seized, trembled, and absolutely ached. I lost my grip on the table. He moved quickly, wrapping an arm behind my back as my body fell limp.

I endured the invading pressure within my core with a slight cry.

Instant. Pleasure.

I had no idea I'd respond to the violation—the conquering masculinity of a man touching, taking, and exploring an unexplored part of me. His breathing shuddered. Mirrored mine.

I either needed another kiss or to scramble for my inhaler.

"I'm going to take you, Sarah," Nicholas whispered. "Again and again. You'll belong to me. You'll offer yourself to me. You will give me *everything.*"

Not everything.

But close.

I smiled. He captured it with a kiss. Stole it with a quick thrust of his finger.

"Secrets, Ms. Atwood?"

"What secret could I keep from my captor?" My voice teased with the same threat that melted from his words like dripping wax.

"I'll learn them."

"I'm sure you will." I lost myself in the golden halo of his gaze. "But, by then? It'll be too late."

"Too late for what?"

"To save yourself from me."

His jaw set. Enough challenges. Enough games. Nicholas Bennett was a gentleman and villain—a man wrapped in the elegance of his status and the power of his name. Beneath the suit and tie, jackets and dress shirts, a feral beast lurked, savoring my every weakness.

I tempted it. I teased it. I offered myself to it with spread legs and a wetness that revealed just how badly I'd lost against his prowess.

Nicholas wanted more from me than threats and promises.

He wanted me.

He wanted to watch me surrender and cry out for him and him only.

I was helpless to refuse.

My body ached without permission. It clenched and fought and bound itself in a passion that squeezed the more I resisted.

He thrust a finger within me. Testing my responses. Laughing at my desperation.

Higher and higher—desperate and twisted— shameless and refusing, I trembled and realized just how much power Nicholas Bennett wielded over me.

I was in trouble.

The pleasure was as inescapable as him.

I silenced my cry. My body took what it needed and devoured what he forced upon me. He watched as I jerked and tumbled, plummeted from the highest heights of desire to the lowest crest of base pleasure.

He withdrew as I shook, and the mew that slipped from my clenched jaw wasn't gratitude or profanity—but a sense of loss and regret that he released me. I trembled, hard, practically crashing to the floor as my clenching body demanded more. Something terrible and *necessary*.

What did I do?

What did I just *offer?*

Sanity returned, and with it every shame. I flushed, fiercer than ever. Nicholas didn't miss a single rise of my chest or loose lock of hair from my ponytail.

I pushed from him and hopped off the table. My legs nearly crumbled beneath me. I panted for breath.

Nicholas surveyed his prize and offered me the inhaler.

God damn it.

I rushed past him, darting up the stairs to my room too slowly to escape the realizations of my temptation.

I'd never be able to resist Nicholas Bennett.

And now he knew it.

CHAPTER THIRTEEN
SARAH

The Bennetts served dinner at precisely eight o'clock, and I wasn't permitted to decline the invitation. My luck had run out on me, leaving me trapped at the table.

I took my seat in silence. Darius preferred that. No one spoke. The roast beef tasted of ash and the mashed potatoes paste. The clinking silverware scratched hard against the plates. Reed didn't eat either. He also didn't look at me.

His avoidance was my first warning something was wrong.

Very wrong.

It had only been a day since Nicholas trapped me, touched me, and nearly destroyed me. I spent twenty-four hours hiding in my room, sleeping to replenish some strength. I felt a little better, I woke in the morning with Nicholas's name on my lips. My nap in the afternoon ended with a new ache between my legs.

And now, my troubles were only beginning.

"Doctor Rimes visited you today, my dear." Darius bit through his meat and licked the bloody juices from his lip. I didn't answer. "He tells me you are doing well."

I waited and tensed, as if I could turn a salad fork into a trident.

"It's time."

Even Max stopped eating. I didn't understand.

"Time?" I asked.

"For your breeding."

The fork dropped.

Nicholas sipped his wine. I watched the goblet from the corner of my vision, studied the strong hands that grasped the frosted glass. Those hands had touched me. Pleasured me.

Tormented me.

"She hasn't fully recovered." Nicholas swirled the crimson liquid. "Would it be wise? The strain might prompt another attack."

"Nonsense." Darius tossed his napkin onto his plate. "Her only job is to spread her legs. If she fights and becomes ill, she'll have only herself to blame."

"She will fight."

"Then we'll bind her to the bed."

My heart thundered.

They wouldn't dare.

They wouldn't be so cruel.

Darius slipped from his chair. I didn't make it away from the table.

His hand snaked through my hair. Reed stood, but Max hissed his name and forced him to sit. I panted in Darius's clutches. He shook my head, pulling me around with a sadistic satisfaction.

Not a sound emerged from my clenched lips.

"Go upstairs. Bathe. Then wait in bed for your brother."

That slimy, grating way he said it. He got off on the idea of abusing his step-daughter with the incestuous threat.

But Nicholas wasn't my brother. He wasn't my ally. And he would never be my lover.

"You'll regret this." My whisper shouted within the dining room. Reed clutched his fists and stared down. Max returned to his roast beef.

Nicholas sipped his wine, unfazed, as though his father had simply prattled on about his day attempting to undermine my family's corporation.

"Upstairs, my dear," Darius said. "Quiet now. No sense aggravating your condition."

I shoved away from Darius.

These men were eager to breed me. Not only would they ruin me forever, they'd steal my *child* once they were done.

What the hell was I supposed to do? Scream? He was right. That would prompt another attack. Escape was a dream. I'd never outrun them, not while the stairs still winded me and panting long sentences revealed just how weak I was.

"For Christ's sake, drug her at least," Reed said.

Darius shook his head. "She deserves this lesson. It will teach her to respect her family."

I'd never respect them. "No drugs. I plan to remember this torture so I can return it tenfold."

"Upstairs, child." Darius twisted his smile into a sneer. "Don't keep your brother waiting."

My false confidence burned through me the instant I hid in my bathroom. What flakes of bravado remained charred to cinders in my rage.

I started the shower if only for the comfort of the steam, but I stepped within to bide my time.

Was. This. Worth. It.

I still didn't know. I had a plan. Dodgy, like everything I tried to do. Risky, but my father told me everything in the world came with risks—capital, market, corporate. No great accomplishment was completely protected and free from failure.

I had one chance to end the Bennetts once and for all.

I rested against the shower door.

At least I wouldn't die.

They'd hurt me, but I was far too valuable to lose. Still, the dread coiled in my stomach. I heaved with chills despite the swirling steam.

What scared me more: The loss of control…or giving that control to Nicholas?

Nothing more dangerous existed than passion. Passion confused hatred with lust and transformed resistance into submission. I had no defense against Nicholas, not when my own instincts twisted my enemy's threats into aching promises of pleasure.

I slammed my hand against the shower handle. The water trickled off. I let the air dry me.

The heat didn't diminish.

Nicholas Bennett waited for me.

I swaddled in a robe and returned to my room. Darius greasy excitement terrified me, as though he already witnessed the crime and relished in every glorious moment of my undoing. My fingers tangled in the robe. I tied the knot tighter. It wouldn't save me.

"You'll behave for your brother, won't you, my dear?" His voice crawled over my skin. I wished I could leap back into the shower just to wash the filth from me. "I don't expect it to be pleasant, but certainly you understand what's expected."

Max and Reed remained silent, poised near the door, preventing my escape.

One step-brother.

I could handle one man.

I could turn off my mind, forget myself, and abandon hope for a short while. I had a purpose for being here. I'd sacrifice my body, my virginity, to protect my family. I'd take one man if it meant defending my father's legacy.

Darius tugged the restraints from behind the bed.

The fear nearly dropped me to my knees.

Oh, no. No, no, no.

"Nicholas," he said. "If you would."

"Wait," I whispered. "I don't…"

Nicholas did as his father commanded, and I hated him for it. Hated the hands that pulled me closer to the bed and the melodic voice that ordered me to stay quiet.

I tried again, appealing to Nicholas for any sort of compassion. "No restraints. That's too humiliating."

"Which part of this wasn't humiliating?" Darius laughed. "You're fortunate we haven't chained you in the basement, naked and rolling in your own dirt. Instead we give you our home, our food, our beds. You deserve nothing of our treatment."

Nicholas ignored his father. He loosened the knot on my robe.

The silk fell to the floor.

I would never be used to such exposure.

Darius hummed as he studied me. "If you were mine, I wouldn't release you from my bed until every inch of your cunt stuffed with my seed. You'd be bred before the night was out."

My airway threatened to close.

Not now. He'd have no pity on me now.

Nicholas wasn't Darius, but I still froze as he grabbed my hand. I tugged away, but his fingers dug into my wrist, no doubt testing for the fluttering pulse beating in his grip. He pulled me to the bed. The softness of his words did not disguise the vulgar request.

"On your back, Sarah," Nicholas said. "You'll be more comfortable."

Hardly. I stared at the restraints—the thick bands of leather chained to the bed posts.

"I can't fight you." I stared only at the horrifying bindings. "Why are you doing this?"

He pushed me down. "I won't ask again."

"Stop bitching!" Darius reached to strike me, but Nicholas prevented the blow. The gold in his eyes hardened to amber. A warning.

Nicholas had never lost his temper. He never threatened, never raised his voice.

Darius beat me, Max intimidated me, and even Reed's solid muscle daunted me, but the flash of impatience in Nicholas's poise struck me to my core.

Nicholas was the last person in the world I ever wanted to cross.

But to survive this? I had to deceive him.

I sat on the bed. He took my left wrist and fastened it with the ugly leather straps. His fingers gentled as I looked away. Soft presses. A confusing touch. He didn't let the restraints cut into my skin.

Yesterday when he touched me, I didn't need cuffs to degrade myself.

"Reed." Darius snapped his name. "Restrain her other hand."

I stiffened. So did Reed.

Darius hadn't asked Max, the one Bennett most likely to get hard from such cruelty. It was deliberate. Reed wasn't like his brothers. He took honest care of me when I was recovering, and he did it without Nicholas's sensual stare or Max's aggression.

Darius hissed as he repeated the order.

Reed had been kind, so I spared him from his father's wrath if only to endure it myself.

I extended my hand.

He said nothing, wrapping the leather over my wrist with a cold yank. The cuff dug into my skin. He didn't fix it.

My breasts exposed, bared and unprotected. I struggled to sit cross-legged.

Darius snorted. He seized my ankles and stretched me flat across the mattress. I bit my whimper as he spread my legs. My slit revealed to them, but Nicholas prevented him from restraining my legs. The leather cuffs hardly reached my feet. I was too tiny for their deviant punishment.

My chest betrayed me, puffing with hyperventilated gasps. I stared at the ceiling as Darius petted my knee. His fingers didn't stop. They grazed up, up, up. I stilled until he scratched a rough hangnail over my thigh. The flinch shoved him away. The slap to my stomach forced a squeal from my lips.

"Sensitive?" He poked my belly, low. Hard. "Not to worry, my dear. The doctor said that was a sign of ovulation."

I twisted, but he smacked again, this time aiming for my breasts just to watch me squirm. A second and third smack hurt, but then he gripped my nipple, twisting until I shrieked and struggled against the restraints.

"You listen to me, slut," Darius whispered. "Tonight is the first night of your new life. Starting now, you are nothing more than a whore. A body to fuck and a womb to fill. Get used to a cock shoved in your pussy. You'll be fucked like the little bitch you are until you swell with a child. Do you understand?"

"Fuck you."

"Unfortunately." He released my nipple with a cruel tug. "I've made my vows. The privilege of your breeding belongs to your brothers. Serve them well, and we'll be kind. If you are disobedient, I promise you'll remain in pain every moment of every day." Darius's smile caressed as invasive as any rape. "Continue to fight, and I *will* fuck you myself."

I had no reason to doubt him. Nicholas shifted to my side. It was the first time I feared he'd never be close enough.

Whatever bastard mind-games Nicholas played yesterday, whatever part of me he won, whatever slice of my pride he captured for his own—at least he hadn't hurt me.

Just the opposite. He frightened me. Touched me. Stole my sanity. But Nicholas didn't bind me to the bed so he could beat me into submission.

Darius tied me down because he liked my pain.

My step-father was a living, breathing embodiment of hell. Whatever strength I reserved for my ordeal wouldn't be enough to survive anything he would do to me.

I searched for Nicholas. Despite me naked, writhing, and bound to the bed for his pleasure, he didn't look at me. He tensed, watching his father. The tension crackled against my skin.

Max grunted. "I got better things to do than listen to her scream. Nick can figure it out from here."

The violence etched into Darius's expression diminished, though the hardness in his pants threatened me more than any word he uttered.

"My dear, I trust you won't disturb the entire household?" He joined Reed and Max and laughed as he passed from the room. "You are far too pretty to gag."

The door closed.

The steps faded.

And I was left to Nicholas's mercy.

I twisted against the restraints, crossing my legs to hide from him. "Let me go. I swear to God—"

"Shh." His voice mellowed without the presence of his family. "None of that."

"Nicholas, this isn't right. You can't do this."

"Didn't my father just tell you to behave?"

How did he tame me so easily? His hand grazed my thigh, tracing where Darius had touched. The goose bumps were nothing like the curdling blisters of Darius's appraisal.

A warmth shot through me.

No. Nicholas's touch was even worse.

"I won't untie you," he said. "Don't ask again."

"*Why?*"

He palmed my hip. I should have hated how thoroughly he memorized me. My curves. The dip across my navel. The softness between my legs.

"You're very beautiful," he said. "Delicate."

"I'm uncomfortable."

"Oh, I can make you very comfortable."

I shivered, hating that it was a good, fuzzy sensation that parted my lips. "I don't like your idea of comfort."

"You liked it last night."

I had no answer for my behavior. "Once. That's all."

"That would be the true crime, Sarah. To watch you come for me only once?"

This wasn't happening. "What are you going to do?"

"I've already told you what I plan." The suit jacket came off. The first time he had been so undone before me. The black vest beneath tailored fit his frame—just as strong and broad without the benefit of the jacket. I stilled as the button popped open. His white dress shirt tensed against his thick biceps. "You remember, Sarah."

I tested the restraints. Tight. "I didn't think you were serious."

"I won't ever lie to you."

That was a comfort, coming from the clothed man prowling around me as I lay restrained, nude and helpless.

His hand tickled, tapping a soft path from my knee along my side. I looked away as the goose bumps teased too close to my breast, tightening the mistreated bud.

"My father is not a gentle man," Nicholas said. I arched as he cupped my sore breast, claiming the entirety of my flesh in his palm. The heat was soothing, but the relief centered deep inside me, tucked into a core that clenched to life despite the horrors of my treatment. "I won't hurt you."

I ignored the fluttering within my belly. "Why?"

"Because you're going to like this. You're going to ask for this. You'll beg for me, and I will please you."

The top button of his shirt popped open. The second followed, revealing hard skin, smooth with the tautness of firm muscle and masculine power. Nicholas moved quickly, draping the material off his broad shoulders.

A body like his should never have hid within so many layers of clothing.

God, he was strong. He thickened with muscle—not the bulky, intimidating form of Max, but a lean build. Enough to impress, more than enough to frighten, and just the perfect amount to completely dominate, with or without restraints.

So why was he covered in scars? Thin white stripes of memorized pain struck everywhere—his shoulders, chest, back. But they extended no further than what was obscured by his suit.

He had been beaten. Severely. Repeatedly. But not for some years.

No wonder he held himself with such dignified poise and served his father in any capacity the monster demanded. He had no choice.

I exhaled as he lurked before me, standing at my feet and examining all of my body.

"Open your legs," he whispered. "Don't hide from me."

I shook my head.

"I won't ask twice."

He'd have to get used to disappointment.

The belt unbuckled with a soft click. I flinched as the leather tugged from his pants. He folded the strip within his hand.

"You said you wouldn't hurt me." My voice wavered.

"I said I wouldn't need to." He leaned over me, tracing my flushing skin with the teasing lick of the leather. "You won't misbehave, will you?"

My breathing shuddered, but not from the illness. "What if I do?"

The lash was quick, nothing more than a flick of his wrist. The belt didn't sting, but I gasped all the same. He chuckled, and the rumbling cadence of his amusement seared through my core.

"I dislike pain," He said. The belt wove over my skin, tugging as the rough edge dragged across a hardening nipple. "Why fight me? This is an unwinnable battle. You're restrained. I'm free. You're naked. I'm in control." His smile bared his teeth. I craved to feel them sink within my neck once more. "You like that."

"I don't."

"You've already submitted to me, Sarah. Denying it to yourself only delays your pleasure."

"Why are you tormenting me? Just take what you want and leave."

He leaned closer, the belt bopping under my chin to raise my gaze.

"What I want is your pleasure, Sarah."

Why did I believe him?

"I want to watch you moan. Beg. Whine." He tapped the leather against my breast. He didn't hurt me, though he was strong enough to flay me without effort. Instead, the leather teased, sending shivers through me head to toe only to center, forcing the sensation between my legs. "I'll watch you come again and again until you are too weak to resist when I claim you."

"You're going to fuck me?"

"Oh, yes. Many times."

"And you'll…"

He lashed with a tease over my tummy. Flat and trembling, where his intentions hoped to spill.

"I'll come inside you." His voice altered, rasped with an animalistic growl. "You will be mine, Sarah Atwood. My prisoner. My prize. My toy." He flicked lower, tickling the silky slit I tried to hide with twisting thighs. "My ultimate conquest."

He tapped with the belt. The soft strike rattled me. Every touch, every vibration cast by the kiss of the leather softened my resistance.

I knew what he was doing.

God, I even knew what he planned.

But I couldn't stop myself from imagining it, wondering about it…wanting it.

"Spread your legs," he whispered again. "You won't be disappointed."

"I can't. Don't make me do this."

"Then do it willingly."

His voice dipped as low as the belt. A single smack arched me up. The surprise untensed my body. He had his opening, and the leather struck what I desperately tried to keep secret and safe. The belt hit rough on my clit, and I whimpered against the slick slap that echoed my pleasure within the room.

"Submit, Sarah." The bed shifted as he settled on the mattress. "Don't resist me, not when I can offer you so much."

I swallowed as his hand rested over my belly, drifting lower and lower until his fingers covered the heat radiating from my bare slit. I squeezed my thighs tight, but the tiny crease was no match for his will. The flick of his finger arched my back, and, without realizing just how quickly I lost the second battle with Nicholas Bennett, I spread my legs.

He was on me in an instant. He lowered his body until his hot breath panted over my exposed pussy.

I fought the restraints—too harsh to escape and too frustratingly short to ease the ache he summoned inside me.

"So beautiful," Nicholas murmured. "I would keep you bound forever—tied up and tucked away, just for me."

And he'd probably do it too. Nothing stopped a Bennett. Not rules. Not laws. Not common morality. He hovered close to my slit, gazing over my vulnerable, fragile form.

Why didn't he end it?

The moment he touched my skin would be the instant I'd lose myself forever in my own regret and hunger. He understood that. I dreaded it.

So what stopped him?

He tortured without the belt or a harsh word. Every second trapped in his power passed in a dozen eternities, ensnaring me in a remorseless need. The terror faded. The injustice and cruelty was lost within the praise of his words and gentle brush of his hands. I shivered.

Nothing made sense.

Somehow, bound and naked, weakened and helpless, it wasn't Nicholas I no longer trusted.

I didn't trust myself.

"Tell me," Nicholas said, patient, curled in his web and waiting for me to tangle in his trap. "Tell me, and I'll give you everything."

An admission. My consent. My dignity?

This was a dangerous game we played. I licked my lips, wishing it were his kiss once more.

"P—please."

His chuckle would have humiliated me had my broken pride not been immediately healed by the sudden, desperate, passionate kiss he placed directly on my trembling pussy.

I nearly bolted from the bed, but the restraints held me as tightly as his sudden grip upon my hips. He forced my legs wider, jerking my body to where he had access to every fold and petal, soft secret and dripping wetness.

His lips never left my skin. His tongue danced over my slit, batting my clit, and dipping down low to taste the part of me bound explicitly for his delight.

I squirmed. He squeezed my legs and held me down.

He chuckled as I moaned and suckled harder against my throbbing, overwhelmed slit.

I arched in sudden panic.

He'd won.

I hated that he was right. Hated that he read me so easily. Hated that he controlled my desire.

And I was so grateful he promised not to hurt me that his violation actually buzzed through my head like a stolen gift.

I battled against the leather cuffs. My step-family lurked in the estate, eager for any scream or cry I might have uttered. Instead, I gasped. Shuddered. Lost my voice in an aching plea and twisted my hips for more attention. I no longer wished to escape his relentless pursuit. I had never imagined how delicious a skilled tongue would feel pressed within a part of me I woefully neglected.

First his touch. Then his kiss?

Only one mystery remained about my body, my reactions, and my untampered passion.

He'd take my virginity.

I came immediately as I envisioned just how raw and deliberate Nicholas would be.

No warning. No explanation. I tensed until I swore everything he did, everything he said, everything he *made* me do ripped me into a million shattered pieces only to rebuild into an aching, fragile replica of my former self—midway between shattering and flaking into perfect oblivion.

He growled.

It was my first warning.

I quivered and fell limp. My wrists flattened against the mattress, restraints and all. I didn't have the strength to move or fight. I didn't have the courage to bluff an excuse for coming so easily against his mouth. I didn't have any way to defend myself or any reason to deny him.

Nicholas rose, his hands ripping over the zipper to his pants.

That was the second warning.

In the hazy glow framing my vision, a man possessed with lust and overwhelmed with power stood over my prone body. His trousers fell away.

Third warning.

The ultimate warning.

Every thought suddenly silenced in my mind, and the quiet realization deafened me.

Twice now Nicholas had teased me into pleasure.

Twice now he had twisted my resistance and proved a primal need existed within my nature.

He owned my attraction and wove a power over me. I knew what he planned next.

His cock hardened, jutting between his legs with every threat he promised and every masculine command he'd wield. I stared at the thickness.

What was I thinking?

He moved between my legs, stroking the thickening shaft.

Bare.

Because he meant to do more than fuck me.

Rape. Mate. Breed.

All animalistic urges. Nothing sensitive. Nothing sweet. Nothing for my benefit except the pleasure of being used, fucked, and taken by a man for his ultimate intentions.

I had to tell him.

Before this went any farther. Before someone realized the truth.

Before they realized no matter the pleasure, no matter the restraints, no matter the dangerous attraction, I was still in control.

I had to tell him.

I had to stop this.

I had to...

Nicholas leaned over me, positioning the thick head of his cock against my quivering slit.

He wasn't going to stop now.

No matter what I said or what I revealed.

I shut my mouth and wrapped my hands around the restraints' chains.

"Submit," he whispered. "Do you trust me?"

"No." Every word wavered. "Can you trust me?"

"What's not to trust?"

"Everything."

"You are a risk worth taking." He studied my body, how my hips arched to meet his, how his cock pushed against my glistening slit. "And I will take you, Sarah. Again and again until I'm certain you'll forever belong to me."

He pushed forward, capturing my shock with a kiss as forceful as his thrust.

I expected pain.

I expected humiliation.

I expected ruin, sorrow, and loss.

His eyes widened, the golden softness as much a gift as his thick arms protecting me from the world. He filled me too suddenly, and I cried out. But the sting of my virginity wasn't stolen in a violent act of cruelty.

He claimed me.

And...I claimed him.

Our bodies melded, combined, and locked in a sudden and shared passion so consuming I stopped breathing, he stilled, and we shared an absolute shudder of *peace*.

No more fighting. No battles. My body surrendered while his protected. My heat welcomed him. His thickness commanded me.

He stole me, but nothing about the ravishing heat frightened me. The blooming pleasure overwhelmed the quick slice that assaulted my virginity. His movements tested me, and my gratitude lashed over him as though I held the belt and struck his sensitive and wanting skin.

Another movement. Another sigh. Another wave of acceptance.

"Please." I whispered, but this time, I didn't beg for my freedom. "*Please.*"

"A cry for mercy?" His words rasped with a waning control.

"Don't you dare take mercy on me, Nicholas Bennett."

"I never intended to."

His kiss silenced my whimpers, my thoughts, and my fading control.

His cock stirred within me—deeper than I ever imagined I could be taken. My legs wrapped over his hips. He seized everything I gave and demanded whatever I dared to hide.

His muscles strained. His forearms flexed as he dug his fingers into the mattress. He stared at my helpless form, bouncing against the blankets and nearly breaking for more of his godly torment.

How did something so vulgar become so beautiful?

Passion and desire destroyed everything ugly and banished whatever fear I possessed.

I lied to him.

He asked if I trusted him.

The answer was yes. With everything. With my body. My pleasure. The imprisonment. His advice. I trusted him to keep me safe. To fill me with the courage I lost combating his father and to reassure me with pleasure when the restraints stole my strength.

He hadn't released me. I became his own personal deviancy as he thrust again and again within my clenching core.

He fucked me.

He took me.

He'd try to breed me.

I didn't understand the carnal need, but I understood a man like Nicholas. He was unchallenged, dominating his opponents through sheer strength of will. This time, I was the opponent. He fucked me with a bare cock and planned to seed me if only to defy the world and claim me for his own.

I had to tell him.

He kissed me again, and the secret was buried.

We tightened together. My hands curled into fists, tugging at the restraints, demanding to touch and hold and imbed myself upon the man who controlled me. He sunk us deeper into the bed. His body pounded against mine in a blind fury of passion.

My surrender ripped through me.

The cresting intensity rushed with such ferocity I feared the crumbling, aching crush of my body. I gave him everything in a moment, a single blistering fraction of time that darkened the world and captured me within the golden hush of his possession. Nothing prevented it. Nothing prepared me for it.

I came, and Nicholas's growl would have shaken the foundation of the estate, crumbling the brick and mortar I'd threatened.

I offered more of my hips, of my tightness, of my taken virginity, and he lost himself in me.

A heat splashed inside me, filling me, coating me, jetting deeper and deeper as Nicholas buried himself as completely as he could. Body against body, skin flushed against skin. I arched and gasped, losing my breath and not caring if it ever returned.

I cried out just as the Bennetts expected, but only Nicholas's name passed beyond my lips, as secret as a kiss and as forsaken as my pride.

Oh, God.

He had come inside me.

And my pleasure rippled as I clenched against the utter dominance of my body.

My frantic breathing and rolling shudders frightened me. He flicked his fingers through the restraints to release me from the bindings.

As if he thought I'd run, he captured me in his arms. We sunk into the bed, entwined in a kiss and sweaty from a coupling that had been the most terrifying and amazing experience of my life. I clung to him, staring into his amber, flashing eyes with no fear, no hostility, and no cowering plea ever to escape his arms.

He said nothing but tucked me onto my side, pulling the comforter up to cover my nudity. He laid beside me in silence. Cradling me. Soothing me. Soothing himself.

He thought I'd be shocked. Devastated. Frightened by the seed tucked in my belly and the implications of his mounting.

I sighed into the pillows as his finger traced a delicate path over skin that needed something rougher and more demanding than gentleness.

I wasn't frightened.

I feared nothing, not now that I understood how strongly I could submit, and just how much *power* I held over the men who presumed to own me.

I had lost the battle. Unequivocally. Almost intentionally.

But Nicholas Bennett?

He lost the war.

CHAPTER FOURTEEN
NICHOLAS

Sarah Atwood slept in my arms.

Soundless. Peaceful. Tamed, for once in her life.

It took every reserve of my patience and strength to break her without losing her. I shouldn't have held back.

She defeated me first.

I counted the easy breaths which passed through her lips, puffy and pink. They had yet to curl into a smile for me. She sated my lust, and fucking her fulfilled my primal urges in a single moment of unrepentant and bountiful bliss. But I wasn't satisfied.

I wanted her smile.

I wanted her trust.

I wanted her to understand.

I wasn't an unreasonable man. Selfish, but not a fool. The girl hadn't believed I would bed her, even after my father abused, terrorized, and humiliated her.

But I never doubted for a second that I would take her. I tied her down and took her virginity. Her first taste of passion, and she struggled against leather wrist cuffs. I spread her legs, but her surrender was as elusive as whatever secrets she hid from me.

Her body complied. Her words admitted her place. But her mind? She was stronger than I anticipated, more beautiful than I imagined, and fiercer than any I'd ever encountered.

And so I held my step-sister down, fucked her like a ravaging animal, and filled her with my every intent to breed her with my child.

Then she slept in my arms.

The daughter of my family's greatest enemy, ruined and pleasured, clung to the arm I draped over her waist.

The sun had yet to rise. I preferred the darkness, but Sarah's pale blonde hair acted as the only bright and wholesome revelation in the room. How innocent could one woman be?

I stirred. As much as I longed to remain pressed inside her for the night, I had untied her. I kissed her without the cuffs and held her secure, offering her safety while my mind raged with the conquering, masculine high of chaotic pleasure.

I meant to protect and comfort her. And yet, I kept her still so she wouldn't spill my seed by escaping the bed.

Just the thought hardened me.

She called me cruel.

I believed her.

She labeled me a demon.

What defense could I give?

She claimed she didn't trust me.

She lied.

How many times would I be forced to destroy her innocence?

She wiggled. The greatest and worst temptation in my world cuddled against me. During the taking, I'd gripped the mattress instead of her, fearing the severity of my lust. In the predawn darkness, the absolute stillness of secret between night and day, a delicate and fierce woman rested in my grasp. I'd already stolen her once.

Tasted. Claimed. Seeded.

One crime committed, another tempted.

My hand wove over her hip. She sighed. My fingers teased for warmth in the cradle between her legs. Her hips edged closer. I flicked my finger against her clit, reveling in the slickness I left within her.

Sarah mewed.

It was the only sound I craved.

The tip of my finger traced a tiny circle. She panted awake, but my strength pinned her between my chest, hardening cock, and teasing touch. I'd offer her such a reward for just a moment of obedience.

Her hand gripped my wrist. I didn't let her push me away. Another few circles and she fell limp. Those perfect lips parted once more. She breathed my name. It was the only word that rivaled the simple thrill of her protests.

I nibbled her ear and she rewarded me with a sweet shiver. "Tell me how this feels."

"Invasive."

I chuckled. "It's soft, Sarah. Warm and wet."

Her words wavered. "Haven't you tormented me enough?"

"Never. You enjoy the torment too much."

Her wetness betrayed her. My cock throbbed for a taste of her. I'd take anything that would ease the rage in me, pacify my need, and silence the demon that demanded another cruel claiming.

But I doubted anything could quell that dark instinct. A raw passion burned my veins and blinded me to everything humane and respectable.

I angled her hips against me. Her words silenced as the head of my cock pushed once more into her tender, inexperienced body. Too weak to deny me and too slick to prevent me, I thrust. The violation shocked her. She tensed, gripping my hands, holding her breath, fluttering with a rabid pulse that tickled against my chest,

I pushed.

She shuddered in a soundless wave of pleasure.

And I had her once again. The tightness fractured me, crumbling away my honor and searing me with the savage determination.

"You will be mine," I whispered, as if she had any doubt. "From this moment. You belong *only* to me. Your body. Your pleasure." I tested her, watching as she pawed against the thickness spreading her apart. "Everything you are will be mine."

Her nails sunk into my arms. "You'll never have all of me."

"You can't fight me."

"I'm not," She whispered through threaded gasps. "You've captured me. You've won all you can. But it was never a fair game, Nicholas."

"I decide what's fair." My teeth pinched against her neck. "And I decide the rules."

"Not this time."

"Always. From this moment on."

I thrust harder. She accepted me. Her chest puffed in excitement. Her perfect breasts, kissed with the delicate raspberry buds, captured in my hand. She whimpered and tightened around me, and the pleasure rolled from the base of my spine. I blinded myself to everything but her.

I lusted for her innocence and softness, and I took the petite wisp of her body and every feminine curve that made her irresistible.

And still, the agonizing realization stalked me. No matter how hard I fucked her, how firmly I held her, or how many demands I forced on her, Sarah Atwood was stronger than I expected.

Her submission came naturally, but I'd never break her.

I no longer wanted to break her.

Her panting desperation twisted my control. She arched against me, and I slammed as deeply as my cock would fit.

My orgasm shadowed hers.

I grunted and emptied myself in her, again and again. She squeezed me and came. Her pussy milked my throbbing cock, greedily accepting my seed into her core.

Nothing compared. Years of self-sacrifice and protection to ensure the Bennett line wasn't tarnished by whatever woman happened across my path, and now? I released inside Sarah, perfect and tantalizing.

It was a shame she didn't want it.

A crime that I did it.

And a crisis of conscience that I felt no remorse in satisfying my desire.

Her panted breaths ended with a cough. The sound stilled my heart.

I pulled from Sarah before she was ready, and her soft, protesting murmur refueled my passion. I ignored my unrelenting hardness and stood, rifling through the pocket of my suit jacket. Her inhaler tucked safe inside, hidden from her provided she asked politely, sweetly, and obediently for the right to breathe.

My father's wishes disgusted me. I handed her the inhaler. She hesitantly took the medication.

Sarah said nothing, watching as I collected myself and disguised my evil in the civilized suit and coat. Her cheeks flushed as she tucked the blanket along her body. She acted as though I hadn't memorized every last inch of her slim form.

"How long do you think you can keep me here, Nicholas?" Her voice softened, heavy with satisfaction. "How long will you hide me away and tie me to beds and take me?"

"Forever."

"You know that isn't true."

"I'll make it so."

She bit her lip. "You can't keep me captive, and you can't keep me from finding your family's crimes. This won't last."

The only crime my family committed rested within the bed, seeded with my lust. But Sarah was right. It wouldn't last. Sooner or later she'd understand the truth about her father, the dire circumstance of her position, and how dangerous her life had become.

So I'd keep her tucked away. Hidden from the world. Protected from my family.

Sated with my cock.

"Sarah Atwood, I've decided no one else will touch you."

Her amusement was a bluff of hope. "Darius already decided everything about my fate. I was yours last night. He'll feed me to Max today. He'll make Reed take me tomorrow." Her voice lowered. "Strategic concessions? You had your turn."

The fury billowed within me, a hot rage of jealousy I had no right to experience for my family's prisoner. I ground my jaw.

"I'm the heir to the Bennett fortune. This estate. The company. The family—and everything in it—belongs to me. That includes you." I paused. "Behave yourself, be respectful. Act obedient for once, and I will rectify this."

"Why?"

The stirring returned. It wouldn't be controlled, and I'd never explain it. Instinct and logic warred within me, and the animalistic passion mauled every bit of humanity away.

"Because the child you'll carry will be mine. I'll have my fortune, my company, and you for my pleasure."

Now I earned her smile, but the sweetness wasn't meant for me.

"You are a Bennett. You've stolen, beaten, and broken every piece of land, every company, and every person you've ever wanted. No one has ever defeated you. No one has ever stopped you." She had my attention. "Until me."

"A challenge, Ms. Atwood?"

"You're no challenge to me."

"Will you wait here, or should I restrain you again?"

She snuggled in the blankets, matching my need heartbeat for heartbeat. "I'm your captive, trapped in this home. What harm could I possibly do?"

Entirely too much in the opinion of my father.

I said nothing but returned to my room, showered, shaved, and dressed as though I were a successful businessman and not a prowling creature of the night.

Sarah was a problem. Her words and defiance entertained me, but it would enrage my father—and I wouldn't be able to protect her from his retaliation. He threatened her, promised that my brothers and I would rape and impregnate her, and I saw it in her eyes.

Fear.

My father offered a woman to us, and she became a perverted family secret that would topple the entire Bennett Corporation. When marrying into the Atwoods didn't secure his fortune, he exploited his step-daughter, a girl he neither loved nor pitied. Provided she breathed—provided she told us when she *couldn't* breathe—he'd be satisfied. But given the option, Sarah Atwood would be beaten and starved, raped and tortured, stored in the dark and left to conceive in utter misery.

I'd never let it happen.

My father awaited me in his office. Seven o'clock, not a minute late, as he rigorously cropped into my hide as a child. I settled across from his desk. He scowled at his email, but spared a moment to meet my gaze.

Nothing but cruelty existed within his presence. His was a hardness he taught me to mimic, something to replicate and pass on. If we succeeded, the Atwood-Bennett heir would no doubt encompass every lesson, every beating, every brutal warning we endured as children. When to speak. When to act. When to think.

And, above all else, to obey him without question.

"Is it done?" He asked.

I nodded.

His excitement crawled upon my skin. "Did she bleed?"

"She was a virgin."

"Was she behaved?"

The memory teased me with a warmth forbidden within my father's office. Despite the fireplace and windows, the room maintained a perpetual frost, as if the poison of our company's products sliced through those uninitiated to his pestilence.

"She was compliant," I said. An understatement.

"Unharmed?"

"Of course."

He snorted. "She won't respect you if she doesn't fear you, son."

"She respects me. She understands just what is anticipated during her stay with us."

"Good." His attention returned to the computer. A dismissal. I waited. A long moment passed as I dared to interrupt his work once more. "Yes?"

"She will be mine."

The monitor clicked off. "Yours?"

"Yes."

"Go on."

I folded my hands. "Sarah Atwood is the sole heir to the Atwood fortune. I am the first born Bennett. A child would secure both worlds, both companies, both reputable family names. Should she conceive, the boy would be my successor. Should it not be my own blood?"

"Bennett blood is Bennett blood."

"Then Max can have the company. Or Reed." I read his expression. Neither option pleased him. "I am willing to take the girl and do what must be done."

"Of course you are," my father nodded. "And if these circumstances were altered, *if* we had more time, I would permit it."

"There's plenty of time."

He snapped his chair upright. "No. Mark Atwood wormed his way into the heart of our investments and stole, bought, and bribed more influence than we ever imagined. Taking the girl, forcing an heir, is of utter importance. Our company is in distress, and Atwood Industries and her wealth must pass to us."

That I understood. I steeled my expression. "All the more reason to secure her trust. If I tame her, keep her under my control, she may not resist us."

"She might be complacent, but once she turns twenty-one, she'll be unstoppable." He exhaled. "She isn't just an opportunity to grow our wealth, Nicholas. She will conceive the collateral we need to save our fucking family."

"All the more reason to keep her for myself. I don't frighten her, but if she is raped by us all, she'll never work with us. She'll turn against the family."

"She's already against us, Nicholas. It's foolish we even let her walk the halls unrestrained."

"She is helpless here."

"Perhaps a door will be unlocked or a phone left untended. Perhaps she'll shatter another window and escape again. She is a *liability*." He rapped his fingers on the table. "I preferred it when she couldn't breathe."

I didn't. "I can control her."

"Three men will impregnate a woman faster than one." He grinned. "You're a Bennett, my son, but you aren't Superman."

"Give me a month."

"You're serious?"

"I want the girl. I want the child. I'll take the risk and build my legacy the way I see fit."

My father stared through me. I had nothing to hide. No shame in demanding what was rightfully mine. I didn't fear the moments I spent tangled within Sarah's embrace. It'd reveal only lust and domination, especially to a man who understood nothing else.

"Will you ensure she behaves?" My father asked.

"Yes."

"Can you breed her?"

"I'm certain of it."

"So be it." He lifted his chin. "But we have very little time before this crashes around us, Nicholas. The investors are nervous. The clock is ticking, and our allies shrink by the moment."

If only he knew. "I understand."

"Don't disappoint me."

I would, sooner rather than later. I eagerly awaited the day.

"Of course, Dad," I said. "I'd do anything for this family."

CHAPTER FIFTEEN
SARAH

It was time to move.

Unfortunately, I tucked deep in the blankets and reveled in the cascading warmth left in Nicholas's wake. I lost too much time in a dreamless, contented nap. I woke achy and dazed. A part of me hoped Nicholas would return.

I silenced that insanity and stuffed it deep, deep down. No doubt he'd still reach those secrets.

I wasn't wasting any more time. I peeked from my doorway. Silence greeted me. The stillness hung heavy in the halls—a foreboding barrier that almost convinced me to camp in my room like Nicholas ordered.

Wasn't gonna happen.

I showered and dressed in protective jeans. No more helpless pawing within their territory like an invalid in baby pink pajamas.

The game changed. Everything changed. I prepared for the wrong outcome. Nothing happened the way I imagined, and I didn't know if I was better for it or not.

I slipped from my room, pulling the door tight. The Bennett estate was carved from the stoic coldness of the masonry itself. No laughter or joy echoed in the halls.

When they were boys, Josiah and Mike invented stair-sledding and tore up Mom's hardwood just before Mike broke his collarbone. And every spring, Mom pumped classic rock from the living room loud enough to hear it outside as she planted flowers. Once, I hid a goat in my closet for a week—until he snuck into dad's office, ate half of his laptop's keyboard, and did terrible things to his office chair.

My house was a flurry of activity—a farm, a business, a lively home full of noise and excitement. The day it quieted was the worst day of my life.

The same depressing stillness drifted within the corridors of the Bennett Estate.

I thought rage would lead me as I tested the secrets of the mansion. Instead, I endured an insufferable curiosity. It wouldn't help me as I faced the serpent and searched for the right place to slice in his slippery underbelly. Somewhere inside Darius Bennett's sanctuary was proof that my father's death came at his hands. Even worse, Darius still had my research journal. It was a crime far worse than offering me to his sons.

Twice he attempted to destroy my family. He failed with my father—the farm hadn't fallen and the fortune hadn't passed to him when he tricked my mother into marrying him. He also failed with my journal—the experiments were only part of the ideas I had, the plans I drew, and the projects I believed could aid Atwood Industries and every agricultural business struggling in an arid region.

His third and final attempt to end us would fail too.

No matter how I responded to Nicholas, I had the upper hand.

Except my mind still dizzied with the softness of his breath upon my slit, the weight of his body thrusting into mine, and the utter oblivion of peace that crushed me in pleasure under his touch.

He ordered me to obey him and remain in my room, quiet and out of the way. To protect me? To own me? Probably just to confuse me.

Damn Bennetts.

The hall window faced the front of the estate. A limo came and went. Nicholas hadn't returned. I avoided Max. Reed hadn't come to visit and I doubted he would, not after that terrible moment when he tightened the restraints around my wrist and let Darius slam me into bed.

The solitude was fine. I'd take this tour of their estate alone.

The first door was locked.

As was the second.

And third.

They disabled the elevator at the end of the hall.

Why bother building such a lavish mansion if everything was bolted shut?

No one rushed at me as I tip-toed across the stairs. I stole through the foyer to the hidden rooms tucked behind the parlors and dining halls, kitchens and libraries.

Darius's office spanned the rear of the mansion, looming at the end of a windowless, escapeless hall. The heavy oak door arched tall, closed tight and foreboding. I swallowed.

It had to be in there. Answers. Evidence. What belonged to me and what would make every abuse worth the suffering.

I listened, but only the low hum of air forced through the register rumbled within the corridor.

Now or never.

I slunk along the wall, reaching for the knob as though testing for fire on the other side. I wouldn't doubt if a blazing flame awaited me. Darius was a demon, and he'd sour the ground with brimstone wherever he lurked. He was evil. I saw it, experienced it, fought it.

And it scared me more than I dared to admit.

Locked, like everything else in my prison. The thickness in my chest wasn't good. I held my breath as I tempted fate, or maybe fate had taken my breath from me. I sighed. Darius wasn't on the estate, but nothing would stop me from getting into his office.

I pulled two bobby pins from my hair and stripped their plastic buds with my teeth. When we were younger, my brothers broke most of my hairpins on the locked closet in our parent's bedroom. They promised to tell me what they tried to steal from Dad when I got older, but I figured it out when I hit the right age.

The pin bent and fit into the lock. I tensed as it jiggled. The tumblers clinked like an avalanche of stone. No one shouted. No one came to stop me.

The door popped open. I shifted inside before anyone witnessed my trespass.

The office might have been Darius's heart and soul if he possessed either human quality. Part library, part conference room, part throne. His desk loomed in the corner of the room, surveying the gardens, the pool, the patio outside his windows. He'd ripped up the forest and replaced beauty with garish granite and imported plants, bent and broken to his will, like everything else in the godforsaken house.

I dove over his chair. The desk spanned an elegant L shape with a dozen drawers. Cabinets stretched behind me, bordering the walls and hiding more compartments and cubbies. I nudged the keyboard. The computer was locked, of course. I didn't dare mess with it. I respected myself too much to imagine what Darius's sordid mind might have concocted for a password.

I ripped the first drawer open and accidentally scattered pens and paperclips. I swore, fumbling over the dropped rubber bands that snapped my fingers as I tried to gather them. My vision blurred, and I smacked my head under the desk.

"Damn it."

Just being in his office terrified me. Touching what he touched. Sitting where he sat as he decided who would molest me first. I sucked in a breath and coughed as it stuck awkwardly in my chest.

Not a good sign. I forced myself to move slower.

I replaced the drawer with a soft click. The papers on his desk revealed nothing. A contract. A color quarterly report stuffed under a gold and marble clock.

No pictures of his family? No trinkets or memorabilia?

I doubted his computer desktop was filled with a collage of my step-brothers as little boys, running on a beach or climbing around the Santa Cruz Mountains. Hell, I couldn't imagine it, but I hardly understood Nicholas Bennett now. I couldn't picture him as a child.

Just as I couldn't imagine what our son might look like.

The trembling returned.

The search was supposed to distract me, not force my thoughts into the mire that was the bedroom's tossed blankets and discarded clothing.

He slept beside me all night. Why the hell would he do that?

I still felt his warmth, imagined his touch, and wetted for whatever else he wished to give. I hadn't protested when he woke me by entering me again. He simply answered a prayer I offered in my dream. Had he not taken me, I might have asked for it anyway.

Of all the foolish, incomprehensible, *dangerous* things I ever did, offering myself to Nicholas would only end in my ruin.

And yet I knew I'd do it again.

"Idiot," I whispered. "Probably have brain damage from the attack or something."

The drawer next to Darius's computer housed only tax information for the house. The second drawer contained copies of important documents—insurance, birth certificates. I pulled a paper from an older folder.

A death certificate.

Helena Bennett. 1998.

Nicholas's mother?

I tucked it into the folders. Not the memento I would have kept.

The chair tripped me as I clattered to the bottom drawer. I bit my profanity and yanked the door. A manila folder rested over a collection of other papers and leather binders. I recognized my handwriting on the paper that slipped from the pile.

My research.

"Son of a bitch."

I lifted the folder. It contained every scrap of my research journal.

Ripped from the book.

Photocopied.

Vandalized.

The journal had been stripped. Undoubtedly scanned and cataloged and critiqued by *his* research team at whatever division of Bennett Agricultural Supply he deemed fit.

This violation prickled my skin more than any touch, lick, or bite. Nicholas's desire coated me from the inside, but I hated the bile thickening in my stomach more.

I flipped through the pages. It was all there though mostly out of order. They even copied my doodles and bubble letters scrawled in the margins of the notebook when I got too tired to read the figures on my labs.

My life was in this research—everything that had been me before my family died. I had a plan. A future in a field that I liked and something I was good at. Something that would have made Dad proud. Cutting edge, ridiculously bad-ass fields that would have helped us.

I reorganized the pages, but the newer the date, the less data I had. Numbers and graphs trickled away. A message from Mike scribbled in the corner—a note about Dad's chemo. Another page passed. I wrote a phone number for the funeral home. I flipped again. The numbers were unreadable. I had to redo the experiment after drinking too much when Mom announced her engagement. Another page. A scribble of dress sizes and shoe dyes Mom requested for the wedding.

Then a blank page.

Mike and Josiah's plane crash.

The research stopped. The numbers now scrawled between phone messages and dates and endless acronyms of the divisions I was supposed to oversee and the directors I was supposed to help and the endless wills and bonds and assets and liabilities I was supposed to deal with.

A yellow highlighter scrawled through one of the columns I listed. Darius marked something.

I squinted.

Josmik Holdings.

Son of a bitch.

How the *hell* did he keep finding information about the holding? Everything my brothers did was so tied up in wills and trusts I hardly had the authority to run the company, and that was before I opened my mouth and proclaimed Atwood Industries untouchable except for my male heir.

Great idea.

Darius Bennett knew something about Josmik Holdings. My stomach tensed. That was my key. It wasn't like I'd find a bloody knife stashed around his office to proclaim his guilt in my father's death. But money was a weapon that couldn't be washed in bleach or buried in the backyard, deep and secret.

If I could get information about my brothers' financial secrets—if I learned what they did with all the money they spent—I'd find the evidence of Dad's murder. Maybe Josiah and Mike had already figured it out, and the proof waited for me to find it.

I took my research. The originals were probably in a safety deposit box somewhere, but at least I had something. One mystery solved. How the hell was I supposed to solve the other?

What if I couldn't prove anything that would implicate Darius in Dad's death?

The door's handle clicked.

The bile rushed into my mouth. It wouldn't matter now, not if Darius killed me for breaking into his office.

I tucked the folder under my arm. The door opened.

I bolted.

Darius roared as I ducked through the doorway, skirting under his arm. He swung, but his fist only clipped my shoulder. I didn't stop.

Except I had nowhere to run.

"Little fucking *cunt!*"

His bellow rumbled over the mansion. I sprinted, but my chest tightened almost immediately. I wasn't recovered enough to marathon around the estate. I avoided the steps and rushed into the kitchen. Darius's boots slammed behind me.

How was a man his age so fast?

I scooted around the marble island and dove over the counter, clasping the handle of the chef's knife imbedded in the butcher's block. The steel rang as I unsheathed it. Darius stilled under the kitchen's archway. He shed his suit jacket and quietly rolled up his sleeves.

I regretted not grabbing the cleaver.

The grey in his hair hadn't slowed him, and the cracking of his knuckles heralded a charge. He was older, but his sons were built like him. Strong. Fit. Etched from stone and just as unbreakable. I brandished the knife before me, crossing my arms over the folder.

"I should have tied you down like a little whore." Darius stepped closer. "Gagged your mouth and plugged your ass. Left your cunt exposed for the only goddamned reason you're of any use to anyone."

"Get away from me." I aimed the knife like I knew what I was doing. "I swear to God, I'll hurt you."

"My dear, you've never truly experienced pain. It's about time someone showed you."

He lunged. Instinct won. I turned from him and screamed, kicking at his ankle and sprinting even as he grabbed a lock of my hair. The sting forced tears, but I didn't stop.

I slid around the corner to the dining hall and ducked behind a thick chaise tucked in the front parlor. The dark material stretched to the ground, and I fell to the carpet, pressing my face against the elegant design and silencing my hitching breath with a hand over my mouth.

Darius swore, raging down the hall. The powder room door crashed against the wall before slamming shut with a hideous crack. I ducked farther down, my fingers trembling over the knife.

Christ.

What the hell was I supposed to do?

My mind blanked in terror. Only one thought broke through the panic.

Nicholas.

Where was Nicholas?

I peeked over the couch. Darius's fury overturned chairs within the smoking room. I had a decent head start for the stairs. Upstairs had closets to hide in. Dark corners.

I'd have to use the knife.

I almost heaved.

I hurried over the chaise and scrambled through the parlor. I wasn't watching where I ran. I searched over my shoulder for Darius and crashed into a solid chest instead. Someone seized my wrist and twisted. The blade dropped to the floor.

Reed.

He clapped a hand over my mouth before I screamed. I fought his grip, but he shook his head, the questions in his voice icing over as he realized my cheeks wetted with tears. I clutched the folder.

I protested as he peeled the research from my hands, but he released me. "Downstairs."

He picked the knife off the floor and shoved the folder within the couch cushions.

"*Downstairs*," he hissed.

I stepped away. He continued down the hall, calling to his father.

"Hey! Why the hell is everyone screaming?"

Reed, dear-heart of the Bennett clan and a friend who deserved a better partner at Mario Kart. I hurried down the stairs as he delayed Darius.

Not that I knew where I was going.

The estate was huge, a sprawling complex of marble, granite, and hardened masonry. The polished steps glittered gold in false warmth. I leapt down the last three stairs and turned hard to my right.

Nope.

The room spawned into a giant gym, lit by fluorescents and cluttered with weights and machines and no easy way to escape.

I turned, losing myself in a game room. Promising, but too open. A plasma television built into the wall, surrounded by black leather furniture perfect for the Bennett's man cave.

A beautiful bar was captured in the glow of an unlit fireplace. I ducked into the corner. I couldn't hide under the poker or ping pong table. The room housed pinball machines and old arcade styled games that looked much easier on an iPhone. I'd be spotted behind them.

I swore and hid in the bathroom, crouching between the toilet and sink like a damn coward.

I shivered. Reed would protect me just as well as Nicholas. I hoped.

Stay in the room. Goddamn, I hated that he was right.

But Nicholas wouldn't let his father hurt me. Not after all the declarations masquerading as endearments. If he wanted me, if I was supposed to be *his*, he'd have to prove it by protecting me.

I'd never fight my step-brothers again if they kept me safe from Darius Bennett.

Reed shouted as the lights flickered on in the game room. I wound myself into a tight ball. It did nothing.

Darius's foot cracked through the door. The wood splintered over me, as sharp as the dragging clutch of his nails against my shoulder. Reed called for him as he heaved me from the bathroom.

"You little bitch!"

Darius tossed me against the pool table. I crept backward but lost a fight with my lungs. I didn't dare run as I sputtered and coughed. Reed hadn't moved to intercept his father.

He wouldn't abandon me. He wouldn't let Darius…

"Get on your knees," Darius growled.

"Dad," Reed said. "Easy. She's still sick."

"She's not sick. She's dead. On your fucking *knees.*"

I didn't move. Reed edged closer, but he didn't have Max's aggression or Nicholas's demeanor. Darius ignored him. He grabbed a pool cue from the display against the wall. Reed lunged for me. He didn't make it.

The pool cue slammed against my back, driving me to the floor in a flash of pain. The stick splintered in two. I screamed.

Didn't matter.

Darius had another.

I covered my head as a second strike rained over me. The third lashed my shoulder, thudding hard against bone and instantly welting. I struggled, but Darius ceased his beating only to point the cue at Reed.

"One step, boy, and I fuck her ass with it, do you understand?"

Reed swore. "Jesus Christ, she's just a *kid!* Let her up!"

The cue slammed against me. I rolled, but Darius crushed the second stick against my ribs. My vision flashed white. My chest heaved without air.

"She's not a kid. She's your sister, our fucking *whore.*" Darius seized the broken cue and lifted me by my shirt. I fought against his arms. "And it's time she learned her goddamned place in this family."

CHAPTER SIXTEEN
NICHOLAS

Sarah screamed.

Terrified. Trapped.

Pained.

I kicked the chair from my desk and slammed the phone console. The conference call had been on speakerphone, and her shrieking silenced the conversation. I batted the phone off the hook and offered a false chuckle.

"Excuse me, gentlemen." My hand cracked the receiver. "I need to postpone this meeting. I'll email you a time when we can next convene."

I crashed the phone onto the cradle.

Sarah screamed again. The haunted agony in her voice would shatter bone.

Or maybe that already happened.

No woman screamed like that without cause.

I sprinted from my office, jogging the steps two at a time to the foyer. Max peeled from around the corner, bare chested and wet from the shower. He tugged his pants over his hips.

"Dad's got her." Max dried his face. "Jesus."

I didn't answer, and I didn't wait for my brother to limp down the stairs.

Sarah had quieted, but that didn't mean she wasn't hurt.

Or worse.

I knew what my father planned for her. The sexual abuse was left to his sons—as though he offered us a gift. He expected our savagery over a woman without the strength or ability to protect herself.

And yes, part of me enjoyed that.

Part of me wanted nothing more than to have taken her again—forced her to her knees if only to hear that timid, uncertain mew of my name as my cock sunk within her.

But I hadn't made her scream.

Or cry.

And I'd never, ever hurt her.

My father wouldn't understand that, but he hadn't held her, tasted her, breathed her. He hadn't experienced her heat or how beautiful she looked arched in pleasure as her body milked every ounce of desire from me.

And he would *never* experience that.

The rage seared through me. Hot, white, deliberate flashes of hatred and disgust blinded my sight. I hadn't run through the halls of the estate since I was a child—since my father slammed me against the wall and slapped me across the face while reminding me Bennetts didn't run. Others waited for *us*. And so they did wait. My family waited while my mother rushed me to the dentist to repair my broken molar from his swipe.

Sarah's cries shrilled in the game room. I launched inside as my father tangled her within his arms, tearing the clothing from her flailing, *bruised* body. He hauled her around the waist, forcing her against the pool table. He didn't stop as she gasped in a shocked pain. The tattered shirt ripped from her shoulders. She kicked as he reached for her pants. He slapped her face.

"What's happening here?"

I didn't swear. I didn't attack. I didn't even look at my fucking brother as Reed paced the room, begging him to be careful with the girl. My father's assault slowed. He parted from Sarah's spread legs just as he finally managed to unbutton her jeans.

She didn't roll away when he turned. I didn't know if she could.

Shatters of the pool cues splintered over the floor. A leather chair toppled before the television. Broken glass glittered on the bar.

My father's knuckles bled.

Sarah coughed.

"Your sister misbehaved."

Goddamn it.

I gritted my teeth. I *told* her to remain in her room. She promised.

But the Atwoods never were trustworthy. I learned that lesson seventeen years ago, and I prided myself on never allowing their false words to determine the future of my company or to interfere with the safety of my family.

But Sarah Atwood wasn't Mark.

She didn't realize the power she held or the threat she posed or how everything she represented would eventually destroy our empire.

She was just a girl. Tiny. Fragile. Stubborn.

Passionate and strong.

And my father would break her for it.

I should have left her retrained. It would have been an act of compassionate foresight. Instead, it was my weakness that trapped her within his arms.

"What has she done?" I asked.

Sarah stirred, her fingers grasping the pool table for leverage to slide away. My father hadn't granted her permission to move. He raised a hand. She screamed before it pitted in her gut. Reed grabbed my arm as I rushed the table. The only good he did so far.

"You little sister trespassed where she didn't belong."

I frowned. It was his second incestuous reference. Either he knew how uncomfortable it made Sarah, or he liked the implication more than I realized.

His trousers tented. It sickened me. Violence enthralled him, and the helpless girl groaning under his hand would only excite him.

"She broke into my office." He teased her with the jagged edge of a broken pool cue. "Attempted to steal some of my belongings."

"*My*...journal..." Sarah gasped.

My father thrust the splintered cue at her throat. He pushed until she whimpered.

"Sarah, quiet," Reed said. "Just stay quiet."

Was she suicidal? The idiot girl would willingly climb into the lion's den and hope the prowling beast wouldn't rip her to shreds?

"Little girls aren't supposed to leave the bedroom." My father licked his lips. He jerked the button of her jeans open, gripping the denim. "From now on, we'll have to ensure you can't get out of bed."

"Let me talk with her," I said. My heart pounded white sparks of fury as Sarah struggled to prevent my father from removing her jeans. "I'll find whatever it was she stole."

"So will I."

The pants ripped down. Her pale panties clashed against the violent red felt of the table. She scrambled backward. The shattered pool cue jammed between her legs.

My father scowled. "Either she apologizes, returns what she took, and proves her obedience, or…"

The wood pressed hard against the gentle cotton of her panties. My stomach pitched. Every shred of rationality drained from my blood, my mind, my muscle.

"I'll dig my fucking way to her goddamned womb and make sure a Bennett jerks off in there."

"I'll take care of this." My voice hollowed as Sarah trembled against the bite of the wood. "Leave her to me."

"No." My father ripped the bra from her shoulders. The panties tore next. "I'll teach this lesson."

Helpless.

Fucking helpless.

Sarah pawed the pool table. Her bare skin had been a gift, hidden from view in the darkness of the night, wrapped around me in the morning. Every secret exposed, every little heat and slickening petal a treasure reserved for me.

She shrieked, kicking and punching and attempting to cover herself. Now her nudity wasn't a gift. It wasn't beautiful.

It was agonizing.

A thick strip of wood rested at my feet. I picked it up, spinning the shard within my fingers. Sarah yelped as my father pinned her neck against the table, slapping her breasts twice, three times, just to watch the blossoming pink bruise spread over a dark welt left by the pool cue.

He'd hurt her. He'd *kill* her.

And the only way to stop him existed in a pool of blood.

My heartbeat thudded in my ears.

The wood cracked in my hand.

I lunged forward.

Max's punch to my kidney nearly toppled me to the ground. He pitched the splinter away and shoved me aside.

"Dad." Max curled his hands within the towel wrapped over his shoulders. He brushed it through his wet hair. "I was supposed to fuck her tonight. I'll take care of her."

Reed helped me to my feet, though my murderous intent burst for Max instead. He expected it. The simple shake of his head warned me.

My stomach heaved.

Was I really about to kill my father?

Jesus.

My father arched an eyebrow. "Can you handle her, Max?"

My brother shrugged. "I tend to be a disciplinarian by nature. I'll ensure she learns her lesson before, during, and after I breed her."

Sarah shook her head. My father uncurled the hand from her throat.

I didn't recognize my voice. "I thought we had an arrangement."

"Nicholas, the situation has changed." He stroked Sarah's side, brushing his hands along her lower belly. She flinched as he parted the soft folds of her slit. "The girl must be disciplined properly to learn her place within our home."

"I can teach her."

He nodded. "Son, she will learn how to behave once she's impregnated. We can't delay it, not if she's acting out. Pain is an excellent motivator."

A shard of glass dropped from Reed's hand. He hid his bloody palm in his pocket.

"Max'll do it," Reed said. "I trust his abilities. His girls are always so…" He held my gaze. "Respectful."

My father grinned. "A man after my own heart."

Max stared at the naked, trembling girl. "I'm just old-fashioned. I teach women to respect me before I bed them."

I tasted blood. Reed's stare was enough of a warning.

Max would take her then.

Punish her.

Beat her.

Fuck her.

And I knew why. The frustration would shatter my bones, rend my muscles, and choke me on the unspoken profanities.

My father would forever scar Sarah Atwood.

At least Max would leave her alive.

My father released Sarah and tugged on his suit, brushing away the straying bits of glass and wood from his rampage. His demeanor once again encompassed a sense of composed calm, but I saw through shell of a man. Evil lurked behind his passive nod.

"She's yours then, Max," he said. "Do with her what you will."

Sarah tucked her legs under her as she struggled to escape the pool table. Max snapped his fingers at Reed.

"Borrow your belt?" He asked.

Reed had no problem offering Sarah up, but the son of a bitch would give us away. His delay lasted a second too long. Max sneered, but Reed moved before he barked the order again. His hands jerked over the belt. He tossed it to Max. He turned, but my father's command prevented him from escaping.

"You will watch this," he said.

We all would.

We all deserved to suffer.

Max tested the leather belt, but the loop he created wasn't meant to lash her. Sarah flinched and shielded her face as though she expected a strike.

Her eyes flashed pale, wide and terrified.

My heart would shatter with her. She didn't know it, couldn't possibly understand it, but sacrificing her to my brother was the only way she'd live to hear my apology.

Sarah flinched from Max, but she couldn't escape his authority. The belt jerked over her neck. She fought. Ripped at the leather, struggled to get away.

"Enough." Max had no patience. He immediately tightened it too hard around her throat. Sarah choked, but she should have been accustomed to losing her breath. She went still. Max waited, counting the passing seconds as he earned her fear.

Sarah gasped as he finally let her breathe. He fashioned the belt into a leash and tugged.

"Come with me, baby," he said. "Follow close."

She no longer looked at me. Her shoulders sagged. Abandoned.

I'd have taken the pain to spare her what was coming.

Max helped her from the pool table, an arm around her waist. She crumpled to her feet, but attempted to rise. Max gently twisted his fingers in her hair and tugged on the leash.

"No, no," he whispered. "Crawl for me."

She shuddered. My father laughed. Reed met my stare.

A plea to stay quiet.

Strength to endure it.

The unspoken order to hide my rage to protect the girl.

And I'd do it. I'd let Max ruin her if only because Sarah Atwood clawed her way under my skin and burrowed deep where she didn't belong. Her fight, her desire, her delirious heat. She filled my head with unnecessary confusion and dirtied my fingers with dirt from her grave.

Keeping her for myself was a dangerous lust. My father would have noticed. Every second she spent wrapped in my arms was more reason for him to steal her and leave her bloody and broken. To him, Sarah wasn't a woman. She was an enemy to be bred and a fortune to acquire. Her womb was the only reason she lived, and she was fortunate for the opportunity to offer it to us.

The Mediterranean styled bar set apart from the game room with rolling arches and lavish tiles. Max wrapped the belt over a column and forced Sarah to straddle the marble. He tangled her hands in the bound leather and pushed her forward until she pressed her breasts hard into the stone.

"Flogger or crop?" Max played with her hair, carefully tugging it from under the leash so as not to pinch her.

Sarah shook her head. He patted her cheek and asked again. Her bare shoulders trembled as she clutched the column.

"Flogger. Or. Crop?"

Her voice wavered. "I...don't know the difference."

The poor girl.

My father laughed. "Flog her. It'll teach a greater lesson."

He settled within a leather chair, admiring how Sarah curled around the column. She cradled against it, either trying to break through or find a way to hide her nudity.

I should have stopped it. I should have taken her, let her cling to me, protected her. But my father watched for signs of disobedience. He expected my fight.

Now was not a time to challenge him. Not with the plans I had in motion, and the deals I made in the quiet dark of betrayal. More was at stake than the lovely paleness of Sarah's unbroken skin. Billions of dollars, each and every penny depending on his life.

If he believed I was anything but his devoted heir, the company would fall.

And if he thought I forged any sort of loyalty to Sarah Atwood, the girl would be flayed alive.

Had I plunged that wooden shard into his side, we'd have lost everything—the company, the money, and our freedom for the crime.

Sarah unwillingly sacrificed another innocence for the Bennett family.

Max grazed the soft skin along her back. She winced as his hand drifted low, just barely touching the curve of her ass. He pushed her high onto her knees, encouraging her with a whisper.

"I'll return," he said. "Stay still, baby."

Max moved quickly, nodding to our father and limping only once he believed no one looked. I distracted myself at the bar, preparing three tumblers of whiskey. My father accepted the glass with a grin. He gestured to the seat beside him.

Sarah couldn't see me behind her, but I saw everything. I'd watch it all. Every bite of the flogger. Every blossoming bruise. Every cry.

And I'd make sure this was her last punishment.

Max returned, and Sarah flinched with each of his lumbering, uneven steps. She squeezed the column.

"Max, please…" Her whisper hadn't broken yet. The shadow of pride lingered in her plea, like she bargained for her freedom. "Don't hurt me. I'll behave. I'll go to my room. I won't bother anyone—"

The flogger whistled before it struck. Sarah's words curled into a surprised, blistered scream. She slammed against the column, but the belt prevented her from escaping. She crumpled. Max gripped her hair and moved her back into place.

"You aren't to make a sound," he said.

My father snorted. "Make her scream. Let her realize no one will come to save her."

"No." Max stared at the pink welts creeping over her back. He rubbed a hand over the tender area. "She gives me a headache."

Sarah would be silent if we forced her to scream, and she'd shriek if we demanded she remained quiet. She swore between gasped breaths, but the insults lessened as Max called to me.

"Nick?" He waved a hand. "Your tie?"

He was smarter than my father believed. He took Reed's belt, my tie, and he bluffed him into thinking we got off on the charade. The designer tie was one of many, but at least it looked as good resting between Sarah's lips as it did complimenting my suits.

The dark silk knotted within the pale blonde of Sarah's hair. She fought it, only until the tickle of the flogger brushed her side. Max praised her behavior.

She wouldn't be passive for long.

He stood and surveyed his prey. Max wasn't a subtle man. I understood his preferences even if I didn't particularly share his methods. The flogger flicked over his hands.

Sarah wasn't prepared for his strike.

The leather kissed her skin before biting. A jagged crisscross of welts rose from where he previously hit. Her cry muffled. Both Max and my father enjoyed it. Reed downed his whiskey without a sound.

Another swipe.

Sarah jerked, and Max wove his hand over her neck, brushing her fine blonde hair to admire the redness he created.

A third hit.

Sarah coughed over my tie. Whatever she said was lost within the struggle. It hadn't been polite. I credited Max's forethought in gagging her.

The fourth hit startled her.

The fifth pained her.

And the six drove her to tears.

She sunk against the column, gasping for air and fighting to stretch the aching skin flushing her back. Her fight earned her no mercy, no pity. The belt only tightened around her neck.

The next strikes crippled her in a breathless agony. Quick flicks of Max's wrist sliced her skin. The leather wrapped over her sides and tucked against her thighs. It nipped the sensitive welts already abused from my father's assault.

Max flogged her, but his attack was less severe than the beating with the pool cue.

How the hell could my father hurt such a delicate creature?

The whiskey soured, but its fire extinguished whatever foolish pride might have prevented any more of the spectacle.

Sarah should have known the consequences.

She shouldn't have left her room.

She shouldn't have tested me, teased me, enthralled me with her touch.

I should never have let her go.

Her weeping drove my father to the edge of his seat. His hands wove over themselves, as though imagining touching her bruised skin. I trembled in a untested fury.

Max knew what to do. Another strike conquered Sarah. She sunk to the floor when her knees no longer supported her. She didn't bother hiding her breasts. Her legs twisted, but the pink promise between her thighs flashed to everyone.

The temptation destroyed us all.

Sarah couldn't fight. She wouldn't struggle. She'd offer before the flogger touched her again.

I would have taken it. Not a man alive wouldn't have launched, buried himself inside her, and marked her for his own.

I wondered if she'd ever forgive us.

I wondered more when I started to care.

The flogger dropped. Max's quick glance was enough of a warning.

"She's ready." He seized the belt and released her from the column. "I'll keep her in one piece."

My father surveyed her injuries once more. "She's meant to be bred. Do whatever you wish, but seed her cunt when you're done."

"Of course."

Sarah gripped the leather around her neck as we rose. Reed disappeared. I lingered, buttoning my jacket. She fumed in spitting hatred. Her teeth ground against the tie.

Sarah imagined it was me.

It was the first logical thought the girl had.

And I'd let her hate me. I'd let her curse me. I'd let her blame me.

What was about to happen would be far worse than enduring her temper.

I left Sarah Atwood, naked and helpless, within the arms of my brother.

And I could do nothing to protect her from his desire.

CHAPTER SEVENTEEN
SARAH

They left me alone with Max.

I sunk against the column. The belt around my neck constricted.

I didn't want to be flogged anymore. I hated my nudity. I ground my teeth into the tie. It tasted of salt. Tears. Humiliation.

How *dare* they beat me?

I expected it from Darius Bennett. Hell, I was surprised I still lived. The chase through the house only delayed his rage. I should have realized the hunt excited him.

I had no idea it would thrill his second son as well.

Max gifted me a sanctuary to recover from my asthma attack, and he anticipated my needs in the hospital. But that didn't make him an ally, and I'd forever regret even considering that any Bennett might have helped me. My step-father controlled everyone and everything within the estate.

No one would help me. No one would save me. They all would eventually hurt me.

Including Nicholas.

Foolishness bound me to the column, not the leather belt strapped around my neck. I was beaten because of my idiocy, arrogance, and naivety.

It was my fault I now faced Maxwell Bennett.

But I thanked my every fading fortune that I was not at Darius's mercy.

"Are you hurting, baby?" Max unraveled Nicholas's tie. I debated staying quiet.

I wasn't that strong. "What do you think?"

The flogger rose and fell before I prepared for it. The leather lashes stung against my heated skin. I yelped, crashing against the marble.

"I think you should be more respectful," he said.

"Hard to respect a man wielding a weapon."

"I'll use my hand if you prefer."

"You're a monster."

Max circled me. He bent at the waist, tipping my chin with the flogger. The soft leather surprised me. It burned like fire against my back, but teased like a caress when he wished it. I tried to hide my breasts.

"I asked if you were hurt." His voice edged hard. Not the conquering cadence of Nicholas. A touch of violence and threat shadowed his words.

Max wasn't wearing a shirt, though the sleeves of tattoos and tribal thorns obscured most of his skin. The ink practically pulsed in the sheer strength of his form. Muscle upon muscle. Whatever he did wasn't a workout, it was obsession, a compulsion to become bigger, stronger. I wasn't ashamed that my gaze drifted over his body, away from the dark severity of his features and onto the remorseless strength pooling in the twitching of his pecs, the steady breathing rocking his abs, and lower.

A thick V defined his hips, and his hardness held his trousers upon his waist.

He favored one leg. Had my hands not been tied, I might have struck at his injury. But I behaved. Even with a bad leg, I wasn't fast enough to escape from a man so fiercely sculpted.

"Sarah," he said. "Tell me if you're okay."

Like he deserved to know. "I'm still breathing."

"I'll take it."

The flogger jerked away. I flinched with it.

I wished he'd release the belt around my neck. Instead he made me crawl to him as he sat in one of the leather chairs.

He tugged the leash, forcing me between his legs. He admired my nudity and all the shivers that rolled over me. The belt pinched before I considered popping him where it counted. I forced myself still, hoping he wouldn't strangle me in some perverted kink I didn't understand.

"You haven't thank me," he said.

"Why would I *thank* you?"

"I just saved your life, baby."

I shivered. "You beat me."

"And had it been my father, you'd be raped with a broken pool cue, beaten, and left to bleed out in the garage." He jiggled the belt and smirked. It didn't soften his expression. I didn't think anything would. "You'd be dead, *sis*. So you better thank me for saving your beautiful ass."

Christ, he was telling the truth.

Darius would have murdered me.

But what did Max expect in exchange for his kindness?

"Thank you," I whispered.

"Good girl."

"Can you let me go now?"

"Not a chance."

I kicked. The leash tugged, and I fell deeper into his lap. My bare breasts pushed against his legs.

"I didn't say to move," he warned.

"Max, please."

"Please, what?" He laughed. "You don't get it, do you?"

"Get what?"

"That *this*?" He caressed the belt wrapped over my neck. "*This* is your life now."

"It doesn't have to be," I whispered. "You don't have to do this. You could let me go."

"Did Nick let you go last night?"

I didn't look away in time. He saw my blush. Worse, he felt me tense. Max sensed every bit of betrayal and anger, confusion and blame I pitted on his brother.

"I didn't think so," he said. "Nick does what's *expected* of him. Always did. Always will."

"It doesn't matter what he did. Forget him."

"Can you?"

"Max, I'm asking you. Please. You don't have to...to..."

"Fuck you?" He studied my body. The flick of his eyes over my bare form was every bit as humiliating and degrading as he could make it. "Yes. I do."

"Why?"

"Because my father *expects* it." He jerked the belt. I resisted, but he tugged and toppled me on his chest. My palms rested against his muscle. His whisper added yet another tension around my neck. "And because I want to fuck you."

"You want to hurt me?"

"You've been calling the Bennetts monsters ever since we met. Consider this your validation."

"You could be different."

"I'll only say this once, baby." Max drew me closer. "I'm not Nicholas."

"I never said you were."

"But that's the problem, isn't it?"

"I don't know what you're talking about."

"Of course you don't."

The heat from his body passed into me. I shouldn't have gotten that close. I didn't understand what was happening. His muscles flexed. The panic fogged my mind.

He'd break me in two.

"Do you get off on this?" I whispered. "Beating women?"

"Yes."

"Why?"

"What's not to like?" Max shifted me to the floor. He kicked at my knee and adjusted the belt, forcing me to sit with my legs open.

He saw everything. I raced the twisting of my stomach to cover myself before the shame colored me pink.

"You're a beautiful woman," Max said. "And you're helpless. I enjoy that."

"Monster."

"You like it too, baby."

His words resonated deep within my belly. I didn't cower as he loomed over me, not when he would have liked it, gotten off on it, and used it against me. I braved his dark gaze.

I wish I hadn't looked.

"I don't like this," I said.

"You've already submitted to me."

"You're delusional."

"I'll show you."

The flogger danced across his hand. I whimpered as it crossed over my chest, catching my nipple within the sting of the leather.

"You like the fight," he said. "You like resisting. Challenging us. Thinking you have a choice."

"I do have a choice."

"You *don't*." He silenced me with another slice of the flogger against my belly. "And the sooner you realize it, the safer you'll be."

"I'd rather be in danger than become a toy for a Bennett."

"Then you'll be both, and you'll still lose."

The damn leather again. I yelped as he struck only to watch my body welt. I hid a lot of things, but the sting was as impossible to conceal as the streaks of pink spread in its wake. It wasn't fair.

"Are you afraid of me, baby?" He asked.

Why lie?

"Yes."

"Good."

I tensed as he stood, preparing for the inevitable strike of the flogger. It didn't come. Instead, he grunted and rubbed his thigh.

Even he couldn't hide everything. I took a chance.

"What happened to your leg?" The weapon didn't crash down. He permitted my question, though his harsh sneer faded within a tense moment.

"What do you think?"

He kept his hair cropped short. Worked out. Inked most of his body. Held his head high.

"Military accident." I said. "You got hurt in the army."

"Reserves. And no. I never saw any action." He tapped his leg. "Titanium rods. Shattered my femur, knee, tibia, and fibula, shredded everything, in a car crash. They should have taken the damn leg."

An anger shadowed his admission. I braced myself as the flogger rose again to punish me for my curiosity. The leather didn't strike. He rolled it over my arms, my side. A shiver caught me.

How did something painful still feel so soft?

"You have no idea what's happened, do you, baby? Not in this house. Not in our lives."

I swallowed. "So explain it to me."

He didn't. The flogger rushed down, striking my back once more. I bent forward, unintentionally offering him just another bit of sensitive skin to claim, another moment to watch me groan.

He didn't hit as hard, and the sting washed away too quickly. I feared the warmth it left behind more than the bite.

Another hit.

I bit my lip, but the gasp still mewed too much. Max twisted the ends of the flogger and pushed. I flushed as my chest presented to him.

The leather kissed my breasts. The sharp prickle morphed into something…different.

My core clenched.

What was happening to me?

"I need your help," Max said. The flogger snapped again, but the confusion shielded me from the pain. "And I'll make you a deal to get it."

"...What?"

The flogger cracked harder.

"Don't move. Don't open your fucking mouth. You're going to listen now, and you're going to think long and hard about what's best for you."

Another hit, this one grazing my belly. The fine trail of the leather dipped a little too low. A sharp peck struck between my legs. I collapsed onto the floor. Max didn't care.

The heat didn't either.

A rush of dizzying adrenaline protected my sensitive slit. I shuddered as it rolled over me. It hurt. It warmed.

It tingled.

"What can I offer you?" I swallowed. "You're the one with the whip—"

He hit. Harder. I cried out against the stinging crash of the leather. He hadn't broken skin. Hadn't bruised me. Hadn't seriously harmed me. But the stings dug deep, like Max understood the raw ache his instrument caused. I shuddered against the next smack.

"It's a *flogger*, baby. Get used to it. You'll be experiencing it a lot. Does that scare you?"

Depended on who held the weapon. I didn't answer.

He tickled the leather through his fingers. "Listen, Sarah. Be smart about this. You are going to do everything I say."

"Why?"

"Because if you submit to me, if you swear you won't resist me…" The flogger pressed against my lips. He waited for me to kiss it. I obeyed only to keep him talking. "Then I can make it so that I am the only one who hurts you every again."

"I don't…." My words faded. "Is that supposed to *comfort* me?"

He bent down, his bad leg awkwardly supporting him. No matter how unsteady his step, the darkness of his expression, thickness of his jaw, and intensity of his presence revealed a man far stronger than just the physical strength bulking his muscles. I might have cowered in his stare, but I saw no cruelty. None of Darius's blind hatred. Sadism, but no brutality.

"If I hurt you, I can protect you." Max whispered.

"That doesn't make any sense."

"I'll tell my father I'll take complete control over your discipline, and he'll agree."

He was lying. Had to be. "Yeah, and Nicholas said he would be the only man to fuck me. What makes you think you can convince Darius?"

"Nicholas pushed his luck, and my father hates when people question him." Max brushed my cheek. "But he would let me be the one to break you."

"Why?"

"Because hurting people is all my father trusts me to do. I'm the second born. I scavenge for whatever piece of the company I'm allowed to claim. Nick has an image to maintain. I get what he doesn't want dirtying his hands."

None of this made any sense. I picked my words with caution.

"What if I say no?"

"Then the next time you act out, my father will take pleasure in satisfying every last vendetta he has against your family."

"And how would you help me?"

The flogger tickled my breasts. My nipples hardened against the gentle tail.

"I don't want to kill you. I want to break you. Watch you submit. Keep you quiet and tame while everything comes undone."

"As appealing as that sounds..." I steadied myself. "I'm not choosing which Bennett I prefer to beat me."

"Do you want my father to hurt you?"

"Do *you*?" I didn't bother fighting the leash. "No? Then don't offer to hurt me *for* him, just stop Darius from doing this!"

"We can't."

"No. You *won't*. There's a difference, and I'm the one who gets hurt because of it."

"We've all earned our beatings, baby. Believe me." Max's grip might have broken the flogger in half. He swore, twisting the leather. His eyes darkened. "Will you help me?"

"I can't do anything for you."

"Yes, you can. He needs you to behave."

"Who?"

The flogger cracked hard. I gasped as Max growled over my pain.

"Nicholas."

The heat ground within me. His name shivered over my every welt and ache.

Max didn't give me time to recover. "You have to be compliant. You have to obey us and do as we say even if it means getting fucked like a little whore. Make my father think you've given up. Let him believe he's won."

"*Why?*"

"Because Nick is plotting a takeover of the Bennett Corporation."

The shock pounded my chest like an instant asthma attack. My first breath was ravaged by sheer, perverted excitement. It bound my pain and melted it into beautiful relief.

I stared at Max. "Are you serious?"

"My father is running our company into the ground. We're losing money. Losing investors. Nick isn't a man to inherit a problem. He's taking control now."

"Why are you telling me this?" I asked.

"You aren't a threat to us, baby."

"I must be, or I wouldn't be your prisoner. You wouldn't be asking for my submission. I wouldn't be..." I quieted over the words. "I wouldn't be bred by you."

"Mark sealed your fate. Don't blame us for taking what is offered."

"It's *not* offered."

"Isn't it?" Max brushed his hand through my hair. "What would you give to see Darius Bennett humiliated by his own sons? Dethroned and cast aside. Left with nothing?"

I practically salivated at the fantasy.

"What is that worth to you?" Max asked.

"Everything."

"Is it worth your submission?" His words curled over my neck, tighter than the belt. He tested just how badly the stirring rage built within me. "Would you spread your legs and let us fuck you, fill you?"

"I thought I didn't have a choice."

"You don't. Not in this. But you have an opportunity."

"What opportunity?"

Max pushed me down, twisting me until I rested on my hands and knees. I squirmed, but his hold on the belt held me steady, exposed and vulnerable.

"You can enjoy this."

He could see my every curve. Every shudder. Every single part of me I had kept secret until the Bennetts captured me, stripped me, and tasted me.

He didn't caress me. His hand struck my ass, hard.

It should have hurt.

It should have mortified me.

It should have enraged me.

But the proposition was too good to be true.

Darius Bennett, displaced by his own son. A secret takeover, a humiliating and degrading act of aggression that made resting naked and exposed on my hands and knees seem pleasant in comparison.

"Will you submit?" Max whispered.

His hand warmed over my flesh. The fingers drifted too close to my slit. I squirmed—mostly to escape, but a part of me desperately needed a reassuring touch.

He spanked me again. My cry echoed in the room.

"What will you do if I submit?" I asked.

"I'll fuck you, baby."

"But…why? If Nicholas takes over—"

"I'm not Nicholas."

The warning was sealed with a harder strike. I shuddered, my fingers digging into the carpet. Max wove his hand over my body, touching every place I had been bruised or welted. He didn't offer his touch to soothe me. He explored. Pushing. Pinching. Earning my protesting squeals and watching as I twisted in my own agony.

Was it agony?

Nicholas didn't frighten me. He had no need, not when a single touch, his heated glance, and the oppressive weight of his body over mine dominated me so thoroughly. I allowed myself the pleasure of submitting to a man so formidable, confident, and *assertive* that it wasn't humiliating. It was *right*.

But Max?

He beat me, and whatever natural reaction I had for Nicholas mirrored in the stinging bite of Max's hand. The constant strikes confused me. Slap after slap stung, but my skin faded the harshness into a heated protection. What began as pain and fear prickled away, leaving only the pure sensation of his aggression.

I swallowed. "Nicholas didn't hurt me."

Max's hands gripped my hips. His hardness ground against me.

"Baby, I'm always going to hurt you."

I believed him.

"If you do this for me, no one else will ever lay a hand on you. I promise. Every lash, every spank, every agony will belong to me."

His words tangled in my mind. How could something so horrible reassure me?

"Can you really promise that?"

"My father is looking for a reason to frighten you," he said. I stilled as his hand looped over my waist, traveling down, down, down. "And he knows I can and will frighten you."

He captured my slit in his hand and smacked it hard enough to earn my squeal.

I flinched away, but his fingers found every humiliating and earned wetness caused by his attention. I whimpered, but he ignored my protest. His touch wasn't possessive like Nicholas's. He sought my clit and rubbed. Hard.

Why did I get wet for him? His intentions were dark. His hand ground my most sensitive area, just to watch how my body pulsed and shivered. I arched as he thrust a finger within me. The tightness gripped him, and I prayed he didn't feel my shudder.

A fool's prayer.

The quick pleasure enhanced the flogger's bite. Every sensation—pain and pleasure—centered deep inside me. His finger sunk in deep and captured the confusing feelings.

"I'm going to fuck you," Max admitted. "Are you gonna fight me?"

"I don't know."

He tested me, withdrawing slowly enough to earn a protesting moan.

"Listen to me, Sarah. We need you to behave. You can distract my father so Nick can make his deals and take this company. That means you doing what we brought you here to do. Last long enough, and we'll keep you safe."

His hand slipped back to my stomach, caressing the part of me he thought he'd own.

"Not a bad trade, baby. You give us an heir, and we get rid of my father. He won't be able to hurt you or your family ever again. That's worth a little fuck, isn't it?"

He had no idea.

What should have been a punishment and horror became my greatest opportunity.

My head rested upon my hands, and my fallen hair hid a revealing smile.

Max demanded I submit, but he didn't know the power that submission offered me. I'd do anything to protect my family—that included indulging the Bennetts.

And it also meant deceiving them.

I bit my lip, hiding the tease in my voice. "I…guess I have no choice."

"You never did, baby."

His growl heated the air. His hands claimed my hips once more. The leash tugged, and he pushed my head against the carpet.

I shuddered. He wasn't like Nicholas. Not in his demands. Not in the way he positioned me and readied himself for the taking.

I pinched my eyes shut as his pants unzipped. My stomach fluttered, and I counted my staggering heartbeats. It'd be quick. Hard, but I could handle hard. Nicholas was gentle, but even his strokes had verged on overwhelming.

My core clenched in a good way. In anticipation.

I took an unsteady breath. It was all the permission I could give.

Max's cock pierced inside me.

And the undeniable pleasure of his invasion shocked us both.

I hadn't prepared to accept his entire raging thickness—not so soon after Nicholas claimed my virginity and took me in the morning. I stretched, and the heat blistered through me. His cock filled me in an instant.

I groaned. So did Max.

It didn't hurt.

The slickness coating my thighs betrayed me. Whatever Max did, whatever games he played and pain he caused, wasn't the sadism I expected. I thought he'd want me to hurt and cry and beg. God, was I wrong.

Max forced my submission and rewarded my surrender with pleasure. He grunted, slamming deeper inside of me as my body rejected everything sane and logical and embraced the ache created from his hands.

He twisted my pain. Max invaded my mind and shattered my every hope of self-preservation.

What should have disgusted me heated my blood.

What might have harmed me wetted me in preparation.

I didn't submit because I chose to surrender. I submitted because I *had* to. Because Max was too powerful, too strong, too overwhelming to refuse. I reacted to protect myself, forging desire from fear.

I quivered under him. My fingers clenched in the carpet, and his thick arms pinned me, teasing with the leash binding me to his body. But I was too small to oppose him and too weak to escape from the barrage of his thrusts. I'd never be able to fight him.

But I wouldn't have to.

Max promised he'd be the one to hurt me. And I believed that promise. I held onto that promise. It was easier to fear one man than defend myself against Darius's unbridled, murderous rage.

Max wasn't Nicholas.

His pace drove me to the floor. His strength slammed against me, as if he wished to hear the scrape of air from my lungs as he fucked. I had no support. No hope. No escape from his thrusts.

Who would choose to escape such passion?

The untamed and wild dominance stole my fear. I couldn't fight, and I couldn't stop the swirling tightness from crippling my body with the shadow of pleasure's final crest. I fell limp as Max demanded it from me. He positioned my hips to steal my strength. His cock reduced me to a trembling, shivering, desperate shade of myself. I whimpered as my pussy claimed even more of his thickening length.

So different from Nicholas. So much rougher than Nicholas.

Just as pleasurable. Just as confusing.

Was this always how Max fucked? Did he take his pleasure from women as they writhed and begged and *endured?* This wasn't sex, it was aggression. He thrived on the power taken from spread legs and animalistic mounting.

I wished it hadn't excited me.

I wished my core hadn't squeezed.

Max picked me up, holding me against him as his hips drove his cock deeper, harder, faster, unending.

His hand twisted under me, and his fingers teased the sensitive, aching nub. He flicked my clit and thrust faster as I murmured in protest and encouragement.

"Come for me, baby," he whispered.

I shook my head.

"You said you'd submit."

I said a lot of things. I couldn't remember any of it now. Max slapped my thigh. The sharp pain dizzied me. I accidentally clenched, and we both surged with the sudden bliss. His cock slowed as I fought the intrusion. He liked that and slapped again.

"You'll lose this fight," he warned. "Take me. Come on me. Let me break you."

He couldn't. I was already broken—enraptured and bewildered and absolutely lost in the Bennett's power.

"Sarah," Max panted my name. "You gotta trust me. I'll keep you safe. I'll give you pleasure. I'll protect you."

I had no idea what he'd done to me, but one undeniable truth existed in his rampage.

I believed Max. And I believed him when he promised Nicholas could end the Bennett cruelty once and for all.

Nicholas's victory was worth offering myself to his brother.

The orgasm was meant to shatter, break, and destroy me.

The pleasure only strengthened me and revealed both of us to each other.

I couldn't breathe. It didn't matter. The agony that teased me was better served in utter silence. I arched and tensed as Max pinned me to his chest. I let the humiliation of his punishment coil into something primal and natural. Again and again he struck me. I offered my wetness and reveled in the enraged pounding of his cock.

His final thrusts lost me in a haze of passion.

I surrendered to pleasure.

He came.

The squeeze of his hands would bruise my hips. The shudder of his body would forever sear in my mind. The shared passion would bind me to him in a way I didn't understand.

This was submission. So different from the bond with Nicholas, and yet, so physical with Max.

His endless heat jetted within me. Again and again, as desperate and forceful as Nicholas. Max fucked as though he were determined to be the one who claimed my body for his own. And maybe he was. The Bennetts promised many things—my safety, my protection—but they all wanted something damning in return.

I fell onto the carpet as Max pulled away. A shiver of delicious pleasure rolled though me. I wondered if he'd touch me again.

He didn't.

Sadist.

I panted, trying to force myself up. The adrenaline and indulgence swirled into a dizzying promise of peace, but the aching bruises and welts crossing my skin tightened with each passing moment.

I'd hurt soon.

It didn't scare me.

Max tugged the belt from my neck, his fingers rubbed where the leather had bruised.

"You won't regret this, baby," he said between harsh breaths. "Nick's got a plan. If it works, my father won't ever harm you again."

"But you will."

"I'll have to."

I briefly touched his hand, but the intimacy frightened me more than anything Darius might have done. I looked down, seizing the moment of submission, the control he so desired over me.

The control all the Bennetts wished they had.

"Do this for us," he whispered. "Let us take you and accept what happens to your body. You'll earn your revenge over my father."

I already had it.

Nicholas secured it for me. If I survived, I could have it all. I'd win.

And, while I waited, my step-brothers promised me the pleasure of a lifetime.

"I'll help you," I said. "However I can."

My conscience prickled. I ignored it as Max hiked me in his arms to carry me to my room. He grunted against his leg, but I admired his determination. The injury should have slowed him, just like my asthma complicated everything. But Max wouldn't let an illness or injury define him. I knew the feeling.

He didn't hide his limp.

Christ. He trusted me.

Who was making the worse decision—me or my stepbrothers? I only hoped I'd earn their forgiveness as easily as their trust, if only so I'd live to see the end of this madness.

But deception was the only way to survive. Until I could punish Darius, see him rot in jail, and watch him suffer at the hands of his eldest son, I'd have to keep my secrets from my step-brothers.

But mine wasn't a secret that would stay hidden for long.

CHAPTER EIGHTEEN
NICHOLAS

My brother was a dead man.

I crashed through his doors, cracking the frame against the heel of my hand. The bone might have splintered as much as the wood. I didn't care.

Max possessed an animalistic strength, but he wasn't quick. I hauled him from a chair and jerked him enough to unbalance his good leg. His glass of whiskey shattered against the floor.

I slammed him into the wall and cursed.

"The fuck is wrong with you?" Max swung at me.

I wasn't as easy a target as the girl. I dodged, shoving my forearm into his throat. Max grimaced, but he ceased struggling.

"Get your shit together." He held my stare. "And get your fucking hands off of me."

"Did you hurt her?"

"What?"

I pressed harder. "Did you *hurt* her?"

"Jesus Christ," Max hissed.

I let him up, watching with mindless satisfaction as he rubbed the soreness from his neck—not unlike the leash he strapped over hers.

The belt had bitten into Sarah's pale skin. She'd be bruised for days. Everywhere. Her back. Her neck. Her entire *body*.

Wherever Max touched, blood followed. Bruises, broken bones, threats, anger, violence.

And Sarah endured it all.

"Answer the question," I said, before imagining her pain drove me insane. "Did you hurt her?"

"You saw what I did. Take a wild guess."

"Did you fuck her?"

Now he laughed. "Holy shit, Nick. What the hell broke in your head?"

"I won't ask again."

Max ignored me. He limped—more noticeably than usual—to the muted TV. The World War II documentary shut off. A half bottle of whiskey rested on the table. He poured another drink. As if he hadn't already damaged his leg, Max worked each night to destroy his liver as well.

"You're losing it over an *Atwood*." Max offered me a tumbler. I declined. "Not even the right one. She never should have gotten involved in this."

"Doesn't matter," I said. "We need her."

"Some of us more than others."

"Did you traumatize her?"

"Probably."

I exhaled instead of swearing. No sense revealing more of my aggravation, not when I already threatened my brother with the same physical violence he inflicted on the girl.

"I had her. It was under control." My voice lowered. "I tamed her."

Max snorted. "You never had her."

I expected the challenge from Sarah, not my brother. He clinked an ice cube in his drink.

"None of us *have* her," he said. "She's got something she's hiding. Thinks she's untouchable. She says one thing, believes another, and defies us with every breath she takes." He sipped the whiskey. "Any punishment that happens is her own damn fault. She'll be lucky to survive."

I knocked the glass from his hand.

"She has to survive!"

Max wasn't deterred. He drank straight from the bottle instead.

"Get some perspective," he warned. "Either have a drink or get the hell out of the house. If he sees you like this—"

I growled. "Like what?"

"Like you care about what happens to her."

"Of course I care! Everything hinges on her. Our wealth. Our company."

"Then why are you worried? Between what Dad did and what I finished, she's not going anywhere. She's probably sleeping it off now."

I didn't dare imagine it. Just the possibility rent my mind. The beating was savage, and Max's punishment severe.

What happened after?

The softness I claimed during the night might have been defiled.

She might have screamed instead of moaned. Bled instead of warmed. Cried instead of experiencing the crested bliss she deserved.

I told her to stay in her room.

Why the hell hadn't she listened to me?

"She learned her lesson," Max said. "She's not *tame*. Not yet. But she won't cause problems."

"How do you know?"

"When I got her on her knees, I made a deal."

I didn't get blood on my suits. He was fortunate. I said nothing.

"I told her I'd keep her safe if she lays low, lets things happen, gives in to us," Max said. "She agreed."

"*You'll* keep her safe?"

"You want Dad beating her? He knows what I like. He'll give her to me. Let me rough her up when she gets it in her head to fight us."

"So you'll be the one to abuse her."

"The only one to *discipline* her." He saluted me with the bottle. "Come on, Nick. This is why Dad keeps me around. I inflict the pain. Our little sister will learn pretty fucking quick how to behave, and if it gets her the fuck away from Dad? I count that as a win."

"Until you hurt her."

"She was always going to get hurt."

I didn't answer. Max frowned. He leaned forward, balancing the whiskey on his bad leg. The alcohol gave him too much courage and not enough common sense.

"This isn't about me." His laugh grated against the sudden silence of his suite. "Jesus, Nick. Are you fucking *jealous*?"

The conversation wasn't productive. "Sober up."

"We're not done." Max lurched to his feet, preventing my exit. He stepped too close, stared at little too hard. "You come into my room. Slam me against the wall. Fight. You answer my goddamned question."

"I don't have to answer to you."

Max laughed. "No. You never did, did you?"

"Why should I?"

"You're absolutely right." He extended his arms. "You. Nicholas. The eldest son. The heir. The future of the Bennett Corporation. Who am I to you?"

The drink held him. It wasn't my brother talking.

Then again, I wasn't feeling much like myself either.

"This is fucking amazing," Max said. "I've spent twenty-seven years living in your goddamned *shadow*. Who the fuck would have thought that *you*, of all people, would be jealous of Darius Bennett's crippled son?"

"You aren't crippled."

"Might as well be." Max slammed a hand against his leg. It hurt him. He was too drunk to care. "We all have our roles to play, Nick. You're the heir, the company is yours. I was supposed to enroll at West Point. Make the family look good and serve the country. I was born just to take the heat off of you when our billions bribed whatever goddamned politician we chose." He shrugged. "It didn't happen that way, and Dad's never let me forget it. And neither will you."

"You're drunk."

"And you've always believed you were better than me."

I said nothing.

"All those deals you created and friends you made and negotiations you settled and companies you acquired..." Max coughed over a swig of his drink. "Who wouldn't be impressed? But what about the men we bribed? Those guys I had to scare. The blood I spilled? Who did that for you? Who stained their soul for you? Who is the one son-of-a-bitch who took that fall so you would be…*praised*."

"We do everything for this *family*," I said. "I've always done everything for this family."

"You thought she'd be yours."

I stilled. Max edged closer. "You thought you could organize this takeover yourself. Kidnap the girl. Steal her fortune, company, and body. You'd get it all if you could just *control the girl*." He snickered. "And you can't."

"I will."

"You know what the best part of all this is?" Max asked.

"I suppose you'll tell me."

"I've spent my every waking moment working for this family so you could benefit, and I've never once complained." He laughed. "*You're* the one who told me to do this to Sarah Atwood. You're the one who said she *had* to be fucked and bred. We had to make a goddamned bastard child so we could claim her company and save our asses. Reed bitched. I told you it was dangerous. But you…" He pointed to his broken door. "You rush into my room and accuse me of hurting the girl when I was just doing what you asked of me, like I *always* do."

And if he knew why, we'd all be in danger. He was right. My father didn't need a reason to cast off the weak. Originally, I made the sacrifice and resigned myself to the crime. I accepted that the beautiful girl trapped in her room would be raped, again and again, until our satisfaction grew within her womb.

And now?

Max stared at me. "Listen to me, Nick. I'm not gonna challenge you. And I'll do whatever vile and bloody crime this family requires. But…" His smile bared teeth. "Sarah will give us her son. That child will become the newest generation of the Bennett family."

Max leaned close. "I'm not going to stop until I'm sure that Sarah Atwood's bastard is *mine*. You can have the company. The glory. The fame. None of it will matter because it will be *my* son who takes it from you. And Christ, that'll fucking eat you alive."

Never.

I didn't answer him. It didn't deserve an answer. It would never *be* answered.

I slammed the door behind me.

My brother presumed to take what was mine?

Unacceptable.

Sarah Atwood belonged to me. Her body. Her submission. Her womb. Everything.

I shouldn't have gone to her, not raging from my brother's insubordination. Not so soon after Max had parted from her.

It was selfish, even to learn if she was safe, see if she had been harmed, and know if she were frightened.

My motivations weren't honorable.

I didn't act to protect her. I hunted her only to ensure she'd survived. And I'd rescue her—if only to become the man who'd ultimately break her.

I had no idea what I'd find in her room.

A terrified woman.

A beaten and broken girl.

An armed and violent Atwood diving for my jugular.

I entered and found nothing.

Her bedroom was dark, the bed unmade and a pile of tattered clothing tossed haphazardly in the garbage. A robe rested over the blankets.

The bathroom door pulled up, but the steam escaped from the sliver she forgot to close. The shower pattered inside. I edged open the door. The heat clouded my already sickened mind. Thick, rolling fog permeated everything, concealing tiles and mirrors and obscuring everything that might have revealed me.

She waited in the heat, trapped in the thick air and wrapped in a soft cocoon of quiet. Peace that I eagerly shattered.

Whatever had happened hadn't broken her.

She hummed a soft song, and the heavy steam carried a creamy, fruit-kissed scent that watered my mouth as though I had already seized a bite of her. I cast off my jacket. Slipped the tie from around my neck.

Her cough stilled my heart. The rasp was too harsh for her delicate frame.

All rational thought dissolved within the steam and swirling heat. I pushed the door aside and captured Sarah's scream with a clapped hand over her lips.

She flailed, but I pinned her chest to the wall and drove my body against hers, trapping her between the marble tile and pulsing shower.

The water practically scalded me. I didn't care. The suit clung to my shoulders, and the heavy press of my pants ached with the raging hardness that came alive within sight of Sarah, naked and dripping.

I had her in my grasp, exposed for my inspection.

Her body flushed in the heat, but not enough. Thick welts damaged the perfection of her skin. Jarring bruises jutted over her side and ribs from the pool cue so expertly aimed by my father. Hidden beneath the pale blonde locks of her hair, her creamy neck blossomed with a sinister mark.

My brother hadn't even removed the belt when he fucked her.

Sarah Atwood called the Bennetts mad.

The truth must have hurt as much as her punishment.

The marks on her skin, the heat of the shower, and her pale blue eyes would drown me in savagery. Her knees scuffed with carpet burns. I imagined her under Max. He took her like a barbarian.

He took her how *I* longed to take her.

Every inch of her perfection and every marred bruise and scratch enraged me. I turned her around, revealing her beautiful chest, flattened belly, and the soft silk between her legs. She hadn't been spared. A single lash looped over a raspberry pink nipple.

What had he done to her?

"Nicholas, leave me alone."

She dared to take that tone? She hoped a little pout and hardening her timid voice would deter me from utter perfection?

I grasped her cheek, tangled my hand in her hair, and dipped her head for my kiss.

I wouldn't permit her to give me an order, and I'd steal her last breath just to taste how valiantly she fought against me.

"Were you harmed?" I grunted as she pushed my chest. She arched, but it only exposed her neck. I dove, nipping at the spreading bruises staining her paleness.

"Harmed?" She groaned against my lips. "He *beat* me."

"Did he…hurt you?"

She swallowed. "You know better than to ask me that."

Yes. He hurt her. I watched him beat her. I watched as she struggled against the strike of leather against her flesh.

Of course that hurt her.

It wasn't my question.

"No," I whispered. "What did he do to you?"

Her eyebrow rose, a perfect peak that tempted and challenged.

"You mean when you left me with Max? When you abandoned me for my *punishment?*"

"Yes."

"I think you can guess."

"I'm not guessing. You will tell me." I heaved a frustrated breath as she quieted. I didn't recognize my voice. I didn't recognize the words. "Please, tell me what he did to you."

"Before or after he fucked me?"

Rage.

The fiery blindness of gut-wrenching rage flashed in my vision and stole every chill from my body. I erupted in heat and molten agony.

Max called it jealousy.

It wasn't.

This was something more primal than jealousy. It was need. Obsession. A staked territory and an intrusion of the most mortal mistake.

I launched at Sarah, grasping her injuries and her curves, her softness and the aching slit she could no longer hide from me. She weighed nothing. I lifted her against the wall and edged between her thighs. I threatened her with my lust and forced her legs to wrap over my waist.

Sarah's hands tangled in my shirt. I should have ripped the damn thing off. I didn't need clothes anymore. Why would I ever barricade myself from the woman writhing against me? She arched for me, murmuring my name. I grasped for my zipper and struck her silken slit with a knuckle.

It wasn't only her desire that slickened her.

A primitive fury clawed at me. Max came inside of her.

"You're mine," I growled. "Don't forget that, Sarah Atwood. You belong to me."

"Are you sure?" She whispered.

She tempted a fate she'd never escape. I tensed. "What did he do to you?"

"You can figure it out."

"Did you come?"

Her expression shifted. The pink kissed her cheeks, but she didn't look away.

"He didn't hurt me."

"Wasn't my question."

My cock released from my pants. She panted for it. I licked her bottom lip.

"Tell me if you came on him."

She gripped me tighter. "You don't deserve to know, Nicholas Bennett."

It was like she got off on challenging me. Like she didn't understand the game she played or how desperately foolish her resistance would be.

I didn't give her a reprieve. I didn't ask if she were ready. I didn't even grant her a moment to adjust.

I slammed inside of her, taking every last inch of the body my brother tried to claim.

She arched, scratching at me in the pitted heat of my aggression. Her moan shrilled, but the pounding water and closed doors of the estate would prevent anyone from hearing how she cried my name.

Her tightness gripped me. Her heat drowned me. Her slickness infuriated me. My brother didn't deserve to take root within the sanctity of her body. I thrust hard. Instinctual. Demanding. Each forceful push and deliberate pull cleansed her of the past moments and centered her completely on me.

Sarah clutched me as I pinned her against the stone. She shook. Her eyes glazed with excitement, but she flared with a heat that seared through me.

"I made a deal with Max," she whispered. Her words chopped as I thrust deeper at the mention of his name. "Why didn't you tell me?"

My cock was too hard and her body too broken for me to concentrate on anything but taking her for my own. I silenced her with a kiss. She resisted.

"Nick, what are you planning?"

As if fucking one of the most beautiful, temptingly forbidden women in the world wasn't enough, she demanded I reveal what madness I devised. The sheer power in my plan, the absolute carnage it'd cause and the wealth it'd generate would have hardened me without her heat clutching my cock.

"You don't deserve to know, Sarah Atwood."

Her breathless groan earned my grin—a predatory bite that should have frightened her. Instead she shuddered and pushed against me, trying to unpin herself from my length.

It wouldn't happen.

I fucked her harder, forcing her arms over my shoulder and driving her again and again against the wall until her welted and bruised back punished her for me. She embraced me, whimpering into my neck as the wracking pleasure weakened her within my hold. She panted and cursed me and kissed my neck as my hardness thickened for her.

"You're going to take over the Bennett Corporation." Her words brushed my skin with silk and sandpaper. "Why?"

"I have to."

"Bennetts don't turn on each other."

I slowed, propping her against the wall to watch the rising of her chest. My movements drew more waves of pleasure from her. She stared at me, wide-eyed, eager.

Waiting.

It wasn't an opportunity to capitalize on my family's misfortune. She genuinely wanted to know what I thought.

She wouldn't like the answer.

"I had no choice." I kissed her lips, her chin, her neck. "You played your hand. I played mine."

"But your father—"

"My father demanded we imprison and rape you," I whispered. "And, had I not convinced Max and Reed to fuck you, he would have killed them."

Sarah stiffened. I didn't let her escape. It destroyed me more than it hurt her, and the only sanity and reason I could find was buried with her warmth. I moved faster. She shook her head.

"He…he'll *kill* them?"

"I need you, Sarah. More than you know."

"Nick, you can't…your father wants you to *breed* me."

"And I will."

"No, listen—"

"You have to let this happen. You have to let them take you, and we have to impregnate you." I kissed her again. Her lips parted. "I will do everything I can to overtake my father, but it depends on you. *Everyone's* safety depends on you."

"Nick, you don't under—" She groaned. "How can you ask this of me?"

"Because Reed will never fuck you. He'll refuse." I slowed my movements. "And if he doesn't take you, my father will."

She tugged me closer. Just the thought terrified her. She couldn't imagine the horror, but I knew exactly what my father would do to her.

He'd kill her. He'd kill Reed. He'd kill Max.

And I'd be left with everything and nothing.

"You have to convince Reed to take you even if he means he'll be the one to…" I cursed the thought. "Even if he's the one to give you a son. I'd rather he claims you—"

"No one is claiming me."

Odd words for the woman imbedded on my cock. I thrust deep just to watch as her head fell back. The dark bruises on her neck exposed her shattered innocence and re-forged strength.

"You're wrong." I held her tight, grinding as deeply within her pussy as I could get. "You are made to be claimed. Built to be taken. Ready to be bred."

Her smile quivered. "And if I'm not?"

"It won't matter. I'll have you anyway."

She shuddered. The heat pitched within me, and her parted lips whispered my name and secrets and truths I had no patience to hear. I seized her mouth and buried inside her, losing myself with a perfect heat, a stolen body, and my own ragged obsession demanding every ounce of my seed be lost in her tightness.

Sarah arched as I did. Cried out as I grunted. Submitted as I took.

The heat seared inside her. Jet after jet, promise after promise, intent after intent.

Sarah Atwood would be mine.

Her body would warm for me. Her will would break. Her pleasure would submit to mine.

And the child she'd conceive would belong to me.

I'd possess her completely—mind, body, and soul; past, present, and future; in defiance or utter obedience.

If she didn't conquer me first.

CHAPTER NINETEEN
SARAH

I was to be nude at all times.

Darius's perversions weren't sated while he watched Max beat me.

The instructions came in the morning. No clothing. No covers. Nothing but the brush of cold air against my aching skin.

The remnants of the punishment striped me with bruises. Darius inflicted the worst of it. My ribs screamed from the strike with the cue, and Max's flogger did the rest. What hadn't been jostled and pitched, beaten and broken, was driven into the shower wall again and again within Nicholas's feral thrusting.

I despised Nicholas for leaving me with Max.

I hated that he returned to mark me as his.

And I silently begged he wouldn't leave me alone for the night.

He did, and I slept, but it wasn't enough. I needed all of my strength for Darius's next demand. It was Reed's turn to fuck me, and the thought scared the hell out of all of us.

I didn't fear Reed. He vowed never to hurt me, but I had no idea how he'd react. It was just as likely he wouldn't touch me. Or, in his kindness, he'd deny his urges and tempt his father to take his stead.

And so I was naked, and I hoped my body would appeal to a base impulse buried deep in my step-brother.

Darius offered me a new gift.

"A proper collar, my dear." He snapped the leather into place, forcing me to my knees before him. Max handed him a leash—leather, tailored, and remorselessly expensive. "You will crawl for your brothers. Bend over when they say. Present when they order. Take their cocks when they wish."

I didn't dare glance to Nicholas, standing silently at his father's side. I'd already been fucked when they wanted to take me, positioned the way they longed to see me, and filled with their every dark desire.

Except I knew something Darius didn't.

Secrets that would tear the Bennetts apart.

Secrets my family would have killed to learn. For years, Dad longed to watch Darius Bennett writhe like the worm he was. He didn't live to see it.

But I would.

Darius passed Reed the leash. He held it too tightly. I coughed and edged closer to his legs.

"She's all yours, son."

Darius reserved no patience for Reed. His stare bore through him, just as fierce and unforgiving as the flogger stuffed in Max's pocket.

Reed wrapped the leash in his hand, pulling me closer, as though that would protect me from his father. It wouldn't. Nothing would. But I was glad he did it.

"You will fuck her," Darius said. "Think you can figure it out?"

Reed tensed. "Yeah, I got an idea of how it's done."

"You will come inside her."

"I don't need instructions."

"Are you sure?"

Reed said nothing. Darius scowled.

"Don't worry." Max snapped the flogger with a sadistic precision. The leather cracked against my side. I lurched onto Reed. He nearly dropped the leash. "Her pussy's so tight you couldn't pull out if you wanted to."

My stomach prickled with sickness. The insult came so easily. I curled my fists, hiding the roughened carpet burns from when he took me.

Nicholas pulled his phone and answered an email, as though he didn't even care that his youngest brother held me by a leash and Max gloated his victory over me.

God, I was trusting *Bennetts*.

Nothing could be more dangerous, but I wallowed through indignity and regained an ounce of control. It'd be worth it. It had to be.

Reed tugged the lead, leaving his father with a humbled nod. I attempted to rise.

Max slashed the flogger again. I dropped to the floor.

Nicholas's bronze eyes briefly passed over me.

"Crawl," Max said. "It suits you."

I shivered. The heavy darkness in his voice carried the same authority as it did on my knees yesterday. He didn't do it to correct me. He played a game for his father.

But what was he thinking? His order would only discourage Reed. I tugged his pant leg to offer my reassurance. Reed ignored me.

The hardwood hurt against my raw knees and hands, but it wasn't as bad as where my skin pulled tight over the welts and bruises. I had to crawl slowly, and I knew, without a doubt, every Bennett savored the view of my slit as my hips rolled.

I flushed under my step-brothers' gazes, but I loathed that Darius saw. He didn't deserve the sight. Not that my step-brothers did either.

What was I getting myself into?

I inched over the carpet, stumbling as Reed's pace increased. He didn't look at me, and the hard jade in his eyes was not the Reed I knew lingering beneath the shell of the Bennett name. I jerked to keep up with him.

Nicholas walked by my side to the stairs.

I didn't want to know how he matched my speed so effortlessly.

I didn't want to know why his presence soothed my jumbled nerves.

Every strike that bit my skin faded under his touch. Every humiliation transcended shame and morphed into a beautiful expression of utter lust in his embrace. But every secret I kept from him burdened me with a horrible weight.

I should have told him before all this happened. Before Max and the beating, before Reed damned himself to a darkness he didn't deserve.

Before I'd shuddered in absolute pleasure in Nicholas's arms.

Instead, I kept my mouth shut, and now wasn't the time to blab secrets and jeopardize everything.

We reached the stairs. Reed swore as I timidly attempted to push myself along the marble. He reached down, hauled me into his arms, and then settled me over his shoulder.

The leash swung free. I didn't know what to do. I grabbed it, clinging to the leather as Reed adjusted me against his body.

"Reed, make her crawl." Darius's displeasure echoed in the hall. "How else do you plan to teach her respect?"

"I'm gonna fuck her, aren't I?" He said. I held tight to him as a simmering rage tensed the muscles pinning me against him. "Christ, all this voyeur shit is getting old. I got her from here."

His shoulder dug into my bruised ribs, but Reed didn't let me go until he reached his suite. The door slammed behind us. He tossed me on the sofa and immediately covered me with a shirt that missed the hamper by two weeks.

"Wear that." He turned so I could dress. "And take the fucking collar off."

I tugged the shirt on, catching his scent of salt and ocean. Reed's hair bleached light in the sun. His suite was decorated with surf boards and pictures of reefs and corals. Newspaper clippings and blog posts framed his sea-side décor. I didn't have to ask why all of his photos were taken when he was a teenager. The surfer in Reed existed in a world before college and Bennett responsibilities.

I unraveled the leash as Reed sunk into the chair before the TV. He didn't turn it on.

"I haven't been in any of your rooms before."

I was reduced to small-talk. My summer finishing classes never taught me how to engage a man ordered to rape and impregnate me. They always were a waste of money.

285

"This isn't my room," he said.

"But—"

"I have a penthouse in San Jose and a home on the coast—Half Moon Bay, for the surfing." He gestured toward the surfboard on his wall. "But, my father decided that we should all be under the same roof to accommodate our *guest*."

I hated the edge in his voice. He didn't look at me. Didn't move. Didn't even glance at my bare legs tucked under me as I sat. His shirt hung loose over my curves.

It should have comforted me.

I felt as exposed as ever.

I wasn't naked, but it was close enough. Stripped and vulnerable and forced into a situation neither of us could handle.

Except instead of trembling under Nicholas's touch or tensing for Max's punishments, I had nothing forcing us together except Darius's expectations.

Darius would hurt me if Reed didn't fulfill his duty. And he'd kill my step-brother if I couldn't convince him to hurt me.

I had no idea how to protect either of us.

"I won't fight you," I whispered.

Reed's eyes blazed a dark, furious green—not nearly as regal as Nicholas's constant composure or Max's haunting reprimand.

"I don't want to do this to you, Sarah."

"I'll be okay. I can handle it."

"I can't."

"You won't hurt me."

"That's not the point."

I folded my hands before I clenched my fists. My words were too forceful.

"I'll just…lay there. I promise. I'll look away."

"Jesus *Christ*." He stood, knocking over the coffee table with a sudden kick. His hands wove through his hair. "You think that's how I want you? Just *lying* there? Enduring it?"

"We don't have a choice."

"Maybe I'll be the reasonable one. Maybe I'll be a fucking man and not rape you."

"But your father will." I wrapped my arms over my chest. "And I don't…it's not an option."

"Of course it's not." Reed snapped. "But instead you'll spread your legs for me with no issues?"

Who were we kidding? I laughed. "We're all gonna have issues because of this."

That wasn't the right answer. Reed exhaled. I froze as every hesitance coiling in his soul turned to suspicion.

"What aren't you telling us?"

My stomach tightened.

Everything.

Nothing I could tell them. Not yet. I hardened my voice, hedging the question.

"I'm not a helpless little girl," I said. "I know what I'm doing."

"So it's all part of the plan to get raped by your step-brothers?"

"If that's what it takes."

"Takes for *what?*"

I didn't even know anymore. Everything they had done, every way I had been touched, every moment I spent beneath Nicholas dizzied me with stark confusion.

I'd see Darius Bennett decimated.

I thought this was the only way to do it.

Reed paced his suite. He grabbed a bottle of rum from a cabinet, but he didn't drink.

He swore. "You have no idea what's happening."

Apparently not. He wasn't the first of my step-brothers to allude to something darker, something frightening lurking unspoken and undiscovered within the estate. I didn't like it.

"So tell me," I said.

"It wouldn't matter."

"Maybe it would." I bit my lip. "I know Nicholas is planning to take over the Bennett Corporation. He's pushing Darius out."

Reed laughed. "It won't work. My father is too connected. Too powerful."

"Nick is dedicated."

"Nick is as power-hungry as my father. He'll do whatever he can, however he can, to get what he wants." He held my gaze for the first time. "He does nothing out of kindness. The sooner you realize that, the safer you'll be."

"I'm not afraid of Nick."

"You should be."

"I'll handle him."

"Sure." Reed perked an eyebrow. It wasn't a playful gesture. "It's all fun and taboo and naughty. Fucking in secret and pretending to hate him."

"I'm not—"

"You're safe until you get in his way. And, Sarah? You're already in his way. You are the single greatest threat to the Bennett Empire, and you don't even realize it."

"Funny." My patience evaporated. "Hard to be a threat when you're captured, fucked, and bred."

"That's the beauty of it," Reed said. "You don't have to do a damn thing. We'll burn ourselves to the ground."

He paced again. I covered my thighs with the couch's pillow and dug my fingers into the stuffing.

"What are you talking about?" I didn't like his frustration. The sincerity of his voice hollowed, jagged and frustrated. "Reed, what are you hiding?"

"You first."

I lied. "I have no secrets."

"Then I guess I don't either."

"Reed, please."

"Do you know how fucked up my family is?" He asked.

I tugged on the leash. "I have an idea."

"My childhood was nothing but pain and misery. Nick made it out unscathed. Max got it the worst. But…" He tapped his right ear. "I lost most of my hearing from one good clip against the head. My tie wasn't fashioned correctly in a family picture. My father found that… unacceptable."

None of it surprised me. Was that why he was scarred? "I'm sorry."

"We survived. He groomed Nick to be the heir. Max was supposed to go into the military, but I guess you figured out how that ended." He paused. "I admire you."

"You do?"

Reed crossed to the TV stand and pawed through the video games stacked inside. He tossed me my smuggled research journal. It was only the copy I stole, but I clutched it just the same.

"You're passionate about what you want to do," he said. "I wish I had that choice."

I tapped the folder. He didn't know the half of it. "My dad encouraged me to go into genetics."

"Yeah. I get how that works. I'm the third son."

I shrugged.

"The Bennetts are an old family, and we adhere to certain traditions. The eldest is the heir to the fortune. The second son enters the military and honors his family's name. The third…" He smirked. "Clergy. I took over what my mother did. Charity work. Ensuring the Bennett name shines like gold while we hold a woman prisoner in our rooms for our pleasure."

"You have a choice. You can escape Darius." I clutched at the pillow in my lap. I was so close. "I *know* he had something to do with my father's death."

"Sarah."

"Help me. Nick's takeover will ruin him, but if I could just find out the truth—"

"Stop," Reed held up a hand. "Don't make me pick a side. I like you, Sarah, but you won't like me if you keep pushing."

Goddamn it. I looked away. Suddenly, his shirt wasn't long enough. I tugged it further down and adjusted the pillow. He noticed.

"Did…" He asked the question softly. "Did they hurt you? When they took you?"

"No."

"I'm afraid I will. It scares the shit out of me."

He wasn't lying. I sighed.

"Nick was gentle, and Max wasn't frightening. You won't hurt me. You aren't Darius."

He fell onto the sofa. "That's the problem. He *expects* things from me."

"He has a lot of expectations for his sons."

"We're all gonna get hurt by this. I hate seeing you in pain."

"Don't worry about me."

He sighed. "I gotta. Especially when I know what I have to do."

The silence crawled over me. I dreaded it more than any touch.

"Maybe we can fake it?" I asked.

Reed snickered. "My father anticipated that. He doesn't think I'll rape you."

"I already said I wouldn't fight."

That didn't help. "I'm not the Bennett you want, Sarah. Don't pretend."

Dangerous territory. I didn't like where the conversation headed. My fingers threaded through the buttons on the shirt. I didn't take it off, but I was tempted, if only to distract Reed from stumbling on any other secret I wasn't ready to admit.

Enough games. Enough torment. Delaying it wouldn't help either of us, and it wouldn't protect Reed from his father.

It didn't protect me.

I steadied my voice. "How do you...Should I lie on the bed?"

Goosebumps prickled over my skin. Reed silenced. His jaw tensed, and he stood so suddenly I flinched, the memory of too many strikes with a flogger all too real. He didn't apologize.

"Bed's fine."

Reed didn't wait for me. I heaved a silent breath and softly padded after him. His shirt just barely covered my curves, hardly hiding the last traces of lashed welts still coloring the back of my thighs.

Why was this so hard?

Nicholas took me bound to the bed, wrapped in his arms the next morning, and slammed against the shower wall. Max beat me into a puddle of myself and seized what remained.

But this was Reed.

Reed.

Warm, caring, and somehow *good* Reed.

Max might have promised his protection through sadism, and Nicholas challenged me in every conceivable way, but I recovered from the asthma attack with Reed. Played video games with him. Watched movies.

He was a nice guy.

A sweet guy.

A *friend.*

And I'd break as soon as he laid over me, filled me, and claimed me with every deviancy his brothers possessed.

His room flooded with brightness—white and clean and washed in the crystal blue of the ocean. The warmth faded as he pulled his shirt over his head. I might have admired his perfect beach body had the darkened tan of his skin not been sullied by the flicks of his scars. The same injuries adorned Nicholas and Max.

What had Darius done to his sons? And why did he have such power over them as grown men in possession of every wealth, luxury, and opportunity?

"Do you…" A flutter of panic built within me. I coughed it away. "Should I undress?"

"What do you want?" Reed asked.

Nicholas.

"I just want this to be okay."

"You think this is ever going to be okay?" His voice chilled with the classic Bennett threat. "Do you think you'll be able to return to your life once this is done? Do you know what we plan to do to you?"

"I figured it out."

"I'm supposed to hold you down. Fuck you. *Finish* in you."

I nodded.

"You know I'm supposed to knock you up?"

"Who are you convincing?" I asked. "Me or you?"

"Why aren't you *scared*?"

I answered him with every honesty. "Because I can't let myself get scared."

I'd make this easy for him, before he had any more questions or pried into something I couldn't reveal. The stress thickened the breath in my chest, but Nicholas's warning replayed in my mind. I wasn't going to let Darius Bennett win. He wouldn't hurt my step-brothers, and he sure as hell wasn't going to touch me.

I pulled the shirt over my head. The material fluttered to the ground.

I didn't hide myself—not even as the chill of the room stiffened my nipples. His eyes feasted on me, studying the swell of my breasts, the trimness of my waist, and the bared and silken patch that so enthralled his brothers.

"I'm not asking for romance," I said. "Let's just do it so Darius doesn't have reason to suspect anything. So he doesn't hurt me. Let him live this perverse fantasy long enough for Nicholas to do what he has to do to free me."

"You're never going to be free," Reed sighed. "If you think Nick will release you once my father steps down, you're in more trouble than you realize."

The back of my knees collided with the bed. I didn't know I retreated.

Reed wasn't as intimidating as his brothers—he was younger, brighter, and acted as though he actually meant to spread warmth with his single, amused dimple.

But that didn't mean he wasn't as strong, fierce, and overwhelming as the Bennett name demanded. His scars hardened him. Without his smile whatever violence caused the trauma to his face and neck proved Reed was just as tough as his brothers.

He stood lithe and graceful, possessing a perfect balance of strength and playful arrogance. As he breathed, the muscles over his chest tensed. Not nearly as defined as Max, and not as inherent as Nicholas. A swimmer's strength.

He hardened.

My nudity had the desired effect.

"On my back?" I asked.

"Why are you being so damned formal? Did you ask Nick how he should fuck you?"

I wasn't about to tolerate his tone. "Nick tied me down when he took my virginity. Max choked me with a leash. Sorry if I think you might have a particular position in mind."

"Should I get some restraints?"

"I don't know." I shrugged. "Should you?"

"For Christ's sake, Sarah."

"You tell me! I'm trying to make this easy on us."

"Easy?" His voice rose. "You think this is *easy* for me?"

"I'm sorry if you're uncomfortable." I rolled my eyes. "I'll *try* to be more sensitive—"

"Goddamn it!" Reed pushed me onto the bed.

I didn't appreciate the force. I ground my teeth.

"I'm trying to help."

"*Help?*"

My voice edged with impatience. "I knew this was going to be hard for you. Excuse me for trying to ease you into it."

Reed stepped away, laughing and swearing in the same breath. His grin widened, but the coldness prickled my spine.

"Holy shit, Sarah, don't you get it?"

"Get what?"

"Do you think I don't *want* to take you?" The word echoed against his room. He stared at me. "Sarah, my every goddamned thought anymore is how *badly* I want to fuck you!"

I stiffened.

Uh-oh.

Reed turned from me to kick an ottoman from his path. He paced, ignoring me on the bed though he found my reflection from the mirror hanging on his wall.

"I have been fantasizing about this since we first captured you."

I didn't answer. I didn't think I could.

Reed groaned. "Christ, I've counted the hours until I get my turn!"

I twisted my legs under me. My voice weakened.

"But...you didn't...You've been defending me?"

"Fuck." Reed slammed a hand against the wall. The mirror fell. That was fine. My wide-eyed reflection revealed entirely too much of my shock. It didn't calm Reed. Nothing would.

"I know it's wrong," he said. "The *last* thing I should ever imagine is fucking you. But every night I'm dreaming about sinking inside you. Sarah, you have no idea what you do to me."

Obviously.

I tensed as he approached. He pushed me, dropping me against the blankets with the faintest touch.

"Here's the *sickest* part." He fell to his knees beside the bed and gripped my hips. I yelped as he tugged me to the edge and exposed every part of me. I didn't fight. I didn't even cover myself as he spread my legs and groaned at the first gaze of my slit. "I shouldn't want you. You're my fucking *sister*."

Those types of thoughts didn't help anyone sleep at night. I shook my head.

"*Step*-sister, Reed." Why the hell did I try to correct him? It didn't calm him. If anything, it made him more...aggressive.

"Like it matters. You're family. I shouldn't imagine fucking you. Filling you."

My hands cupped his on my hips. The warmth surged through me, far too close to my vulnerable pussy waiting just inches from Reed.

"Maybe we should talk about this..." I whispered.

"What's to talk about?" Reed's voice layered with a heavy desire as he stared at me. His attention was every bit as overwhelming as Nicholas's presence or Max's strikes. The shudder surprised me. "I shouldn't want to taste you. To touch you. To take you. But I do. Know why?"

I shook my head. He didn't see.

"Because *I'm not supposed to.* You're my sister. You're my prisoner. You're a fantasy no reasonable man would ever imagine. It's...*forbidden.*"

His words tickled my skin. I whimpered as he licked without warning—a single, long taste of my spread slit. I arched. He dropped a hand over my belly to keep me still.

I wasn't trying to get away.

"Look at you." He murmured over a mouthful of me. A shiver quivered me against his tongue. "You're absolutely helpless."

"I didn't think you'd like that."

He licked me again. "Who wouldn't? You're here. Beautiful. Fucking softer than any other woman I've ever..."

I arched as he sunk his tongue within me. My confusion wound tight. I shifted away. He didn't let me go.

"Know what's even worse?" He whispered. "Know what makes me every bit as evil and depraved as my father?"

My voice couldn't steady. "You aren't."

"I am." His tongue toyed with me. I wasn't ready for pleasure. I wasn't ready for his admission. "He wants us to use you. He expects us to *breed* you. And, God, Sarah, nothing gets me harder than thinking about what I might do to you."

I tensed. He expected it. His attention turned fervent, suckling and licking at my core as I panted against his ravishment.

"I'd love to hold you down, fuck you, come inside, and keep you in my bed until I'm certain it's my child growing inside you."

So did all the Bennetts. It was a universal trait—some sort of masculine need to dominate and oppress, to claim and capture, to taste and tease. I expected it from Nicholas. I understood Max's aggression.

But Reed?

I didn't think he had such thoughts.

"I won't molest you," he breathed.

The words vibrated against my clit. I gasped. "I think you already are."

"Then I won't indulge any more than I already am."

I groaned as his tongue struck against me once more. "It'd be hard to get me pregnant then."

He adjusted himself, unzipping his pants and taking his hardness in his hand. His lips sealed over my clit, and the rolling intensity drove me to silence.

"I'm not going to hurt you."

Jesus, he was far from hurting me.

I hadn't expected any pleasure from Reed, even though his brothers seized me, tormented me, and dragged me through layer after layer of relentless bliss. I imagined awkward thrusting, hollow shame, and frustrating moments trapped within my own mind as his heat forced inside me.

But Reed was generous outside the bedroom. Why did I think he'd be any different with my legs spread and body offered? I gripped the mattress and fought the revealing groans that threatened to escape my parted lips. Reed's insistence overwhelmed what fragile defense I mounted.

I fell limp against the bed.

Why did sex with three men—three *Bennetts*—feel this damn good? I should have been mortified. I should have been emotionally scarred, thoroughly damaged, and shadowed for the rest of my life.

Was something wrong with me?

Was something wrong with them?

The shuddering rumbled within me, and I couldn't stop it. Nothing I did short of fighting Reed and escaping his fixation would have stopped it.

Reed anticipated my every tremble. He caught my lust, bound me with sensation, and relentlessly chased my hips as I bucked against the blankets. It didn't matter. He commanded my body and took what he wanted.

And he wanted my pleasure.

I arched and crashed and shredded myself. The brightness of the room haloed in my vision. Sweet tingles and darker consequences gifted my orgasm to Reed. I offered as easily as he seized, and I had no idea what he'd expect in return.

I hadn't imagined this.

I hadn't hoped for this.

My fear faded in the trembling shock of his attention. I gently laughed. Of course Reed would be gentle and kind, even after revealing his darkness. I panted.

Reed lapped at the wetness between my legs. I shifted as the strike of his tongue lashed like the flogger. He had me convulsing, and I kicked at his side.

He groaned but didn't release my clit from between his lips.

He nipped instead.

"Again," he ordered.

I covered my face with my hands as the pink flush betrayed how wonderfully skilled he was with his kisses. But another orgasm?

Maybe Reed was as ambitious as Nicholas.

"Just…a minute…" I whispered.

"*Again.*"

He suckled. Hard. I pushed to my elbows and jerked away, but Reed's hand was quicker. He forced me down on the bed, warned me with a muttered growl, and then returned to feasting between my legs.

"Reed…wait…"

He didn't listen. Reed didn't just ravish. He suffocated me in my own desire.

I was in trouble.

He moaned as I twisted and ached. My voice cracked as I cried out against his torment. He flipped his tongue over my clit, winding it again and again until I pulled at the blankets in crippled agony.

He'd torture me with pleasure and call it kindness.

"Reed, *please!*"

I edged up on the bed. He was stronger than me. His hands gripped my hips, and he tugged me to his mouth. His tongue whipped me, testing my tightness. I moaned for mercy.

Like all Bennetts, Reed didn't understand the word.

He pinned me against the bed with one hand. His other furiously pumped his cock, stroking me in time to the pistoning tongue he teased inside me.

I gasped.

He wouldn't fuck me.

The thought relieved and disappointed me.

He pleasured himself as he savored me, offering me the delicious bliss he denied himself.

Sweet, idiot Reed.

I arched again, biting my lip as painful shudders cracked through me. I wasn't strong enough to resist him—not after the asthma, the stress of his brothers' attention, and the pain that still struck me from the punishments. I cried out into the room, dug my hands into the blankets, eased away from his devouring.

It didn't matter.

Reed captured me as thoroughly as Nicholas and as aggressively as Max.

And, like them, he wouldn't let me go.

A second orgasm crested over me, layering my skin in a sheen of exhausted sweat.

He didn't *stop*.

"Again." His tongue and lips and words would dissolve me. "Again, Sarah. Enjoy this."

Was it enjoyable? My body hummed and fought and offered more and more of my wetness for him to taste. Pain lashed with pleasure, tightening over my chest in an artificial restraint that would either kill me with intensity or worship me in rapture.

I couldn't think. My breath rasped between shrill groans and begging for more or less or God only knew. The heat chilled me with shivers, and the trembles burned me against the sheets wrinkling in my clutches.

And still his tongue savored and stole and adored.

"Don't ever stop coming for me, Sarah." Reed's order flicked at the end of his tongue.

Who was I to refuse?

The third peek cracked my voice and lost my words to moaned nonsense.

My body rested heavy against the bed, spent and exhausted and thoroughly fucked without Reed once pressing his thickness within my desperate core. I ceased struggling if only to ensure I could still breathe without fracturing into delirious pieces.

Reed groaned against me, tasting every shiver. His voice turned rough. He pumped his cock harder. Faster. A punishment.

"Sarah…" He warned. "I gotta do it…"

He might have slit my throat then and I would have thanked him. His weight shifted over the bed, and his movements jerked hard. His cock thickened in his hand. It throbbed against his palm. The angry red head pulsed.

I quivered beneath him as he edged between my legs.

"Quick," he promised. "I'll put it in and come. I promise. I won't do anything else."

I nearly wept.

Was it possible to be tortured with compassion?

Maybe it was his plan all along. Sweet, kind Reed—more of sadist than Max and a greater manipulator than Nicholas.

Maybe he wanted me to beg.

Maybe he wanted to watch as I wound myself tight in stress, exhaustion, and confusion.

Maybe he planned it as my greatest humiliation of all.

Or maybe he was just Reed, and he wanted to protect me.

His cock hesitated at my entrance for only a moment before his grunted instinct seized control. His movements stretched me open inch by thickening inch, as though he were afraid he'd hurt me.

He'd drive me insane.

I shattered with sensitivity. I arched my hips and stole the rest of his length before he dared to thrust within me. His groan mirrored my own. I clutched at his hands on my waist, struggling to hold onto anything that would grind me against his fullness.

"Fuck," he swore again and again. "God damn, Sarah. I gotta come."

I squirmed against the bed. "Don't."

"I'm sorry. I can't—I have to—"

He didn't understand. Damn the blind fool. He had no idea. He'd make me say it.

I gasped. "Don't *stop!*"

Reed stiffened. His hands dug into my flesh—the first time he hurt me and he didn't even realize it.

"*What?*"

"Just take me," I whispered. "It's good, Reed. Don't stop now."

"I…" His words cut with guilt. "I can't do that to you."

His cock already imbedded me. I shifted, driving him deeper. Our bodies tensed. It wouldn't be long. Not now, not since I had been torn apart and fit back together and his urges tightened his every muscle.

"You aren't hurting me," I whispered. "Take me."

He swore. His grip hurt, but his thrust broke with his own hesitance. He nearly pulled out. My hips reflexively shifted, offering more to him. The shudder thundered over me.

He wasn't cruel enough to leave me to Darius.

But if he stopped, Reed Bennett was just as merciless as his brothers.

He seized my hips and wrapped me in his arms. I yelped as he rolled, falling onto his back and letting his cock pierce me from below. I fell awkwardly over him. The timid rocking of my hips was a moment of pure instinct.

"You like it?" He gritted his teeth. "Then I'll give it."

"You like it too."

"Too much."

I moved over him, but I hardly had the strength to find a real rhythm. I shrugged as his cock throbbed within me. Reed helped. He held me tight and guided me in place, drawing me against his thick demand.

"You're absolutely beautiful," he whispered.

"I bet you say that to all your step-sisters."

I giggled as he groaned. His hands tightened over my waist. He drew me against his cock, pumping me up and down until I squeezed him too much to accept anything but pleasure.

I was on top, but he didn't give me an ounce of control. He allowed me to set the pace, only because my timid motions teased his cock. He helped me as my inexperience trapped me with a possessing fullness and no idea how to ease the tension within me. I begged my step-brother to fuck me, and he savored my shame and chased away my fear.

His reward pounded me from below, and I spread my legs to grant him every access.

"I can't hold back," Reed whispered. "You know what I gotta do."

The cresting pleasure seized control of me too.

He'd do the same thing Nicholas did with the same fury Max had thrust.

They planned to claim me. They thought they'd fuck me, conquer me, and watch as the evidence of their mounting proclaimed them a master over me.

Christ, if they knew.

I sunk deeper against Reed, taking every bit of ecstasy I could steal from the Bennett under my spell. I hadn't meant to seduce them or be seduced. And I never planned to take satisfaction with their desire. I intended to mislead, destroy, and ruin them.

How easily they did the same to me.

I dug my fingers into Reed's shoulders, breaking myself in a stolen orgasm I didn't deserve and he didn't give. His words grunted into a feral growl, and he seized my hips, driving me down upon his thickness as he jetted.

Thick. Hot. Consuming.

Useless.

We bound together, shuddering in time and moving in breathless demand against each other. The crushing pleasure tormented us, and, when my first full breath returned to me, I met Reed's stare with as much gratitude as trepidation.

But he hadn't figured it out.

None of them had.

And the greasy guilt of the secret stained me from the inside.

He rolled me off of him immediately. His breathing rattled, but he tucked himself within his pants and tossed his discarded shirt at me.

He turned while I dressed.

My heart clenched. I couldn't imagine losing the beginning of what friendship we had.

"Reed..." I fumbled with the material, pitching it over my head. "Wait. Talk to me."

"Sarah, don't move." He clutched his phone. "I have to...he asked for proof."

Oh.

Ew.

He guided me into the bed. It was the first time I fought him and closed my legs. I covered my face and sunk into the blanket.

"But..." I grunted. "This isn't..."

"I know."

The phone's camera clicked, and my stomach almost heaved with it. But the humiliation was quick, and I didn't have to see it. Reed tossed the phone away. I pinched my legs shut once more as he pawed through a drawer next to his bed. He pushed a folder into my hands.

"That's for you," he said.

I hadn't caught my breath or steadied my fluttering heart. Reed panted, leaning against the wall on a muscular arm. We shared a shiver even parted from each other.

Flipping through the folder's contents exhausted me. I couldn't focus, but I recognized the scrawling insignia and faded lettering.

"You're giving me *one* share of the Bennett Corporation?" I perked an eyebrow. "So...you fuck me, then you insult me?"

For the first time in days, Reed's smile returned—a beaming, mischievous grin that soothed the thoughts and fears jumbling inside me.

"Never know when that'll come in handy," he said.

I arched an eyebrow. "Do I get voting rights?"

His amusement faded for only a moment. "Ask Nick."

"I'll just make sure my accountant labels this stock as *risky.*"

"You'd be surprised."

He quieted.

"What is it?" I asked.

"Forget it."

Reed sighed and returned to the bed, scooping me in his arms before I could sneak away. He pulled me to his chest, and I crashed against his salty, sea-tempted scent. It wasn't bad. Oddly comforting. He found the last show we'd watched on Netflix during my stay in the theater and settled in before the television.

None of this was normal, but I appreciated it, especially as my legs had yet to stop trembling from his delivered passion.

I let him wrap his arm around me, even smirking as he kissed my forehead. He didn't draw his attention from the TV.

"I know I'm not Nicholas—"

"Reed—"

"And I know you'll never think of me as your brother."

I swallowed.

"But I'll take care of you just the same. No matter what happens here, no matter who is the one that…" He shrugged. "You're not gonna get hurt. I won't let it happen."

I snuggled against his chest. "Goddamn it."

"What?"

I stole the remote from him. "I never wanted a Bennett for an ally."

"You got one."

For now.

I didn't have only Reed. I had all three of them under my thumb, in my possession, and stricken with my lust.

And yet, the sudden allegiance with my step-brothers filled me with dread. They expected more from me than I could give, and I needed more from them than they knew.

What the hell would happen when they realized the game I played?

And how badly would it hurt when they abandoned me?

CHAPTER TWENTY
NICHOLAS

I never considered myself a criminal.

Ambitious——yes.

Determined——of course.

Ruthless? One had to be merciless in our line of work. To succeed and achieve both survival and wealth, ruthlessness was a common trait and necessary evil.

I also never considered myself gentle.

Sarah Atwood dined at our dinner table——naked, for our pleasure.

And it had been my idea.

To protect her, she needed to learn humility. I tried to shame a woman who had no reason to be ashamed by her utter perfection. But how else was I supposed to assume my authority over a woman who wielded the power to force me to my knees with a single word?

Every flush of delicate, pink innocence that haloed her body pitted my stomach. Three men had taken her. My father expected her to be humiliated and lost, broken by our strength and damaged by our violence.

He wanted us to rape her. Hurt her. Ruin her.

The only thing Sarah Atwood did was ruin us.

And I had no idea how she did it.

The collar secured around her neck—her only adornment. She arranged the table cloth over her lap and covered her breasts with an awkward arm. She abandoned her dinner and left her bread uncut to preserve her useless modesty. Instead, she fiddled with her fork, clattering it to the plate when the air conditioning rattled through the silent dining hall.

She yipped a breath and searched over her shoulder for the root of her fear.

"My father won't be joining us." I sipped my wine. "He remained at the office this evening."

I admired her courage though she wasn't brave enough to admit how he terrified her. The tension shivered from her body. She gulped her wine and earned Reed's smirk as her arm accidentally revealed a sinfully pink nipple.

"I'd like to get dressed," she said.

I sliced my steak. The bloody juice soaked a mound of mashed potatoes. Sarah picked at her salad.

"No," I said.

Reed shifted. Max perked an eyebrow.

None of it mattered.

Sarah bristled, waiting for my explanation. She wouldn't receive it.

"I'll strip if he comes back," she offered.

"I said no."

"*Why?*"

I chuckled. "Don't you think three men would prefer the company of a naked woman?"

Reed nodded. "Steak and tits. It's not a bad deal."

"You're unbelievable." Sarah's glance silenced Reed's chuckle. "You think this will humiliate me?"

"Yes," I said.

"Fine." Her arms dropped and her beautiful chest puffed proud. Her attention fell to Max. He no longer focused on the food. "Can you please pass the butter?"

Max's grin issued the challenge. "No."

"Christ."

"Come get it."

Sarah stiffened. We waited. She tossed her napkin and stood.

My cock couldn't harden any more. The softness of her skin still marred with bruises, but the pale tease of her body held more power over us than any command, whipping, or restraint.

I might have ordered her to strip, but she bared our souls with a single sway of her hips. She circled the table, leaned over Max, and waited for my approval. Her breasts brushed Max's arm. He grinned.

She didn't tease. Sarah dared.

I tamed my jealousy with a bottle of wine and fierce devotion to my brothers, but Sarah still devastated my control.

I entertained a fantasy of tossing her over the table, breaking glasses and pitching dishes from my path. I'd rut her right there. Let my brothers watch as I earned her squeals, forced her to come, and filled her with my authority.

Max took her, but I buried myself within her almost immediately, marking her again as mine.

311

Reed had his taste, but I had yet to take her again. It would be rectified.

Sarah hoarded the butter and sipped the last drops of her drink. Reed casually shifted the bottle toward him as she reached for it.

She sighed. "Reed, may I have some more wine?"

"Nope. You'll have to come around."

"You guys are acting like children."

"Most fun I've had since this afternoon." He gave her a grin, dimple and all.

She didn't react, but in her caution, she revealed everything.

After all the deviancies we forced upon her, it was Reed who triggered her shame.

What had he done that drove her to silence? My brother wasn't cruel. My father doubted he'd even touch the girl. How did she convince him to fuck her?

A moment passed. Max scraped his fork against his plate. Reed surrendered and offered a refill.

The stillness laced with a perverted inelegance.

"So." Reed was never one for awkward silences. The wine glugged into her glass. "Which one of us was the best fuck?"

Sarah choked.

"I'm not answering that!"

"Why not?"

"Why *not?*" She covered her face. "Because you guys *forced* me into bed!"

"I'm just curious."

"And you'll stay curious."

Max dropped his fork. The flogger wasn't a usual utensil at our table, but he rubbed the leather anyway. It rested next to his plate. His grin pinned her in place, though she fixed on the weapon.

"I'm curious too," Max said.

Reed folded his arms behind his head, forsaking his dinner. "Come on. What's it gonna hurt? We all had you, so who was the best?"

I didn't speak. Sarah's eyes flicked to me in a moment of weakness before looking anywhere else.

She'd deny me.

That was fine.

All the more reason to return to her tonight and recover what was rightfully mine.

"Stroke your own egos," she said. "You all raped me like fine, upstanding gentlemen."

Reed laughed. "And you liked it."

Max's voice lowered. "Be a good girl and answer the question, and maybe we'll do it again."

I sipped my wine. "There is no *maybe*."

Sarah's shudder didn't go unnoticed. My brothers and I shared the same smile.

The little Atwood, trapped within the Bennett's lair. She tried to hide the tightening of her nipples, the rise of her chest, squirm of her hips. Her puffy lips parted only enough to let the tip of her tongue tease over the plumpness I longed to bite.

"You were all…" Her voice wavered, but not in fear. "Good."

"Just *good?*" Max expected more.

She cleared her throat and sipped her water. The glass condensed, and she rested the chilled goblet over her breast. Her nipple teased harder, a little nub begging for attention.

"Well…Reed was very…" Her eyebrow perked. "*Attentive.*"

Reed grinned, tilting his chair with a cocky flourish. "I aim to please."

Sarah waited for me. I said nothing, gesturing with my wine for her to continue.

"And Max…" She bit her lip. "He was *demanding.*"

The flogger edged into his grip. Sarah exhaled a heated breath.

So she had liked his treatment. My little Sarah, taken in hand.

She was a fragile thing—delicate and timid and perfectly submissive to me. I hadn't needed to be attentive, and I never required a flogger.

When Sarah's hesitant glance fell to me, I knew exactly how she felt about our embrace.

Because I felt it too.

She was *flawless.*

From her whispered breaths to her silken, heated core. Every inch of her body was created for me, and it was by my grace and patience I let my brothers have a fleeting moment with perfection.

No matter how much Reed had offered her, or how intense Max's strikes had been, Sarah Atwood belonged to me.

She knew it.

They knew it.

And she'd never escape me.

"And Nicholas." Sarah flushed. The deeper the pink, the harder I became. "He was…passionate?"

It wasn't the word she meant.

I'd have to correct it. Soon. Just so she understood how *passionate* I was.

"So." Reed leaned in, flashing his dimple. "When do we try again?"

"Classy." Sarah tossed her bread at him. "Eat your dinner."

"Rather eat something else."

"Reed, I swear to God."

"Get used to it, baby." Max shared Reed's enthusiasm. "You got off easy before."

"Stop making puns!"

"Little girl, the fun's just starting."

Sarah tucked a fallen lock of blonde hair behind her ear. If possible, she looked even gentler. A trapped fairy fluttering at our table. But she ignored my brothers.

"You can't keep doing this," she said.

"Why not?" Reed stabbed his steak. "Working so far."

"This isn't *working*. This is insanity. You guys can't keep me here forever."

Max shrugged. "We don't have to. Just until we knock you up."

Sarah said nothing. It wasn't as though she had forgotten the purpose of her stay, but she stiffened like it was the first time she had understood our intentions.

Like it was the first time she considered it.

And she still wasn't afraid.

Why was that?

"It's not going to work." She tried to scold us. "This plan is foolish. And...and cruel. And impractical."

"This will work, provided you are amenable to it," I said.

"Yeah, well..." She attempted diplomacy and failed. "I'm not. This got out of hand. And...we've all done things that I'm sure we'll regret sooner rather than later."

"Doubtful."

"You're working on the takeover, Nick. Once you have the company, you won't have a use for me anymore."

It wasn't true. We needed her more than she understood, more than she could have possibly realized. And I couldn't tell her why.

"Sarah, we'll take care of you," I said. "We'll provide for you, protect you, and ensure you are comfortable. In return, we ask only for your cooperation."

She huffed. "It's not cooperation. You're keeping me prisoner. There's no reason for it. You know I'll do whatever you want to take down Darius, but you don't have to..."

"What?"

"You don't have to rape me anymore."

"Have we ever raped you?"

She touched her collar. "Did you ever give me a choice? You're keeping me here against my will. You've made me drop out of school. Forced me to take a leave of absence from my *job*. You won't even let me leave the grounds."

"And you won't. Not yet."

"Are you listening to yourself?" She appealed to Reed and Max but earned the same silence. "You guys don't understand what you're doing. This plan isn't going to work."

"Why?" A prickling suspicion tingled in my gut. I trusted my instinct in business, and I didn't like how frantic Sarah's breath rumbled in her chest. "What's wrong with our plan?"

"I can't…" Her voice wavered with hesitance. She swore and looked away. "It's insane. You can't hold a woman against her will and *breed* her like savages."

"You said you understood. You promised your submission."

"And you had it for those nights," she said. "I did my part. Now you have to do what's right and help me find evidence of my father's murder."

How was I supposed to find what didn't exist? "Sarah—"

She anticipated my argument. Her hand slammed against the table. "People are going to start questioning where I am. They'll wonder what happened to me, where I've been, and when I'm coming back. How do you plan to fight that?"

Reed shifted. Max gestured for me to field the question.

The family heir had many rights—I just never expected breaking an innocent girl's heart to be one of my responsibilities.

"Your mother has spoken on your behalf," I said. The thought sickened me, but I downed my wine to fortify my resolve. "She's explained the severity of your asthma to your Board of Directors. She convinced them you're still sick and seeking additional help."

"At Darius's request, no doubt."

"Sarah, you sealed your own fate when you revealed the clause in your father's will. You aren't in control anymore, you're a figurehead."

"I'm still in charge."

"Not with the leave of absence. Your Board controls hiring now, and they've begun nominating new candidates for CEO."

"How do you know that?"

"I answer your emails."

Her jaw clenched. "How dare you."

I exhaled. "No one expected you to take the company. Sarah, you're a twenty-year-old girl with no business experience. If a billionaire heiress suddenly drops from the public eye following a family tragedy and severe health issues, no one will question it. Your company, the public? They won't miss you because no one will realize you aren't exactly where you're meant to be."

"You son of a bitch." She kicked away from the table. "I can't believe I ever…"

Trusted me?

Not a single moment passed that I hadn't shared the same disbelief.

She stalked from the dining room. Max and Reed exchanged a glance.

"That could have gone smoother," Max said. "Let's see you fuck her now—get that heir without her kicking the shit out of you."

I silently swore. An aggression wove within me, ignited by the pure instinct rampaging my thoughts. She ran. I would chase. The adrenaline surged. The urge to claim her as my own poisoned me. Everything was at my fingertips. The girl. Both companies. The ultimate wealth.

I could do it.

I could have it all.

But it depended on *her*.

How had the Bennetts fallen so far that our survival depended on our greatest enemy?

But Sarah wasn't her father. She wasn't a monster. She was a beautiful, spirited, unbroken woman who surrendered under my touch and still fought me as though she had an escape.

Or a secret?

The thought burned me. Something gave her courage beyond what she should have possessed. My father terrified her. Our goal disgusted her. And yet she offered herself without a fight.

She accepted us, came for us, even *flirted* with us, and it wasn't because she thought she'd seduce us and learn a family secret that labeled Darius Bennett a murderer. She had something else up her sleeve—even when we ripped the clothing from her.

I tossed my napkin to the table. "Excuse me."

Reed laughed. "She's gonna tear your throat out."

"I'll be on my guard." I hesitated only to drink the rest of my wine in hopes it'd dull the animalistic urge to chase, seize, and dominate.

Sarah dressed before I rapped on her door. She expected my intrusion. As I entered, her robe closed, securing in an ugly knot.

The restraints still tickled her bed, dark leather tempting the delicate pink of her sheets. She followed my gaze.

"Forget it, Nicholas Bennett. You lost that privilege."

"You're lucky we give you the freedom to go unbound."

She pointed to the leash strewn across the bay window. "You want to bind me? Go ahead. It wouldn't surprise me."

"Sarah."

"Do you even understand how fucked up this is?" Her blue eyes paled so beautifully when she was frightened. If I was a better man, I might have taken her in my arms and comforted her against every nightmare I inflicted. "Please tell me you know it isn't right."

"Of course it isn't right. But this is how it has to be."

"Why?"

"We knew this wasn't fair, Sarah."

"I want to go home."

It was the first time she said it. I knew the demand would hurt.

I didn't know how badly.

Her plea twisted, barbed, and bled me like a blade to the side. It wasn't the need in her voice that agonized me. It was my refusal that ripped out our hearts.

"This is your home now."

Sarah gnawed her lip. I'd kiss her if only to spare her quiet whimper. "Don't do this. I told you I would help. I protected your brothers. I gave myself to you. Why are you torturing me when you're so close to taking the Bennett Corporation?"

Because I wasn't anywhere near close enough.

And every moment spent arguing instead of taking her was another second, minute, hour, day, week, month that sped us closer to disaster.

"I have to do this," I said.

"You don't."

"You have no idea what's at stake, Sarah."

"Then *tell me*!" Her frustration caught in her chest. She coughed, harsh and painful. "You haven't told me the full truth."

"Neither have you."

Silence. She stepped back. Her voice hollowed.

"Am I just a prisoner? Am I just someone to breed and toss away? Or...am I...?"

I didn't answer. She braced to run, but I didn't hold her in place. She restrained herself.

"What am I to you?" She whispered. "Honestly, Nick."

What was she?

Everything.

My torment. My salvation. She was the one woman in this world capable of culling my greed, allaying my ambition, and restoring my conscience. She was a delicacy more tempting than money, power, and success.

But she was also the greatest threat to the empire I planned to build, and she had no idea why.

"Dangerous," I said. "You're a danger to everything."

"That's not what I meant."

"You are mine." My voice lowered. "Anything else is irrelevant."

Her breath escaped in a tremble as I touched her cheek. The heat burned my fingertips. She promised a more treacherous warmth, one that would lose me within her forever.

"You have a choice…" Her whisper silenced over my kiss. She eased away as my lips teased her chin, her neck, the hollow of her throat. "I'll offer it once."

"I'll take everything you offer."

She braced against me as I moved to the bed. Her legs locked. I growled low in my throat. She froze, but she wasn't frightened.

"We share something," she said. "You feel it too. A bond. I think that deserves honesty."

"I agree."

Her fingers curled over my arms. She wetted her lip, expecting another kiss.

"I can either be your friend, your step-sister, maybe…*more?*" Her words caught over a word she didn't dare speak. "Or, I can belong to you in that perverted way and fight you with my every breath."

"An ally or a slave?"

"Make a choice, Nick. And you better make the right one."

An Atwood for an ally.

Sarah for a lover.

The perfect woman for something *more*—a relationship full of warmth and compassion, built on a mutual trust. Such a luxury was denied to my family.

Every muscle flexed hard within me.

Who was she to force me to choose?

What power did she think she had?

The thought crushed me. She had the authority. Sarah was everything I wanted.

But if she knew what power she possessed, the revenge she could take, the lives she'd ruin—Sarah would rip out my heart to destroy the Bennetts brick by brick just as she promised.

She could give me every choice, every chance, but it wouldn't change what I had to do.

I had to protect my family.

I had to protect it from her.

And she'd never forgive me.

Her stolen kiss was a moment to savor. She eagerly surrendered, and the heat passed between us in a delicate, peaceful, uncomplicated promise.

I pulled away, only to nibble her bottom lip. She moaned.

It would be the last delight she'd offer willingly.

"You belong to me." My words fell upon her like the strike of a hand. "From now until the day you give me my heir."

It wasn't the illness that took her breath.

I hoped I wouldn't be the one to stop her heart.

"You are mine, Sarah Atwood."

CHAPTER TWENTY-ONE
SARAH

"Are you ready to behave?"

Darius expected an answer? I gnawed over the ball gag—the ugly, horrible, humiliating piece of rubber clenched between my teeth. My jaw ached. My bare chest covered in my drool. Gross.

Darius, of course, loved it.

My step-brothers did nothing to prevent it.

I blinked against the blindfold. It was a good thing I couldn't see them. The trip to the wine cellar wasn't pleasant, and Max's strikes with the flogger layered me in tears.

Was it worth it?

Probably not.

The profanity aimed at Darius hadn't helped me, eased my rage, or moved Nicholas in any profound manner.

The next time I acted out, the next time Darius dared to stroke my breast when we sat down for dinner, I'd plunge a knife through his hand.

The *next time*.

I ground my teeth against the gag. The pain did nothing to quell the rage bubbling within me.

Even I started thinking in terms of *next time*.

Then again, it wasn't hard to imagine a *next time* when my step-family bound, blindfolded, and gagged me, then tossed me naked into a wine cellar. My arms tied over my head and screamed with strain. The flogger's bite did its job, but the chill hurt more.

In two days, my world shifted from delirious pleasures to untold horrors.

My step-brothers hadn't touched me since my fight with Nicholas, but Darius planned many things. I'd be damned if I let any of them near.

"Messy, messy." Darius pulled the gag from my mouth. "Filthy girl. Be good, and we might let you take a bath."

My jaw *hurt*. The blindfold ripped off. Even the gentle light of the wine cellar shocked me. I preferred the darkness over Darius.

"Cold?" He asked. His hands brushed over my goose bumps. The chill of the cellar hardened my nipples. He liked that. I flinched as he squeezed too hard. "Apologize for being naughty, my dear."

I stayed silent. Max approached, twisting the flogger in his hand. Darius nodded. The snap of the leather struck my breasts. I lost my balance, and my arms jerked. The bindings hurt more than the weapon.

Max was too good at this. Reed exhaled, but he said nothing. It was probably for the best. His father could sniff out weakness, and I didn't need his bullshit promises to protect me.

The Bennetts spoke only lies.

Lies and betrayal and hatred.

"Apologize, Sarah." Nicholas checked his watch. "We're on a schedule."

I fought against the chains binding me to the wine case. I'd either rush him or pull the damn shelves down and end my misery.

I refused to look at him.

I loathed the caramel rumble of his voice. I hated his penetrating eyes searching my body.

He allowed his father to rage over me.

What the hell happened to the Nicholas who woke me with whispers and promises? The Nick who rushed into my shower and took me in the scalding water in passionate, conquering lust?

How did he possess me with such unrelenting desire...and then toss me away?

Why the hell had I ever let him get that close?

I offered him a part of me. I warmed with the possibility of a connection more secure than chains and stronger than lust.

And I thought—I felt—as though he would understand. We were both heirs. We fell to the mercy of our families and the burdens that encompassed such honors. I thought he would help me.

But Bennetts only helped themselves.

The damn room was too cold. I shivered, and my mouth dried. I was hungry and thirsty. How long did they keep me tied up? Hours? It had to be.

But I'd survive it. Their cruelty burned through my confusion. I was finally thinking clearly.

My stomach threatened to heave as Darius spanked my ass. His fingers dug into my soft flesh.

"Tell Daddy you're sorry."

Oh, he was a freak.

His little incest perversion was getting weirder. Darius got off on it, and every time I reacted to the terms it made the game more fun for him.

"You aren't my father," I whispered. "Get away from me."

"But I am your father now, my dear." His excitement turned lecherous. "Did you disappoint Mark the way you disappoint me?"

"Let me go."

"Good thing he's dead." Darius stared at the crest between my legs. "Imagine how he'd react if he knew you were too busy getting fucked by your brothers to manage his company."

I yelled, but the flogger bit before Darius raised a hand. The tears came too fast.

"Apologize, girl," Darius said.

I hated myself. I hated him.

"Sorry."

"Sorry, *what?*"

I wished to be gagged again. "Sorry, sir."

Darius laughed. "Oh, nothing that formal, my dear. Try again."

My stomach rolled. Reed and Max shifted, but Nicholas didn't react.

Heartless fucking bastard.

"Sorry...*Dad.*"

"Good girl."

I shivered again. Uncontrollable. I'd throw up, but they hadn't given me anything to eat since I mouthed off. Max released the restraints on my wrists. My arms fell, and, as the blood trickled into them, I crumpled in half, cowering to ease the pain.

Darius kicked my side. "Get up," he said. "We'll let you rest."

A kindness?

No way. Darius set only traps.

I refused Reed's hand and struggled to my feet. My chest tightened from the constant pressure of the bindings holding my arms up. I longed to grip my inhaler, just to be prepared and know I had it under control. I bit my lip instead.

I'd never ask for it. No sense degrading myself twice.

They led me up the stairs. I stole a towel and cleaned my chin and chest from what I drooled over the gag. Darius prevented my escape upstairs. He pinched a nerve above my elbow and ordered me into the nearest powder room.

He pushed me inside. My heart thundered. He reached into his pocket, and I expected a gun.

"My dear, if you would." Darius handed me a pink box. "Quickly now."

It wasn't a weapon. I flipped the box over.

"You've got to be kidding me."

The pregnancy test was name brand and guaranteed for early results.

"Forget it," I said.

Darius grabbed my hair. He threw me into the wall and sneered as I lost my balance. I crumpled to the floor. He pitched the test at my chest.

"My sons' part in this is done," Darius said. He pointed to my step-brothers, lingering in the hall. "They fucked and seeded you. Let's see if you've done your job."

"You are all insane," I said. "Let me out of here."

"Sarah, my dear. We are only asking for a little cooperation."

That word again.

They asked for my pride, my dignity, and my family's lasting legacy.

They deserved none of it.

"You will take this test, or my sons will bind you to the floor and fuck you until you're raw, bruised, and visibly swelling with a child. That might take some time."

I hoped he didn't see me tremble.

"One of these options is more pleasant than the other." He smiled. "If not as satisfying."

He would order them to do it. And I knew, with every betraying confidence, he'd earn their obedience. I'd fight. They'd overpower me. Max would beat me, Reed would endanger himself to save me, and Nicholas would drive me to the brink of insanity, wrapped in his heat, scent, and cruelty.

And it wouldn't be like the last time I offered myself.

No surrendering. No kindness. No...desiring them.

It'd hurt.

And I didn't want to hurt anymore. I wanted time to rest, to plan, and to hide in the darkness for a few minutes.

I wanted my heart to stop breaking.

I shrugged. "Fine. I'll take it."

Darius didn't move. Neither did my step-brothers. I exhaled.

"I said I'll take it." I stared at the box. "Give me a minute to figure it out. I've never taken one before."

Reed snickered. "You pee on it."

"Thanks."

Darius bowed his head. "We'll wait."

The cold shock pitted inside me.

Oh, God. No way. He didn't think that he'd *stay*?

I cleared my throat. "I need my…privacy."

"No, you don't."

The box crushed under my hand. "I *agreed*."

"So take the test."

What the hell was wrong with this family? "Not…in front of you!"

"How else will we be assured you've taken it properly?"

I'd throw up before I did…that in front of an audience. In front of my *step-family*.

In front of Nicholas.

I shivered. This was worse than the beatings and the bindings, the gags and even being restrained for my first experience with a man. The fear prickled through me.

I swallowed the tremble in my voice.

"We're waiting," Darius said. He reveled in my discomfort. "You were in the cellar for hours. I assumed you'd be grateful to use the facilities like a civilized woman instead of a pet whore."

No end existed for their depravity. No matter how hard I fought, how badly I struggled to preserve even a fraction of my pride, the Bennetts sensed my weaknesses.

I did *not* want to do this.

What kind of a man forced a woman to humiliate herself in such a way?

I had even allowed them to touch me. My skin crawled.

Never again.

"Fine."

Darius nodded. I ripped open the cardboard and pulled the test kit. The box and wrapper pitched into the garbage. I clutched the applicator.

How was I supposed to do this?

It was beyond mortification. It'd be a moment of utter, horrid submission to a perversion I didn't think existed beyond the far corners of the internet.

But at least it'd be quick, and it'd be over, and they would be disappointed.

That gave me a little courage, despite the bile threatening my pride.

Darius expected this to be the end. I was fucked by three men during a dangerous time of the month and filled by them all. The test should have been the final blow. Dehumanize me, strip my privacy.

He'd watch as I suffered through taking the test then crumbled at the result.

But only because he thought I was pregnant.

Maybe after the shock wore off, I'd jam the damn stick down his throat.

Reed had the decency to look away. Max braced with the flogger like I'd make a break for it.

And Nicholas?

He watched.

He waited for this exact moment since the first day he kidnapped me.

He *wanted* me to be pregnant, needed it badly as his father did. And why not? I was nothing to him but a name and a womb. Not Sarah, but Atwood. Not lover, but woman.

My weakness for him, the momentary break where I thought I might have *trusted* a Bennett, still gave him power over me.

Nicholas Bennett sold his soul to steal my family's fortune.

I waited for his moment of sweet disappointment.

My fingers trembled over the applicator. A creeping blush pinkened parts of me I didn't know could reveal my embarrassment.

"Get on with it." Darius clutched the door frame.

I had no way to hide. I took a breath before an attack made it more sickening.

I sat and hated my nudity.

They waited. Eager. Desperate.

I pinched my eyes shut and tried to think of anything but how the gentle trickle sealed some sort of perverted, horrible fate with the Bennetts. It was worse than the bindings. Worse than threatened rape, than Darius's touch.

I didn't mean for the light sob to escape—more a fit of anger than genuine shame. But it happened, and I couldn't take it back. I finished, cleaned, and stood, pitching the applicator onto the counter and slamming a hand against the handle.

"Two minutes," Darius said. "Easy, my dear. This might be a happy occasion."

It would be.

For me.

I washed my trembling hands, pretending not to notice how close the Bennetts crowded within the doorway to the powder room.

I also ignored the stick. The box. The instructions. Even the time. Reed counted, though his silent numbers audibly rushed toward the end. He nudged Nicholas.

"Okay," he said. "Check it."

I didn't help. Nicholas edged in front of his father. His eyes caught mine in the mirror.

I rewarded the false warmth of his golden gaze with a knowing perk of my eyebrow.

"Negative," he said.

My mouth dropped in mock surprise. "*Really*? No way?"

"*Negative*?" Darius ripped the applicator from his son's hand. "How the hell is that possible. All three of you fucked her."

I sighed. "Well, you know how these things go."

The men stood in a stunned silence. I escaped from the powder room and shrugged.

"There's a lot of things that factor into it. Stress and diet and environment. Sometimes getting raped repeatedly by your own brothers just won't do it."

"Enough," Nicholas said. "We'll take another one in a few days. It's still early."

He didn't understand. He didn't *want* to understand.

"I'll piss on everything you give me, Nicholas Bennett, it won't change a thing."

Darius checked his watch. "Nicholas, handle this. I have a meeting."

I grinned as my step-father bristled, stomping from the room. I called after him with a sweet smile.

"Bye, *Dad.*"

"Jesus Christ." Nicholas took my hand. I jerked, but he hauled me into the smoking room. He hissed at Max and Reed, and they chased after Darius.

I fought him, but Nicholas tossed me on the couch and covered me with a blanket. The door slammed shut. His mocha voice strained over an ill-concealed anger.

"Are you insane? My father looks for reasons to hurt you!"

"Everyone's hurt me lately." I wrapped the blanket over my breasts. "Why shouldn't Darius have a chance too?"

"Don't tempt him. It's dangerous."

"Dangerous enough that he'd beat me, strip me, and force his sons upon me?" I waited for Nicholas to show one ounce of remorse. That damn stillness. He'd turn to stone before betraying what he thought. "I think I understand just how dangerous he is."

"You give him a chance, and he will burn you alive, Sarah."

"Then why doesn't he?"

"Because you're still useful to us. He threw you in a sixty degree cellar for *three* hours today because you insulted him. And that's him holding back."

I curled my arms over the blanket. The fuzzy warmth calmed me, hiding everything Nicholas had seen, touched, and taken before I realized I slept with the devil.

"You said it yourself. He's going to keep me alive. He wants my *child.*"

"No. He's punishing the Atwoods. Breeding you is just part of his sadism."

I gritted my teeth. "Hasn't he already done enough? I'm trapped here. My brothers are dead. He killed my father."

"He never touched your father."

Liar.

The son of a bitch liar looked me directly in the eyes with a cinnamon promise and melting voice and *lied to me.*

He had no shame, no honor, no dignity.

There wasn't a profanity strong enough.

"He didn't murder your father, Sarah," Nicholas said.

My chest tightened, stealing my words from me. That was good. He didn't deserve a single sound from my lips.

"Do you want to know how your father died? Do you *really* want to know?"

Nicholas leaned in, his arms pressing into the sofa. He trapped me and still spoke lies.

"Your father died from *natural* causes. He died because he had complications from the cancer."

"How dare you."

"He *died*," Nicholas continued, "because he was an old man who endured more chemotherapy than he could withstand. He went into remission, but he died because his body was *weakened*."

"That's not true."

"You are looking for someone to blame. You've imagined every way you could pin his death on the Bennetts."

"Because Darius killed him!"

"No. That's not the reason." Nicholas stared at me, through me, into me. "You weren't as close to your father as you thought you were."

"Let me up."

"He didn't love you as much as you loved him."

I yelled, but my voice broke. "How dare you!"

"Mark Atwood didn't name you in his will. He passed every *cent* of the family's fortune to his *sons*."

"They were older than me!"

"But he wrote no provision for you. No trusts. Nothing! He left the money, company, and land to Josiah and Michael. He let them decide if you were worth a pittance."

"You have no idea what you're talking about."

"He had plans for you. Just like my father had plans for me and my brothers. You were meant for R&D. Always. He put you in science camps and tutoring. He forced you to choose genetics as your field of study."

"He didn't force me," I said.

"You did it because *he* wanted you to. Because you did everything to get noticed by your father, and he paid absolutely no attention to you beyond what he could profit."

"I don't have to listen to this."

Nicholas frowned. "If you knew what he had planned for your research? What he already did? You wouldn't have stepped foot in that lab. You'd be *relieved* my father stole your research journal."

The pain in my chest was more than just the asthma catching my breath. I accidentally clutched my neck. Nicholas pulled a spare inhaler from his pocket. He held it up before handing it to me.

"Your father hid your asthma. Why?"

I didn't take a hit of the medicine. "Because it was *my* illness. Why share what weakens us?"

"He was ashamed of you."

"I swear to God, if you don't stop talking *right now*—"

"Mark Atwood wanted a son," he said. "A third son. To mirror the Bennetts. Instead he had you. He made do with what he was given."

"My father loved me."

"He was incapable of love."

"What the hell would a Bennett know about compassion?" My lungs would crush before they allowed a scream. I tried anyway. "You're a monster, Nick. You're twisting his memory."

"He was twisted when he was alive."

I trembled. Everywhere. Why didn't he just beat me? Hurt me? Break my heart again?

Anything but this.

"You're lying," I said. "Every word is a lie. You're trying to confuse me, but I know Darius killed my father."

"I wish he had."

I slapped him. Nicholas didn't react. He took my hand, and I whimpered in rage and fear and a helpless urge to strike him again.

"My father isn't the murderer." His voice lowered. "Yours is."

I stilled. Both of us heaved useless breaths. I shook my head.

"What are you talking about?"

"Mark Atwood is a murderer."

"That's not true."

The gold in his eyes faded into a murky, dire sorrow that coated me in forlorn misery. I lost him in that moment, a memory that stole him to a place that frightened him more than his father.

"Mark Atwood murdered my mother."

He should have just struck me. I gripped the couch.

The Bennetts never told the truth. They never followed through on their words. He was lying.

He had to be.

"I was twelve years old. Max was ten. Reed eight. We weren't supposed to be in the car with her."

"*Car?*"

"The crash took her life and nearly killed my brothers as well."

"I don't understand. How did my father murder your mother if she died in a car crash?"

Nicholas didn't hesitate. Sincerity frosted his voice. "He paid a laborer from your farm to sever the break line. Once the job was done, Mark reported him as one of the many illegal day workers under your employ and had him deported."

"Bullshit."

"We didn't realize the car was compromised until she hit the highway. By that point, there was nothing we could do." A soft echo of pain shadowed his words. I didn't want to listen anymore. "The car flipped twice before landing in an embankment. I was thrown clear. My brothers weren't as lucky."

I tried to escape. He held me against the sofa.

"I saved Max first because he screamed the most."

"Oh, God."

"I dove into the wreckage and chiseled my brother from between the seats. His leg was pinned and turned to jelly. It dislocated as I pulled him out." His voice hollowed. "He never passed out. Not even when the paramedics vomited in the grass after realizing every bone in his right leg was pulverized."

Christ.

Max's limp. The crash. His plans for the military.

"Reed was trapped. His face broke through the glass. He had major lacerations, so bad I could see his jaw through his cheek. He went into shock before I even got him out of his seatbelt. Nearly died on the way to the hospital." He paused. "Ask him how many plastic surgeons we saw before they could piece his face together well enough for him to smile."

God. Reed only had one dimple. The scars had faded, but I hadn't asked how he got them.

Nicholas's pain manifested in a quiet anger. I trembled in his silence.

He was a good liar. A really good liar.

He had to be *lying*.

"And my mother…" He heaved a breath. "I saved my brothers before going after her because she would have wanted me to help them before her. It was how I was raised. I was the oldest, and I had a responsibility to take care of them."

I couldn't handle any more. He didn't let me look away.

"The car caught on fire before I could free her, and the flames spread too fast for me to do anything. I didn't get close before it was engulfed." He hesitated but forced through the memory. "I heard her screaming."

"Oh god, Nick. I'm so sorry."

"I don't need an Atwood's pity."

"It's not pity." I said. "It's sympathy. No one should have to experience that."

A shaking breath rattled his body before exhaling into nothing.

"Your father was evil and heartless," he said. "He murdered my mother, and it still wasn't enough. Everything he did was meant to hurt my family."

"I'm sorry about your mother," I whispered. "But my father wasn't the man you're saying he is."

"I'm not wasting my breath convincing you. What happened, happened. Nothing can change it."

Callous. Cold. Like all the Bennetts.

"And if it is true?" I let the question linger. "Does that justify what you're doing to me?"

Nicholas hesitated. The pain in his expression mirrored mine. I clutched the inhaler.

I wished I could hold him instead.

"It has to."

A final strike. My heart thudded in hope only to shatter upon his cruelty. Nicholas said nothing else. He rose and left me to my medication. At least he knew not to ask if the tightness in my chest was the illness or the agony of his total abandonment.

"Sarah, for Christ's sake."

Dad stole the inhaler from my hand and pitched it into the living room. The few engineers he guided into his office flinched as the case shattered against the wall.

"We're Atwoods. We don't wheeze. Do that somewhere no one can see."

Mike picked up the inhaler and tugged me from Dad's meeting and into the bathroom where the cigarette smoke hadn't permeated.

"Don't worry, Sprout." Mike winked at me. "One day, I'll be in charge. And you can huff and puff anywhere you want."

I wasted the medicine on a sob.

The second dose helped, but it didn't ease the grinding nausea eroding my stomach. I held tight to the blanket.

Nicholas Bennett was a liar.

He hadn't helped me, he hadn't protected me, and he used me only for his own gain.

I couldn't believe a word he said. I wouldn't. Not when everything that happened to me within their grasp was meant to break my spirit.

It hadn't worked.

He hadn't won, even after he and his brothers took turns attempting to ruin me.

I lived, and I would keep on living because Nicholas Bennett was a *liar*.

I wouldn't believe his deception.

Not when I endured everything they stole, abused, and hurt to defend the name of a monster.

CHAPTER TWENTY-TWO
SARAH

I'd never find evidence that Darius killed my father.

Nothing incriminating existed in the Bennett Estate. The only crimes within its walls were the ones they did to me.

The ones I did to myself.

I thought I could handle it. I imagined walking into a den of depraved beasts and staring evil in the eye until I got the answers I wanted and the respect I deserved.

Hard lessons.

I wouldn't discover a bloody weapon in Darius's drawers, but the Bennetts obsessed over something else. The company. Wealth. My family.

Maybe I wouldn't find proof of murder, but money was just as damning. I had to follow that trail.

It was the only option I had left.

I snuck through the estate, ensuring Max's suite door was pushed tightly closed before I edged into the theater. The Playstation 4 had an internet browser. Something the Bennetts obviously didn't remember.

I hadn't had a chance to use the console alone, and I counted the seconds it took to power on. I swore at the damn controller as the cursor inched across the screen and typed the URL character by aching character.

I held my breath. The email client popped up. I checked the clock. I probably had less than ten minutes to get my answers and rush back to the room before they realized I had access to the outside world. I couldn't imagine the punishment if they caught me.

Of all the people in the world to contact, I emailed my lawyer.

God, I was getting corporate.

Anthony, I need everything on Josmik Holdings. Now. –S

Radio silence was not conducive to a proper attorney/client relationship. Anthony's response came immediately.

S—Are you safe? Your mother said you were staying with the Bennetts. I can be there by the afternoon to get you home. –A

Anthony had a sixth sense for danger. Usually it worked well in negotiations, but I couldn't let him jeopardize my mother's safety to rescue me from Darius's torment.

A—I've got it under control. Don't come. Need an answer –S

We wasted time. I jiggled the controller and begged the screen for something to pop up.

S—Nothing's available to us. Whatever deal your brothers made existed outside my firm. Got information on a secret trust. They didn't want you to know.–A

The hairs on my neck rose. Something lurked within Josmik holdings that terrified every one of the Bennetts. So why did my brothers hide it from me?

A—The Bennetts have more information on Josmik than us. They know something. Why?—S

The email replied immediately.

S—They must be involved in the trust. Your brothers were working on a business plan—I don't know what. They disregarded most of my advice after your father died.—A

Damn. I thumped my head against the controller.

I had another question, but each press of the letters twisted me into a greater knot. I stole my inhaler from my pocket before I pressed send. I preferred the tight coughing over the dread clutching my chest.

A—Helena Bennett died in a car crash in 1998. Do you know anything about it?—S

I refreshed the browser twice. Three times. Nothing returned. I checked the time. My step-family never wasted the day, not when there was money to earn. Each second past seven o'clock gave them cause to look for me. I refreshed again, my heart stalling as the email appeared.

Sarah—I don't advise questions of that nature. Forget you asked it.

Like hell. I responded quick.

Why?

I held my breath until the email flashed.

Because you won't like what you find.—A

"Goddamn it."

I tossed the controller.

I didn't trust Nicholas Bennett, his brothers, or his father, but Anthony? My father relied more on our attorney than his damn oncologists.

Sickness washed over me. I flipped the Playstation off and rushed from the theater, bolting to my room just as my stomach heaved. I fell to the bathroom floor.

My father—a murderer?

It wasn't possible. My father wasn't terribly kind, but he didn't have time for kindness. He worked hard for the company—for the family. There wasn't a crime in that.

And he hated the Bennetts, but he would *never* have tried to murder them.

Not a woman.

Certainly not her young children.

No one could be that evil.

The memory buried deep. My mother rushing into my room when I was little. Three, not even four years old. Mike and Josiah tagged along, sleepy and irritable.

"Up, Sarah. Get up." Mom sang Grandma's milking song for the cows to get me out of bed. "We have to go. Off the farm."

But I liked the farm. She tugged a little book bag filled with clothes over my shoulders and told me we were going on vacation.

I yelled and stomped and ran from her. She shouted, but Dad welcomed me with open arms. Mom hurried after me with tear-stained cheeks and a flurry of angry words I wasn't allowed to repeat.

"Take your sister." Dad pushed me at Josiah. "Beth, we need to talk."

"It's on the news," she spat. "She's dead."

The door slammed. Mike covered my ears as the smack echoed and Mom yelped.

Dad's voice carried.

"Good."

I threw up again as someone's steps echoed against the tile. I didn't bother hiding.

"Go away, Nick."

It wasn't Nicholas.

"Your sickness might have been a good sign had I not seen the test, my dear." Darius waited as I struggled to my feet.

My stomach heaved again. "What do you want?"

He wetted a washcloth with warm water and passed it to me. I took it, hesitantly.

"Do you want to know the truth about your father?" He asked.

My throat closed. What kind of trick was this?

I met his toad brown eyes and shook my head.

"I don't trust a word you say."

Darius tugged on the sleeves of his suit, adjusting the diamond cufflinks that he wore even within the privacy of his own home.

"Get dressed."

Not the order I expected from him. "Why?"

"Because you're coming with me today."

"Where?"

His smile trembled my gut. "We're going to the Bennett Corporation Headquarters. I have something to show you."

I shook my head. "I'm fine here."

"Do you want to know the real Mark Atwood?" Darius buttoned his suit. "You have ten minutes to get ready before I rescind my offer. Dress professionally, Sarah. You're representing your family."

Damn it.

Was he serious? He'd take me to the main office? Why?

The answer hit me harder than any of his strikes.

We'd be alone.

Separated from my step-brothers.

Away from Nicholas's intervention, Max's promised abuse, and Reed's kindness.

He bribed me with secrets about my family, but I feared he'd lead me straight into hell.

Anthony's warning and Nicholas's revelation churned my stomach. I was certain—absolutely certain—Darius was responsible for Dad's death. But now? A creeping fear punctured through me.

Christ.

What if I was wrong?

What if I was taken and fucked, seduced and abused for...*nothing*?

The sickness returned. I didn't let it out. I pushed beyond Darius and dove for my wardrobe.

He handed me the outfit he preferred. The skirt did nothing to settle my stomach.

But I had only one way to find out what happened. One way to end the insanity. I'd give Darius one opportunity to tell me the truth, and God help him if he lied.

I wasn't fighting for my father's legacy anymore.

I'd thrive on my own revenge.

I didn't trust Darius, but I followed him to the limo parked outside. He answered a call as soon as the driver had his instructions. I scrunched in my seat as far from him as I could without offering him the satisfaction of watching me squirm.

The road twisted and turned for miles without pavement markings. No cars rumbled near for twenty minutes, and every mile traveled within the wilderness stole another flake of my courage. Darius probably hoped I'd be demoralized by the distance, the isolation.

The joke was on him. I wrecked my own confidence, dashed upon a foolish belief that I could protect myself from his demons.

His phone buzzed again. He brushed a finger over my arm.

"She's with me." He hummed. "Consider it a…bring your daughter to work day."

"Get off of me," I hissed.

Darius smirked and ended his call. "Your brother. Checking up on you."

I didn't ask which one. It didn't matter. I guessed. Darius sneered.

"You fucked him more than once, didn't you, you little slut?"

I didn't answer.

He chuckled. "Thought you could ensnare him? Thought you'd seduce him, and he'd fall in love with you and release you from our custody?"

"*Seduce* him? If I recall …" I threaded my words in bitterness. "I was the one tied to the bed."

"He doesn't care for you, and he never will. You are nothing but a cunt for Nicholas to fuck."

So I learned.

I didn't react.

"You weren't impregnated this month, my dear." Darius looped a lock of my hair behind my ear. "But I assure you, my sons were raised with Bennett ambition. We always get what we want."

I had no reason to doubt him, especially as his eldest son stood at his side. Nicholas could rot in hell, but he was still an ally. I said nothing about our encounters. It'd kill me, but I'd protect him as long as he stole the Bennett Corporation and humiliated his father.

The ride to San Jose prickled with an unsavory silence. I ignored Darius as he answered emails and took calls, but his attention wasn't on his cell. He stared at me. Searched over my curves. Shifted against the bulge in his pants as we drew nearer to the headquarters.

No matter how much I hated my step-brothers, their desire had been just that. Desire. And in my moments of weakness, I shared it.

But everything Darius did, every word he said, and every breath he took riddled with bestial sadism. The limo parked, and he attempted to take my hand. I leapt out as the driver opened the door.

The Bennett Corporation compound was housed on its own plot of land in the middle of the city—a five story complex of modern architecture and classy design. Enough people wandered the street to make escaping easy, especially as a police officer parked one block away.

Darius took my elbow and squeezed.

"It would be unwise," he whispered. "Painful to you, and certainly a tragedy on your poor mother. Come with me. Don't make me regret this trust."

I didn't trust him, but I still followed.

A marbled and ostentatious foyer welcomed us into the heart of the Bennett Corporation. Artificial light and chlorine kissed fountains decorated the lobby. The ceilings stretched multiple stories, but they painted it a fake blue. Suits and ties and heels and skirts filled the morning rush of employees to their offices. A stale whiff of coffee permeated from the kiosk parked within an imitation jungle of ferns and flowers.

Was everything the Bennetts touched fake?

When my family went to work, they toiled outside, in the real plants under an honest blue sky and prayed for the water that freely tumbled from the Bennetts' fountain.

Then again, my father spent more and more time trapped in our company's offices. And I hadn't touched soil in years—not when most of my experiments were conducted within the RNA of the crop, not in tilled dirt.

Darius reserved a private elevator as CEO and owner. He pulled me inside, ignoring the nods and well-wished good mornings from his employees. I shuddered as he refused to release my hand.

The elevator moved too slowly. I studied the mirrored panels.

I was still bruised—pale and tiny next to the greying demon that possessed enough strength to overpower me and reveal my rage and grief and damning emotions I tried to hide.

The doors opened. The silence of his private floor descended like another gag stuffed in my mouth. My skin brushed with goose bumps, and every rational thought barraged my head with warnings to stay tucked within the elevator.

"Come with me, my dear." Darius bargained with blood. "You'll appreciate this."

I swallowed, immediately regretting the breath that refused to squeeze from my lungs.

Our steps echoed in the vast hall, and Darius led me to the thick, spanning door that sealed me inside his office. The sterile space existed only for efficiency and business. The windows spanned the entire office, but the stark light that trickled in fell cold upon the black leather furniture.

He offered me a seat before the sprawling executive desk.

He claimed the throne behind it.

And smiled.

"It's been some time since an Atwood graced my office," Darius said.

"I'm here. Let's talk."

He didn't offer me coffee or water. His phone blinked on do-not-disturb. I winced as I realized how tightly I crossed my legs.

"I wish to...clear my name," Darius said. "You believe I am responsible for Mark Atwood's death."

"Yes." I stated it strongly, even as the conviction faded in my head.

"I didn't."

I expected as much.

"Nicholas told you about his mother?"

I ground my jaw. "He said that my father hired the man who severed her car's break line."

"It's true."

"Do you have proof?"

Darius folded his hands. "If I had enough to convict him, he'd be in jail now, rotting away for taking my wife and nearly murdering my sons."

"I can't prove you killed my dad, and you can't prove he killed your wife," I said. "What's the point of this? It's getting us nowhere."

"My dear, I told you. I wish to clear my name." Darius stared at me. "And to damn his."

He ruffled through a file next to his desk and offered me candid pictures of a farm. Photos of alfalfa and corn, potatoes and onions— each plant thriving in a cracked soil that shouldn't have sustained such quality. He allowed me to read the documentation attached to the file.

"Transgenetic drought-resistant crops grown on an African farming collective." I flipped the page. "This is a non-profit project?"

Darius nodded. "Keep reading."

The scientific journals revealed the program's experiments into a specific genome of the plants they cultivated. My heart fluttered at their results.

Hearty plants, durable crops, seeds that'd withstand arid climates and a product relatively unscathed by the harsh conditions of its growth.

"Similar to your research?" Darius asked.

I wouldn't rise to his challenge.

"Similar, but not exact," I said. "It's what I planned to study when I finished my degree."

"Yes, it is." Darius absently studied a photo. "Your father realized it."

"My father was always interested in my research."

"No, my dear," Darius laughed. "He was interested in *progress. Profit.* Your research was secondary to his goals."

"You don't know anything about my father. He committed to R&D because he understood the environmental threats facing the agricultural business in the west."

"Spun better than a PR department," he chuckled. "Your father cared only for his own business and farm. Everything he did and every penny he spent was meant to profit only the Atwoods."

"This research," I tapped the folder, "and the experiments I did? It'd help everybody."

"He didn't help anyone, only himself." Darius pulled another folder from his desk. "This should be illuminating."

I opened the folder.

My heart sunk.

"One of your father's first initiatives was forging an R&D team to study, create, and *patent* specific genes that would benefit his company. Once the genes were secured and the product created and the money tucked safely within his bank account, he ensured no other laboratory studied anything similar to what he patented." Darius took a great satisfaction in my trembling. "How many of Atwood's development products are actually on the market?"

None. I cleared my throat.

"It wasn't part of our business plan," I said. "The past few years we focused on the water shortages and droughts. My father got sick, and we didn't have the initiative we needed to…to…"

"Benefit every farmer in southern California? To offer products and produce that would revolutionize agriculture?"

"The science was new. My father didn't understand it."

"Yes, he did. Your father knew exactly what the science meant. And that's why he squashed it."

The folder trembled in my hand. I continued reading.

The farming collective with their beautiful plants and healthy, lovely vegetables.

Sued and dismantled for *patent violations.*

I thumbed through the rest of the papers. Not just one project squashed.

Dozens.

Non-profit companies and university research.

Small labs and large industries.

Individuals.

Charities.

When someone researched anything even remotely similar to our patents and developments, Dad descended with an army of lawyers and dozens of lawsuits claiming our work had been *infringed.*

The most recent suit stabbed through my chest. The African initiative—a non-profit attempting to stop hunger and grant sustainability to rural and desperate villages—sued, dismantled, and pending restitution.

Dad cited *my* research as the cause to shut them down.

He used *my* name.

"Your father knew the value of that research. He also knew how pivotal it would become." Darius leaned over the desk. "But why release a revolutionary product before the market is sufficiently desperate?"

"No." I seized a breath. "This was just…protecting the research. He wouldn't have hid it. He was sick. He couldn't take on this many projects. But if he hadn't died—"

"Sarah, he planned to sit on your projects and the science that would literally save hundreds of thousands of lives from hunger."

"It's not true."

"Like a proper businessman, Mark Atwood knew he'd earn more from the products when they were *in demand.* Ever wonder why your father invested *so much* in political super PACs and organizations? Those groups lobbied for farmers' tax breaks, subsidies, and all the irrigation water they needed to drown their drought-ridden lands with water-demanding crops despite the harsh environment not supporting their product."

Darius plucked the folder from my hands and replaced it in his desk. "Your father planned to wring southern California dry, profit from the crops he sent overseas to rot in storage, and patent and hide the one solution that would ease the demand on the environment and provide hungry people around the world the means to feed themselves."

I trembled.

"Sarah!" Dad was mad. I hid in the doorway. He'd shout just as loudly if I approached his desk or waited in my room. "You worked on our research in the university lab!"

Only once. I entered the results, that was all. Dad raged, running his hand over a bald head. He forgot he lost his hair to the chemo last week.

"It was just an Excel sheet," I said. "I'm sorry, Dad."

"Never take our work out of the lab!" He didn't have the energy to slam a fist on the table. He could hardly even raise his voice. "If the school finds it—"

"They won't."

"If they find it, they'll claim it for themselves. Any work done within the University is their property! You could have cost this family millions, Sarah! Billions!"

"I…I didn't mean to."

"You never mean to." He sighed. "Sarah, I don't know how you're ever going to help this family when I'm gone."

"Dad, you aren't dying."

"Good. Because I certainly can't trust you, now can I?"

"You can. I promise."

He waved a shaking hand. "It's fine, Sprout. I should have expected this. Just be more careful and go to bed."

I didn't let him see me cry.

"I'm sorry, Dad. I love you."

"Yeah. Goodnight."

Darius's smile only grew.

"Your father was *ruthless*, my dear. He was violent. Vindictive. And he was obsessed with my family. The car crash was only one opportunity he took to harm us. Our warehouses were constantly damaged with vandalism and violence. One of his migrant workers was to be charged after he attempted arson on a *fertilizer* factory in Texas. Do you know what happened when he was arrested?"

My voice weakened. "My father had him deported too?"

"Your father had him murdered in his jail cell."

No.

I clutched the arm of the chair as Darius laughed.

"You didn't know your father at all, did you, my dear?"

I closed my eyes. It didn't help. The room swirled and tilted, and I suffered through a wavering breath that did nothing to ease the strain building in my chest.

Was it true? Nicholas's pain was too real, and Anthony's warning too abrupt.

I searched through reluctant memories.

Dad's late nights at the office.

The patents he forced me to file.

Mom's arguments. The time she tried to leave. The black eye when he didn't let her.

He taught me nothing about the business.

He never included me in meetings.

He posed for pictures only with Josiah and Mike.

He hadn't named me in his will.

God. What the hell had I done?

I adopted his work ethic and ambition, but I inherited something worse. His *hatred*. I shared his every loathing heartbeat for the Bennetts, and, in my blindness, I trapped myself in their grasp.

Darius rose from the desk. He circled behind me, but I didn't notice until his hands rested upon my shoulders.

The goose bumps returned. I shrugged, but it didn't cast him away.

"I understand. It's difficult to hear."

And he loved every second of my torment. The breaking of my heart was a far more effective punishment than any gag or flogger or bindings.

His fingers pressed hard.

I stiffened.

"And now you see why we have taken you in. Given you a new family."

I swallowed. "Don't twist it. You kidnapped me."

"Only to do what must be done." He petted my hair. "Your father spent his life attempting to suppress the Bennett Corporation. It's time we had our revenge and take what is due to us."

"Your fight was with him. I've done nothing to your family."

"Sins of the father…" Darius chuckled. "My dear, I've been lenient with you, if only because I anticipated it would be difficult for such a young girl to understand her new place in this family." His fingers dug into me. "No longer, Sarah. You have a very important role to play for my sons, and I will not accept any further disobedience."

"If you think I'll let any of this happen without a fight, you're as insane as you are cruel."

"Cruel? I haven't been cruel *yet*."

I didn't have time to prepare. The backhand blinded me. I stumbled, but Darius caught me before I tumbled from the chair.

It wasn't a kindness.

He forced me over his desk.

The shock of the wood struck under my lungs, prying the air from me in a painful wretch. Darius pulled my hair and slammed my head against the desk as I twisted to escape.

The slam blitzed me with pain. I stilled. Blinked. Heaved.

Nothing came out.

A darkness warred with the light from his windows.

"Since the beginning, you've been a nuisance in my household," Darius hissed. "I've given you too much freedom, and you've bewitched my sons. They've taken pity on you. It ends now."

"Maybe your sons aren't monsters."

"Maybe they didn't fuck you enough." Darius's strike wasn't a spank. He meant to hurt. I lurched over the desk, but he spoke over my shout. "Your life is going to change, Sarah. We were benevolent, but you didn't show the proper gratitude."

"You beat me."

"I didn't kill you." He leaned over me, his breath foul against my face. "I offer you my generosity, and in return? You refused to give me a grandson. That disappoints me."

"Get used to it."

"I will not rest until you are swollen, broken, and pregnant."

"I'll kill you before that happens."

"Like father, like daughter." He sighed. "You only respond to violence."

His hands groped my hips. His touch was nothing like the gentle brush of his sons' exploration. He gripped me.

The sickness rose again. I batted his hands away with a shriek. He ripped my hair back.

"You've been a naughty girl, my dear." Darius slapped my ass again, eager to listen for my screaming. I didn't recognize my fear or my frantic cries when he pitched my skirt up and pulled my panties to my knees. "Your father should have taught you better manners. Not to worry. Your new Daddy will help you become a proper little whore."

I fought against the desk but earned only another brutal strike that seared me with hot tears. I kicked. Darius dodged. A third strike.

"Let go of me!" I struggled. He hit again. I shrieked. "Don't touch me!"

Why was I even screaming?

Why was I wasting air?

Darius had no respect for me, and his grip bound me with every evil he promised. I tensed for another swipe. He beat my head against the desk, laughing as the force echoed in his office. The pain cracked through me. I weakened, and my vision darkened.

It wouldn't be enough.

It would never be enough to dull the horror of what Darius planned.

Agony burst within my chest. The panic surged with an instant asthma attack, and I wheezed against my futile scream. His fingers prodded. I squeezed my eyes shut.

This wasn't supposed to happen.

They had *promised.* Each one of them.

Reed swore he'd protect me like a real brother.

Max vowed he'd be the only one who would ever hurt me.

And Nicholas?

Darius forced a finger in me with a grunted profanity. The sensation nauseated me.

Nicholas said I would belong to him.

I was *his.*

He promised it, again and again. He whispered it while I was in his arms and he growled it while he came inside me, filling me with his every devotion.

I was supposed to be *his.*

Darius spat. The hot spittle trickled over my skin. He withdrew his hand only to force the wetness between my legs.

I struggled.

No.

Not between my legs.

He didn't aim for my slit.

"I took a vow with your mother."

Darius caressed my hips, my curves, my behind. Every touch prickled like a thousand needles, burned like spilled wax, and ached like his relentless strikes.

What he planned would hurt far worse.

"I won't disrespect her honor by knocking up my step-daughter."

"So don't hurt me," I whispered.

"You only seem to understand your place when you're imbedded on a cock." Darius hauled me up by my hair. His sausage fingers pressed hard against a part of me that hadn't been touched. I *never* wanted to be touched there. A shiver rolled over my spine. "This lesson will benefit us both. I love to hear an Atwood scream."

His finger jammed inside that most vulnerable part of me.

And I screamed.

God, did I scream.

The violation was nothing like what my step-brothers forced upon me. Where their touches had been passionate and meant to tease, Darius intended to rip me apart from the inside.

The tears fell and my whimpering begging filled the office. I swatted at his arms, twisted from his grip to escape.

His hold on my hair was too harsh. He ripped out of me only to spit again, forcing his wetness over my budded entrance. He shifted.

His zipper tugged down.

My mind splintered.

I screamed, even without the invasion of his finger.

He liked that, but I didn't know what else to do.

Darius Bennett wanted me to suffer, and he'd deliver that torment with his cock. He'd brutalize and sodomize me for his own perverse enjoyment.

I'd never known a fear like this.

Not when I watched the smoldering wreckage of my brothers' plane crash on the news.

Not while my step-brothers chased me through the city streets and wrecked my car within the desolate stretch of my family's property.

Not even when I realized how badly it hurt that Nicholas abandoned me.

I couldn't move.

I couldn't breathe.

I clutched the desk as though it were the only means to protect me, but the arresting terror wouldn't let me escape. The desk angled my hips up for Darius. In my horror, I offered him every access to a part of me that should have never been touched.

I pleaded with Darius to fuck me anywhere but *there*.

"This won't be pleasant for you." His words already crawled within me, twisting and clawing a way for the rest of him to enter. "But from now on, nothing will be pleasant for you. The sooner you realize, the easier your life will become."

The fat head of his cock pushed against me so suddenly I had no time to fight.

My nail splintered as I tried to claw away.

His hips thrust forward. My body refused in a wave of nauseating pain. He smacked my ass and tried again.

The agony shredded through me.

My scream begged for mercy, but Darius managed only to hurt me, not to imbed himself. He swore and ground against my hips.

My vision darkened.

Why wouldn't I just pass out?

My world would end in incomprehensible misery.

I didn't understand the shouting. Darius jerked, releasing me before any of his grotesque length sullied my violated body.

I scrambled away, hauling myself over the desk and across the polished wood in a blaze of utter panic. The floor captured me as I tumbled. I kicked my panties away before they tangled around my ankles.

I collapsed against the wall and tugged my skirt down, down, down.

Nicholas pitched Darius into his chair and slammed a fist against his jaw. Darius spit a tooth onto the floor.

"What the hell is the matter with you?" He yelled. "You can hear her screaming from the *elevator!*"

Darius roared, but Nicholas punched again. He seethed, leering over his father with a menace I didn't recognize. I curled into a tight ball and shuddered.

"Do you want everyone in this building to know you're raping your step-daughter?" He heaved an unsteady breath. "They'll call the police, haul her off, and we'll lose her for-fucking-ever?" Nicholas seized a handful of Darius's suit and shook. "How the hell would we survive then?"

The coldness damned me.

Nicholas saved me.

But for what?

To protect me? To spare me pain? To take me as his?

Or to ensure his investment hadn't been compromised?

I stumbled to my feet. Darius sneered at me—disappointed he hadn't rutted me into pained, ruined submission.

"She misbehaved."

"Then let Max handle it before you kill her and jeopardize the entire company."

Nicholas kicked his father's chair. He rolled, striking the window.

Not nearly hard enough. He deserved nothing but broken glass and a ten story fall to Hell.

"I'm taking her home," Nicholas growled. "Put your cock away. You almost cost us everything."

Nicholas gripped my arm. I struggled, but the panic and pain, exhaustion and utter terror leaded my reactions. I wept as the door closed. Darius sealed inside, trapped in his own frustration and sadism.

The elevator closed. Nicholas didn't release me.

I hadn't expected his kiss.

I didn't think I'd warm to his touch.

I never knew he could be so gentle.

He cupped my cheeks and shuddered, dropping his forehead against mine and surrendering to a trembled fear that rivaled my own.

"Jesus, Sarah." He kissed me again. I clutched at his arms. "You have to stop me, and you have to stop me now."

"Stop you?"

"Tell me you need me. Ask me to hold you. Beg me to stay."

I stared into his eyes, lost in the protective gold. "Why?"

His breath panted in raw agony.

"Because if you let me go, I'll kill my fucking father for hurting you."

CHAPTER TWENTY-THREE
NICHOLAS

Rage.

I never experienced true rage before.

This was worse than anger. More violent than wrath. Less civilized than madness.

Hearing her scream iced my core. Witnessing how he tried to violate her clawed through everything composed, guarded, and rational inside me.

I hit him.

And it felt good.

It wasn't enough.

I had never wanted blood before—not even when my mother died in front of me and my brothers howled in agony. Then, I wanted what all Bennetts craved.

Retribution. Justice. Revenge.

But I never murdered.

Not until my father touched what wasn't his, hurt what he had no right to harm, and attempted to take what I'd already claimed.

Sarah refused my help until we reached the safety of my Mercedes. I helped her into the seat. She grimaced as she repositioned her skirt over her thighs.

We left her panties in my father's office.

If I wasn't careful, I'd wreck the car in a fit of unbridled fury.

I clutched the wheel but took her hand before she cowered too far from me. I kissed her delicate fingers. She trembled, but her breathing worried me even more, especially as she wasted her breath on crass insults reserved for my father.

I hated that I hadn't cared enough for the woman in my possession to learn the signs and triggers of her illness. That was my fault.

"How is your asthma?" I asked. "Can you last until we're home?"

"*My* home?" She shivered, but the steel in her eyes hardened the blue into refined grey.

Her life would be nothing but disappointment caused by my cowardice.

"No."

Sarah's lip quivered. "Yeah. I'll be fine."

I doubted it, but I knew better than to argue with Sarah Atwood.

The silence pierced my head in a migraine of regret. The fear still held me. I'd forever endure nightmares about what might have happened. Reality finally struck both of us. She realized her fate. I saw what would become of my beautiful, brave Sarah once my father sated his lust.

The one thing she asked of us was to protect her from my father.

I failed her.

I should have protected her. She wasn't hurt because I was too preoccupied with my own plans for her and my company. My father hadn't outplayed us. I wasn't weak or out of options.

I failed Sarah because I hid from her.

Nothing used to frighten me in this world, not when I had the wealth, power, and ambition to overcome any challenge. But I met my match.

I surrendered to Sarah Atwood.

She bound me so tightly in beauty and gentleness and grace I'd relinquished every means of escape. Her words teased. Her lips enthralled. Her body tempted.

My enemy. My opponent. My step-sister.

She'd forever destroy what had been the Bennett Empire, and, for the first time, *I didn't care.*

I lost myself within her, and I'd give my name, my inheritance, and my last breath just for a chance to hold, taste, and love her.

Even if it was only for the fleeting moments while I kept her captive in my life.

I trapped her at the estate, scooping her into my arms and carrying her into her prison. She squirmed. She wanted to scrape her pride together, patchwork but functional. How she always survived.

Sarah protested, but her fingers curled into my suit. She held on as tight to me as I clung to her.

I'd never let her go again.

I hadn't allowed her to trespass in my wing or explore my suite, and I didn't grant her the opportunity now. I locked the door behind us and delivered her right to my bed.

Sarah trembled in the center of the classic poster bed—king sized for me but absurdly large for my captured fairy. She sunk onto the black sheets, her hair the only bit of pale brightness I'd permit in my bedroom. She glowed within the dark walls and draperies. My decor didn't suit the little farm girl clutching the blankets. Then again, nothing inside the Bennett estate did. Sarah adapted to everything we forced upon her—her room, her schedule, her body.

I approached, cupping her face and studying the damned bruises that stained her perfect skin.

Who could mar such beauty?

"I'm so sorry," I whispered. "Can you forgive me?"

Sarah straddled the edge even when no one challenged her. She wept with desperation, but her voice hardened with every foolish resistance she reserved for me.

"Depends," she said. "What are you apologizing for?"

Dangerous question.

"For my father. For letting him take you. For him almost hurting you."

I leaned in. She permitted my closeness, but the kiss broke over her rasped sigh. I cursed myself for forcing it, but she pushed forward, taking a deeper, gentler press of my lips.

She'd draw the very blood out of me with that kiss.

"Give me more than that apology, Nick," she whispered. "Tell me there's a soul in there somewhere."

My soul died, broken, bruised, and hurt than the girl trembling before me. She wasn't ready to hear my true confession, and I wasn't ready to reveal it.

"I'm sorry that I need you to be mine." I touched her cheek. She leaned into my hand. "Nothing else makes sense. You are more than my captive, Sarah, but every beat of my heart is a living agony when you are not trapped under me."

She looked away. I hated losing that kindness.

"I want to trust you," she whispered.

"Then trust me. I know I am a monster, but I'm *your* monster. I swear I will do everything I can to protect you."

"Tell me why I'm really here." Sarah didn't realize she gently rocked herself. "You stole me. Imprisoned me. Kept me here. Planned to *breed* me, but it isn't just to steal the company. I know it isn't. Tell me. What are you hiding from me?"

I wasn't the only one with secrets. Mine would ruin lives. Hers?

"You have to share yours first," I said.

"Who says I have a secret?"

I searched her expression. "Today was the first time you showed any real fear."

"And today was the first time you dared to oppose your father."

It was the truth, and I didn't know what would come of it.

But she wanted secrets, and I couldn't give them. It wasn't just her at risk. My family, our future, the very livelihood of a multi-billion dollar business rested upon our decisions and depended on our crimes. If she knew, if she *acted*, my father would do worse than rape her.

I knelt beside the bed, pulling her close. "I can't tell you. It isn't safe."

"*Nothing* is safe, Nick. Not here. Not trapped between restraints and floggers and passed around for three men to be used and fucked and…"

"I'll protect you. So will Max and Reed. I swear to you, Sarah. Trust us. Do this for us. Be here for us, and I'll find a way to free you."

"Do it *now*."

The soft plea refueled the helpless rage simmering under my skin.

"Nick, please, I'm asking you as a sister and a friend and someone…" Her voice trembled over the aching truth. "Someone who is falling in love with you. Please, let me go."

"Sarah…"

"I can't be here anymore. I thought I had this under control. I thought I'd handle it."

"You *can*."

She dug her fingers into the bed. Why was it so damned dark in here? I couldn't see her face, I didn't know if she was crying. How was I supposed to console her?

"Everything is wrong." Her words choked. "I thought I was doing this for my father. I wanted to redeem him. I tried to honor him."

The crushing heartache in her voice tempered my rage. I pulled her close, letting her wrap her arms around me in whatever way she needed—friend, brother, lover. It didn't matter anymore. I let her cry, and she let me see her weakness without fear.

"I'm sorry," I said. "You shouldn't have learned like this."

"I could survive this when it was to protect the Atwoods. But now?"

"You can still survive this."

"But *why?*" Her voice hardened. "Why put myself through this torture?"

"Is it torture?"

"Your father tried to rape me."

It was selfish. I held her tighter.

"I won't ever hurt you," I promised.

"Every minute with you is pain."

"But you're strong enough to take it, Sarah. I know you are."

She sank deeper into my arms. "You aren't giving me a choice, Nicholas Bennett. Am I always going to be your prisoner?"

"If that's the way to keep you here, so be it."

"That's not fair."

No. It wasn't, but I was beyond *fair*. The rules of the world—the laws and morals, principles and ethics—didn't apply to us. To me. My name, my money, and my power offered something more than what normal men possessed. Sarah Atwood could beg and plead, and I would never let her go.

If only because I feared that she wouldn't come back to me.

And that made me more of a threat to her than even my father's vengeance.

Sarah's whisper begged for the wrong things. She should have asked for affection, devotion, and seduction. Those I offered. But *mercy?*

Mercy didn't exist within my embrace, and forgiveness would never rest within her heart.

"Nick, if you love me—"

"I do."

She shuddered. "Then *please.*"

She couldn't support herself any longer. I laid beside her, cradling her against my chest. She clutched at me, the tears damp on her cheek. I stoked her hair, rubbed her back, accepted her warmth.

But I wouldn't let her escape from my possession.

"I hate to cause you pain," I whispered.

"It will always end in pain," Sarah said. "Nothing can survive this, Nicholas. Our families have hated each other for generations. Your father will stop at nothing to break me. You refuse to let me go." She rolled over only to bury her head in my chest. "Even if this were different…you're my *step-brother*. God, everything about this is wrong. We have nothing to keep us together and everything that will drive us apart."

"Trust me."

"We'll never trust each other. We'll never let ourselves."

"Then depend on me. Know that I will find a way to keep you safe."

"Even from you?"

"Especially from me."

Sarah burrowed deeper. She fit perfectly against me, snuggled against my jacket and digging her fingers in my shirt. Her breathing shuddered only as she drifted into a fitful sleep. The horrors of her day hadn't stolen her courage, but that didn't mean she hadn't been scarred.

The Sarah Atwood who challenged me, fought me, and forced me to confront the depths of my sins hadn't escaped unscathed.

I feared for her.

It was the wrong thing to fear.

Sarah never needed my pity or my strength, my kindness or my pledge of foolish love.

She needed only to wait for me to fall asleep.

***

I woke suddenly. She was gone, and, in the hazy panic of my fatigue, I burst from the bed fearing she had been taken by my father.

I rushed from the bedroom.

She wasn't in my suite, and the door opened into the hall. My blood chilled.

Would she always refuse stay where I put her?

I prepared for battle, already texting my brothers with an order to find her before my father did. I was wrong to worry for her. My office door propped open—the lock picked by a clever hand of someone who learned her lesson from the last time she spied on what wasn't hers.

This time, she didn't focus on Darius's office.

The heir had the same information.

I was too late to stop her from finding it all.

She sat at my desk—papers strewn across the top, folders opened, the computer on and my email displayed for her to study.

Her scowl darkened with every step I took. I waited before the desk.

"*A secret trust*," she said. "My brothers had a *secret trust* built specifically for an inheritance in my name when I turn twenty-one."

And so we began the descent into Hell.

"Josmik Holdings," I said.

"Josmik *fucking* Holdings."

I waited as she pitched a folder at me.

"My brothers negotiated with your *Board of Directors*."

I exhaled. "Your father and brothers held a proxy takeover of the Bennett Corporation. They contacted our private investors and offered them an exorbitant amount of money to betray my family and promise their shares to the Atwoods."

Sarah's voice shrilled with shock, rage, and utter surprise. "And they *succeeded?*"

"Some of them. When your brothers died, the deal stagnated. You were named the beneficiary of a secret trust only to be accessed when you turned twenty-one. They tried to protect you by limiting your involvement."

"This isn't happening."

"In less than a year, the trust will be available to you." The words bittered in my mouth. "Your brothers secured a large quantity of our stock. That's why we're holding you here. That's why we planned to keep you."

Sarah laughed—a frantic, frightened laugh that crippled her against my desk. She stared at me, her voice a light waver against the darkness.

"You son of a bitch," she whispered. "You knew this all along."

"I did."

"In ten months, I'll possess a *controlling interest* in the Bennett Corporation."

I said nothing. I had nothing to say, nothing to do, and no hope to offer my family save for the depravity we forced on Sarah Atwood.

We could hurt her, terrorize her, abuse her, and it wouldn't make a damn difference.

In less than a year, it would be us begging for her mercy.

Sarah Atwood would control the Bennett Corporation.

CHAPTER TWENTY-FOUR
SARAH

My step-brothers paced Nicholas's office.

Reed sunk into a chair and held his head in his hands. Max stole a bottle of whiskey from a hidden cabinet under the window. Nicholas remained still, as always.

He was the only one who dared watch me.

"You hid this from me," I said. The realization refused to stick.

They didn't answer. I pitched the folder and all its damning contents on the table.

"You *hid* this from me!"

I didn't know who I yelled at——my step-brothers or my real family.

Stocks. Investments. Secret trusts and hidden agendas and proxy wars to steal and punish and humiliate.

And my father won.

My brothers won.

They secured the deals. *Somehow.* They approached the right members on the board and convinced them to hand over their stocks in exchange for...

So much money.

Damn it.

Mike and Josiah didn't waste the money. They spent every cent they could get—every penny that might have been reinvested in the farm, in crops, in *research*—and they used it to punish the Bennetts.

Our families would do anything to hurt the other. Burn money. Murder. Ruin futures.

Kidnap and betray the one innocent person who had no idea any of it was happening.

"*This* is why you stole me," I said. "You kidnapped me and devastated my life because of this deal."

Nicholas nodded. "Yes."

"Why didn't you tell me?" I covered my face. "You've beaten me. Fucked me. Kept me locked in a goddamned basement. You father almost raped me today."

Reed and Max stiffened.

"Yeah." I lost my nerve as they paled. "When he took me to your company and told me all the dirty little secrets about my father and what a monster he was. He tried to rape me. He almost f—fucked my...my..."

I couldn't say it.

Had Nicholas not been there, not saved me, held me, and hid me away within his arms, I wouldn't have survived both the revelations about my horrible father and the torment of Darius's touch.

I thought my life was over.

Instead?

"I've won," I said. "You can't do a thing to me now. I've won."

Nicholas's whisper was gentle, but it didn't dull the pain of loving a man who held me captive. His every word enthralled me, but the darkness and mistaken trust would damn me forever.

I didn't care.

The excitement burned within me.

I won. I had nothing to fear from the Bennetts.

And the surge of raw, uncompromising victory sealed my first real smile in weeks.

My step-brothers didn't share my excitement, but they didn't understand. All the battles, all the stubborn defiance, and all the endless warring now had an *end*.

Why did Nicholas hold me prisoner when I'd be his willingly?

"Sarah," he said. "Forget what you saw. It makes no difference."

I grinned. His words resonated within my head, twisted to punish him instead. "Why are you fighting me, Nicholas Bennett? It's over."

He took my hand. The heat from his touch burned through me, surging with the whirling, coiling emotions of my discovery. I'd cry. I'd laugh. I'd leap into his arms and let him comfort me and take me in the promise of our newfound freedom.

"It's never going to end," he whispered. "You know what we have to do to you."

"You aren't serious."

"We wanted Atwood Industries out of greed, but we *need* it for our security."

My stomach dropped.

Now I understood.

"You're trying to breed me so I'll trade the *baby* for Josmik Holdings."

"Unless we find a way to block the trade and retain our investor's shares, keeping you was always a failsafe to ensure the company didn't fall."

Max said nothing, sipping his whiskey. Reed paced without looking at me.

I let Nicholas pull me into a hug, holding me tight as he plotted his ways to force my surrender.

"I'm sorry," he said. "I hated to deceive you. But I swear, you *will* be kept safe. Protected. Loved. Even in this ugliness, I won't let you get hurt."

I didn't answer.

Had none of them listened to me? Watched me?

Why hadn't they tried to understand a single thing about me?

They freaked about the asthma and obsessed over the calendar for the proper time to fuck me, but they never stopped to *think*.

To *ask*.

Why didn't they realize how strange it was that I'd let *three* men— my step-*brothers*—force me into bed with the intent to breed me like an animal?

"You guys…don't know, do you?" I shifted from Nicholas, holding each of their gazes. "I mean, you never thought it was possible."

"That what was possible?" Nicholas asked.

"That you could rape me as many times as you wanted, and it wouldn't matter."

"I'm sorry, Sarah. I am. But it will happen. It has to happen."

I didn't answer, not because I feared the finality in Nicholas's decision or because, regardless of how wicked his words were, I felt coveted in his possession.

The game had been frightening and seductive.

But now it was done.

They should have realized. So much suffering might have been avoided.

Did I ruin everything or save myself?

How to begin?

"When I was eleven years old, I was rushed to the hospital for severe abdominal pain," I said. My step-brothers shared a puzzled silence. "My father didn't believe me when I said I hurt, so I didn't get to the hospital quickly enough."

They didn't answer. I perked an eyebrow.

"Ovarian cysts are unusual for someone that young."

Nicholas darkened. I waited. They didn't move. They still didn't understand.

"There were complications. Internal damage to my fallopian tubes from when the cysts burst."

I tensed until I thought every bone in my body would crack under the strain of their stares.

"I'm *infertile*, guys. There won't be a male heir for Atwood Industries because I can't get pregnant. And *that* is a secret only my mother knows. I'm surprised she didn't tell Darius."

I expected victory to taste sweeter. Reed was the first to start laughing. A rushed, bewildered laugh that muffled as he rubbed his face.

"Holy shit." He grinned. "We're *fucked*."

Max poured another drink. "No. She is."

I extended my arms. "There is nothing you can do to me now. I have every advantage. Atwood Industries still belongs to me, and in a year, I'll have the controlling interest in your company."

Max didn't flinch. "We can stop some of the sales. You'll only retain a portion."

Reed tucked his hands behind his head. His wink stunned me to silence.

"No. I'll give her control. She has one of my shares. She can buy the rest."

Nicholas spun, his eyes a molten, charred amber. "*What?*"

"Fuck it." Reed said the words slow, staring at his brother. "I'll take the money and run. Get as far from this fucking lunatic asylum as I can. I told you, I'm not going to be a part of this. When Sarah turns twenty-one, she'll get my stock too, and she can burn this fucking family to the ground for all I care."

Max leapt over the couch and reared to punch. Nicholas hauled him off before Reed took aim for Max's bad leg. He forced them apart and turned to me with a wild stare. He ripped his jacket off, but his motions weren't meant to frighten me.

They frightened him.

"Everyone stop." He ordered. "Stop and *fucking* listen to me."

I hated the frustration in his voice. "Nick, I'm sorry I didn't tell you, but—"

"Quiet." The snap in his words struck like a whip. "You have no idea what you've just done. No idea at all. You're still thinking of this as a *rivalry*. As a way to punish the Bennetts and redeem some sort of pride for your family." He swore again. "You just lost whatever chance you had of surviving this."

"But it's over—"

"My father will never let the Bennett Corporation fall to Atwood control."

"He doesn't have a choice."

Nicholas's expression hardened, fierce and shadowed with rage.

"Yes, he does."

I retreated as Nicholas stalked toward me, his words punctuated with each echoing step.

"My father will torture you. He'll beat you, starve you, rape you, and inflict every horrific torment he can devise to force you to sell." He breathed, wild and fierce. "There won't be a damn thing I can do to save you."

"Saved from what?"

"He's going to kill you, Sarah."

The shiver rocked me. I fell against the desk.

"You said your father wasn't a murderer," I whispered.

"I said he *hadn't* murdered." Nicholas curled his hands into fists. "Not that he wouldn't. He wants the heir, but he'll protect the family first. If he finds out you're infertile and there's no way to trade for the stock, he will kill you to save the company."

"Christ." Reed stole the whiskey from Max. He swore after the gulp. "What the fuck are we supposed to do?"

"He'll kill you too, Reed," Max said. "Selling your shares? Are you an idiot? If you die, your portion reverts back to the family. He'd slice your throat before letting you make a deal with Sarah."

"He'll do it anyway," Nicholas said. My heart thudded with a newfound sorrow. I didn't want to think about it—didn't want to imagine them in danger. "Dad forced me to convince you to help. That's why I pushed you to take Sarah. If you didn't, he said he'd kill you. I believed him."

Enough blood threatened to spill. Reed and Max stared at their brother. My tears prickled.

Would *any* of us survive this?

What was left to win?

Nicholas sighed. "Sarah, if you aren't pregnant by the time you're twenty-one, my father will murder you to avoid losing the company."

"But…I can't. The doctors said…"

"Did they say there was a chance?" Reed asked.

"Slim, if any at all." I wasn't about to give them hope. "But it won't happen. I have to get away from Darius. That's the only thing we can do."

Max snorted. "You can't hide from my father. No one can. There's too much money and power. He'll hunt you like a dog. If he found the man who killed our mother hiding in the middle of Central America, he'll find a little Atwood billionaire, no matter where she goes."

"Then I'll sell the stock. You can have your fucking company."

"It's not about the stock." Nicholas approached, gently stroking my cheek. "It's about *your* family. He'll protect the Bennetts until his dying breath, but he'll kill to hurt you."

Christ.

Nicholas was right.

I saw it in Darius's eyes. Felt it in his urge to degrade me. He tried, and he failed, but I knew the Bennetts well enough to realize they'd never stop, never surrender, and never allow someone like me—a woman they saw as no challenge—to gain control over them.

I gritted my teeth.

I'd never surrender to Darius Bennett.

And neither would Nicholas.

"We should kill him," I whispered. I couldn't believe the words slipped from my lips. "Darius. Before he kills me."

"Darius Bennett is the CEO of one of the largest and wealthiest privately owned corporations in the world," Nicholas said. "He can't be murdered. Not without starting major investigations into our family and company. It would be a media phenomenon, and every law enforcement agency on the West Coast would descend on us." He exhaled. "His will is clear if he dies of unnatural causes. We'd lose everything."

Max narrowed his eyes. "How do you know that?"

"You don't think I've planned it? Thought about it?" Nicholas gestured towards me. "He kidnapped an innocent woman and plotted with her innocence. That isn't a man who deserves to live, but he's a man who must if we want to save our company and inheritances."

"So what do we do?" Max asked.

"We'll move on the takeover. My father doesn't know that Sarah's learned about her inheritance. We'll keep it a secret."

Reed swore. "That means we can't give him reason to believe she's infertile."

"No," Nicholas agreed. "We can't."

The silence hung.

I knew what they wanted, and it wasn't to free me.

The excitement fueled his strength.

"Sarah."

He brushed his hand over my cheek. I wished I hadn't shuddered. I was strong, but I'd never be strong enough to resist him, to fight him, to deny my every surrender to him.

And he knew it.

Max and Reed knew it.

And that was why my victory would ultimately end in defeat—a sweet, desperate defeat that'd forever bind me within his clutches.

"I'll protect you," he said. "We'll all protect you."

Promises. Always promises.

Only this time, I believed him.

Without the secrets restraining us, and with the ticking clock measuring my life in single, frightening moments of possession, I had no reason not to trust Nicholas Bennett.

"But it won't work," I whispered. "Keeping me here is a mistake."

"It's only our option," he said. "The longer you're here, the easier we can convince my father that you are our prisoner, the easier it will be to keep you alive."

"And when I don't get pregnant?"

"Leave that to me."

"We can't *fake* it."

"Who said we'd fake it?"

The panic and fear, adrenaline and excitement poisoned me into quivered confusion. Nicholas's touch provided the simple antidote.

Trust.

Devotion.

Passion.

I stilled. "But…you can take me as often as you can—"

"I plan on it."

The fierce dedication in his words blistered me with heat. I blushed, but my perked eyebrow offered him a challenge.

"How?" I whispered. "You've all had me, and I didn't get pregnant."

"Then I try again." Nicholas's voice rumbled low and thick. "And again. And again. Every day."

"Every day?"

He seized my hair, pulling my head back to expose my neck. His lips pressed hard against my throat, and I flushed as I caught the gaze of my step-brothers, stunned to silence.

"You're not going anywhere, Sarah Atwood." His breath heated my skin. "The safest place for you is right here. In my arms. In my bed. I'll protect you. I'll take you, and I'll ensure you're carrying my child before my father has cause to harm you."

"You're insane."

"And you're mine."

His hands tightened against me, capturing me in a kiss before I could struggle away. Max and Reed watched in silent shock.

Nicholas didn't care.

I gasped as he pushed me against his desk. He forced me down with that Bennett arrogance promising a dark, twisted, and primal act. It dominated us both.

Reed called our names. Nicholas didn't look at him, his jaw clenching as he explored my prone body. He palmed my thigh, but I knew better than to refuse him.

He opened my legs and stepped between.

"Don't move."

Did he command me or his brothers?

"This is the beginning of the real takeover, Sarah. You belong to me. Your body. Your future. Your safety."

My skirt peeled down. He ripped open the buttons of my blouse.

My breathing shuddered as the bra tugged away.

My step-brothers saw everything.

I paled, but my struggling ceased as his hand crept along my chest, sealing tight against my neck.

"Don't fight me," he whispered. "We've already had you. You know what we expect."

The thought was once horrifying. Now it shivered through me. I'd never deny the sheer animalistic instinct roaring through him.

I won.

I'd keep my company and protect myself by threatening their empire. Nicholas demanded an heir, but my body would never betray me, not even to their hedonistic and primal desires.

I had won.

And my prize for my conquest?

Nicholas's love.

Max's aggression.

Reed's kindness.

The possibilities and pleasures, victories and *empowerment* dizzied me.

Three men. Three step-brothers. Three protectors.

Three lovers?

Nicholas's urges might have once shamed me. Instead, I welcomed his hand against my neck, and surrendered to the instinctual submission of a woman possessed within the strength of her man.

He admired me. His hardness pressed against my slit.

He moved to his zipper. I searched for Max and Reed.

Would he really take me in front of his brothers?

The answer came suddenly, a quick, fierce, demanding stroke of his cock directly into my core.

I arched, my gasp fading to a low groan.

His cock stretched me, filled me, and claimed me, and I only arched against the desk to accept more of his length.

My face flushed, but I'd never resist Nicholas again. His brothers watched his savage thrusts within my body, listened to my gasped moans.

And they waited with fierce stares and fiercer intent.

Hungry.

This was wrong.

God, everything about it was wrong.

I shouldn't have let him do this. Welcoming him with such betraying wetness only sealed his command over me. I wanted to be free.

I wanted to be his.

I wanted everything he couldn't give me—his love, my freedom, even his promise to be with me forever.

I groaned. He was my step-brother.

A Bennett.

My family's worst enemy.

And I wanted nothing more than for him to lose himself within me.

"This is your life from now on." Nicholas grunted as his motions were meant to take, not tease. I bounced against the desk, held in place only by a grip that would have been cruel had it not delivered me to pleasure. "You will be mine. Taken. Used. Fucked and filled until you're bred, and nothing is going to prevent us from getting what we need."

His words weren't kind, but I didn't care.

I felt the emotion behind them.

The anger. The devotion.

The utter fear that even his basest urges wouldn't be able to save me from the hell he created.

He kissed me. I whimpered against him, struck by the ferocious gold of his gaze.

His cock drove inside me. I grasped him, clenching over every offered inch of his depraved protection. I couldn't hide my thrill, not when Nicholas knew exactly how to hold me down and force me to accept his love the only way he'd offer it.

He fucked with brute strength. Claimed me with unrepentant dominance. Nicholas tangled us in a passion so twisted he'd capture me, ravish me in front of his brothers, and claim me as his captive all to prove his devotion.

I tensed. I'd never fight him. He assaulted me on his desk, his aggressive thrusts brutal and frightening. But I accepted him and every shudder that bound me to his lust.

He promised he'd protect me.

The orgasm overwhelmed me within his strikes. I crumbled against him, offering my hips despite my silent and tempted step-brothers watching as he pounded me.

I cried out, whispering his name, drawn into utter pleasure and the sheer intensity of his strength.

A surge of heat jetted inside me. Nicholas claimed me, forced my submission, and offered me his adoration. He shuddered over me, but his words excited me more than his raging aggression.

"I love you," he growled. "More than you can possibly know. I'll do whatever it takes to protect you, even if it means sharing your body to save your life."

I panted, but Nicholas didn't give me time to rest. He hauled me off the desk and faced his brothers. I was forced to my knees before them—trembling, weak, and slick with his claiming.

"Everything has changed," Nicholas said. "We have no time. If we want to save her life, Sarah has to conceive."

Max and Reed hadn't moved, but their eyes feasted over my every quivering movement. I shuddered, looking up to Nicholas—so stern and still it was as though he hadn't spilled his every secret and longing inside of me.

"This isn't about pride or ego." His authority drew his brothers' attention away from me. "This is about ensuring her survival. I need your help."

I twisted my fingers in the carpet. My body hadn't broken the haze of pleasure. The thrill whipped me, and the raw aggression and arrogance of his conquering left me breathless.

Nothing would stop Nicholas Bennett from securing his heir and path to the Atwood fortune.

He'd do it by taking me until I surrendered in my own selfish desire.

Then he'd offer what remained to his brothers.

He spoke the truth. I belonged to him.

And what should have terrified me only sealed my fate in endless passion and strict, unforgiving pleasure.

He pushed me forward. I fell onto my hands, bowing to my step-brothers as the air thickened with their own instinctual urge to dominate and take.

Nicholas's voice growled with ambition, hardened with challenge, and threatened with lust.

"Who's next?"

The End

Coming Summer 2015

CONTROLLING

INTERESTS

THE LEGACY SERIES BOOK TWO

BY: LANA GRAYSON

My life became pleasure and pain.
My world, mysteries and lies.

Submission was survival.

But how long could we hide the truth?
And how much blood would spill to keep it secret?.

ACKNOWLEDGMENTS

Well, this book was a little different. First off, thank you to everyone who promises not to tell my parents what I wrote. _Pinky swear_!

I had a ton of interest in this story, and I sincerely thank everyone for volunteering for ARCs and sharing posts and just being awesome. Stick with me, kids. I have so many books planned, and I can't wait to share them with you. Thank you for reading!

And honestly, I have to thank everyone who listened to me hem, haw, panic, and generally freak about every little detail of this book—the short list includes Kelley, Kaylee, Jess, Pepper, Cora, Sabrina, Rebecca, Jamie, and my poor husband. Seriously, thank you for your support and encouragement because, without you guys, I would have chickened out a long time ago.

Kelley, Kaylee, and Jess—I owe you guys big for helping to beta. <3

Not included in this list is LC, but just because I spared her the book's gory details doesn't mean she wasn't there for me every step of the way sending me stickers and reminding me to take breaks every once in a while. The advice is appreciated, if not always heeded.

And to my husband—I started out this full-time writing career promising breakfasts in the morning, a day of writing, then making a nice dinner in the evenings with time to just relax with him. So…that didn't happen. Two weeks of fourteen hour days is difficult, but he's awesome enough to not only understand, he also enables the insanity. I think I say I owe every book to him, but it's true. He's pretty much the only reason I'm able to do this. Plus, he gave me the name "Darius Bennett." I mean. What's love if not helping to name naming your antagonist?

Brit, Breann, and Kati—We had our dinner! Let's do it again! Ashley, same for you. <3

And I also want to thank Rebecca Berto for all her help designing my covers. Gorgeous!! And special thanks to Love Between The Sheets for helping to organize my tour on such short notice! Thank you, guys!

Thank you all so much!

Other Works By Lana Grayson:

Warlord – Anathema MC Series #1

Trapped...

For twenty-one years, Rose Darnell desperately searched for a way out of the Anathema MC, but the only thing more dangerous than the desecrated club is the rival chapter manipulating Rose into starting a war.

Bound to a world of bloodied knuckles and drug money, Rose is determined to use her musical talent to escape her abusive father and overbearing brothers. A chance audition would free Rose from the outlaw 1%, but her brothers ensnare her within Anathema's shadow.

A rival club threatens Rose, and only Anathema's President, Thorne Radek, can protect her from the bloodshed.

Betrayed...

A traitor lurks within the brotherhood, and Thorne will burn the world to scorch the rat. When an innocent diva with baby-bunny eyes and dark secrets needs his help, Thorne volunteers to protect the girl and secures his ultimate bait to lure out the traitor.

Thorne may be the only man who ever distracted Rose from her music, but his obsession with the club's betrayal endangers the one woman easing his desire for vengeance.

Helping Thorne find the traitor will damn more than the club.

It will tear Rose's family apart...

Exiled – Anathema MC Series #2

Excommunicated...

Exiled from the Anathema MC, Brew Darnell escaped the bullet only to face the unforgiving solitude of the road. With no future before him, Brew battles his past and vows to protect the one he loves the only way he can—by hunting the man who destroyed his family, devastated the Anathema MC, and betrayed every promise he ever made.

Saved...

Trapped in an abusive relationship with a sadistic biker, Martini Wright learned to manipulate, controlling her boyfriend's temper with a wink and a smile...until she's traded as collateral to a rival MC. Her captor, Brew, has never trafficked a woman before, and Martini intends to exploit his guilty secrets to escape. Caught in the middle of a gang war, Brew and Martini fight a dangerous attraction—a second chance to heal from the mistakes of their past if they can confess the terrible truth.

Redeemed...

Brew failed his family before, but Martini can still be saved. With redemption delivered at the edge of a blade, Brew must choose who to rescue—the one he already lost...or the love he never deserved.

Made in the USA
Coppell, TX
17 October 2020